Worlds of the Lords

by Bryan Lee Gregory

First Edition, October 2014

Copyright 2014 by Bryan Lee Gregory

Cover art by Jeremy Gregory

All Rights Reserved

ISBN-13: 978-1502456854

-Books by Bryan Lee Gregory -

The Bladesmen Lords Trilogy

Lord of the City
City of the Lords
Worlds of the Lords

Editor's Note:

Due to the extensive amount of Bladesmen language used in this story, we have helpfully translated it where it occurs. Quotations in this language are prefaced by a *. For example, instead of the common Bladesmen farewell "*Anya Delinn!*", this book would read "*Blades sharp!"

Book 1

~ Viala ~

Chapter 1 – Rebellion

　　I had expected a normal day of meeting with ambassadors at my husband's side, settled in at my desk with a cup of hot tea to wake me up as I read another stale report on the Lords I was supposed to talk to. With no warning I felt a thundering impact against the warding spells I maintained around the Council offices. The protective magic held, barely, but I could feel the massive stone building shift around me. I fell forward onto my desk, dropping the papers I had in my hand. From elsewhere in the building I heard screams along with the deep groan of granite blocks rubbing against each other.

　　It took me only a moment to recover. I felt adrenaline coursing through my body and triggered a burst of energy to reinforce the magical shielding I always maintained around myself. At the same time I sent a quick mental message out to anyone within miles of the City, attuned so it would only be picked up by humans.

　　Another explosion shook the plaza outside. Once more my wards held, though I could feel them buckling under the strain. It could only be a coordinated attack from multiple rebellious Lords; no single enemy could have damaged my protections so quickly. Those leaders of the Bladesmen may be able to muster more offense than a human Archmagess like myself, but my defenses were the most potent this world had ever seen - barring those from my daughter, Ikami, but she was something unique.

I realized that my thoughts were wandering - the attacks must have been more jarring than I thought. An instant's concentration brought a lifetime of discipline into play and I was ready to fight. I pushed my chair back and swept into the corridor leading towards the grand entryway, pushing other humans and Bladesmen aside as I started to jog towards the plaza at the center of the City. I executed a quick mental scan of the area while moving. No fewer than ten Bladesmen Lords were nearby - one nearly dead on the steps of the Council building outside - but I recognized only one of them. That didn't mean that the others were hostile, since we'd had innumerable visitors in the last few months as other Bladesmen nations set up embassies here in the City, but I was worried that even if we outnumbered the attackers we wouldn't be able to effectively coordinate a defense.

Another attack struck the building just as I made it to the huge granite entryway. The ornately carved wooden doors lay sundered with smoke rising from their shattered remains. This time my wards broke and I cried out involuntarily from the backlash - the pain of a lost spell could be incapacitating to the uninitiated. I was too experienced to let it faze me for long, though, and pushed through the agony to pull myself into the doorway proper. Grey clouds of stone dust and mortar filled the air nearby, and I had to wipe my eyes before I could make out what was happening below.

The City square was filled with carnage. Bodies lay sprawled here and there, bright red splashes of blood picking up clusters of grey where dust had collected on their surface. With a shock I recognized Councilwoman Jerana on the steps only a few feet away from me, nearly cut in half from an enemy spell. I knew she was dead without checking; nobody could have survived such an assault. I steeled my jaw, determined to grieve later over the friend with whom I'd worked for decades.

Bladesmen struggled with one another in a chaotic melee in the center of the square. Although I couldn't clearly see the small spikes around their faces the rest of their forms were distinctive, sword-length blades of bone jutting from their elbows and shins as they fought in flashes of white and red. A few human guards had joined in with longswords, though I had no idea how they could tell friend from foe. Three human mages were working in concert with Lord Wesnoq on the far side of the plaza, protecting themselves from repeated blasts of force by two Lords in the center of the struggle. My vision nearly went red as I recognized Lord Randell standing next to them directing their efforts - the leader of the entire rebellion was right there in front of me, and by the looks of it he'd somehow made it into the City with four other Lords and a host of common Bladesmen guards.

    I threw my arm forward and released a powerful blast of air. It scythed into the melee, knocking everyone to their knees - even the Lords around Randell. The enemy leader staggered for a moment before catching himself on the shoulder of one of his allies. We locked gazes and I sent a mental message to him, promising untold agonies for what he'd done. For a moment the rest of the world seemed to stop as we struggled with each other's mental protections; we each tried to worm our way into our opponent's mind to do what damage we could.

    Randell was a powerful Lord but I was consumed by anger at his gall in assaulting the very center of our defenses. I summoned everything I had and slammed a nail of red-hot energy into his mind, breaching his defenses and causing him to fall onto the pavement screaming in agony. A flash of victory surged through me for an instant before he somehow gathered enough focus to teleport himself away. I could hear an audible pop as the vacant air collapsed around where he had been a moment before just as I slammed a whip of pure energy down onto the stones where he'd fallen. They cracked under the impact and one of the enemy Lords cried out as the crackling force caught him sideways, slicing a dark line across his dirty robes. The impact left a bright red mark across his chest welling blood.

    Contrary to my expectations the other four rebellious

Lords didn't flee with their master. The two who weren't focused on Wesnoq and his helpers turned towards me and sent dual beams of pure destructive light lancing forwards. In my haste to strike Randell down I had neglected to reinforce my personal shields and I was saved from being struck only by the shifting dust in the air. It scattered enough of the attack that my remaining defenses weakly deflected the rest, though I reeled backwards from the assault all the same.

As I pulled myself inside the crumbling entrance of the Council building to rebuild my wards, trusting that the building would be safer than standing out in the open, I felt a mental message from someone I knew better than anyone else in the world. I opened my mind to my husband of a quarter century, Kenton, the love of my life who had stood with me through thick and thin.

I'm trapped in my office, he sent calmly. Nobody else would have sensed the anxiety behind the message but he couldn't quite hide it from me. *I'm holding the stones above me as long as I can, but I don't know if I can keep the room intact if another blast hits the building.*

There's still four Lords in the plaza attacking us, I replied with concern. *I'll do my best to keep them distracted from the building. Where's Cordell?*

He's on his way with three skiffs - that's all he could find nearby with mages onboard to receive messages. Go, my love - just try to keep the fighting away from the building. It can't take much more, and I know there are others in here who don't have my abilities.

I sent a feeling of reassurance, then dove around the corner of the doorway and slapped a shield up into the air around me. Sure enough, the enemy Lords had been waiting for me and two more beams of deadly light sliced over my head. My shield took the impact and deflected it up away from the building, though my chest constricted for a moment with the stress of keeping the spell intact. I scurried to the side away from the Council building, hating to look so undignified but having more important things to worry about at the moment.

I could sense two other Bladesmen Lords standing

ahead of me, holding their own protections up but not joining either side of the battle. I continued to keep the building protected and ran forward while I reached out to them with my mind, politely requesting entrance through their shields so that we could converse through magical means. I felt their minds reach out carefully to meet mine, being sure to open nothing more than necessary for communication.

*Ah, the human Lord, one of them said guardedly in the Bladesmen language. *What is happening here?

*This is the doing of the rebel Randell and his people, I sent back sharply. *Why are you just standing around? Help us work against them.

*We were not sure who was where, the other replied with an arrogant overtone. *While I do not sympathize with the rebels - we would not be here if we did - I do not believe that assisting in the human defense was part of the necessary agreement for setting up an embassy here. Indeed, I find your lack of proper preparation -

I cut him off angrily. *This is why the Lady Ikami - **my daughter** - is working to bring us all together against the rebels, because they have been terrorizing those who are willing to work together for peace. The City is her home and she will not take kindly to those who do not help in its defense. I took a deep breath to calm myself, pushing more energy up to deflect further attacks from the enemy Lords. This should be Kenton's work - he was the diplomat, not me! I had to remind myself that right now I needed these two. Whatever other Lords had been in the area had fled, leaving only Wesnoq, these two, and the four attackers in the center of the plaza. I continued to run in a crouch from one point to another, holing up behind the broken remains of the plaza's fountains and columns to let them absorb some of the attacks.

The first Lord replied more politely. *I would not want to anger Lady Ikami. I will assist you. Your protective spells are quite puissant - defend us both and I will keep those Lords busy.

*You may do so, but I will stay out of it, the second Lord sent haughtily, then withdrew from the conversation and physically stepped away from the other Lord. A moment later he disappeared with the familiar crack of teleportation.

Thank you, I sent back to the first. By now I had nearly reached him and I extended my wards to both of us, though my reserves were rapidly running low. If my attackers had been able to see me clearly as I darted between places of cover I would have been dead by now, I admitted to myself grimly.

In a display of utmost trust, the other Lord withdrew all power from his own defenses and sent out a sweep of energy that slapped both of the enemy Lords aside for a moment. I was impressed, both with his confidence in my protections and with the display of power. Once more the fighting around the center of the plaza stopped for a moment as the combatants regained their feet. My heart shuddered as I saw how many loyal soldiers lay dead on the ground, though at the same time the rebel commoners had been greatly reduced.

A squadron of City soldiers had just made it to the far side of the square, having run up from somewhere nearby. In a disciplined display of training the Bladesmen contingent lined up to the sides of the humans, ready to protect them from any flanking attack, while the humans calmly strung their bows and pulled arrows with thick heads from over their shoulders. I recognized Fuel-tipped arrows and sent a quick message to my companion to try and protect the arrows on their way in. He replied with a sense of acknowledgement and I felt his focus fly to that side of the square.

The friendly soldiers in the center recognized what was happening and fell backwards, lying down and covering their heads. The rebel Bladesmen pulled up in confusion, not sure what was coming but not daring to go after their suddenly prone opponents. Taking advantage of the momentary lull, the enemy Lords started pummeling my shields while one of the human mages near Lord Wesnoq wavered and fell, the magical strain proving too much for him.

My eyes watered as I struggled to keep the unknown Lord and myself both covered, but somehow I kept my wards up though I could feel the air nearby heating up to a worrying degree from the attacks. Just then the squad across the way loosed their flight of arrows and I willed them to strike true, though I couldn't spare a shred of energy to guide them onwards. Fortunately, the Lord working with me understood what to do and sent a curving burst around to weaken the enemy formation's shields on the far side facing the soldiers' attack.

The first arrow struck the back of an enemy Lord just to the left of his spine. Bladesmen Lords are notoriously tough, but a Fuel-tipped arrow explodes with the force of a hundred hammer blows. I caught a look of shock on the Lords' face as he fell to the ground, his torso twisting unnaturally as a gaping hole was blown in his side. The blast wave set the other arrows off in a ripping series of cracks, wrecking the rebel formation and killing most of the common Bladesmen they'd brought with them. The other three Lords were thrown to the sides with varying degrees of wounds. Three final cracks echoed across the square as they teleported away, leaving their comrade in his final death throes.

My vision was dazzled with the flashes of the arrow payloads exploding and I had to blink a few times to steady my view again. The ringing in my ears took longer to go away, but within moments I realized that the plaza had fallen silent except for the moans of the wounded and dying. The Lord next to me reached out a hand and I took it with thanks, letting him pull me to my feet.

"It is good to fight you with," he said in a deep voice, his words heavily accented. I was surprised - it was rare to find a Lord who was willing to learn the human tongue, even if his command of it was incomplete. "My name was Lord Jabnoss. Your name was?"

"Is," I corrected, breathing heavily. "My name is Archmagess Viala." A disturbing creak reminded me of the crisis in the Council building and I looked at it with worry - its facade was blasted and broken, shards of stone covering the plaza for twenty feet in front of it. "Can you help me get people safely out of the building?"

He nodded after a moment's concentration and we set off into the dangerously unsafe structure. Behind me I heard the familiar thump of an airship engine and I sensed my son Cordell ordering people around in the plaza - he must have seen me head into the building. I felt a surge of pride - he had been elected a Councilor only two months ago, and he was already proving able to take command of a situation.

A few minutes later I was able to clear the rubble from Kenton's office enough for him to get out. He was exhausted from the strain of holding half a ton of stone above him; while he was a powerful mage in his own right, he would never come close to what a Bladesmen Lord or an Archmage like myself was capable of. We stood facing each other in the dimly lit corridor for a moment before speaking, granite dust sparkling in the air.

"You look a bit of a mess, my dear," he said finally.

I laughed. Nobody but Kenton would be able to make me smile in such a situation. It only lasted a moment, though. "Kenton - Jerana's dead. So is another visiting Lord, I don't know who. We got one of them though."

He digested this news for a moment, then nodded. "They hit us hard right where it hurts. Nobody's going to trust the City's safety after this attack."

I swept around with my mind and sensed Lord Jabnoss escorting the last few survivors out the front entrance. Kenton and I linked arms and started walking back out of the building as it settled around us. "Ikami can't be everywhere at once," I said with a sigh. "They would never have dared approach if she'd been here."

My husband nodded as we came to the top of the steps and looked around. By now two squads of soldiers were collecting the injured and carrying them to the hospital nearby - it had somehow remained undamaged. Kenton and I sat down wearily, coated in grey dust from head to toe, and sat in silence as we thought about those we had lost today and where to go from here.

Chapter 2 – Protection

    By the time Ikami teleported herself back home eight hours later most of the mess had been cleaned up. No other could have crossed the continent so rapidly but by now we were used to my daughter's exploits and nobody made mention of it. She joined us in grieving for those we had lost, Jerana being the closest to the family. The Councilwoman and Kenton had worked together for many years and my husband had learned much from her even after he became Head Councilor.

    I still burned with rage, but where I would have lashed out when I was younger I was old enough now to let it simmer inside of me until the proper time had arrived. Late that evening the four of us sat around a small table in Cordell's house not far from the plaza. The only other person to eat with us was the Bladesman Lord Ather, who might as well have been family - he had come with Kenton and I when we had fled the human world nearly twenty-five years before. Now our homeland was overrun with Bladesmen from this very continent, while we humans were refugees who had given up our homes for good.

    We ate in silence until, at a gesture from Kenton, the last servant nodded and left us alone. My love cleared his throat and all attention was on him - he had that effect, though he swore up and down he didn't know how he did it.

    "The Council has decided to wait until tomorrow morning to meet out of respect for the dead. We'll need to determine how to communicate what happened today to the rest of the continent, and how to reassure the Lords here that we can keep the City safe."

At the mention of safety I traded a glance with Ikami. She and I were the only human Archmages alive, although her power - combined with that of a Bladesman Lord, her biological father who was dead for two years now - far surpassed that of an Archmage or Lord. It was due to her intervention that the politics of this world were changing, though the rebels hoped to redirect the course of history back to the ceaseless wars that she'd stopped. I was proud of what she'd accomplished; I could admit that to myself now though deep inside I still felt some hurt and resentment when I looked at her. It reminded me of the terrible circumstances of her conception and birth, a time during which I had been held in a magical coma.

But now was not the time to think of that. I looked over my daughter's young face with concern. Though only eighteen, the last year had been difficult on her and she had been forced into adulthood earlier than she should have been. Her Bladesmen heritage showed in the tiny spikes surrounding her face, making her look exotic more than anything else. The left side of her head remained terribly scarred, though it was much improved from when Cordell had found her underneath the remnants of the City of the Lords after she had done battle with her sire. Most of her hair had regrown and with some careful magical treatments from friendly Lords she had regained all of her motor functions, though her miniature right forearm blade no longer had a matching twin.

Ikami sighed and shook her head. "If I had been here, they would never had dared attack. We all know that the problem is that I can't be everywhere at once. I've been jumping across the four continents for months, settling feuds and convincing reticent Lords to stop giving aid to the rebels. There's at least forty of them left, and Randell keeps on the move just as much as I do to stir up trouble wherever he can." I felt my face twitching into a smile at her words, so similar to my own thoughts earlier.

"Could you put a Shield Wall up around the City, like you had back in the human world?" asked Ather, steepling his hands under his chin. His right forearm blade was missing, long gone in the accident which had claimed the life of my mentor Mastermage Dural and set in motion the chain of actions which had nearly killed my daughter and had rebalanced the center of power in this world to our City. In an oddly appropriate way Ather's missing blade mirrored Ikami's, the two injuries reflecting the beginning and end of those events.

Realizing that he was waiting for me to answer, I shook my head. "Randell and his companions must have snuck in with the other arrivals sometime in the last few days. Even if we found a way to screen everyone through a checkpoint, Ikami and I would be the only ones able to raise or lower an entrance in the shield. We can't run a City that way."

Kenton nodded. "Besides, we're trying to convince the various nations to open embassies here and set up the City as the center of politics. We can't let anywhere else fill the vacuum of power left by the destruction of the City of the Lords. We have to show that we are safe while remaining open to talk and trade, and a Shield Wall would only accomplish the opposite."

My son set down the cup he'd been idly playing with and frowned. "Speaking of the City of the Lords - Ikami, what's happening there? The last we heard was two weeks ago when Lord Lim sent a message saying that the ruins were acting up again."

"I was there just yesterday. He and Haren have set up a research camp not far from the crater. There's still far too much energy being released there to make sense of anything yet. Between the thousands of warding spells that backlashed and the mountain of Fuel that I used to destroy it, that damn crater is going to be sending out magical shockwaves for a thousand years." She grimaced and continued, "Lim and Abel are worried that the power is building up and might be released at some point in an unpleasant way."

"*Lord* Lim and *Lord* Abel, dear," I reminded her with a

slight smile.

"How unpleasant?" Ather asked, leaning forward.

"Extremely," she replied with a sigh. "I need to spend more time there to try and figure out if I can bleed off some of what's building up. Nobody else can so much as marshal a spark of power in the crater. You've been there, you know how it is."

We all nodded. Every one of us had experienced the swirling vortex that remained in the ruins of the once proud city, and any spells attempted there were muddled even when cast miles away from it. I shuddered inside to think of what might happen should it decide to detonate unpredictably.

Ikami continued in a frustrated tone. "Trouble is, I don't have any time to spend looking at it! Randell and his friends are causing too much trouble, and there's still dozens of Lords around who aren't happy with the way things are heading. They're helping the rebels every time we turn our backs." I didn't prompt her to properly title Lord Randell as I had Lim and Abel - the man was a rebel and deserved no respect from anyone.

"Four friendly Lords are now keeping a constant eye out for any teleportations within a hundred miles, at least," Cordell said with a frown. "That's something."

"Kenton, do you think that you and the Council will be able to calm the Lords currently in the City?" asked Ather.

My husband nodded. "Yes, but only this once. If it happens again, I'm afraid we'll lose many of them who are on the fence. In the long term we're setting up a strong system, but right now it's built of twigs and any errant gust could send us straight back where we were a year ago, with the entire continent up in arms and spoiling for a fight."

"We have to take the fight to Randell directly," I said flatly. "That bastard needs to die."

My husband frowned at my choice of words but Cordell spoke up first. "You know as well as we do that he moves around too much. By now he could be anywhere within a thousand miles of here and every day he could teleport two or three times again if he's willing to push himself. He's proven that he's no coward, but he knows that nobody can win a straight fight with Kami." He reached over and grasped his sister's scarred hand, giving her a warm smile. There wasn't a jealous bone in Cordell's body, a blessing for which I had been thankful every day while the two were growing up.

Kenton somehow took command of the conversation effortlessly again, drawing our attention without a single obvious gesture. I couldn't help but admire the way he could control a room. "Viala, I know how angry you are with him. We all are. But perhaps the time has come to try and seek peace with the rebellion. They've lost nearly a dozen of their own, and at some point they have to be getting weary of the fight as much as we are."

"No! We can't make peace with those - " I retorted, but Kenton cut me off in a tone that he rarely took with me.

"I'm sorry, love, but it's the only way we can settle this quickly. I'd rather find some compromise with them than lose another friend, and we can't afford to let them keep terrorizing the entire continent like this. You know it as well as I."

I grated my teeth together, glaring at him. He didn't give an inch, knowing my temper well enough to wait me out. After a few moments I took a deep breath and forced myself to reply in a calmer tone. "They won't go for it. They'll never accept Ikami's justice, and we won't allow anything less."

"They might accept exile," Ather said quietly. "There are several large islands which have few inhabitants. We let them move there and do what they like with their followers, barring them from returning to the four continents."

"Better yet, send them back to the human world," Cordell said with a hollow laugh. "Let them sort things out with the other Lords who usurped our home."

Ikami stared at him with a calculating look on her face. I could tell that wheels were turning in her mind and wondered what she was thinking. Before I could ask Kenton spoke up. "Tomorrow I'll advise the Council to try reaching out to the rebels and suing for peace. Ather, I think that exile to one of those islands would be entirely acceptable to all involved. It's an excellent idea."

I frowned but remained quiet for the time being. Later, after the dishes had been cleared, Ikami asked me to go with her to the drawing room to talk alone. I shut the door behind us and turned to face my daughter, wondering what she wanted to say.

She settled into a chair and gestured for me to sit next to her. "Mom - I wanted to say that I think you're right. Randell probably won't stop until he's dead. But Dad's right, too - we need to at least try to negotiate with them. It's been two years since we've talked to them face to face. Maybe they're ready to give up. At least we can try to strip some of his support away."

I settled back in the chair and shook my head. "They'll never agree to it. You're all wasting your time."

Ikami smiled. "We'll see. I can only hope. Anyways, I wanted to talk about protection for now. I heard from Wesnoq - excuse me, *Lord* Wesnoq - what happened at the plaza. That was well done. Dad and Cord will make a diplomat of you yet."

Once I would have bristled at her tone but now I could appreciate the compliment she was giving me. Ever since I'd almost lost her we'd had a completely different relationship. I could see past the circumstances of her conception now and appreciate the incredible young woman she'd grown into. At times I felt like I'd lost seventeen years of my life to another person, one full of anger and hatred and resentment at what had been done to her. That person still reared her head inside of me sometimes, but I had mastered her and was better for it.

"The Council building will need a lot of work. Nearly half of it is ruined, and I can't vouch for the strength of the other half. At least the Council table survived." The table was one of the few great works of art accomplished by humans after the Bladesmen had invaded our home world, a massive oak platform twelve feet across on its surface. Human Archmages had kept it safe and preserved for more than a century.

"I hear that Gregor already has plans for installing some

new plumbing when the rebuilding is finished," Ikami replied with a laugh. Gregor was an old friend of ours, the visionary engineer who had developed the first plans for the airships which had given us control of the skies. I wasn't surprised to learn that he was worried more about schematics for a new project than grieving over the dead.

"What can we do to protect the new building better? If they get in again, they'll try and ruin it for good. It's a symbol of everything your father is trying to accomplish." Asking my daughter for advice was something else that I'd never been able to do until recently. It felt good to treat her as a peer, though at times I still had difficulty with the concept.

"That's what I was thinking about. I know you put wards around your office - and I'm glad you did; without them the whole building might have collapsed in their first assault - but the whole plaza needs to be protected. I'll focus on putting some protective spells into the area. I wanted to go over an idea that I had - I think that if we set up wards linked to a preexisting supply of Fuel, we might be able to get them to get more powerful when they are triggered instead of using up all their energy quickly. At least until the Fuel is gone, anyways."

I leaned forward, interested in the idea. "You and I are the only ones who would be able to do it. Even if the enemy Lords learned about the idea, they couldn't copy it and they'd have a hell of a time dismantling the spells."

She nodded, obviously excited. "Lords can't use Fuel to power spells like we can. Look, here's how the trigger could be set up..."

We talked late into the night. Every time I worked with Ikami I marveled at her mind and I was finally in a place to take pride in her accomplishments. Despite her origins, she was the product of our family and friends. My children were grown - and I could relate to them as adults, no matter how difficult that transition had been.

Chapter 3 – Tracking

Unsurprisingly, the Council agreed with Kenton in their meeting the next morning. We had to come together in an auxiliary office, the Council building needing weeks or months of repairs. Kenton used this constant reminder of what had happened to help convince them to try and contact Randell. He had a way of presenting his ideas that always seemed like they were the most obvious solution. It drove me wild sometimes when he did it to me, to where I'd take a contrary position just to stymie him for the spite of it. Ours was never a boring relationship.

Ikami was to send a mental message blanketing the entire continent later that afternoon. Anyone else would have needed days of preparation and an entire team of Lords or Archmages sharing their power; Ikami was ready to do it alone after only a few minutes of concentration. Her call to Randell would reverberate across thousands of miles, ensuring that every Lord knew we were ready for peace - hopefully causing the remaining undecideds to perhaps step back from supporting the rebels in causing more havoc.

Right after the Council meeting adjourned and my daughter agreed to send the message requesting parlay I pulled Kenton aside into the private office he'd taken over from the secretary who had used it until yesterday. I started in right away, not giving him a chance to speak first. "You know I don't agree with this, love, but we're past that. I have an idea that might help settle the issue but I need your help."

Kenton was clearly suspicious with my sudden cooperation; it was written all over his face. "And what's that, dear?" he asked.

"We don't know how the rebels will respond or even how long it will take. But from what we know of Randell I wouldn't be surprised if he replied right away. He'll be hundreds of miles from here, if not further, and no Lord would be able to track him back to where he is from his reply. So he'll feel perfectly safe, tucked away in whatever friendly little nation is giving him harbor."

"But I'm damn good at following magical traces," he followed, knowing exactly where I was going. "You know I haven't had much time to practice magic in the last couple of years, Viala."

I smiled. "I know you, Kenton. You're still better at it than anyone else in the City. Most of the Bladesmen still have no idea just how accurate and fast you can be if you have sufficient power backing you. It would take a lot of power to search across that distance, sure, and by the time you got anywhere nearby the traces would be gone. If I backed you with everything I had, though, I bet you could pinpoint exactly where that bastard is hiding."

"And then?" he pressed, his eyes saying that he understood precisely what I wanted.

"And then, if his answer isn't good enough, Ather teleports a team of us there and we nail the bastard to the wall." I took a deep breath and continued. "You want to give him a chance, I understand that. But Kenton, we both know that he's never going to give up without a fight. He's not the type to submit. Neither are we. We're just on the right side of this one and he's not."

He gave a bitter laugh. "I'm sure he thinks the same thing."

I shrugged. "Ikami is on our side, and that makes us right."

"Sometimes, my dear, I just don't understand you." He

sighed and leaned back against the wall, crossing his arms across his chest. "This time, though, I'm afraid that I do. He hit the City hard, and we can't afford too many more of his disruptions. The Lords bowed to Ikami once, but even without the rebels it's a huge task keeping them all moving in the same direction without fights breaking out right and left. They've lived in a culture of war for thousands of years, and not many understand the concepts of conciliation and compromise yet. The rebels certainly don't - they're the worst holdouts from the old days, and I have to admit that part of me agrees with you. Entirely."

I smiled and leaned forward to give him a kiss. "Then you'll do it?"

He nodded. "Though I fear I will regret it, yes, I will. I'm not committing to any more than just trying to find him, mind you - anything else will depend on how he responds."

With that settled, I called for lunch and we ate together while talking over the day's business. I would be heavily involved in building some new defenses around the City with Ikami's help, while Kenton had scheduled meetings with the most influential visiting Lords to try and soothe their ruffled feathers and convince them that continuing a permanent embassy here was the right thing to do. Neither task would be easy or quick, but I probably had it better - magic didn't need careful negotiations to be convinced.

I spent the next few hours helping the construction crews safely dismantle wards in the Council building that were getting in the way. It was delicate work that kept my mind off what would happen when Randell was contacted, a blessing that I appreciated whenever I took a break and found myself fretting. It was an aspect of my mind that I hated but had never been able to get rid of. I'd never worried about things so much as a girl, but it seemed to be part of being a parent even though I knew that Ikami would be in no danger during her attempt.

Finally the appointed hour rolled around and I headed out to meet the others involved. There weren't many of us; really, Ikami was the only one who was needed, but Cordell and

Ather had requested to be present along with several Council members and the Lords Wesnoq and Jabnoss as representatives of the other nations just in case the rebels sent an immediate reply. Ikami had chosen a field not far from the City with a tall tree in it. It seemed to have some significance to both of my children, as I caught them sharing a look and some private mental communication when I showed up, but they just shook their heads and smiled when I asked them what they were talking about. Kenton and I settled down on the dirt not far from Ikami while the other onlookers stood a few yards further back and talked quietly to each other while they waited.

Ikami closed her eyes and leaned back against the tree. Next to me I could sense Kenton focus on her with his mind, summoning up the magical senses that had always come naturally to me. The power she was assembling was breathtaking, her reserves orders of magnitude beyond what any other Lord or Archmage could draw in. Despite careful study by many Lords - some overt, some surreptitious - it was still a mystery how her origins had resulted in such prodigious magical force. Her magic had the flavor of both Bladesmen and human spells, magnified far beyond what anyone had thought possible before she had been born.

It took her only minutes to prepare the spell. I could faintly sense her drawing the tiniest filaments of Fuel out of the ground nearby, generating even more power from traces of the mineral in that uniquely human way that none but a human Archmage could perform. I smiled, feeling a comforting warmth in the knowledge that this was one thing that I had taught her, something special that only the two of us shared.

Without warning the carefully built-up power burst forth from her, leaving no traces in the physical world but blindingly powerful to those of us with magical sight. I only caught part of the message; Ikami had attuned it specifically to Bladesmen Lords to spare the human mages nearby the full impact. Even so I saw both Kenton and Cordell wincing out of the corner of my vision, while I had to reinforce my own mental protections to shield myself from the sheer magical force. Traces of the specific words whipped through my consciousness in the Bladesmen language - *... *Randell, presence for a parlay is... protected passage... bring the fighting to an end... safe place set aside for... lands where no interference... judgment from... terms for discussion...*

Of the three Lords who had asked to be present, Ather seemed to be doing the best though even he showed a grimace at the strength of the message. Wesnoq's eyes were closed as he tried to maintain his calm against the magical storm with deep breaths and meditation, while Jabnoss was openly cringing and had one hand against his forehead. I had no doubt that Ikami's communication had blanketed the entire continent, demonstrating her strength yet again not only to the rebels but to the dozens of Lords who were kept in line only through fear of my daughter's wrath.

As soon as she was done I touched Kenton's shoulder and started sending him pure magical power, as much as I could summon. He nodded without opening his eyes and I felt his focus drifting upwards, ready to sense any incoming response directed to Ikami. He was among the most naturally potent of the human mages, but without my energy backing him he couldn't send his senses more than a few hundred miles away. We'd had enough adventures together when we were younger to know his limits and reinforcing him with my power was a familiar sensation though we'd never done it for quite this purpose before.

It was only minutes before I felt Kenton's mind pricking up at something incoming. When feeding another mage power one's own senses are dulled and limited, so I couldn't immediately focus on what he had, but as soon as his mind darted to intercept I could feel the message as well as he could. Sure enough, the contact came from Lord Randell directly. I could tell that his own power was being augmented by at least one other Lord to give him extra range and the impression of more potency.

Kenton didn't waste a moment. I skimmed Randell's message as we sped backwards along its path, my husband tracking it like a bloodhound at breathtaking speed to pinpoint its origin. I knew that we had only seconds before the rebel leader finished his statement.

I address this to those who would support the Tyrant Ikami and her illegitimate rule of the continent...

Far below us in the real world I dimly sensed the countryside racing by but couldn't make sense of our direction. Suddenly I recognized Lord Pan's magical spark flicker by below us and realized that we had already passed Rainshye, the nation we'd fought and defeated not long after coming to this world for refuge. Kenton's own strength was already flagging; he wasn't used to sending his mind darting so swiftly. I fed him more of my reserves and pushed him along with a sense of urgency.

...Many of us Lords refuse to recognize her violent coup. She slew hundreds of our kind in a vile act that will never be forgotten...

We had to be over Ganshe by now. Somewhere below us, the Bladesman commoner Dalt was working to help redraw the ways of her country. The onetime rulers of that nation had oppressed the commoners, using their magical power to crush any resistance to their authoritarian ways. Dalt had helped Cordell escape capture there just a year before and the two had bonded during their long trip to the City of the Lords. Without her help, Cordell would never have saved Ikami. I owed the Bladeswoman a deep debt that someday, I swore to myself, I would find a way to repay. For now, I imagined her somewhere far below, oblivious to the magical actions playing out thousands of feet above her.

...Still, despite her villainous ways, we recognize that this war has harmed many of the just and rightful Lords who truly rule our race...

A great river flashed by and I knew that we'd passed beyond the borders of Ganshe, crossing to the far side of the River Gan that gave that nation its name. Now we were in unknown lands - a great desert where nations had once lived prosperously. Cordell had told us of the insane Lord that lived somewhere in the waste, but Ikami had not yet had time to track him down and bring him to heel.

*...*We refuse her terms of exile and surrender, but would be willing to meet under a flag of truce to discuss how the current bloodshed might be ended...*

We were getting close. The message was stronger than ever and Kenton was following it faster than I'd imagined possible. We were halfway across the continent by now; I hoped that we didn't have much farther to go as I felt my own stamina fading. Even an Archmage's power has limits, and I knew that I couldn't continue to push Kenton for long. Behind us I could sense the thin thread connecting us to our bodies hundreds of miles away, growing weaker by the moment.

...In one week's time we will send another missive to those who would arbitrate in the retired Lords' stead with a time and place to meet. Until then, we will remain peaceful and expect the Tyrant's forces to do the same.

With that, the sending ended abruptly. *No!* I cried mentally to my husband, but I had nothing more to give. I felt his mind darting to and fro in a frenzy until a moment later he responded.

Home, he sent with a sense of deep exhaustion, and with our last gasps of power we fled back along the threads of our minds. The journey seemed to take forever and I realized just how far I'd stretched myself - I hadn't used that much power since the war with Rainshye twenty years before. After too long a time my focus slammed back into my body and I blinked, the world blurry and confused.

It took several moments before I realized that I was being held up by friendly hands, surrounded by a babble of concerned voices. "I'm all right," I croaked, straining to sit up on my own. I hated appearing helpless; from my earliest memories I remembered being told over and over that an Archmage cannot show weakness without endangering the entire City.

Next to me I saw Kenton flat on his back; Ikami was squeezing water from the very air into a steady drip over his mouth to revive him. Ather sat nearby in a trance and I faintly sensed his mind probing at Kenton to make sure he was unharmed. After a few seconds' examination he opened his eyes and looked at me, nodding gravely. "He will recover."

"What did you do, Mom?" Cordell asked, searching my face to make sure I was doing all right. "I haven't seen you this pale... well, ever."

I took a deep breath and glanced around. Speaking quietly so that only the five of us could hear, I replied, "We tried to follow Randell's message back to where he was."

"That's crazy," Ikami replied immediately. "Nobody could do that, not even me."

Cordell shook his head. "I don't know about that, Kami. Dad can find damn near anything. With Mom backing him up..." He hesitated for a moment, then continued, "Why didn't you ask for more help? I'm sure Ather and I could have lent more power. The two of you are spent."

I reached over and took Kenton's hand. His clammy skin made me shudder involuntarily but I only clasped it harder. "You know I couldn't have made him try if he didn't think it was worth it. Randell is somewhere far to the west, beyond Ganshe. Maybe beyond the desert. We didn't get far enough," I finished with a deep bitterness.

"We did," Kenton said faintly from beside me. Cordell, Ikami and I all jumped a little at his voice though Ather didn't react at all - crafty bugger; he must have known that Kenton was awake the whole time. "Right before we fell back I found him. He's in a cave under the desert. I know exactly where he's hiding, with a handful of other Lords there too."

I smiled, feeling a sudden rush of satisfaction. "We've got him," I whispered. Our long fight was finally about to end.

Chapter 4 – Disputes

Cordell looked back and forth between his father and I. "He agreed to a parlay, though. In a week we can talk it out and find some way to peace."

I glanced at Ather, who returned only an impassive stare. I replied, "Randell also refused to consider Ikami's terms. He won't agree to anything we want, and if he stays on any of the four continents you know that he'll keep stirring up trouble. Neither of us is willing to back down and it's just going to end with more fighting."

Ikami frowned. "The Council said to try negotiating, Mom. We need to give it a shot."

I shook my head ferociously. "We know where he's hiding now! We could end this rebellion today. Right now. Ikami, you could do it yourself - one teleport; nobody else could make that distance in one jump. Finish the whole thing."

My daughter looked back and forth between Kenton and I, clearly at a loss as to what to do. Kenton's eyes were still closed, and I could tell that his breaths were labored. "Dad... what should I do?" Ikami asked quietly.

"Oh, my dear girl... If only I knew," he replied with a sigh. "I fear that your mother is right. There was no reconciliation in Randell's words, and his tone contained nothing but defiance. He killed Jerana," he finished simply. The Councilor had been a friend of the family for many years; I still hadn't really felt her death sink in, and his words hit home with all of us.

"Come on, Dad," Cordell replied with more passion in his voice. "This isn't right. Let's get you back to the City where you can rest up and we can plan out how we want to approach the parlay." He stood and looked around at the rest of us, then frowned when nobody else got to their feet.

"Cordell, this might be the only chance we have to hit them. How much damage is another year of this fighting going to do? What do you think will happen if they hit the City again?" I asked him angrily. "They're not going to give up any more than we would!"

Our son looked at Ather. "Lord Ather. Don't tell me that you agree with what Mom's suggesting. It's against everything you and Dad taught me about what we should do."

The Lord frowned and shook his head. "I cannot help you, Cordell. I do not agree with what your mother is suggesting, nor can I be sure that her statements are without merit. I will do whatever the Head Councilor asks - that is the oath that I swore many years ago, and I will not betray it now." He shrugged and continued, "I know that you are troubled by this; you were named after me and I feel the same misgivings."

Cordell - whose second name was indeed that of our Bladesman friend - balled his fists in frustration. "I can't believe I'm not getting anywhere. What's wrong with all of you?" He turned directly towards Kenton and crouched down. "Dad, look at me. Look at me and tell me that you're honestly considering this."

My husband opened his eyes wearily and looked at his son directly. "Yes, Cordell, I am. If I were simply a Councilor or mage or ambassador, I would be just as appalled by the idea of breaking a parlay. I can't say that I enjoy the concept. But I'm Head Councilor, and with that title comes the duty to protect the City above all other things - even my own morals. The more I think about it the more I think Viala is right. The Rebels won't give up, and we can't afford another year of fighting back and forth across the continent." He hesitated, then continued, "This may well be a choice that will save hundreds or thousands of lives in the long run. How can I choose otherwise?"

Cordell looked ill. He turned to me and growled, "I always knew you were bloodthirsty, Mother, but I never realized just how much." After a shake of his head he turned towards Kenton and Ather. "But to hear this from the two of you... I thought better of you both." With that he spun around and stalked back towards the City, his spine straight and proud.

"He's your son," I said with a sigh.

My comment didn't produce the chuckle I was hoping for. "This is ugly business," my husband said quietly. "I'll talk to the Council, but we have to move fast if we're going to do this. Ikami?"

She nodded. "I don't like this either, but I'm willing to be more pragmatic about it than Cord. I'll do it myself - no need for anyone else to risk it. Randell can't have enough Lords around him to worry me." Our daughter stood up and looked around, counting quietly to herself, then pointed to the Council members watching us and waved them over.

The distinguished elder Bladesman General Teyo arrived first, faster to react than the others despite the cane he needed due to a wound acquired several months ago in a fight against the rebels. He looked back and forth at our expressions, then nodded before speaking in the Bladesman language. "*I don't know what you're planning, but you have my support. I trust you."

Kenton smiled and reached an arm up to clasp the other's hand. "*Thank you, General." Teyo was one of the Bladesmen who had come with us from the human world, and had been elected to the Council - the first of his kind - just three months ago.

Five other Council members joined us a moment later. I frowned - we needed one more to make a quorum of two-thirds. We'd have to head back and wait. "Friends, here is the situation," I started. "Head Councilor Kenton has found the exact location of Randell and many of his fellow rebel Lords. With permission of the Council, Ikami can teleport there and end this war in a moment."

They looked at each other, surprised. "I thought we were asking to parlay?" one of them ventured, a younger Councilor who I didn't yet know well. I realized that they still had no idea that Randell had even sent a message back.

"I did," Ikami replied. "He answered immediately. He didn't agree to our requirements, but -"

"Without agreement to Ikami's terms, we can't accept anything they'd offer," I said, cutting her off before she could mention that Randell had wanted to set up a meeting. Ikami's eyes went wide as she realized what I'd done, but she shut her mouth and stayed quiet. Lord Ather gave me a penetrating look, gauging my determination, but also chose to not speak up. "We have to hit the rebels immediately before they flee to another location that we don't know about. There's no time to lose."

The Council members traded looks. "In that case, we have to strike them while we can," Teyo said, this time in the human language for the benefit of those Councilors who didn't speak his own tongue. "I would fully support an immediate attack against the ringleaders." I smiled and bowed my head in respect to him - I'd known we would have his support from the beginning.

In moments the other Councilors had given their agreement as well. "That's it," Kenton said softly from where he still lay on the ground. "Councilor Jerana's position has not yet been filled, which means that us seven constitute sufficient votes to pass the motion. Ikami... you may proceed."

I blinked, startled. I hadn't realized that the rules worked that way. In the back of my mind I thanked Jerana for one last contribution to the City that she'd worked tirelessly on behalf of.

Our daughter nodded grimly. "Let's get this done, then." She rose up into the air a dozen feet, flying easily on her own magical power in a way that no other being could accomplish without using nearly everything they had. "Dad - send me the path I need to follow."

Kenton nodded and closed his eyes again. A moment later Ikami took a deep breath. "I'm ready. Anything else-"

Suddenly she cocked her head to the side as though she was listening to something. I frowned and concentrated. Sure enough, I could sense the faintest spark of a message reaching her from somewhere far distant. Only Ikami would have been able to understand something so depleted. Her eyes grew round. "Oh, damn!" she cried. "I can't go after Randell - there's something else -" With a familiar crack and a flash of light she vanished.

"What happened?" Kenton asked, blinking and trying to shield his eyes from the sun so he could look up.

"I don't know," I replied worriedly. "Ikami teleported out. There may have been another rebel attack somewhere else."

Teyo frowned, looking around. "That only makes it more vital that we execute their leaders while we know where they are. The Lady Ikami is the only one who could do so, however."

I looked over at Ather. "I'm worried about Ikami, but the General is right - if we wait for her to get back we may lose this chance. Ather, what do you think?"

Our old friend shook his head. "It is too far for me. We will need several other Lords and some time. Perhaps half an hour to prepare for teleporting? Are you suggesting that you go alone?"

"Viala, there were other Lords there. It wasn't just Randell. You can't do this without help," Kenton said with frustration evident in his tone.

"I'll get a strike team together with whoever is willing to go. I'm not waiting this one out," I said firmly.

"How many?"

"I don't know," he admitted, "but at least two or three others. I know you're strong, my love, but you can't take four Lords on by yourself. We don't have enough humans to hit a group like that, and the Bladesmen can't tolerate teleportation well enough to help out. Maybe we should wait for Ikami to come back."

"I'll get any human mages I can scrounge up from the City. Between them and I we can protect whatever Lords are willing to come long enough for them to recover from the teleportation. Kenton, we have to do this now - we can't wait."

Kenton opened his mouth to protest but I stared him down, daring him to speak, until finally he just shrugged and slumped back against the ground. We were both deeply concerned about Ikami, of course, but the best antidote to that was to keep our minds and bodies focused and busy.

Within an hour I'd assembled two squads of soldiers armed with Fuel-tipped arrows and four human mages, though I hadn't had time to look over their experience too closely. Two Lords from friendly nations had been willing to go along with Ather and I - he had quietly refused to stay behind and guide the teleportation effort. Kenton ground his teeth, clearly pained that he couldn't accompany us, but he had to stay with the five Lords who were sending us. Without his mental guidance they wouldn't be able to put us precisely where we needed to land. Even with so many Lords having time to prepare their energies the teleportation would be fraught with risks; it was not a small group and we were crossing half the continent.

Not for the last time I was reminded just how vital Ikami was to our cause. Without her strength to back it, our fragile alliance would crumble and the Bladesmen world would go back to a chaos of warring nations. At least I was finally doing something important to help, I thought to myself grimly.

In the late afternoon I assembled our team into a compact circle in the center of the City plaza, the humans with arrows nocked ready to fire and the Bladesmen in the center. The Lords would be nearly incapacitated at first, needing hours to recover - the plan was to set us down a half day's walk from the Rebel encampment. Hopefully it would be far enough that they wouldn't sense the spell. Soft pallets had been prepared for the Lords so we could carry them as we went. I fretted that I was forgetting something important, but at the same time every passing minute was a chance for Randell to flee once again.

Just before I gave the final signal to Kenton and the teleporting Lords Cordell ran into the plaza carrying a heavy backpack with him. He waved at us and I held up my arm, signaling to my husband to hold the spell for a moment longer. Our son jogged up to me, panting despite his conditioning, and handed me the pack, gesturing for me to look inside while he caught his breath. I took a peek at the contents and smiled at the sight of a silvery chunk of Fuel the size of my head. Dangerous to carry in the extreme, true, but I could draw on its power to greatly enhance my own abilities.

"Thank you," I said quietly. "I can't believe I didn't think of this myself."

He sighed. "If you're determined to go through with this, I'm not going to let you go empty handed. I still think this is the wrong thing to do - but clearly that's not stopping you. Take me with you and I'll do what I can."

I nodded appreciatively, thanking him with my eyes. My family had never been good at changing their opinions, myself least of all, and I knew how difficult this decision must have been for him. His glance back told me that the matter was far from closed - but keeping us safe was more important than anything else.

I sent one final mental message to Kenton - *I love you* - then gave the final go ahead for our mission. I closed my eyes and waited for the spell, hoping that we could get in and out safely.

With a bright flash through my eyelids and a sudden sense of vertigo, we teleported away.

Chapter 5 – Approach

    I gasped and nearly fell when we materialized without solid ground under our feet. Fortunately the spell had only been an inch or so off target; we landed with a collective grunt on hard packed gravelly sand. I blinked a few times, looking around in the suddenly harsher sunlight. Stark desert stretched in all directions, only a few barren hills and dead trees breaking up the horizon.

    Cordell grunted. "This looks familiar," he said. "I'd hoped to never come back here. Makes me wish Dalt was with us, though she would have hated that teleport."

    I looked over my shoulder at the Lords who had accompanied us. Ather and his companions looked ill; one had already vomited across the stony ground. None of them could maintain any balance. I directed the soldiers to load all three onto the litters we'd brought and directed the group to start marching northwest with no delay.

    After a few minutes of uncomfortable silence I tried to break the ice with my son. "I'm glad you're here, Cordell. You know more about this place than any of us. What do we need to worry about?"

    He thought for a few more steps before speaking, making sure to pitch his voice so everyone could hear. "When Dalt and I had to cross this place, a pack of... things... attacked us near the river. We're far beyond that area, though, so hopefully we won't be needing to deal with them. The Lord of this area, Eklavi, steals power from other Lords to keep this place clear of any life other than what he experiments with. The Council has him on their list of Lords to negotiate with, but he's refused to respond to any requests for diplomacy." Cordell shrugged. "Now that we know he's been sheltering the rebels, I imagine he might move up in the priority list a bit."

"He destroyed the belt Ather made for you, didn't he?" I prompted to keep the conversation going. My son had told us the story of his crossing two years before, of course, but the others in the group didn't know what to expect from this blasted place.

"Yes. We don't know how much power he has stored up here, but he's been alone in this nation for centuries. I'm almost more worried about dealing with him than I am with Randell and his cronies," he said with a sigh.

I could feel magic in the land all around for miles in every direction, lending a solidity to Cordell's descriptions that had been hard to grasp back home. It was a foul place - not just the Bladesmen-tainted magic; I was used to that now. Something terrible had been done here long ago. I doubted that anyone who had experienced this place firsthand would be willing to let Lord Eklavi leave without some justice. An entire nation, kept sterile for centuries.

"Archmagess, forgive me, but should we rotate ethereal watch duties as we travel?" asked one of the human mages politely. Sara was perhaps twenty-five years old, too young to really remember the war with Rainshye. Looking at the other mages with me, I realized with a chill that Cordell and I were the only ones to have seen combat. Everyone had been through years of training and battle drills, of course, but I had a momentary sense of foreboding and worry about their inexperience. Even Cordell's experience with real battles was limited and he'd never fought alongside human forces in the way he'd trained for.

"Yes," I replied awkwardly when I realized the young mage was still waiting for an answer. "That's an excellent idea. Can you take the first shift? We'll trade off every hour to keep people fresh." She nodded and held out her hand to another mage nearby - Harran, I think his name was. Physical contact was common practice for mages who had their minds away from their bodies; one mage could guide another so they could continue to maintain vigilance while making progress in the physical world. The way he tenderly clasped her palm showed that there was more than just training between the two of them.

I reviewed the plans we'd come up with before leaving. For Cordell's benefit I talked them through out loud; it wouldn't hurt to remind everyone else either. "Once we make contact I'm going to focus on maintaining a wide-area shield around the battle to ensure they can't teleport away. Cordell, with this Fuel I should be able to keep some additional protection around us as well. Ather will lead the other two Lords in striking down Randell - the other rebel Lords as well, if they continue to fight, but Randell is the primary target. The soldiers will take two mages with each squad and spread to our sides a little, both to make sure no Bladesmen soldiers get in the way and to keep up the pressure with Fuel-tipped arrows."

My son nodded. "Those are always useful - they're just strong enough that the Lords can't afford to ignore them."

"Dangerous, though," one of the squad sergeants added from nearby. "We're only carrying two per person and we'll try to get rid of them as quickly as possible. We'd appreciate it if you mages can try to keep the blasts away from us - we all know how little it can take to set a chunk of Fuel off, and I've seen too many soldiers lose fingers or hands to an arrow that went off in their grip."

"Liyane, right?" I asked, suddenly recognizing the woman. I hadn't realized she was still in the army - she had fought as a young woman in our war with Rainshye more than twenty years before.

She nodded, clearly gratified to be recognized. "Yes, ma'am. I've been through this before. We'll keep those Lords busy so you can finish them off."

I smiled and nodded in appreciation. There weren't that many veterans still around from those days and it would be very useful to have her in our midst.

    The hours passed slowly. We'd brought plenty of water, but the air was so parched that it felt like the water evaporated before it reached our throats. The soldiers didn't complain, though, their discipline and training showing through the discomfort of the march. The Lords' pallets were passed around every hour; I used trickles of magic to lighten the soldiers' loads as much as possible. We switched the ethereal watch on the same schedule. Cordell and I took turns as well. It was boring but necessary, scanning continuously with magical senses to make sure we weren't discovered by hostile forces before we were ready.

    After nearly five hours I called a halt. We were getting close, according to Kenton's directions, although it had taken longer than I had hoped to reach this point. I couldn't blame my companions; they'd struggled over the brutal terrain without complaint. I could only hope that the rebels were still in place, waiting unsuspecting for our strike.

    The three Bladesmen Lords were able to walk on their own by now and had each kept down some food and water though they were clearly not fully recovered. Lords would generally take a full night's sleep after teleporting before showing their faces and I greatly appreciated their willingness to join me in this mission. The soldiers spread out for a half hours' respite while I stepped aside with the Lords to discuss our position. After a moment's hesitation I waved Cordell over to join us. It was still difficult at times for me to respect the official authority he'd grown into in the last year.

    "*We're a little less than an hour's walk away from the cave entrance that Kenton described," I said slowly in the Bladesmen tongue. While Ather was entirely fluent in our language and had been since we'd met him, the other two were much more comfortable in their own tongue. I was a little worried about this for the coming fight, as not all of our soldiers were bilingual, but there had only been so much time to gather forces before departing from the City.

    "*I assume we don't want to try probing to find out

their defenses?" asked one of the two foreigners. Lord Mavue was a deceptively young-looking Lord who carried his nearly two hundred years well. I knew little about his country, save that it had been a staunch ally ever since Ikami had revealed herself to the Bladesmen world.

"*Kenton stated that he did not see much if anything in the way of warding spells," Ather replied. "*We're more worried about them detecting us on the way in than any traps; remember that they don't think there's any way we could know where they are. So yes, to answer your question, we plan to go in blind."

"*Excuse me, but I'm not sure that's the best idea," Cordell interjected. "*Lord Eklavi is a paranoid old bastard. I've been in one of his hideouts before, and I would expect him to maintain some protections around it at all times. It doesn't matter whether the rebels think they're safe - they're not the ones that live there."

The second foreign Lord, named Bonattel, nodded stiffly to my son in acknowledgement. I knew little about him save that he had come to the City recently from one of the smaller continents, asking to evaluate the prospects for an embassy with us. I had been surprised but gratified when he volunteered to join us on this mission. He still seemed uncomfortable around humans, but I couldn't fault him for jumping in with both feet and trying to understand us better.

"*In that case, I'll try to probe a short distance ahead as we approach. We've seen in the past that Bladesmen wards don't always trigger properly against human magic, so I'm safer off than any of you." I looked around at each Lord in turn, but received no counterargument so I continued. "*Does everyone understand the plan of attack?"

The others nodded, some more hesitantly than others. "*Remember, these rebels have killed numerous Lords over the last year. This is our best chance to stop them. If we fail here, they will continue to attack our allied nations and disrupt everything we are trying to accomplish. They will kill us if they get the chance; Randell has proved that he's willing to butcher innocents if it gets him what he wants. Don't hold back."

Cordell gave me a dirty look, then turned and stepped away. Ather and I traded glances but didn't say anything as the other Lords nodded solemnly.

"*Let's go, then," I said after a deep breath. "*I'm in front."

Chapter 6 – Errors

It wasn't long before we saw a dark shadow at the base of the next hill. By now I had my mental senses probing constantly about ten yards ahead, thankful as always for the accident of birth that had given me the gifts of an Archmage. I needed no guide on *my* arm, easily able to split my focus between the magical realm and the physical one. At the same time I started to gather power inwards, readying myself for a wide-ranging shielding spell not unlike what had protected our City for so many years back in our home world.

As we approached the shadow it was revealed as a long low archway leading down into darkness. The afternoon sunlight angled steeply into our eyes, making it difficult to see very far into the sandstone cavern before us. I quickly scanned the opening and felt only the faintest tethers of long-broken magics, none more recent than a few months ago. I waved to the group behind me that the entryway was clear and continued inwards.

Grey sand and gravel stood out starkly against the reddish stone interior where debris had been tracked a few yards inside by numerous feet before ours. We paused for a moment, letting our eyes adjust while the soldiers lit small oil lanterns - we mages could easily have summoned lights, but that would have risked giving ourselves away too early. The omnipresent defensive spells that every Lord maintained were damped far below their usual potency around me, and I made sure to similarly stifle my own innate defenses. I had been keeping them up automatically for so many years that it was surprisingly difficult to dampen them down. None of us dared to remove our shields completely, of course, but we brought them down to nearly undetectable - and far riskier - levels of power.

Everyone started moving slower once we found ourselves walking on bare stone. The constant low sigh of hot wind over sand outside was replaced by complete stillness except for the echoes of our boot soles scraping against the cavern floor. I could sense the nerves of everyone around me as my own neck hairs rose, sure that an ambush could come at any time.

After one turn we lost all natural lighting and the lanterns cast wildly dancing shadows that tricked the mind. I started at imaginary movements every few feet, and I wasn't alone in that. The passage itself had clearly started off as a natural water-carved fissure long ago but at some point it had been widened out to provide easy access for two people walking side by side. I trailed my fingers along the smooth walls, feeling the soft texture of the sandstone through my fingertips.

Fifty yards in we came upon a split in the passageway. The air had turned chilly and humid, with an icy draft spilling from the right-hand fork indicating a further descent. A whispered conversation with Sergeant Liyane caused me to lead the group left; her study of the smooth stone floor caused her to say with confidence that far more foot traffic had gone that direction. I couldn't make out the signs that she had seen clearly, having always relied on my magical senses for such things.

We proceeded onwards, constantly trying to minimize our sounds. Once or twice more my delicate magical probing revealed the broken strands of old spells but I encountered nothing still active save for the omnipresent magics that infused this entire country. After another twenty stressful minutes of creeping through the underground caves Lord Bonattel tapped on my shoulder. I stopped and turned towards him only to see him gesture ahead urgently. After a moment I caught the same noises he had - faint voices from somewhere in front of us. The soldiers behind us closed the shutters on their lanterns and we waited together, letting our eyes adjust to the near-complete blackness.

Sure enough, after a few minutes in which I could barely keep myself from shaking with anticipation, I was able to make out a faint light filtering down the corridor.

The soldiers behind me strung their bows as quietly as they could while the mages gathered power into themselves. I went through a few of my old exercises to help me focus, willing away the impatience that had been my companion ever since I could remember. Now that the time had come to fight I found it much easier to maintain a sense of serenity, a contrariness in my makeup which had always frustrated Kenton. When everyone was ready I started forward once more, keeping my defenses tightly reined in and barely daring to send my magical senses more than an arm's length ahead.

Before long I could see forward into a much larger cavern. Desks and workbenches littered the area, unidentifiable cobwebbed apparatus intermixed with papers and scrolls on nearly every available surface. In the center of the room a single table had been cleared off and it was around this that six Lords sat on the customary Bladesmen stools deep in conversation. A collection of magical lights spun slowly overhead, illuminating the entire room with a soft creamy glow.

Damn, I thought to myself, this was more than I'd hoped to face. I could make out Lord Randell himself on the far side of the table; for a moment I felt a stab of fear that they would surely spot us but a quick check behind me showed that our group remained well within the shadowed corridor. I looked over at the others and received nods of readiness, some of them grimmer than others.

I quailed under a momentary lack of confidence before reminding myself that I was one of only two Archmages currently alive. Unlike our last encounter with the rebels, we were fully prepared to face them and finish their guerilla war once and for all. A tiny voice in the back of my head wished that my daughter were there; she would have been able to deal with all six Lords without breaking a sweat. Her unexplained absence gnawed at my concentration. Under our original plan none of those behind me would have had to risk themselves.

Decades of training helped me push my worries aside. Drawing a deep breath, I expanded my magical senses throughout the room in an instant and identified the primed defenses on each of the six enemy Lords. Before they could react to my sudden unveiling of power, I raised my own defenses to their most potent state and released the spell I'd been holding for nearly half an hour ever since we'd entered the caverns. Appearing from nowhere, a bright blue glow shot up from the floor to surround the cavern in a human Shield Wall the likes of which had never been seen on this world.

My allies acted only a heartbeat later. The two foreign Lords thrust their arms forward, letting dual beams of deadly green light slice through the air at the nearest enemy. Their focused heat made the chill air react with an unpleasant sizzling noise. Their foe's defenses, only half-raised, lasted barely a second before shattering in a bright flash. The rebel slumped forward, sliced neatly into thirds by the crisscrossing lances of blazing energy.

Lord Ather, who had learned much from us humans over the last twenty years, threw forward a blast of air that sent the entire enemy group tumbling out of their chairs. They struck the floor in a tumble of limbs and broken wood, gaining us a few precious seconds more before they could react. As soon as his wind had calmed for a moment, our human soldiers fired synchronized waves of Fuel-tipped arrows from where they had slipped into the cavern to either side. The human mages smoothed the remaining gusts of air so that the arrows flew straight and true, striking the chaos in the middle of the room with a deafening ripple.

Smoke and flaring lights hid the center of the room for a moment. I risked a quick sweep with my magical senses and found at least three enemy Lords still alive in there, with another two radiating flickering sensations of dying energy. One of them tried teleporting out and for a split second I felt the energy of his spell stretching out towards the roof of the cave. When it contacted the Shield Wall I felt the impact as an almost physical slam; my spell held easily against the strike. The enemy Lord was not so lucky. He clearly hadn't expected my barrier to be there and the feedback was too much for his weakened state. For the first time in my life I felt an enemy Lord die from the total and utter dissolution of his body. He had teleported away - but nothing was left when the spell was prevented from passing out of the cave.

Ather had thrown up a wall of magical energy, preparing for the inevitable counterattack. The other two Lords were blindly firing blasts of flame and light into the smoke, hoping to keep the rebels off balance. Our soldiers had their last volley of explosive arrows strung, waiting for any target to show themselves.

I felt one of the enemy Lords probing my spell, desperately looking for an exit. I reinforced it grimly, determined to not allow any of them to escape. The others had managed to regroup somewhat and two beams of focused power flared through the smoke in our direction. Ather's protection caught one of them, absorbing the enemy assault cleanly, while the other erratically sliced upwards through the cave wall. A stalactite came free, falling just behind some of our soldiers. In a credit to their discipline they barely moved despite the rain of sharp rock chips clattering off their oiled leather armor.

I called out into the cavern, magically amplifying my voice so that it could be heard over the constant blasts and explosions of battle. "*Rebel Lords! Give yourselves up now and we will allow all of you except Randell to plead for your cause. Continue fighting and you will find nothing but death!"

The only response I received was a concentrated blast of power from at least two Lords. There was enough energy behind them to push through Ather's protections, and my own defenses fought to compensate. I sent more energy into them, drawing upon the Fuel in my backpack to keep the Shield Wall in place as well and prevent any escape. Its energy was reassuring, though I was constantly aware of its potential menace should it get struck directly by an enemy attack. There was enough there to collapse this entire cavern if I didn't keep it protected.

My long experience allowed me to keep the blue shell maintained around the periphery of the cavern at the same time as I reinforced my personal defenses and continued sweeping the cavern with magical senses to try and figure out what they were going to do next. The attacks of my companions were keeping two of the enemy Lords busy deflecting attacks, too harried to strike back - but I felt something else building from Randell himself. I tried a few quick jabs of power, but didn't have enough left over to do more than cause his personal wards to light up slightly.

Suddenly I realized where his concentration was - on the walls and ceiling above us. He was working to fracture the stone, a dangerous maneuver that was just as likely to entomb all of us together as strike only us. "Fire everything in there!" I yelled to the soldiers, needing to gain a few moments of distraction so I could counter his efforts. The second - and last - volley of Fuel-tipped arrows flew from our soldiers' bows into the melee in the middle, where another series of explosions showed that at least a few of them had struck deep. One of the enemy Lords stopped casting, though I couldn't spare a moment to determine if he had been killed or just knocked aside for a moment - my full attention was needed on the stone around us.

I sent my mind arrowing deep into the stone, detecting the natural fissures that Randell had been trying to weaken. It had been a sly maneuver; by using the preexisting weaknesses he'd come close to succeeding quickly instead of simply blowing up a few yards of rock directly above us where Ather would have countered it. I felt my brow furrowing in concentration as I stretched to repair the bonds of the rock and forge new ones. Using pure magical energy I forced some of the fractured stone back together, forming and heating it so that the fragments of metal buried deep within melted together to form tiny rods holding the breaks together. Without the Fuel on my back I wouldn't have been able to keep up all of my spells at once, and I resolved to thank Cordell again once this was all done.

A cry from the side made me wince but I couldn't risk leaving what I'd started. I took a few more precious seconds to finish my repairs to the point that Randell would need minutes of constant work to break the stone apart again, then ripped my focus back to my body. I glanced to my right and cringed as I saw a half-dozen soldiers crushed against the wall, unconscious or dead. Sergeant Liyane was among them, blood dripping from her smashed skull.

Ather was regaining his feet, dust and grime covering his body. *Three of them hit me at once,* he sent in a mental message. *I couldn't stop them all.*

I nodded - I knew he'd done his best. I felt him pulling a protective spell together again despite the failure of his first one - his head must be banging like a bell after having his spell broken like that. I winced in sympathy, then pushed aside my grief and sent my mind leaping around the cavern again to better discern the course of battle.

The furniture in the cavern was nearly all burning by now, causing flickering orange light to combine with the blue glow from the shimmering Wall at the periphery. Smoke was collecting at the top of the cavern and everyone was coughing from the fumes. We couldn't see more than twenty or so feet ahead, but I could sense three remaining Lords twice that far into the cavern. Of the other three I could sense nothing; either they'd somehow escaped or all had been slain. I hoped for the latter.

Randell himself was still alive; I recognized the flavor of his spells blasting out of the smoke. His companions were busy fending off the constant assaults of my allies, and the human mages accompanying our soldiers - while far weaker than any

Lord or myself - were helping harry our enemy and keep them busy. I pulled together as much energy as I could and pressed my presence forcefully against Randell's mind, seeking for any crack in his defenses. He could tell I was there, of course; I wasn't trying to hide what I was doing. For a moment our minds connected as his focus flashed across his protective wards to double-check that he was well guarded.

*Go back to your home, human bitch, he snarled at me with a sense of hatred beyond anything I'd ever felt.

*I'm going to butcher you for what you've done, I sent back with venom. **You and your rebels killed my friends, and I'm going to hurt you as much as I can for that.*

Chapter 7 – Hatred

With one last fleeting sensation of rage he wrenched contact away and immediately attacked. A lightning-fast whip of flame struck at me out of the darkness, deflected by my protective spells into a cascade of sparks. Almost simultaneously I sent a tendril of thought trying to worm its way into his mind, but it was blocked by his own wards.

After these opening shots the fight started in earnest. He sent a lance of light directly at my face, guided unerringly back to me through the haze along the line of my own mental probing. At the same time I reached out magically and slammed a blast of wind down on him from above. Our attacks were once again defeated; his protections crackled upwards to redirect my wind into the wall while Ather extended his shielding spells to deflect Randell's strike down into the floor. Shards of white-hot stone burst in all directions for a moment before the deadly beam flickered out.

I pulled some of my focus away from the Shield Wall around the room and struck with renewed vigor, pulling energy from the Fuel on my back to reinforce my strikes. I hammered Randell's mind with repeated blows, any single one of which would have fractured his sanity had they made it through his wards. At the same time I split my attention into the floor below him, pulling its substance apart and slowly weakening it in preparation of blowing the stone apart beneath his feet.

He didn't plan on giving me any time to coordinate my

attacks. Lord Randell was not one to stay on the defensive. I felt his magic slashing at my defenses; he was simultaneously trying to line up a lance of light to beat down my defenses and heat the air around me to the point it would ignite. Ather's magic flickered back and forth, trying to hold off Randell's direct assault while keeping the human soldiers protected, but I could tell he didn't see my enemy's more subtle strike.

My face was flushed with anger and for a moment I forgot that I'd never faced down an enemy Lord like this one on one. I released my hold on the Shield Wall around the cave entirely and used that magical power to siphon the heat away from me before Randell burned us all to cinders. I created a channel in the air between the enemy Lords and my position, visible as a small whirling tornado through the smoke and dust. With a primal scream I forced the superheated air back along the channel and threw every scrap of power I had into it, resulting in a jet of flames running the length of the cavern.

For a moment the entire chamber flickered into light. My allies fell back, covering their faces with cries of pain from the intense heat. The enemy Lords were clearly visible for the first time in minutes, a look of surprise on their faces as they redoubled their defenses towards me. Randell and I locked gazes across the cavern and for one instant I recognized the same hatred on his face that I was feeling towards him. In that moment I knew that I could never have found common cause with him. That recognition fueled my resolve and I pulled everything I could from the power source on my back into blasting the center of the cavern to ash. This was the man who would destroy my entire family if he had the chance, and right now I had the opportunity to stop him once and for all.

One of the enemy Lords' protections failed against my Fuel-powered assault and in that split second he was consumed by the flames. A wailing shriek was all that remained.

Randell's sole remaining ally suddenly disappeared with a crack. Without the Shield Wall in place he'd found a route out of the cavern, teleporting away instead of facing my wrath any longer. Randell's eyes flickered upwards and I knew that he was preparing to teleport as well. I pushed further than I ever had and split my attention back to the ground beneath him where I'd been working earlier, desperate to prevent him from fleeing. I dimly felt my body falling forward onto the hot floor, but somehow assembled just enough extra force to trigger a blast beneath my foe. The weakened stone exploded upwards, sending blisteringly hot shards scything everywhere around Lord Randell.

He instinctively shifted his protective spells downwards to protect his legs from the attack. Before he could realize his error my flames ripped through the top of his wards. They exploded in a ripple of energy, knocking the few remaining tables and chairs away from the center of the room.

Randell met my glare for one last instant, unrepentant, before he was consumed by my anger and blasted into a blackened smear against the cavern wall.

I gasped and released the spell. I'd maintained it for only seconds, but the jet of flame had been of such force that I felt utterly spent even with the additional power I'd siphoned from the Fuel on my back. It was nearly gone, just a few dusty threads remaining of the block which had enabled my human magics to stand up against so many Lords.

My ears rang and lights flared across my vision. It was at least ten seconds before I could hear the moans of pain from those around me. At the same time I realized that my hands hurt, and looked down to see red blisters and burns where I'd fallen onto the floor. The cavern itself was dimly lit by flickering fires off to the sides, all of the enemy Lords' lights having been extinguished long before.

Trembling, I called upon my earliest training and sent a few lights of my own upwards to brighten the chamber. They revealed a hideous charnel ground; the half-burned remains of the first slain enemy Lords were scattered around the room while the stone showed a black glassy reflection where my flames had landed. Of Lord Randell and his last fallen ally there was no sign, their ashes mixed with the soot coating the entire far half of the cave.

"Are you all right?" asked Lord Ather from behind me, coughing with every other word. After two tries to sit up I nodded, my shaking hands betraying the weakness I felt.

I looked around to my sides to see what had become of our own people. Many of the human soldiers sported burns and broken bones, but only a few had perished - Sergeant Liyane and Mage Harran among them. My heart lurched when I saw Sara sobbing over the body of her lover, his torso nearly detached by a slicing beam of magic. Lord Mavue was slumped against the wall, barely conscious but alive. Ather and Bonattel were walking among the wounded, doing what they could with magical healing to make sure that no others died. Bladesmen healing had always been more potent than that of our human magic, so I left them to it while I sent one weak mental tendril around the perimeter of the cavern to make sure we were safe.

It was nearly an hour before our group was ready to travel. Our slain had been wrapped carefully in the cleanest makeshift shrouds we could find and the wounded were as stable as they could be made. I had spent much of the time resting and probing the area to discover what had happened of the original inhabitants. Cordell sat near Sara, whom he'd known from a young age, comforting her as best he could and giving me sorrowful looks whenever our eyes met.

When I couldn't take it any longer I stood up and slowly walked towards the far end of the room. Between the other Lords and myself the cavern was brightly lit by magic, but even so the soot and blast marks seemed to suck up light as I stepped carefully through the wreckage. Despite my best efforts I stirred up plenty of ash and dust from the still-warm floor. I made my way to the far end of the cavern with my companion's voices bouncing off the walls to reach me sounding distorted and foreign. I peered down a dark corridor heading further into the earth, trying to keep my mind off of the slain bodies at the other end of the chamber.

I sensed Cordell stepping up behind me before he spoke, my protective wards prickling in a familiar way at the presence of another mage. "The Lord who lived here before -

Lord Eklavi - there's no way he would have allowed this without stepping in. The rebels must have killed him or driven him out."

"He wouldn't have cut a deal to shelter Randell?"

Cordell shrugged from next to me, looking down the same passageway. "He wouldn't have allowed his precious experiments to be harmed like this. He was insane enough to have thought he could stand against all of us, I think. Eklavi had consumed the power of enough other Lords to give a good fight against anyone short of Kami, but he wouldn't have lasted long against Randell and all of his friends together. If they decided they wanted this land for their own... well, it made a good hiding place until now." He kicked a scrap of debris so that it clattered off the wall.

"Randell's dead now. The rebels who are left won't -"

My son put his hand up to cut me off. "Not now, Mom. Please. People - our friends - are dead back there. They're dead because you wanted to fight instead of talk. Maybe someday I'll understand why you wanted to come here like this, but not today." The sorrow and anger in his voice left me silenced, unable to come up with any response that would have meant a damn thing.

He kicked at the ground again, then paused and leaned over. He came back up with a long belt covered in ashes, somehow still intact despite the destruction around us. "Well I'll be damned," he breathed in an entirely different tone. "Look at this. Do you recognize it?"

I reached over and brushed at some of the soot ineffectually, doing little more than rubbing the color deeper into the still-supple leather. I felt a spark of magic respond to my touch and suddenly realized what this was. "It's your birthday present from Ather," I exclaimed. A smile spread across my face for what felt like the first time since the rebels had struck us back in the City.

"I thought Lord Eklavi had drained its power long ago," he said excitedly. "Look, there's still some magic left in it. It's been more than two years. I hated to give this up so much -

I never imagined it would come back to me." Despite the smears of ash and debris it left on his clothes, he threaded it around his waist and buckled it shut.

"Ather will be happy to see you wearing it again," I said, then hesitated for a moment before continuing in a lower tone. "I know you don't agree with why we came here, Cordell. I hate that we lost people here, but we didn't start this fight. Right now we need to focus on getting home and rebuilding. Can we set this aside for now? Please?"

Cordell looked at me, startled. I didn't say "please" very often. Slowly, he nodded, then put his arm around my shoulders and turned me back towards our friends. We walked back across the cavern, feeling more like family than we had for some time - even if it was only a temporary truce.

Chapter 8 – Reconnection

  Our return journey was difficult. The three Lords and I combined our weary magic to make contact back home across hundreds of miles. They were in no shape to teleport us across such a vast distance so we had to wait for the Lords in the City to bring us back. It was an uncomfortable wait as we crowded together into a tight circle, our dead laid close, so our allies would have to transport as small an area as possible.

  Finally I felt a touch of familiar warning from Kenton, guiding the others to our location. I called out "Get ready!" and had just enough time to close my eyes before magic surrounded our group and flashed us across the miles. An instant later I was breathing fresh air for the first time in hours, realizing only then how deeply the blackened smoke in the cavern had seared itself into our lungs.

  I had to blink for a few seconds to clear the spots from my vision before I recognized Kenton standing in front of me, a concerned look on his face. I nodded and fell into his arms, needing to hold him for a moment before anything else. Even then I resisted the urge to feel the full force of my grief, having been trained since birth to never show weakness in public.

  We were in the plaza at the center of the City, a cold sun shining brightly in the sky above us. There was an unseasonable chill which explained why few people were nearby to witness our return. Construction efforts continued on the Council building, the workers pausing only briefly to look us over before returning to their tasks.

The dead and wounded were taken to the hospital nearby while the three Lords, myself, and Cordell stepped aside. We turned to speak to the Council members and allied Lords who had hurried over after we'd arrived. "Randell is dead," I said bluntly to their questioning faces. "One got away, but four other rebel Lords were also slain." Behind me I heard Lord Ather giving a quiet running translation for those who were more familiar with the Bladesmen tongue.

My audience traded glances of surprise. Lord Jabnoss, the Lord who had helped me a few days ago in the battle at the Council building, spoke up first. "That is good, very good. Other than Lady Ikami at City of Lords, I don't know time where five Lords were slain with no losses of friendly." His accent would have been charming had the subject not been so serious.

"We lost several of our number, actually," Cordell said quietly. "Four soldiers and a human mage."

"Yes, but no Lords?" Jabnoss replied.

My son frowned and I hurried to jump in before he said something to cause an incident. "It was a difficult battle, but we had the advantage of surprise and that made all the difference. We need to consider how to deal with the remaining rebels. They may choose to lash out, though I don't think they'll stay united without Randell."

Cordell swallowed whatever he was going to say with obvious difficulty while the Council members started talking excitedly. Their conversation revolved around how to try and convince the Lords who had been on the brink of siding with Randell back over to work with us. I sent a quick mental message to my son and asked, *Are you all right?*

I thought we'd gotten past this, he sent back in a sour tone. *Lives are counted in more than simply Bladesmen Lords. Does this Lord treat his people well or is he one of those who considers anyone who's not a Lord or Archmage worthless?*

You know we still have a long way to go, I replied with a sense of sadness. *Some of these Lords have treated their people like dirt for centuries. We can force them to listen to the will and ideas of the common Bladesmen, and show them how much we value our own non-magical citizens, and eventually that will show them the advantages of our way.*

Cordell withdrew from the conversation leaving behind a feeling of discontent. I sighed and focused back on the Council's chatter, listening closely to what our allied Lords were saying. Tired as I was, my mind kept drifting until I realized that we still didn't know what had happened to Ikami. I wanted to ask Kenton if they'd had any contact during the hours we'd been gone but had to wait until he was done talking to the others. If I didn't respect his position of Head Councilor how could I expect others to do the same?

It was a long half hour until the impromptu meeting broke up with little being decided. The visiting Lords had said nothing of use other than to clearly state that they supported Lady Ikami and that the rebels must be put down entirely, while the Council had decided that they needed to wait until their contacts elsewhere on the continent could give an update on what the rebel coalition was up to now. Everyone's worst fear was that they would simply pick another leader and continue their guerilla war against us.

As soon as I could I snatched Kenton's arm and pulled him away from the group. He knew what I was going to ask before I opened my mouth, of course, and just shook his head with worry in his eyes. "I don't know, Viala," he said with a sigh. "We haven't heard anything since you left. I'm worried too."

"Could the rebels have struck somewhere else? We know they still have dozens of Lords sworn to their cause."

My husband just shrugged helplessly. "Your guess is as good as mine. Ikami can handle herself, but their strike here hurt a lot. If they hit an allied capitol just as hard we could lose entire nations that are wavering in their support. Look, neither one of us is in any shape to go looking for her right now. All we can do is wait. Tomorrow we can try searching around if we don't hear anything."

I frowned but had to admit that he was right. It was a familiar feeling after so many years of marriage, and he was the only person in the world that I'd put up with having so much insufferable correctness in them. We started walking arm in arm back towards our home, Cordell trailing a few paces behind us still talking to one of the allied Lords. I could catch enough of the conversation to know that they were talking about Ganshe; Cordell was always interested in how well Dalt was doing there.

I'd never been able to tell if there was anything more than friendship between the two of them. Kenton had told me a hundred times to let our children be but I couldn't help but hope Cordell at least would settle down with someone who cared about him at some point. Ikami was still too wild, and it would take a very special person indeed to be able to live with her casual use of power above and beyond anything this world had ever seen. It had taken me years and even now I had to push away feelings of inadequacy whenever she performed miraculous feats without even thinking about it.

The evening dragged by slowly with no word from our daughter. We picked at a dinner together, all attempts at conversation failing, before Cordell finally gave up and headed to his own home after wishing us a good night. Kenton and I slept poorly, both of us tossing and turning all night hoping for any word from Ikami.

This unease continued until late the following morning. Kenton was in his temporary office, trying to focus on the never-ending work of the Head Councilor, while I lent magical support to the Council building repairs. The plaza behind me was busy with normal traffic, the citizens of the City going about their business while ambassadors and diplomats met with their counterparts from other nations throughout the four continents. Today's weather was noticeably warmer and I had just taken off my overcoat during a short break to drink a canteen of water.

Without warning a magical surge rippled through the plaza accompanied by a terrible ripping noise. I instinctively dove forward and raised my personal defenses against whatever attack might be coming, twisting around to look at the center of the square from whence the power had blasted. To my surprise there was no obvious damage. Instead the ripping sound continued, growing in volume until it was deafeningly loud. I recognized the noise just as the portal widened, a shimmering hole in reality nearly a dozen yards across holding steady a few feet above ground level. A few people stood staring at it, slack-jawed, while everyone nearby who had any magical senses whipped up defensive spells just as I had.

Only one person in the world could have built such a thing. With a great relief I recognized Ikami's mind as it reached out towards me and she politely requested mental conversation.

Ikami! Where are you? What has happened?

I'm fine, she replied. *This time, anyways. Look, can you get Dad, Ather, and Wesnoq if he's there? Apashae would be useful too, and Cord can come if he wants. The portal I opened leads to the camp near the City of the Lords. It would be easier to show you what I'm dealing with than try and explain it from afar.*

Are you still on the other side? I asked, suddenly worried. *You sent your presence through the portal instead of across the continent normally?*

Yes, why?

Ikami, what do you think would happen if this portal suddenly shut? This isn't safe! I'll get people and come through, just go back to your body now!

My daughter suddenly realized what I meant. If the portal wasn't perfectly stable her mental presence might be cut off from her body and the thread she used to return would be disconnected, without any direction to find her way back. It was a certain death sentence, just like when a mage stretched too far and their connection back to their body snapped. With a mental shudder at how much she'd risked Ikami sent a sense of apology and slipped her mind away from mine.

I flicked messages out to everyone Ikami had mentioned and asked them to come to the plaza immediately.

Within fifteen minutes everyone was there, Ather having teleported Cordell back from the airship docks a few miles away. When I was asked what was happening I could only shrug helplessly and say that Ikami needed us to join her through the portal still hanging imposingly in midair.

With some trepidation - we'd only used this method of transportation a few times since Ikami had learned how to make them - we proceeded to step through the gateway. I felt slightly ridiculous as I climbed the makeshift steps made of two stools and a park bench, but the feeling fell away as I closed my eyes and stepped forward. It was an unnerving sensation that set my skin to tingling but just as it had before there were no other effects other than instantaneously transporting me clear across the continent. This, more than anything else, showed the difference in scale between Ikami's power and that of other Lords and Archmages.

The air of this side of the portal felt thin and cold, making me wish I'd brought the overcoat which was now thousands of miles away. I stepped forward to make room for Ather. On this side our entrance was aligned perfectly with the ground. My feet fell on hard-packed dirt with only a few dismal strands of grass trying to struggle upwards. We were behind a low hill that I recognized all too well; on the other side was the crater marking the continuing magical disturbance where hundreds of retired Lords had once lived. Around me was the research camp run by the Bladesmen Lords Lim and Abel, dark green tents standing starkly against the patches of snow that clung anywhere a shadow kept them safe against the midday sun.

I stepped forward and grabbed Ikami in a tight hug, then stepped back and looked her over. She looked unharmed, the only signs of injury the long-healed burns and broken bone blade on the left side of her body. "You need to align those things better on the far side," I said in way of greeting.

She smiled back, though lines around her eyes spoke of more exhaustion than I'd seen from her in a year. "I'll work on that," she replied, then her expression turned somber. "I'm sorry I didn't think about the risk of going through the portal like that. I should have sent someone to speak in person."

"Just take it as a lesson that us old-timers still have some wisdom to share with you," I chided gently.

"I'd never imagine otherwise," she said seriously. "I should have known better."

As soon as Cordell came through he rushed between us and grabbed Ikami in an exuberant embrace. Though the two looked completely different - small bony protrusions around Ikami's face left no doubt as to her genetic heritage, even before you noticed the delicate blades protruding from her shins and arm - they were closer than most siblings and I had no doubt that the strength of our family rested in their relationship. If it weren't for Cordell's belief in his sister we never would have gotten her back after she'd faced down the City of the Lords.

Mastermage Apashae, the mage who had taken over training of other humans with the gift of magical power, was the last one through the portal. She smiled at us and nodded, though she and Lord Wesnoq clearly felt somewhat left out from our impromptu family reunion. We walked over to a nearby tent and stepped inside to find a charcoal brazier giving off welcome heat. Lim, a thin Lord who looked nearly skeletal with his lack of obvious fat or muscle, stood up to welcome us with a bow.

Though most of us knew each other reasonably well, there were at least two who didn't. "Lord Lim, this is Mastermage Apashae of the City. I don't believe you've met. Apashae, this is Lord Lim of Tanekyth."

Apashae, a pretty woman in her mid thirties, curtsied with a smile. "I've heard much about your research both here and in Illonye, Lord Lim. It's a pleasure to meet you."

Lim looked at Ikami helplessly and I realized that he was the only one here who couldn't at least understand the human language. Both Kenton and Apashae looked abashed for a moment, then Apashae spoke up in broken Bladesmen. "*Many sorries Lord Lim. I speak your speak now but not quality. Good to meet your Lord self."

He smiled in return and bowed again. "*You speak very well. Thank you - I appreciate your willingness to use a foreign tongue."

We settled in on stools around the warmth. "*I apologize - it's hard to get any long-term spells to stay stable here, otherwise I'd just use magic to keep the camp warm," Ikami said apologetically. "*Thanks, everyone, for coming through so quickly. Lim sent a message to Lord Qamu, who was visiting - never mind, it doesn't matter. Suffice it to say that he got a message to me yesterday through several middlemen. A group of Rebels had showed up here and they were trying to trigger the magic in the crater to, well, blow up."

Lord Lim nodded and continued. "*I could not stop them alone - there were at least half a dozen of them. Lord Abel had headed back to Seratore to make sure his people were doing well so I was alone aside from the maintenance staff. Once I sent my message off I hid out in the hills nearby and used the interference from the crater to stay undetected. All I could do was watch. They were experimenting, trying to see if there was a way to get the magic to overload in what I would call an exceptionally detrimental manner."

"*Ikami spoke to us of how dangerous the energy here is just the other day," Kenton replied gravely.

"*Well, I arrived just in time to stop them," Ikami said. "*Most of them got away but I caught two. They're still here, trapped until the Council decides what to do with them."

"*Trapped?" Apashae asked, clearly unsure that she had translated the word correctly.

"*I stuck their feet in the ground deep within the crater. The little magical energy they can summon down there has to be used to keep from burning up. They're not going anywhere unless I let them out," Ikami assured us.

I smiled. "*Creative," I said approvingly.

"*Let's move on from Kami's methods of punishment," Cordell said with a frown. "*How can we keep this place contained? From what you said the other day, Kami, even without their interference this place might explode on its own at some point."

She nodded. "*Here's what I'm thinking. We can't risk a group of Lords deciding to come here and blow up half the continent, that's for sure. I need to fashion something to use up the crater's power, something long-term that can't be misused." My daughter took a deep breath, looking around at each face in turn, before continuing. "*I want to build a portal back to the human world."

"*What?" Ather asked, as clearly surprised by this suggestion as any of us were.

"*Look, I think I can do it safely," Ikami said, plunging forward with an explanation. "*I know what it took to bring the City here before I was born. Mom, Dad, Ather, Apashae - all of you were there and had some part in it. Lord Wesnoq and Lord Lim, both of you have heard of the terrible slavery that Bladesmen undergo there. We have to go back at some point - we can't let millions of Bladesmen stay like that. A portal is going to be much safer than trying to replicate the transport spell that was used before. It killed your predecessor, Mom, and I'm not going to risk it with you and I the only Archmages to handle the human half of that magic."

"*It's too far," I exclaimed. "*Ikami, I know you're powerful, but you're talking about building a portal to another world entirely."

"*It's not too far if I'm using the power in the crater here," she disagreed. "*If it doesn't work, it will at least buy us a couple of months until the magic builds up again. Maybe three. Just think - with a portal we could send airships back and forth with supplies, we could bring our wounded back home, and we could bring as many forces through as we need. We all know that going back means war - the Lords running the Pact may be few in number but they won't give up easily. By now I'm sure they've fixed things so that their Bladesmen won't obey other Lords, so we'd be facing millions of Bladesmen commoners who won't stop until they're dead. We have to try and free them before that happens, but it won't be easy."

Lord Wesnoq frowned. "*Lady Ikami, your goals are noble. And I agree that at some point this injustice must be remedied. But at the same time you must remember that many Lords here are still grappling with the idea of equality with commoners. Risking their own lives to rescue Bladesmen they've never met will be a difficult proposition to convince them of." He looked around uneasily and continued, "I must confess that I am still getting used to the idea myself, and as you know we of Illonye treated our citizenry much better than many other nations."

Ather spoke next, rubbing his chin thoughtfully. "*I hear you, Lord Wesnoq, but I must disagree. I come from the human world, the only Lord born there who survived. This injustice makes the work of the rebels here pale in comparison. The Pact is pure evil, something beyond the comprehension of even the retired Lords who once lived nearby. Unless you have a better idea of how to harness the energies here, I am at least provisionally in favor of the Lady Ikami's idea."

We all sat back, thinking it through. The best alternative I could come up with was to build a giant Shield Wall around the crater, which would both protect it from the uninvited and leech off its power to hopefully keep it contained. It wasn't a bad idea, and I knew Ikami would have thought of it beforehand - so why didn't she mention it? Without letting my expression betray my intentions, I sent the thinnest of mental probes out towards my daughter and politely requested contact.

Hi Mom, she replied after connecting her mind to mine.

Why not a Shield Wall? I asked without preamble.

She sent a sensation of mirth. *I knew you'd catch on to that,* she replied. *Dad and Cord will, too, once they think about it a bit longer. Maybe Ather as well. Here's the thing - this portal to the human world - I've been thinking about how to get us back there ever since I dealt with the retired Lords. No matter how I turn the problem over in my mind, even with the wealth of magical knowledge I got from - well, you know who I mean. Anyways, I can't figure out a way to do it without risking everyone's lives in the process. It's a miracle that anyone lived through the original spell or the version that you and Ather cast. I can buffer a lot of the magic, but not all of it - somebody's likely to die every time we try and send people back and forth.*

I remembered the Archmage who had trained me when I was young. It had been more than twenty years and I realized I couldn't remember his face anymore. He had died bringing the City here; the magic had been too much for him. It had taken me years to realize how close the spell had come to claiming my life as well.

A portal is the only sane answer if we plan more than a one-way trip - and Mom, as much as I know you and Dad grew up there, that place isn't my home. It never will be. We have to have some means of regular transport and communication or the two worlds will eventually grow apart and lose contact. This power can keep a portal open and stable for centuries. I don't know any other way to do it.

So this might be our only way to really get home, I replied after a moment's thought.

Yes, exactly. The Lords will jump on the idea of a Shield Wall - it's safer for them, and gives them an easy out to avoid thinking of going to the human world. We have to push them into this war with us.

I'm not sure your father will agree, I sent back with a sense of warning.

He might surprise you, Ikami fired back. *He's never forgotten what the Bladesmen back on that world are going through every day. Ather is a constant reminder. It won't be easy, but I think he will agree. And you and I can work on him in the meantime.*

I gave Ikami a feeling of agreement before withdrawing. The entire conversation had taken only seconds, during which the others hadn't spoken a word. I wouldn't be surprised if there were other magical conversations going on right now, but if so everyone kept them constrained enough that I couldn't sense them - just like I'd done with Ikami.

After another minute, Lord Lim shook his head and spoke. "*I confess that I cannot come up with any viable alternative. There is simply too much power here for any lesser spell to contain."

"*The rebels must be settled with before we take any action, one way or another," Wesnoq followed quickly. "*Only then can we look at assembling a force to go through to the human world."

Ikami smiled. "*I agree. Fortunately, most of our allies already have significant armies at the ready to guard against the depredations of Randell and his cronies. Once we have found a solution to the rebels those armies will be ready to go. I know the City's airships are fully armed and ready to fight, though this will be a different battle from what they expected."

Kenton frowned. "*I think we're getting ahead of ourselves. Ikami, do what you can for now to keep the remains of the City of the Lords from blowing up on us. Lord Lim, we'll make sure to send a few extra Lords to help guard this place just in case. The two captured rebels will come back with us to the City where they will be judged and dealt with." He looked at Ather, hesitated for a moment, then finished with, "*And yes, we will start preparing our forces for an expedition back home. It would be a crime to let millions of Bladesmen continue to serve against their will any longer than we must."

Our friend smiled back, an unfamiliar glint in his eye. For an instant I glimpsed the anger that he'd kept suppressed for so many years with the patience of an immortal, then it was gone and he was once again cool and serene. We had lost our home but found a new one here. Ather's people were still back there, alone and forgotten by everyone but him - and now he would finally have a chance to settle the scores of his childhood.

Chapter 9 – Tension

    Our return through Ikami's portal was no more pleasant than the trip out but at least the experience was short. As soon as I emerged I ran into Kenton's back and stumbled on the stones of the plaza, catching myself against his shoulder with a muttered curse. "Please move out of the way so we can come out of that thing, dear," I said with mock sweetness.

    His lack of immediate response gave me pause and I looked around to see what had stopped him. It took only an instant to realize something was dangerously wrong; the normal business of the City center had halted and both human and Bladesmen alike were huddled near the buildings arranged along the outside of the plaza. A group of ten unfamiliar Bladesmen stood only a dozen yards ahead of where we'd emerged from the portal, the powerful magic radiating from them marking them unmistakably as Lords. As soon as I recognized one as the lone Lord who had escaped from our trap a day earlier, I threw my protective spells around both Kenton and myself and braced for an attack. I had no hope of deflecting a barrage from so many, but I only needed to hold out until Ikami came through behind us.

    Ather ran into us and took less time than I had to recognize the dreadful danger of the situation. I pushed hard to extend strong warding spells around him as well and from our many years of working together he knew he could concentrate on offense without a single word being spoken. He threw his arm outwards and gathered energy for an attack, but before he could release his spell Kenton held up his hand and quietly commanded us to stop. Both Ather and I hesitated, glaring at the rebels as though we dared them to start a fight against the three of us.

The Lords on the other side of the standoff stared back with various degrees of anger and defeat in their eyes. One, a Lord I'd never met, shouted across the plaza in the Bladesmen language. "*We will speak only with the Lady Ikami. Until then, we will defend ourselves but begin no battle without provocation."

My husband gave no sign of weakness with his response. "*I am Kenton, the Head Councilor of the City. The City and its allies are willing to negotiate if you release your readied spells and lower your defenses to a more reasonable level. We will not parlay until you do so."

I could sense mental communication darting between the Lords we faced. While we waited I sent my mind dancing around the plaza and the nearby buildings, sensing several allied Lords as well as human mages watching ready from the crowd. I left each with a sense to be ready to attack as soon as an opening appeared; Ikami or I would send a clear signal when to begin the assault. No quarter was to be given.

Behind me the nearly limitless sensation of my daughter's power emerged from the portal. I needed no visual confirmation; Ather and I traded looks and readied ourselves to strike at the slightest sign from Ikami. Her presence rose up above us, coming to a hover perhaps twenty yards in the air. My lips curved into a grim smile, knowing that with her power backing us the odds had completely changed.

We're ready whenever you are, I sent quickly to Ikami. Before I withdrew my mind I felt Kenton sending a trickle of communication upwards. He sent a mental invitation to join the two of them, and an instant later I felt Cordell and Ather connect as well.

I think they are here to surrender, Kenton sent.

I agree, Dad, Cordell answered before I could reply. *Let's *hear them out and get this finished.*

These are the last leaders the Rebels have, I fired back. *We can finish them here and scatter whatever remains. Between these Lords and the ones we slew yesterday there'd be none left to organize their resistance.*

If they're here to parlay we can't just attack them, Cordell sent back with frustration leaking through.

We know they're not going to just give up and happily settle down. They're right here in front of us - this is what we have wanted for months! I didn't understand why we would let this opportunity pass. The whole Council had talked of little else since Randell and his people had started attacking friendly Lords.

I don't know, Mom, Ikami sent uneasily. *I'll do whatever the Council decides - right now, that means Dad. I've been chasing these Lords for what feels like forever, but... Randell's dead.*

I tried to send more but Kenton replied with an authority I didn't want to challenge. *Cordell is right, my love,* he started off. *I have been wrestling with our decision since yesterday - we did not deal in good faith with Randell and we all know it. If we can make up for that here, and settle the rebellion peacefully... Good men and women died yesterday because we attacked instead of talked.*

I choked back my frustration, inwardly wanting to stamp my feet in disgust. *We have to be guided by prudence and wisdom, not conscience,* I replied as evenly as I could. *These Lords will cause trouble down the line.*

Look at them, Mom, Cordell sent back. *Look in their eyes. They're defeated. You did what you needed to yesterday - now let us do our part. We can talk to them and convince them to stop. Enough blood has been shed.*

I almost fired back a scathing reply, but waited for a moment and took a deep breath first. I wanted to believe in Cordell and Kenton's surety, but had no faith in anything we would sign with these rebels. Still... For the sake of my relationship with my son I pulled back for a moment and looked, really looked, at the rebel Lords across from us.

They glared back at me, clearly aware that we were mentally debating what to do about them. And then I saw the despair that Cordell was talking about, a deep loss in their eyes that spoke of utter surrender and defeat. It struck me that they had come here knowing that Ikami could destroy them completely; they'd given up the stealth and guerilla tactics that had kept them alive during their rebellion and come to the center of our power openly.

I didn't send anything more specific than a sense of assent to the group conversation above before settling my mind back into my body. I still kept alert for any sign of action from our enemies but this time it was only as a measure of insurance instead of combat readiness. When the others broke their communication link a few minutes later I stayed out of the way and kept quiet.

Kenton stepped forward and addressed the Lords again. "*I repeat my request - we will negotiate with you once you lower your defenses and release the magic you hold at the ready. You know that the Lady Ikami can overpower you if she so chooses; she serves the Council and will parlay through us."

The rebels looked at each another for a moment, then one by one began to relax their wards. Now would be the time for us to attack, but I held back and made sure the others around the plaza did the same. When they stood before us a moment later, nearly defenseless, they looked around as though feeling naked in public.

My husband nodded. "*Now we will begin. The last time your group arrived it was as enemies who killed innocents in cold blood. What is your purpose today?"

One of them, a Lord I didn't recognize, stepped forward and bowed deeply in Ikami's direction. He then turned back to Kenton and bowed again, though noticeably shallower. "*With Lord Randell's death we have no common cause. We have come to surrender; we have no death wish. We do not agree with the ways that Lady Ikami - and you humans - have brought to our world, but we recognize that we can no longer resist them."

"*We offered Lord Randell a sanctuary on empty islands far from the four continents. The same offer exists for all of you and the others who sympathize with your cause. If you are willing instead to try our ways, we will grant you amnesty though you must know that you will be under probation for many years. If you find a way to live within our rules, respecting all Bladesman - including commoners - and humans alike, you will eventually earn back our trust and become part of our new society." I fidgeted at Kenton's words, uncomfortable at the idea of accepting these Lords back from their pariah status, but knew that this was what he and the Council had discussed.

"*Twelve of the thirty-eight Lords we represent have chosen to accept exile," their representative replied in a proud tone. "*The rest of us, including myself, will accept your amnesty and take whatever terms you give for probation. We are willing to try your new ways, though we make no promises that we can accept them forever. If we find that they are too different for us, may we choose the path of exile at a later date?"

"*So long as you do not commit any crimes before making that choice, that would be acceptable to the Council," my husband replied immediately. "*The Lady Ikami will enforce this agreement; as you all know, she has been chosen by the other Lords on this world as the ultimate arbiter of any disagreements. The Council will draw up full documents for you to sign within a day's time; until then we request that you remain here as honored guests and we invite the other Lords who will sign these agreements to arrive here in the next twenty hours." His tone left no doubt that the invitation was an iron-clad command.

The opposing Lords nodded and bowed one after the other to Kenton and Ikami. I released a sigh of relief and let down some of my shields; the strain of maintaining them across all of us was starting to give me a headache. Cordell looked at me and a moment later I felt his mind politely requesting me to open up to him and converse.

This is the right thing to do, Mom, he sent gently. *I think most of them will get along with us eventually. It will take years, but in the long run we'll be better off this way than fighting them for the next decade* until we finally dig them all out.

I know, I replied wearily. *Or rather, I hope you and your father are right. I am less optimistic than you are but that seems to be a regular state of affairs in our family.*

Cordell gave a faint smile, one of the few I'd seen him give since we had disagreed so strongly about attacking Randell. *That's all right. It seems to work out in the end.* A moment later he shook his head. *One other thing I wanted to say, Mom - we can't keep using Kami as a weapon like this. It's hard on her, though she won't say it.*

She put herself in that position at the City of the Lords, I replied warily. *I don't think we're pushing anything on her. You know the other Lords wouldn't respect the Council one whit without her backing us up.*

It's just... My son frowned, looking down for a moment. *All the killing. It gets to her. I'm... I know that we probably wouldn't have lost anyone if Kami had been able to go deal with Randell yesterday, but in a way I'm glad that we went instead. She has too much blood on her hands already.*

I nodded slowly. *I think I understand what you mean. I wish I could spare her much of what she's had to go through. She's beyond us now, though.*

That's what I'm trying to say, Mom. She's not. She's still Kami, my little sister and your daughter, no matter how powerful she is now. We can never forget that. She needs our help and support more than ever - if she feels alone it will affect everyone in this world, human and Bladesmen alike.

I'll try to remember that, my dear, I sent back slowly. *It's hard sometimes, but you're right.*

Cordell withdrew his mind with one last smile for me. We turned back towards where Kenton and Ather were talking animatedly to the rebel Lords, showing them to the quarters where they would be comfortable prisoners until the agreements were signed. Ikami nodded to me when I looked at my husband's retreating back, reassuring me that they would be looked after just in case some of them changed their minds.

"That came close, didn't it?" Apashae asked from

behind my shoulder. I turned to her and nodded.
"It came very close indeed," I replied quietly.

Chapter 10 – Agreement

Kenton had no trouble bringing the Council into line at a meeting early the next morning. I sat and watched but didn't say anything. About half of the Council members - along with many of the allied Lords who were allowed to join out of respect for the attacks many of them had faced from the rebels - wanted little to do with the supposedly repentant Lords. My husband quieted them down and convinced them that we could gain more by letting our former enemies rejoin the society we were trying to build, provided they were properly monitored of course.

The exiles were another matter. General opinion held that they couldn't be trusted to stay put; a number of Lords insisted that we strike them dead immediately - by which they meant that Ikami should, of course. I didn't like their assumption that they could order my daughter to perform such a task, but Kenton convinced them by showing just how far offshore they would be placed. Ikami was the only one with enough power to make the jump in one hop; she'd drop them off and leave them to build their own society however they liked. Nearly three thousand miles from the four continents, the islands we'd chosen would provide them no escape without outside help. After almost three hours of discussion the Council and our allies grudgingly agreed to Kenton's proposal and the matter was settled. Cordell, sitting next to me, let out an audible sigh of relief as consensus was reached.

The rebellion was formally settled two days later. Thirty-eight Bladesmen Lords stood with varying degrees of reluctance in the center of the City plaza surrounded by nearly a hundred other Lords who wanted to witness the occasion. Many of them didn't bother to contain their smirks and smug looks; I was well aware by now that there was no tradition of graceful victory in this world. Such an assembly hadn't been seen for two years, since Ikami had destroyed the City of the Lords and scattered the few surviving retired Lords across the four continents. Humans and common Bladesmen watched from a public viewing area nearby, behaving much more politely than most of our allies.

Kenton, Lord Wesnoq, and Ikami signed the various documents that the Council's bureaucrats had come up with for the occasion. Each defeated Lord in turn came up and agreed to either permanent exile or careful probation and re-integration to the new world that Ikami had created. Once all the rebels had been processed Ikami closed her eyes and focused inwards. Every mage in the plaza could feel her gathering power; some of the weaker Lords and human mages physically stumbled. In that instant it was as though Ikami had become the center of the earth from which all gravity sprung; the closest thing I'd felt was when I was near the magically unstable remains of the City of the Lords. With no further fanfare the twelve who had chosen exile vanished with flashes of light and loud popping sounds. When my daughter released her breath and let go of her power, I had to blink a few times and gasp for air.

The pale faces of many Lords - allies and rebels alike - clearly displayed which ones had not yet felt Ikami when she was at her most potent. Dozens of Lords working together for days might have been able to accomplish such a feat, but she had taken only seconds and showed no signs of fatigue or apparent effort. She looked around and smiled, though I knew her well enough to see the darkness behind her eyes. She was putting on a show for those assembled here today; my daughter was learning quickly just how important the appearance of easy power could be.

With so many visitors in the City, discussion soon turned to the topic of the human world and the proposed expedition there. To my surprise most of the visiting Lords showed great interest in the prospect. A number of them that would have happily joined in the Pact two years ago proclaimed their love of the common Bladesman today, denouncing the Lords on the human world who kept their kin in slavery. I suspected that they believed they would better prove their loyalty to Ikami by helping in what seemed like an easy mission; most of the conversation revolved around how quickly she would destroy the Lords we would face there. It reached her ears even when she didn't seem to be listening, of course, and before long I caught up to her talking quietly to Cordell.

"Is this how they think it will be?" she asked her brother sadly. "We'll just march in and the Lords will conveniently assemble themselves for me to politely kill?"

He sighed. "It sounds like it. We're back to them not respecting the power of the common Bladesmen. The Pact is going to be a shock to them, I think."

"Without a doubt," I said, stepping into the conversation. "It will be to the two of you, as well - I know you've heard about it for all your lives, but there's nothing that can prepare you for the full impact. Seeing thousands of Bladesmen acting instinctively on the slightest command of one of their leaders... well, it's a sight I'd hoped to never see again. One of our allies can kill hundreds of commoners, but they can't stop thousands or millions."

Cordell nodded grimly. "They don't seem to understand that the commoners under the Pact are innocent. They're being controlled whether they like it or not."

"A few of them do," Ikami said quickly. "Wesnoq and Lim seem to get it, though it took me a while to explain it to them. Several of the others as well. We need to make sure to take as many of those ones as we can. Once we're on the other side of that portal I can't be everywhere at once."

I looked at both of them. "I'm going to go as well... but your father has decided he's going to stay here."

"Dad's always wanted to go back, though," Ikami said with surprise. "Of all of us he feels their plight the strongest."

"He's the Head Councilor, Kami," Cordell replied, laying a hand on her arm. "Somebody has to stay here and keep the four continents in line while you're gone. We'll just have to do a good job for him."

"Ather's coming?" Ikami asked, looking at me. When I nodded she continued, "Good. I can't imagine him sitting out."

"A number of our recently reformed friends have asked to come, too," I said. "They seem to think it will get them off of probation earlier."

Ikami and Cordell looked at each other. "I'm not sure we want them there," she said slowly. "Can we really trust them?"

I shrugged. "It's up to the Council, but I imagine you could veto the idea if you wanted to. It's not like the portal's going to open without your help, dear. Besides, if we need to send anyone out on a riskier mission..."

My son frowned at me. "You wouldn't."

"I damn well would," I snapped back. "You tell me - would you really risk Ather over one of those rebellious bastards? If someone needs to hold off an attacking force while we rescue a crashed airship, you better believe I'm looking at those rebels first."

"They're not rebels anymore, though," Cordell began, but I was having none of it and cut him off.

"Until they prove themselves, they are to me."

"Mom, Cord, please. We don't need to argue this now. Let me think about it and we'll see what the Council says - it might be a moot point. Worry about what we know, okay?"

I shrugged and met Cordell's eyes. After a moment he nodded, though I saw a familiar stubborn look in his gaze that told me this conversation wasn't done. I'd seen it a hundred times in his father and sister; truth be told, I probably gave it more than anyone else in the family. Suddenly I laughed and gathered my children up in a wide hug.

"Come on, let's celebrate! Randell's dead. The rebellion is crushed. Whatever happens tomorrow we've made some huge strides in bringing this place around."

Ikami and Cordell traded startled looks but nodded and came along with me when I started winding my way through the plaza to look for my husband. Half an hour later we were sitting down together in our home, lunch on its way out from the kitchen. The children seemed bewildered by my sudden change of attitude but Kenton took it in stride and smiled as he raised a toast. "To peace!" he cried, and we echoed his sentiment with a clink of glass. For today, at least, we could celebrate a victory.

Chapter 11 – Assembly

    For the next two weeks forces assembled near the City from all over the world. Due to the rebellion many nations had taken to keeping small standing forces of soldiers and these were easily repurposed to the expeditionary army we were building. Ikami was kept busy opening portals to one nation after another, their forces stumbling through with expressions of awe on their faces. Most common Bladesmen had never left the borders of their own country before and soon the farms nearby disappeared under a circus of tents and temporary buildings.

    Planning the whole affair was a monumental task. Many nations had historical rivalries that Ikami had settled only recently, and more than once skirmishes broke out between factions who had been embroiled in conflict for generations. Training and uniting the various groups was a task that General Teyo and General Sanato took on with some reticence but the Council didn't give them any choice in the matter.

    Integrating humans into the various armies was an even more difficult matter. Of all the millions of Bladesmen on the continent very few had ever seen a human. While many saw us as curiosities and creatures of dubious strength, others clearly considered us freaks of nature and dismissed the words of any human soldier put into their army as an advisor. In some cases an insult was only settled by proving that humans could fight as well as Bladesmen. Invariably, once a Bladesman had seen what we could accomplish with our spears, longswords, and bows, their animosity turned to guarded respect and formed the foundation for a better conversation. Those few who refused to consider humans as equals were kicked out, sent home to their lasting shame.

The forces of the City itself were stretched thin. Humans were of great value in battles with Lords since we were nearly immune to the teleportation sickness that all Bladesmen experienced. We didn't have the numbers to work with all of the various countries, however, since our army was tiny compared to what even a middling-sized Bladesmen nation could assemble. Our great equalizer was the power of our airships, which rumbled through the skies above the camp on a regular basis as they were armed and crewed in preparation for the sortie. Stacks of powerful Fuel-tipped ballista bolts were stowed safely beneath oak decks while sails and rigging were carefully inspected and repaired to ensure top performance in dodging the attacks of enemy Lords. Thousands of arrows - both mundane and explosive - were fletched and distributed among our groups.

Several of the friendlier nations were invited to place squads of their Bladesmen on board our zeppelins. This served two purposes - it freed up City soldiers to help coordinate the fight from the ground and impressed the power of our technology upon the visitors. We had learned long before that airships could drop forces off at strategic locations on a battleground, helping focus attacks against enemy leaders and capture whatever objectives we were going after.

Ten ships of the line were outfitted for the mission. Each stretched over three hundred feet long from prow to stern, the black wood of the native trees looking dark and menacing against the clear skies. Three huge engine exhaust ports could be seen at each one's stern, the gigantic rudders connected to the steering column through a cunning series of gears and levers. The only sign of the huge lifting balloon inside each hull was the width and length; despite their girth the only inhabitable space on each side was a single row of cabins and a narrow hallway. They were of varying models, some of them almost twenty years old. One of them had even fought in our war with Rainshye many years before; its sides had been repaired and repainted so that the scars of those battles could no longer be seen.

The zeppelins flew with two skiffs slung underneath each. These were only thirty to forty feet long, their masts left down until needed. They had no interior space at all for people, the entire hull taken up by the balloon which kept it aloft. Most had only a single engine though some of the newest had a much smaller backup engine built in as well. They were sleek and long, much faster than the clumsy-looking skiffs we had built back on the human world. The last of those original ships had died many years ago.

Each airship was an intimidating sight in its own right, and when two or more were together it was awe-inspiring. Even the most jaded Lords couldn't help but be impressed by them, especially when a City denizen - human or Bladesman, it didn't matter - casually mentioned the many battles where an airship had made the difference against an enemy Lord. Several of our allies asked the Council for an airship of their own to which they all received the same answer. We were willing to lend the technological marvels to our friends for several months at a time for assistance in their matters, but City crews would man them and none would be permanently traded - ever.

The experience of so many foreigners made our people pull tighter together. Human and Bladesman had worked side by side for so many years now that it felt natural to consider themselves citizens of the City more than one race or another. Many of our visitors seemed confused by this; they didn't understand why they were rebuffed when they tried to talk to the Bladesmen of the City about how ugly or bizarre the humans were. In a strange way it was comforting. I still remembered how long it had taken for us to work together after escaping from the human world and now we were truly a united force that used each race's strengths to the fullest.

A small force was sent over from Ganshe - which had no ruling Lord at present - and among their number was Dalt, the female Bladesman who had helped Cordell escape when her country was still run by the cruel Lord Onalye and his cronies. The moment Cordell saw her step out of Ikami's portal his eyes lit up and he ran over to sweep her into a wide hug. She laughed, kicking her shins backwards so she wouldn't catch him with their jutting blades while he swung her around in a circle.

"It is good to find you, Cord," she said. Her accent was terrible and her words halting, but she had clearly been practicing our language.

He smiled and nodded. "I've missed you, Dalt. I'm so glad you're here. How are things going?"

"Very glad," she replied. "We run by Council all time now, and food very better for everyone." When she saw me standing nearby her smile became a bit more formal and she let go of Cordell, bowing to greet me politely.

"It's nice to see you, Dalt," I said with a smile.

"Lady Viala, am honored to find - see? - you as well." While she was less timid with her tone than she had been on the other occasions we'd met, she was clearly still unused to speaking with someone she considered the equivalent of a Bladesman Lord. I could see her hands shaking slightly but she did an excellent job of hiding it.

I decided to put her at ease. The poor girl deserved it after everything she'd been through and the work she was doing back in her country. I reached over and gently took her hand, giving the most soothing smile I could. "We all appreciate how you are helping Ganshe recover, dear," I said encouragingly. "I'm sure you and Cordell would like some time - why don't the two of you meet us for dinner later at our home?"

My son smiled at me approvingly from over Dalt's shoulder but she looked panicked for a moment before recovering. "Yes, of course, Lady Viala. I glad to share eat with you."

I nodded politely and waved them off. Once she turned

back to Cordell Dalt was at ease, and the two of them talked animatedly on their way out of the plaza. I went back to helping organize the other forces coming through from Ganshe, showing them to the place in the camp that had been set aside for them. Many had worked at Dalt's side as guerrillas in Ganshe for years and showed a quiet competence that belied their small frames and malnourished bodies. It had only been a few months since they'd been able to live openly and eat a steady diet and they were just starting to gain a healthy weight. From what I'd heard, though, these would be effective fighters to have on our side and I decided to have some of them assigned to an airship or two as a strike force.

    My mind went back to Cordell and Dalt as I worked. More than ever I suspected that there was something going on between them and I hoped to finally get it out of them at dinner that evening. Ikami would help, I was sure; she was as keen to see her brother happy as I was. Even though she was a Bladesman, Dalt seemed to bring my son joy and I was resolved to let him make his own choices in love. I was old-fashioned enough to instinctively look askance upon such a match but wise enough to recognize my feelings and put them aside for the sake of my family. Cordell and I had enough arguments; Dalt would not be one of them.

Chapter 12 – A Moment to Talk

    It was well past dark by the time we all gathered for a meal. Our dinner table was nearly full between Ather, Dalt, and family; I'd decided it would be easier on Dalt's nerves for us to eat in the less formal dining room. The larger room had enough seating for the entire Council plus a few guests and would feel too imposing for the occasion.

    The young Bladeswoman was a mystery to me and I watched her out of the corner of my eye as the first course was served. I'd met her only four times, and despite the fact that she was organizing a new government for her nation she was still overwhelmed by the presence of Lords and their equivalents. Ikami had tried to draw her out of her shell before the meal but was having trouble despite the fact that Dalt had seen my daughter at her absolute worst. It was difficult for me to reconcile the reports I'd heard of her assertive, courageous nature with the mumbling, shy woman that sat in front of me.

    I didn't pay much attention to the conversation at my end of the table until Kenton prodded me in the shoulder. "Are you listening, Viala?" The look of excitement on his face drew my immediate attention.

    "I'm sorry, I wasn't. What were you saying?"

    Ather leaned forward. "Lord Wesnoq and I talked with many of the visiting Lords yesterday. Two of them - Lords Orove and Jabnoss - have done some excellent work on breaking long-term spells. This afternoon we sat down together and worked out a way to break one of the longest lasting spells we've encountered. It took twelve of us, but we did it."

"I've met Lord Jabnoss," I said, my interest piqued. "What did you work on?"

"General Teyo," our friend replied. I'd seldom seen him so excited. "We really, truly did it. The Pact is broken on him."

Ikami dropped her fork at the other end of the table and turned towards us. "Did I hear that right? That's incredible!"

"What so important?" Dalt asked Cordell quietly.

"I told you about the Pact," he replied. "Ather figured out how to suppress it a long time ago but we've never actually been able to remove it - Teyo, and everyone else under the Pact from our old world, still have to follow a direct and absolute order from any Lord whether they want to or not."

"I tried removing it a long time ago," Ikami added. "I couldn't figure out how to do it without... well, without the process being very bad for the person I was working with."

Ather nodded. "It's not a matter of power - well, there's that too, but it's just as much a subtle unwinding of the spell. It's slow and cumbersome, and we can only do one person at a time, but we can finally remove the Pact for good from people."

"Congratulations," Kenton said with a smile. "We - meaning the Council - were worried about having Teyo join the expedition back home with the Pact still on him. This will calm the worries nicely." He waited a moment, then spoke again in a less formal tone. "This means there's real hope for any Bladesmen we rescue on the other side. Do you think you'll be able to refine the process?"

"Hopefully. If we could get one of the Lords who created the Pact to assist, it would speed our efforts dramatically."

My daughter gave a cold smile. "If I get near any of them, I can make them talk." Her eyes glittered hungrily for a moment as she thought of bringing to justice the enemies who had driven us away from our home. I recognized the look and nodded in agreement; there were times when Ikami and I found ourselves in perfect harmony.

Dalt looked back and forth between my daughter and I with a startled look. "It not easy to capture Lords time?"

"Oh, don't worry, Dalt," I said with a wicked smile. "Between Ikami and I we can deal with any Lord who tries to stand and fight. I have scores to settle from many years ago and I'm looking forward to the opportunity."

"How is progress going on your end, Ikami?" Ather asked.

"I think I have everything figured out. Lord Lim has been of great help - he's been looking into the connections between this world and the human one for decades. Between my power and his studies we can build the portal. We actually had a hard time trying to figure out how to direct it to the right spot, but Dad was able to help us out there."

Ather looked at Kenton and raised an eyebrow. Kenton replied, "The issue was one of familiarity. The City itself was in the human world for a century but over the last twenty years we've rebuilt large swathes of it and expanded dramatically. Plants of this world have grown in every crack and crevice and even the insects are now a hybrid of those from our world and this one. Basically, Ikami needed something solidly from the human world that didn't have any contamination from this one, something to help her focus on where the portal needs to open up."

Kenton paused for a moment to take a drink from his glass, then continued, "It turns out that I had just the thing. Remember when we went into Lord Hannon's tower to get the scrolls describing the original human spell that brought Bladesmen there?"

"How could I forget it?" Ather replied levelly. I shivered - we'd nearly died there after I had used up all my power pushing through Hannon's wards. Only Ather's friend Veru had saved us, but it had required killing a Bladesman Lord for the first time.

My husband continued. "I grabbed a sword while we were in his vault. Hannon had collected many curiosities from the days before his people had arrived. This sword had spells on it that had kept it from decaying or corroding; as far as I know it's about the only artifact that was brought here which survives from the ages when humans ruled their own lands."

Ikami picked up the story. "The key thing is that this sword was protected. So far as I can tell every tiny particle of it is still from the human world. Even the spells - though they're fading slowly, year by year - are those of long-dead human Archmages. The sword is exactly what I needed to serve as a guide for the portal."

Kenton nodded. "I never would have guessed the damn thing would be vital for getting back. At the time I thought it might be useful as a weapon or as something to study. We've never been able to find any value to it other than as a curiosity; our modern weapons have far more reach and versatility. I'm glad I kept it now. It might be the only way we get back to our world."

Cordell cleared his throat and spoke. "We're not there yet. Ather, will you and the others be able to remove the compulsions of the Pact from any other Bladesmen before we leave? The more people we have with experience on the human world the better. Every human was trapped behind the Shield Wall for years; your Bladesmen who came with the City are really the only ones with experience in the outside world there."

"Most of those who were under the Pact at the time are too old to go back. Few of the younger folk were ever forced into the spell, so they'll be fine - but even they are in their thirties and forties now." Ather caught my eye and shrugged. "We're getting older. Sometimes I forget that."

I frowned in return. Other than a shattered forearm blade, Ather still looked exactly as he had when we'd met him more than a score of years before while Kenton and I were visibly older. I'd aged reasonably gracefully, but I had no illusions that I looked anything like the girl who had taken flight from the City back when we were looking for a way to save the remnants of the human race. Kenton had more than a few grey hairs by now but in my eyes he was more attractive than ever. I'd given up envying the Lords their near-immortality long ago though every now and then a spark of that jealousy resurfaced.

"Dalt and I were talking earlier," Cordell said to change the conversation. "Do you want to tell them what you told me? It's not my decision, after all."

The Bladeswoman nodded and spoke up, her heavy accent making her words difficult to understand at times. "Ganshe has Council voted built. I come to City with portal help." She paused, clearly looking for the right words. Finally, frustrated, she switched back to the Bladesmen tongue. "*I'm sorry, I'm still not as familiar with your language as I would like. Ganshe is in solid hands now; the new Council has been put in place and is governing far better than our previous rulers ever did. I'm not needed there anymore. I came here for more than just escorting the fighters we're committing to your cause. If you'll have me, I'd like to join the battle. We may not have much to contribute, but we know first hand the evils of slavery and I can think of no nobler cause than what Cordell has told me about." She glanced over at my son and smiled, giving her face a startling and unexpected beauty for an instant before the expression was gone. Cordell's answering look confirmed everything I'd wanted to know about their relationship.

Kenton thought for a moment, tapping his fingers on the table before answering in the human language. "Cordell, we've already agreed to welcome any help Ganshe can afford to send; Dalt falls in that category. Beyond that, though, I have to ask - will having her along impact your participation in any way?" I nodded to my husband appreciatively - he didn't miss much.

Cordell and Dalt looked at each other uncomfortably for a moment. Eventually, Cordell spoke up after some unseen signal had passed between the two of them. "Well, I suppose now is as good a time as any." He reached over and grasped Dalt's hand where it rested next to her plate. "Mom and Dad,

Dalt and I have been involved for several months now. We don't get to see each other often but... well, if things go well, Dalt wants to move here to the City with me."

Ikami had a wide grin on her face. I glanced at her and she shrugged. "I might have helped get Cord back and forth to see Dalt a few times." She gave a rare chuckle and continued, "Maybe more than a few times."

"Did you know about this?" I demanded, turning to Kenton, only to see Ather smiling on the other side of him. Our friend just nodded silently; I knew him well enough to know that he must have been helping Cordell get back and forth to Ganshe as well. "Everyone but me, is that it?"

"Hey, I didn't know either," Kenton said with mock defensiveness.

I sighed and shook my head sadly. "Oh, Dalt, you poor girl. You don't know what you're getting yourself into."

She looked around uneasily, clearly missing some of our family humor. "Is okay?" she whispered to Cordell audibly.

He nodded, clearly pleased. "Everything is great," he replied happily. It was good to see; we'd had a lot to frown about for the last couple of years. Perhaps, I thought to myself, things were going to go right for a while. I looked over at my beloved and held his hand tightly under the table, basking in the glow of a joyful family around me.

Chapter 13 – Traveling Companions

Time seemed to fly by until one day everything was ready. Nearly twenty thousand Bladesmen had been assembled from throughout the allied nations, led by a thousand experienced human and Bladesmen soldiers from the City many of whom remembered our home world. A dozen mighty airships were fueled and armed with a veritable swarm of skiffs zipping around them. Eight Lords had committed to travel through Ikami's portal with us to support the operation; another dozen would guard this side to ensure no hostile forces were able to sneak through - in either direction.

I felt confident in our plans. Even without Ikami we would outnumber the Lords back in the human world; before we left there had only been seven, one of whom was slain during our escape. With any luck our mission could be accomplished quickly with little loss of life. As soon as Ikami and I managed to capture one of the Lords I would have no remorse in attempting to kill the others. Without enemy leaders on the field, hopefully our own Lords would be able to order the common Bladesmen to stop until we could work to remove the Pact from them.

"Stop fidgeting, Mom," Cordell muttered next to me. I focused on the scene before me, where Ikami had opened a gigantic portal from our City to the ruins of the City of the Lords. It was nearly two hundred feet tall, chill air from the other side flowing through to create a layer of fog streaming across the warm plaza. Soldiers were being guided through in groups of twenty while skiffs and airships carefully lined up before gunning their engines and zipping across the continent in a split second.

"I'm just making sure we haven't forgotten anything," I said back to him. "How much more do we have to send through?"

"Another fifteen minutes and pretty much everyone will be on the other side," he replied. I looked around, surprised that it had only taken a few hours. General Sanato had been exceedingly efficient in his planning.

"Good morning," Lord Ather said from nearby. I turned and nodded to him with a smile. "Has Ikami finished reviewing the plans to open the portal to the human world?"

I shrugged and gave a rueful grin. "I'm only her mother. She doesn't discuss hardly anything with me."

Cordell rolled his eyes. "Yes, she's gone over everything she needs to. Once everyone's through this portal, she'll close it down and start focusing on the big one."

We stood and watched the procession for a few more moments in silence. "It still amazes me sometimes what my daughter is able to do so easily," I said softly after some time.

Both Cordell and Ather nodded without saying a word. Her abilities were almost beyond comprehension; something about the unique blending of a human Archmage and a Bladesman Lord had made my daughter into a singular creation. I shivered for a moment at the thought that without her we would have no way of getting back to our home world safely - or returning here if things should go badly.

"It's about time to go," my son said after a bit. General Teyo was waving us forward - it was our turn to step through. I pulled on my heavy coat and immediately started sweating, but I knew I'd be glad of it the moment I went through the portal.

We walked forward and proceeded to pass through without pause. I closed my eyes just as I took the last step, trying to prepare myself for the disorientation I felt every time I went through one of these bizarre magical constructions. The passage was nearly instantaneous despite the momentary dizziness and strange stretched feeling, marked more by the biting chill on the far side than anything else.

I opened my eyes to see a busy military camp being constructed around me. Thousands of tents stretched off to the sides with precision, various officers barking orders and getting everything into shape. We didn't plan to be here for more than a few days, but nobody - even Ikami - could say for sure how long it would take to actually build the portal to the human world or how quickly we could pass through.

"Please, ma'am, step off to the side so the others can come through behind you," a young Bladesman said politely in the human tongue. I nodded and moved forward, getting out of the way of the last few units coming through the portal. Another Bladesman soldier directed us down a few rows to a large command tent where we found a dozen Lords poring over scrolls and making last-minute adjustments to their plans. Ikami was in the middle of it all, talking to Lord Lim and gesturing about some magical theory or another. At the same time a nearly visible cord of magical energy stretched through the air from her body back towards the portal, keeping it open with seemingly no effort on her part despite the prodigious expenditure of power I knew it required.

I stepped forward and gave her a hug as soon as I could get her attention. She smiled at the sight of the three of us, saying, "I'm glad you're finally here. I think I'm almost ready; we're just finishing preparations now. I'll close down the existing portal as soon as everyone is through. Is Dad coming or did he have to stay behind?"

"He's going to come over for at least a couple of days, but he can't stay too long," I replied.

"*As always, it is a pleasure to see you, Lady Viala," Lord Lim said politely in the Bladesman tongue. He bowed to me and I replied likewise.

"We've been talking mostly in the Bladesman language. It's easier for everyone that way," Ikami added.

"*Of course," I replied. "*Lord Lim, and everyone else, it is always good to see allies of the City." Bows were exchanged all around before we could settle in and get down to business. Ikami dove right into the topic at hand.

"*Mom, I'm going to handle most of the spell myself, but there's a few places where the other Lords are going to help out and there's one spot that I could really use another Archmage for assistance. The actual direction of the spell back to the human world will be made much easier if you can lend me your power; I'm already going to be juggling human magic and Bladesman magic separately as much as I can."

"*Can you really separate the different sources like that?" I asked curiously. This wasn't something she'd talked about much in the past.

She shrugged. "*It's never been an issue before. Something that's human, like using Fuel to power my magic, always just comes from that part of me automatically. Teleporting, on the other hand, feels different but it's just as easy. This is the first time that I've really needed to try and keep them separate. If I'm not careful about using only my powers as an Archmage for this specific part of the spell, who knows where the portal will open?"

I nodded. "*I understand, it's just... Look, I'll help however I can. You know that."

"*Thanks," she said with a smile. Her eyes grew distant for a moment, then with an almost audible snap she released the magic keeping the portal to the City open. The magical tension in the air dissipated, causing everyone except Ikami to visibly relax a bit. "*Everyone's through now. We can start anytime."

The Lords in the tent looked around at each other for a moment as though considering what they were about to attempt, then Lord Lim stood up abruptly and started shooing people outside. We followed him and made our way through the camp to its edge, joined along the way by a number of additional Lords and many human mages. Kenton met up with us just as we came to the last row of tents, giving me a moment's warm embrace before we continued hand in hand.

Not far from the camp was a low rise, the last hill separating us from where the City of the Lords had once risen. Ikami led us to the top where we could look down upon the devastation that stretched nearly a mile away from us. Before she'd come here in anger two years ago, a hill had risen in this location capped with a busy city filled with hundreds of retired Lords. They had abused their power and interfered cruelly with the business of the four continents, wielding invisible hands of power to keep the various nations constantly at war with one another until my daughter had come and stopped them.

Now the City of the Lords was no more. It had been razed to the ground, the hill turned into a crater which still smoked and seethed with heat and power even after so long. The ground was glassy and smooth near the center as though the very earth had been fused together by the energy Ikami had released.

Standing atop this crest gave me chills. The crater below us had the wrecked remains of thousands of years worth of Bladesmen spells and wards, intermixed with the several tons of Fuel that Ikami had teleported in to destroy the City. Opening any of my magical senses resulted in a horrendous headache that buffeted my mind and made me feel like I was in the center of a hurricane even though the air was cold and still around us. It affected the Lords the same way; unlike the other human mages we could never completely turn off our magical abilities. None of us were comfortable in such a place; it felt like we were naked and defenseless, unable to access the magic that was our lifeblood. In the few moments we'd stood in clear view of the City ruins I'd felt my usual magical defenses weakening, torn apart by the hungry vortex of power below us.

Ikami took a few steps down into the crater and turned back to address us. "*I know how this place feels to all of you - I can feel it too, gnawing at our energy any way it can. Without some means of releasing its power, this crater will become more and more unstable until something terrible occurs. Our goal here today is twofold - first to prevent that from happening and second to open a path back to the world from whence my parents arrived. If this attempt fails, it will be at least two months before enough energy builds up to try opening the portal again."

She took a deep breath and began to focus her concentration. "*I will try to buffer the power from the crater as much as I can so the rest of you can work on your spells. Those who are not directly involved in building the portal please step back now and give the rest of us some room. We need no distractions during this process."

Kenton leaned over and gave me one last kiss on the cheek before taking a few paces back down the hill with Cordell, most of the other human mages, and a few of the Lords. A few moments later I felt an easing of the pressure from down below and sent my mind outwards to see Ikami's magic giving us the space we needed. I could still sense the boiling energies in the crater pushing against the invisible wall of my daughter's will, but I could now start to work without having to fight every moment to keep my spells intact.

Two dozen Lords began to send their power inwards to Ikami. At the same time she started to pull on the power generated by the ruins of the City down below, able to harness it in a way that was beyond any of the rest of us. Traces of silvery dust filtered upwards, tiny fragments of Fuel which had remained unconsumed in the conflagration she had caused not so long ago.

The air grew utterly motionless and silent, the murmur of the camp behind us and the crackle of the crater below both dulling down as though a thick blanket had been draped around us. Unlike the others involved in the spell I wasn't supposed to join my powers to Ikami's until she specifically requested it. This left me free to send my magical senses drifting nearby, observing what was likely the most potent spell I would ever witness. I had a strange sense of déjà vu, remembering how it had felt more than a score of years ago when I was a young woman helping Archmage Wendel desperately form the magic that let our City escape the approaching Bladesmen hordes.

Memories from those terrible days drifted across my vision, watching many of those I cared about fall around me as we struggled over days to achieve something far inferior to what Ikami would do in hours. I seemed to have been born into an historic age when we worried more about our very existence than any hope of glory or remembrance.

I shook my head as my mind suddenly snapped back into my body. Something about the magic around me was making my thoughts wander; with a shock I looked up and realized that the sun had moved at least two hand spans across the sky. The others around me remained stock still, caught completely in Ikami's magic. Something brushed at the edge of my consciousness and I realized that she was trying to get my attention. I quickly opened myself to her communications.

Mom? Are you alright? This spell is playing hell with my sense of time. How long has it been?

At least an hour or two. You're not the only one, trust me. Do you need me?

Yes, she replied. *Get that sword from Dad and hold it in your hands. I'll channel my power through you so that I can keep every sense of Bladesmen away from the sword. With luck, that will let me guide us back to the exact spot it left the human world.*

I broke off the contact gently and focused once again on the physical world. Turning back towards Kenton felt strange and slow as though I was pushing my way through molasses. Forcing my foot to step forward was extremely difficult, though I couldn't determine why other than as some unexpected side effect to the magic building nearby.

It took me nearly five minutes to take ten steps, each one getting slightly easier. By the time I was within arm's reach of Kenton I could hear normally again and felt the fitful breeze of the prairie pressing against my cheek. He took the final step towards me and frowned, reaching out to pull on my wrists. "What's happening up there? It's been hours and we can't sense anything."

I just shook my head. "I'm not sure, but Ikami doesn't seem worried about it. We need the sword."

He nodded and reached down to his belt, pulling it from a makeshift scabbard. It had a wider blade than our modern weapons. I'd seen it once or twice over the years but Kenton had buried it among his possessions not long after we came to this world. It seemed to remind him of a time that hurt too much to remember and I couldn't blame him for having forgotten it over the decades that had passed. He hesitated a moment before handing it to me, his fingers trailing slowly along the hilt as though saying goodbye to an old acquaintance.

I leaned forward and gave him a kiss then turned back and took a deep breath before beginning the slow ascent back up to Ikami's side. The short distance was deceptive and I felt a faint claustrophobia as the normal sounds of the world once again faded with every step I took. By the end I was nearly grunting against the physical resistance I felt, leaning forward as though into a gale. Reaching forward to present the weapon to my daughter was like pushing into a brick wall and left my muscles quivering with exhaustion.

Ikami reached out and waved her hands over the blade as though it were the simplest thing in the world.

Excellent. I'm ready when you are, Mom, she sent to me a moment later.

Nodding would take too much effort so I simply sent back a feeling of assent. An instant later I felt her building a connection between the sword, myself, and her own magic. I could feel the pent-up pressure of Bladesmen magic held ready behind her, enough magical energy there to blast apart an army. And beyond that was the immense power in the crater below, restrained only by a thread of her concentration. She seemed immensely fragile to hold so much at bay yet at the same time her own power lay untapped beneath the connections she was creating.

This might be disconcerting, Ikami warned all of us. An instant later I felt my mind caught up and thrown to the side, spinning through a black void with no sense of direction. Long years of training kept me from panicking but I felt other Lords behind Ikami flailing outwards with their minds before allowing themselves to be calmed. I had an flickering sensation of immense distance flying behind me, flashing lights appearing and disappearing around me with terrifying alacrity.

I had no sense of time, caught up with everyone else in Ikami's sure magical grip. She kept me buffered from the Lords, using my power only to focus on the sword in my grip. It seemed to be pulling unerringly in whatever direction she was guiding us like a compass needle across the stars. I could dimly sense the Lords' reserves of power being quickly drained, though my own were barely tapped as of yet.

One of the weaker Lords suddenly vanished from the group Ikami was carrying across the void. A sense of concern flashed across the linked minds, but my daughter pushed on with determination. She was starting to pull on my reserves now and I could tell that she was testing her own limits. The other Lords were already pressed as far as they could be. I began to worry, knowing that she couldn't yet tap the power waiting in the crater as all of that would be needed for the portal itself.

In a fraction of a second the impression of a giant orb flashed in front of my magical senses and then we were all there, back above the human world. I recognized the old City plateau below us though I couldn't make out any details with Ikami leading our effort. She seemed to sense that our power was rapidly running low, taking only a moment to send me a flicker of thought: *Is this it?* I replied with a feeling of agreement.

An instant later I felt her steady her concentration and with an immense surge of her own energy grasp hold of the two worlds with her mind. She was stretched across an inconceivable distance for that moment, maintaining focus on the Bladesmen Lords, myself, and the power back at the crater simultaneously.

I was humbled and felt nothing short of awe.

A rush of magic beyond anything I'd experienced surged through Ikami as she unleashed the power from the City of the Lords. The connection between the two worlds solidified and grew under Ikami's guidance until it had a stability we could all feel. By now three more Lords had dropped out of Ikami's link, utterly exhausted of power.

With the magical link successfully built Ikami flitted back across the void to where we still stood at the top of the crater. She dumped our minds back into our bodies abruptly, causing everyone involved to fall flat on their face. I gasped and doubled over, flashing lights flaring across my vision. There was a rushing sound in my ears as the world returned to normal around us.

Kenton ran to my side and knelt down, clearly worried. "Viala? Viala, are you all right?"

I shook my head and put my hand up to my forehead. "I'm going to have a headache for a while, but yes, I'm fine," I said once the world had stopped spinning.

"Did it work?" he asked quietly.

"Yes," I whispered back. "It was... indescribable," I stammered. "I don't know what else to say."

He nodded. "Then all that's left is to build the portal along the connection. Hold on."

I heard Kenton talking to our children nearby but couldn't focus on their conversation over the vertigo I still felt. After several minutes he turned back to me and helped me sit up. I turned to Ikami, the only one who had been caught up in the spell who was back on her feet. She looked dreadful, as though she hadn't slept in a week - but a wide grin spread across her face as she chatted happily with Cordell. She wiped her hands together, sparkling dust all that remained of the sword Kenton had kept for so long without knowing it would eventually be the key to our return.

When she saw me looking at her she turned towards me and exclaimed, "That was amazing! I never imagined... Anyways, I can build the portal as soon as we're ready. It'll be simple compared to what we just went through."

I gave an exhausted smile back. "You make me wish I was twenty again."

Lord Wesnoq, still on his back nearby, gave a ragged

chuckle. "*Archmagess, right now I would be satisfied to be younger than a century. That was an experience I was glad to be a part of... and would be happy to never repeat."

Chapter 14 – The Portal

Despite Ikami's bravado it was several hours before she felt ready to open a portal using the magical pathway we'd prepared. We all needed some water and a short rest away from the crater rim to refresh ourselves. The devouring energies emanating from the ruins might have been noticeably diminished but their presence still clawed at our minds.

The sun had neared the western horizon by the time we had assembled again. This time we came together in the center of the temporary military camp. A chosen vanguard of our soldiers stood geared up and ready to charge through as soon as the portal was prepared. Nobody knew what to expect on the far side; the magic we'd used might have gone entirely undetected - or it could have reverberated across the entire human world. I would proceed through with several Lords and stake out a base camp. Ikami had wanted to follow immediately to ensure safety on the far end but General Teyo had vetoed this request with the flat statement that until we were sure that the portal was entirely stable she must stay on this side of it. It had sparked a row between the two that wasn't yet entirely settled, but I recognized the General's reasoning - from a strategic perspective, if something happened to the portal then Ikami would be the only one who could reconstruct it - and we didn't know if the resources to do so existed on the far side.

In any case, the decision had been made. Ikami would

come through only after half the army had passed to the other side and the portal had been open for at least one entire day. Fret as she might, she would obey the General's decision.

    This time Ikami stood alone to work her magic. Now that the pathway had been prepared she was the sole person able to build a portal to span the gap between this world and the world where I'd been born. I felt both eagerness and trepidation; a part of me wondered whether this expedition was really worth the effort or whether we should be satisfied living as perpetual guests among the Bladesmen here. To reassure myself I looked to Ather and Kenton, both of whose expressions were set and uncompromising. As much as I disliked - no, hated - the Lords who had abused their own folk on the human world for so long, everyone I cared about was here.

    At the same time the thought of vengeance stirred my blood. Our entire race had fled and hid behind a prison of our own making for a hundred years, unable to stand against the united might of the Bladesmen Lords and the commoners who had been enslaved by the Pact. My pride in humanity craved the chance to prove that we were not sniveling cowards. I wouldn't shirk from an opportunity to end the lives of those who had taken over our world, far from it. I'd relish the moment I could stand united with both the other Lords and the sheer power of my daughter on the battlefield.

    A surge of energy drew my attention - Ikami was about to begin. A glance with my magical senses showed a stream of power flowing into Ikami from the direction of the crater. She raised her arms and braced herself, summoning her own reserves to add to the magic she was pulling in from outside. It gathered and churned in an orb in front of her, crackling blue light sparking into the physical world every few seconds.

    It didn't take long before the energy she held constrained was more than anyone else could have controlled. Had I tried what she was doing it would have spun beyond my control, exploding in a catastrophic wave of destruction through the camp. My hair prickled at the sensation of so much potential death held only a few yards away but I gritted my teeth and repeated to myself that I trusted Ikami to keep us safe. A few of the Lords unconsciously took a step or two back, as though that would do something to protect them if she let her focus slip. Magical shields drew into place all around Ikami just in case; I had to force myself to not raise my own instinctively. I didn't want her to feel that I didn't believe in her even for an instant.

The shape of a giant circle formed in the air before Ikami, still only visible to those of us with sensitivity to magic. It was nearly two hundred feet in diameter. I could feel Ikami twisting magical energy along the pathway we'd formed earlier, using it as a guide to anchor the portal she was creating. It was an incredibly complicated spell, not only because of the sheer power involved but because of how she had to split her focus between keeping the assembled power contained and threading magic in and out of the pathway.

I switched my vision back to the physical world and couldn't help but gasp. Threads of lightning connected Ikami's hands and the oval, describing its shape with flickering power and heat. Whenever a spark touched the earth a tiny plume of dirt would burst upwards. The flat plane of the portal began to shimmer and - for lack of a better word - break apart, shreds of chill violet sky being replaced with inky blackness. Air started to rush through, starting as a thin gasp and growing until it soon sounded like a thousand hurricanes were screaming into the gap. Within a minute only darkness was visible within the crackling outline of the portal.

I didn't know what she'd opened the portal into, but it certainly wasn't the human world.

Then, incredibly, Ikami stepped forward and physically reached into the portal. I watched, paralyzed with dread, as her hand disappeared into the blackness. She grimaced but didn't make a sound, still focusing on the magic she continued to weave. The darkness began to shred once more, scraps of blue sky replacing it piece by piece. Ikami pulled back, her hands grasped tightly around strands of light as though physically forcing them into place. The rushing wind began to subside until a few moments later it ceased entirely as the last patches of black were filled in with blue.

I looked with wonder through the shimmering portal and laid eyes on my home world for the first time in more than a score of years. I'd forgotten what a blue sky looked like, I realized, and felt a tear forming at the corner of my eye.

Ikami took three steps backwards and sat down heavily. Clearly exhausted, she waved the first teams forward. Cordell rushed to her side, asking her something that I couldn't make out. She just shook her head and let him pick her up; a moment later they disappeared into a nearby tent.

All other eyes were on the portal. A squad of mixed human and Bladesmen soldiers walked up and in an impressive display of courage stepped through with no hesitation. We could see their backs indistinctly through the hazy surface and everyone assembled on our side held our breath as they moved away from the rift on the far side. A few moments later one of them stepped back through and called out, "It's clear!"

Those were the words we had been waiting for. I couldn't wait any longer and rushed forward along with many of the older humans nearby. Kenton stayed back, a resigned expression on his face - General Sanato had given him the same orders as Teyo had given Ikami; he was too valuable to risk going through right away.

Fortunately neither of them had tried telling me the same thing - or perhaps they just knew I was more stubborn than they were. I reached the portal before anyone else and stepped through, taking care not to touch the crackling energy at ground level.

The transition between worlds wasn't a comfortable one. My body felt as though it was being ripped apart, my nerves fraying even before they could transmit pain. I'd forgotten to close my eyes and had a strange sensation of utter darkness, a lack of light so complete that a sense of despair filled my being. It felt like an eternity before I emerged once again into the physical world filled with brilliant light, my body thrown together once more on the far side of the portal.

My first breath left me coughing. It smelled so very different from the air on the Bladesmen world. I took a moment to recover, then tried taking a slow, deep breath. The slight stink I'd grown used to over so many years was gone, replaced with the sweetest-smelling air I'd ever had the pleasure of breathing. I felt slightly dizzy, the air thinner than what I'd remembered.

I took a few groggy steps to the side as others came through behind me. I had to remember to shade my eyes as I looked upwards, the sun smaller and much brighter than that in the Bladesmen world. Although it was nearly sunset on the other side of the portal, here it was early afternoon. The sky was blue, so blue that I nearly sobbed at the sight of it. I struggled, never one to be emotional, but it suddenly all came pouring back to me - the terrible last few days we'd spent here in the City, casting a desperate spell so powerful it had taken the life of my teacher and many other lesser mages. At times I had despaired, thinking we'd never escape from the hordes descending upon us and wondering if I'd ever see Kenton again while he fought on the front lines to buy us a few more hours to finish our magic.

"I missed it, too," came Ather's familiar voice from next to me. I smiled and wiped tears from my cheeks before turning towards him to nod in appreciation.

"I'd forgotten what it smelled like," I said quietly. "I wonder what the children will think - they've never been here."

"We'll find out in a moment - Cordell should be coming through soon."

We stood next to each other watching as the first few squads made their way through and started setting up defensible positions around us. I realized I hadn't really taken a look around and turned, recognizing that the flat ground where we stood had once been part of the Bladesmen world. It had been exchanged with the land of the City when we'd transported ourselves there. In the intervening years human plants had colonized it, making the boundary line nearly invisible a few hundred yards away. I laughed and pointed to the west. "Look at that, Ather. That line of trees a few miles that way - it's where we had our precious timber stands. We had to cut nearly all of them to build the first airships, but they've regrown so fast." I paused for a moment, lost in thought. "We had so little wood in those days. I'd almost forgotten how we rationed it."

Before Ather had a chance to respond Cordell stepped through the portal. He shook off a momentary dizziness and looked around, spotting us and heading our way. He was panting quickly by the time he'd taken a few steps. "The air is so thin here! How do you breathe this stuff?" he asked, almost gasping from the short walk.

I smiled. "This is good human air, Cordell. You'll get used to it in a few days. Look up! Look at the sky here. It's so beautiful!"

He raised his eyebrows. "I've never seen you this excited, Mom. It's blue - and bright. Give me a few moments." My son's eyes flicked back and forth between Ather and I, then he gently asked, "Did you remember what you're supposed to be doing?"

Ather pulled a face and shook his head. "We got distracted. Viala, shall we?"

I nodded. We were supposed to be scouting the area magically and setting up defenses; my feelings at being back here had taken all my attention. In an instant I sent my mind winging outwards from my body, spinning upwards in a spiral to get a wider view of our surroundings.

The plateau was much as I remembered, though the once sheer bluffs were crumbled and broken to the northwest where we'd fought our last battle on this world before teleporting the City to its new home. Time had softened the scars but they were still visible, a long ramp of earth marking a difficult but passable way to reach the top of the plateau where we stood. The old mining pit was still evident where we'd pulled out the Fuel that kept our magical Shield Wall intact for a century only a few miles away from the City. Abandoned farms across the top of the plateau had been reclaimed by nature over the last twenty years, many of the old houses now roofless though their stone walls had held firm against the elements.

    I'd learned many seeking and searching spells since I was last here and sent my mind questing nearby for any signs of Bladesmen. I didn't sense any and a few minutes' search established that there were no other Lords within a hundred miles of the camp which was quickly being established around the portal. Good enough for now, I decided, then pulled my mind back into my body. Ather's eyes were still unfocused and I decided to let him be for the moment while he continued to search nearby for any hostile presence.

    I looked up just in time to watch the first airship come through. It hovered only a dozen feet above ground level, proceeding out of the portal slowly and majestically. I couldn't help but grin, looking it over and recognizing just how far we'd come since the days of the *Lord of the City*. The *Origin* was nearly half again as large and its lines were sleeker, looking predatory and powerful. It mounted two dozen powerful ballista with Fuel-tipped bolts armed and ready to fire. Three masts rose proudly with City banners fluttering at the tips and a great cheer rose up from the soldiers setting up camp below. Its shadow passed over me and I felt a fierce pride in my people. With creations like this, I thought to myself, how could we find anything other than success?

Chapter 15 – Parting Thoughts

    By the next morning our camp was well fortified. Two ships of the line patrolled the skies overhead, surrounded by a flock of seven skiffs zipping back and forth across the entire plateau. Eight Lords, including Ather, had come through to the human side of the portal and set up a variety of warding spells around the camp. Almost nine thousand soldiers, a mix of Bladesmen and human, spread out from the camp overnight and kept a watchful eye over the edges of the plateau nearby.

    Ather and the other Lords had been experimenting with magic and evaluating how it worked differently in the human world. As the only Lord who had cast spells here before, Ather demonstrated how much easier teleportation was on Bladesmen bodies here - it still produced momentary nausea, but it was far less than the hours of sickness that ensued when Bladesmen were transported by magic in their native world. Other magic proved slightly different as well, and I knew Ikami was looking forward to experimenting on her own once she arrived.

    I took a short trip back through the portal several hours after getting up. Ikami paced back and forth not far away, clearly fretting to come through. As soon as she saw me she begged me to ask Teyo to reconsider - the portal was clearly stable by now, after all, and going a few hours early wouldn't hurt. I laughed and replied that if she wanted to argue with the hard-nosed General she was more than welcome to, but that was a battle I didn't want to take up myself.

It was good to see Kenton again. Whenever we spent nights apart we were reminded of the days when one or the other of us had been swept up in battles and events beyond our control. I held him tightly, burying my face in his shoulder and enjoying the feel of his arms around me. Our love hadn't faded over almost a quarter century of marriage. Although I understood the strategic need for him to stay behind and direct the City while I was off helping to stop the Pact, I was going to miss him for the few weeks we expected the campaign to take.

Just over half of the army was still slated to come through the portal during the day; they'd paused for a few hours so a long line of supplies could be sent through on carts. Crates and barrels of food and arrows proceeded across that inconceivable distance in an instant, rolling through the tear in reality as though it were the most normal thing in the world. I gave Kenton one last squeeze and turned around, ready to head back to the human world and check with General Teyo if he was ready for me to start sprinkling more wards around the edge of the plateau.

A cry from the direction of the portal drew my attention. A woman covered in blood staggered through into the rapidly emptying camp, causing a ripple of alarm as the carts stopped moving. Kenton and I looked at each other then began to run towards the portal. "An attack," the soldier moaned as she clutched her head. Kenton yelled for a medic and handed her off to one of the guards nearby as I sent a surge of power to reinforce my personal wards. I was a few steps ahead of him in reaching the plane of the portal and didn't hesitate, throwing myself through the transition. Light and darkness battered at my consciousness; I could only grit my teeth and try to ignore the flickering sensations to push past the disorientation that came with such travel.

I emerged a moment later into a chaos of screams and explosions. To my left a line of deadly light was spearing upwards, chasing a skiff through the sky. A cloud of dust obscured everything ahead of me where the main camp had spread; I couldn't make out anything other than a sense of constantly firing magic in all directions.

A wave of power slammed into me and I reeled backwards, almost falling through the portal behind me. My wards held but the spell hit the portal with a terrible grinding noise. I turned around and saw it shiver for a moment, great gaps appearing where the portal lost its shape for a moment before it recovered. I saw the blurry shape that I knew must be Kenton rushing towards the portal from the far side and threw my power upwards, trying to protect the portal from any more attacks.

It was no good. The combined power of at least three Bladesmen Lords - none of whose magic I recognized - crashed into the portal simultaneously. My desperate protection broke, leaving me with a crippling headache. The portal wavered once more, shreds of it disappearing back into the indistinct darkness it had been summoned from. I felt the faintest thread of power from Ikami trying to hold it open from the other side, but it was no good. I watched helplessly as my husband breached the barrier of the portal just as it tore apart.

Another attack struck my personal wards and I felt them failing. The strain of keeping them up after having a spell so brutally broken was too much and my vision faded to grey. The last thing I saw was Kenton's hand flying through the air as the portal collapsed with the sound of a thousand waterfalls, blood spraying from his severed wrist across the dry earth of the human world we had returned to after so long.

Book 2

~ Cordell ~

Chapter 16 – Disaster

    One moment everything near the camp was calm. Well, not calm, perhaps, but busy in an organized way as General Teyo and General Sanato proved the value of their weeks of preparation. The morning was clear and warming quickly despite the air that still felt thin and inadequate to my lungs that had grown up with the thicker air of the Bladesmen world.

    That changed in an instant. I was talking to Lord Fian when he suddenly cut off mid sentence and looked upwards, frowning. His eyes grew wide and he shouted a wordless alarm just before an explosion rocked the earth and we grabbed onto each other for balance. My hand tingled as he raised his defenses instinctively; I took a moment longer and had to spend a few precious seconds summoning power and bringing up what shields I could around myself. By the time I was prepared he had already taken off running back towards the portal that stretched high above the camp some distance away.

    I gave chase as screams and orders erupted in every direction. I split my attention between jogging along and searching around myself with my magical senses, stumbling every few steps and cursing myself for not being more on guard. I could feel magical power being unleashed throughout the camp like tiny candles sparking to life all around me, with over a dozen Bladesmen Lords triggering spells nearby. The weaker sensation of common human mages like me was mixed in here and there, but the power we could summon would be of little use individually unless we were able to coordinate our spells.

After I fell to my knees for the second time I gave up trying to focus on both the mundane world and the magic around me. Instead I pelted after Lord Fian, now some distance ahead of me weaving between tents to get back to the portal. Twin bolts of flame suddenly struck a tent to my left and I staggered, throwing my arms up to shield my face from the heat as it washed over me. The hair on my forearms was singed away in an instant but somehow I avoided any more harm than that. I regained my balance and kept running, doing my best to dodge the soldiers jogging in every direction looking for a foe to engage.

Fian had almost reached the clear area near the portal when a flickering beam of green light lanced out of the chaos and cut across his body. It struck his warding spells and sent sparks flying in all directions; Fian tumbled sideways from the impact but other than a slight redness appeared none the worse for wear as he tried to climb back to his feet. I tried not to think about what the beam would have done if it had struck me that directly as I raced to help him as best I could.

Another blast hit him before he could stand up, with another brighter beam connecting from a slightly different angle. He threw his hands forward, trying to brace his magical defenses with everything he had, but it was too much too fast and his wards broke with an audible explosion. The Bladesmen Lord fell backwards, his left leg cleanly severed just above the knee. I reached forward with my own power, throwing everything I had in front of his body.

One of the beams flickered out just before it struck my desperate defense, but the other one struck it head on. I cried out as my paltry protection broke, falling forward onto my shoulders. The backlash was horrific; never before had I had a Lord's power strike mine so directly. I felt tears in my eyes as I skidded to a halt on the dusty ground, unable to see what had happened to the allied Lord in front of me.

Hands grabbed me and roughly hauled me to my feet. I blinked to see a frightened-looking young Bladesman girl in a uniform that looked too big for her; she was holding me up and trying to say something that I couldn't make out. It took me a few moments before I could understand what she was saying.

"*Are you alive? What's wrong? What should we do?" she babbled in the Bladesmen language.

"*I'm ... I'm all right," I said through clenched teeth as I tried to rein in the terrible pain crackling through my head. "*Help me towards the Lord over by the portal - he needs our help."

She nodded and let me lean on her as we made our way towards where I'd last seen Fian. By the time I got there he was surrounded by soldiers turned outwards, ready to dive in front of any attack that might strike them from the dust cloud that now surrounded us. I pushed my way into the middle to where the Lord was sitting up, his face pale but determined. I spared only a glance for the stump of his leg; it was enough to be sure that the attack had cleanly cauterized it and he would survive the injury.

"*Cordell - the portal is being hit," he said with a cough. "*We have to get there and reinforce the Archmagess!"

I looked up, suddenly afraid for Mom, just in time to see her thrown to the ground from a powerful spell. The portal shredded away in front of my eyes, disintegrating from the assault. I could see Mom trying to shout something at the portal and she reached towards it as though telling someone to wait, but it was too late - the portal splintered into uncountable pieces across the sky. Every scrap of magic nearby was pulled into the explosion; I could feel the little power I had left consumed by it while Lord Fian groaned and clutched his head in agony. I could only look on, horrified, as Mom fell backwards and lay unmoving. In a final macabre touch, someone's hand - cleanly severed at the wrist as they tried to dive through - flew out of the portal as it completely collapsed.

It took me at least a minute before I could pull together enough of my senses to send a trickle of magical energy around us in a probe of the area. I dimly sensed flickers of Bladesmen power around the edges of the camp as the Lords who had struck us teleported away, leaving chaos and destruction in their wake.

The soldiers nearby recovered more quickly than any of us with magical power. Two of them - one of whom I recognized as the Bladeswoman from a few minutes before - helped me back to my feet and supported my steps as I gestured towards where Mom lay on the ground, now surrounded by a cluster of worried-looking soldiers.

We reached Mom just as she was lifted onto a stretcher hastily constructed from tent poles and a piece of canvas. I let out a deep breath when I saw that she was breathing; she had no visible injuries other than being paler than usual. Her head lolled senselessly to the side, informing me that trying to speak with her would be fruitless. I grasped her hand tightly for a moment, trying to send her a trickle of magical communication, but after a few seconds of no response gave up and waved the stretcher off towards a medical tent.

With the few scraps of magical power I could pull together I sent my senses outwards to try and gather a sense of what was happening in the camp. I couldn't manage for long against the hideous headache battering the inside of my skull, but it was enough that I could at least recognize the magical signatures of all the Lords in the camp. Last but far from least, I pushed a little harder than I should have to make sure I could find Dalt and reassure myself that she was all right.

Lord Wesnoq and Lord Ather jogged up next to me just as I pulled my senses back into my body. Both of them were sweating from the strain of the short engagement and Wesnoq's elongated armblades had blood dripping down their length. "Is Viala seriously injured? Will she recover?" Ather asked. There were only a few times in my life that I'd heard him forgo use of a proper title.

I nodded. "I think she'll be all right. I didn't see her get hit directly by any enemy attacks, but she was right next to the portal when it closed."

All three of us turned to look at the empty space where the massive gateway home had hovered only a few moments before. "*How long will it take Lady Ikami to reconstruct it?" Wesnoq asked quietly in the Bladesmen tongue.

"*Based on what she said before we left, it will take a few months for the City ruins to generate enough energy to try again," I replied. All three of us knew the answer already, but confirming it out loud drove home what everyone was thinking.

For the foreseeable future we were on our own in hostile territory.

Chapter 17 – Retrenchment

    General Teyo put Lord Jabnoss and Lord Orove on watch while the rest of us assembled late that night. Mom and Fian were both there, pale and trembling but able to contribute. I'd gotten regular updates on how Mom was doing throughout the afternoon but had been too busy trying to help the camp recover to visit her in the medical tent. We traded glances and I sent her a trickle of emotion simply to let her know that I was glad to see her back on her feet.

    I was invited to the command meeting both as a Councilor and as a mage. Mastermage Sciani was the most senior mage in camp and attended in that capacity, while all the other Lords on this side of the portal were in the command tent as well: Wesnoq, Abel, Bilak, Mornali, and Ather. General Sanato had still been on the other side of the portal when it closed but nobody argued with Teyo's right to command the army here. Several other members of his command staff were there as well, none of whom I had more than a passing familiarity with.

    Once everyone had arrived, Teyo nodded to Lord Wesnoq who spoke in the Bladesmen language for everyone's benefit. "*I'll start off with a summary of what happened. At least five enemy Lords - supported by another four from a few miles away - teleported in near the camp. They struck after only a few moments' recovery, showing either that they've figured out a way to alleviate teleportation sickness or that they've trained themselves to push through its effects. In either case, we didn't have nearly enough warning to react."

Faces nodded gravely around the table as the short Lord continued. "*They were each accompanied by a squad of commoners who proceeded to fight without quarter, targeting every human in sight. Their determination was... surprising... to our troops. Meanwhile, the Lords attacked indiscriminately, except for three who targeted the portal specifically. Archmagess, can you continue from there?"

Mom nodded and stood up so everyone could hear her, leaning against a tent pole for support. Her red hair stood out starkly against her deathly pale skin and I could feel how much weaker her magical reserves were than normal. "*I reached the portal just as it was starting to get struck. I tried shielding it but I wasn't able to hold off three Lords, especially without any preparation. They knew just how to hit it to make it collapse. I don't have any doubt that they studied it beforehand, which means that at least one of them had been no more than a few miles away for several hours at some point since it was opened."

It was a chilling thought - that our foes had been nearby, watching us, shielded well enough that we didn't sense them with our magical sweeps. If they could do it once, they could do it again.

Teyo nodded in thanks to Mom, who sat down as quickly as she could while the General continued. "*I understand that they teleported away as soon as the portal closed. Several hundred soldiers died, mostly human, and Lord Fian sacrificed his leg. We don't know what happened on the far side of the portal, though at least one person was partway through when it closed."

Mom glanced at me, a despairing look on her face like I'd never seen. I tried to open a mental line of communication with her to ask what she was thinking, but she just shook her head and kept her mind closed.

"*Currently we have around eight thousand soldiers in

the camp as well as eight Lords, the Archmagess, and nine other human mages. With what came through the portal before it closed, we have supplies for perhaps three weeks."

"That's a lot of mouths to feed," I heard Sciani mutter to himself.

The General nodded and continued. "*I've already sent human-led patrols across the plateau with wagons - perhaps some useful supplies from the exodus twenty years ago can be found. Lord Jabnoss reported a group of wild livestock roaming at the far end of the plateau; I'd like some of the human mages to go with a flight of three skiffs tomorrow to assist in herding them back to the camp for slaughter."

"*General, I can put up a Shield Wall around the plateau with enough Fuel. That will prevent them from teleporting in or out again," Mom suggested.

He sighed. "*Unfortunately, Fuel is one of the commodities in shortest supply. We have several small crates full - fortunately, none of them were struck in the attack - but they are needed for the airships. Other than those, we only have whatever is available on ballista bolts and arrow tips. I do not wish to sacrifice those weapons unless absolutely necessary."

Lord Bilak looked over at Ather and Wesnoq. "*Excuse me. I know that myself and Mornali are on probation here, but it seems that the situation requires extraordinary cooperation. May I make a suggestion?"

After a quick glance to Mom and Ather as though seeking their opinions Teyo nodded to the onetime rebel. Bilak bowed and continued. "*Lord Randell was very concerned about human forces teleporting in and causing trouble. We had conducted some research into methods to stop teleportation into our bases, but eventually abandoned the magic as it would have prevented us from escaping in a time of need. I believe that with assistance from... human magic... we could build something in short order that would at least protect the camp area." The Lord was clearly uncomfortable with the idea of working alongside my race, but I had to give some grudging respect to him for pushing past his views and understanding that he'd thrown his lot in with us one way or the other.

I was suddenly struck by another thought and stood up, waiting politely until General Teyo nodded to acknowledge me. "*I'm sorry, I don't mean to interrupt, but I just realized something. Lord Wesnoq, you mentioned nine Lords. Weren't there supposed to only be seven left here?"

Ather looked uncomfortable as he replied in Wesnoq's stead. "*Yes. That's another item which concerns us greatly. If there's more Lords than we expected, then either they have started allowing other Lords to live past infancy... or they've had some means of transport back and forth over the last twenty years."

I blinked. That could explain how they knew a means to disable the portal so quickly, but would also mean they knew far more about us than we'd expected. I sat down, trying to wrap my head around the idea.

Ather continued. "*Lord Bilak, I would appreciate it if you could talk over your ideas with the Archmagess. I would like to propose another plan. As many of you know, when we left this world a score of years ago, I left behind a few hundred of my followers under the command of Igwer, an associate of mine. I need to travel to the caves they lived in and see if they have survived."

Teyo frowned. "*These were my friends too, Lord Ather, but... it has been a very long time for them to survive while being hunted by the Lords of this world."

My namesake nodded gravely. "*I know... but I cannot simply abandon them if there is any hope that they have survived." He looked around, then added, "*I do not ask anyone else to come with me. We will want no more than a few at most anyways, as we have several teleports to make. That said, I could use someone to watch my back."

It took me only an instant to decide. "*I'll go with you, if you'll have me," I said. "*I'm sure a few of the soldiers will join us as well."

"*Thank you, Cordell. That means a lot to me."

I sent a mental thread of communication to him as he sat back down. *Come on, Uncle Ather,* I said over the link as soon as he accepted it. *I couldn't let you head off on your own.*

Before he could reply Mom's consciousness joined us. *Are you two sure about this? I hate to say it, Ather, but Teyo's right - there's almost no way they could've survived this long.*

I have to try, he sent back simply.

I could almost see Mom's head shaking with a sigh from the emotions tucked into her reply. *You sound just like Kenton sometimes, you know.*

Ather's emotions softened. *That's the best compliment I could imagine. Thank you.*

I know better than to try and persuade you from going, Cordell, Mom sent my way. *You're as stubborn as your father. Just... the two of you take care of each other, all right? Those Lords might be able to sense you teleporting away and they'll start hunting you immediately.*

The two of us are safer together than alone, Mom, you know that. You rest up and don't spend too much on Bilak's plan, got it?

She sent a sense of assent and withdrew. A moment later I was back in my body, trying to catch up to the conversation going on between Teyo and his commanders about troop movements and how to better fortify the camp. We talked for another hour before splitting up. Ather and I headed off together after I gave Mom a quick hug, still sensing something she was holding back but unable to try and pry it out of her with Ather's mission pressing on my mind.

Three soldiers I vaguely recognized ended up accompanying us after offering to join us, well recommended by General Teyo. All three were human; there had been plenty of Bladesmen volunteers (Dalt had been one of them) but if we were going to teleport a few times we needed people who wouldn't be as affected by sickness. We had two men and a woman, hard-bitten veterans all. I quickly threw a few staples into a pack - food and water, a first aid kit, a thin blanket, things like that - and strapped on my sword before meeting Ather and the others a little after midnight.

"We have a long trip ahead of us," he started off in the

human language. "The cave I last saw Igwer and his group in is over two thousand miles east and somewhat north of the plateau here. With only five of us I can jump a few hundred miles each time, but I'll need a rest after each one. Everyone has supplies for a few days?"

We all nodded. The soldiers looked determined and eager to do something after the hit the camp had taken earlier. Each was fully armed with bow, sword, spear, and studded leather armor meant for fast travel. "Then get ready to go," Ather said and closed his eyes. I did the same, sending my mind around on a quick sweep through the camp while the Bladesman Lord sent his consciousness winging across the countryside. After I'd made sure everything here was as calm as it could be I pulled back into my body and readied myself for the inevitable disorientation of teleporting.

A few long seconds later a flash sparked across my retinas and the earth itself shifted below my feet as though suddenly melting. I staggered for an instant as reality settled back into place around me, a loud crack echoing into the distance from our arrival. I blinked, trying to clear the dazzle from my eyes, to see that we'd arrived in a small clearing surrounded by thick firs of a type I'd never seen. Even in the starlight I could see that their needles were lighter than those I had grown up with on the Bladesman world. I ran my fingers along a nearby branch for a moment, feeling the unfamiliar slickness under my skin. *This is the world I should have grown up on,* I thought to myself with a strange wonderment.

The other soldiers were readying a camp around us, pitching a single tent and putting together a few rocks for a small firepit. The night had a slight chill to it but nothing too uncomfortable. Ather was sitting on the ground nearby looking ill, clearly ready to crawl into the tent and try to sleep. I was happy to take first watch while the others rested, feeling far too awake to rest right away.

Stars glittered through the trees above me while I settled against a tree with my blanket thrown over my shoulders. They were completely unfamiliar to me and their colors were subtly different than I expected. Whatever made the sky here so oddly blue was probably responsible for that. It would still feel strange to not see a violet tint when I looked up tomorrow morning. At least I didn't notice the thinness of the air as much anymore; my body seemed to be acclimating faster than my mind.

My thoughts churned through one topic after another, restless and worried. Without Ikami or the portal our entire battle plan was in shambles. My sister was our trump card, the power that would easily eclipse whatever the Lords here could throw at us. With the unexpected additional Lords we were suddenly outnumbered with no chance of reinforcements. When my people had been here before at least they'd had a Shield Wall to protect them.

I forced myself to look at the assets we had. The Lords we'd allied with were strong, though I had trouble trusting the two one-time rebels who had joined us. We'd expected them to be easy to keep an eye on, here to prove themselves and show that they were willing to take risks to avoid being exiled from the Four Continents back home. Instead we had to rely on them as a significant portion of our force - and I worried about their reliability.

We might be able to hold off the enemy Lords with some preparation and the airships, I knew, but there was no way we could survive an assault by the millions of common Bladesmen here. Eventually they would simply drown us in bodies, heedless of the cost due to the Pact. I didn't know what Ather was hoping to accomplish with this mission; the few hundred Bladesmen he'd left wouldn't be able to tip the tide in any significant way even if they had somehow lived.

I continued turning these things over in my mind, hoping to find some solution we hadn't yet thought of but by the time my watch was over I didn't feel I'd made any progress. I woke one of the soldiers and rolled up inside the warm tent, falling asleep to the soft snoring of the man next to me.

Chapter 18 – A Search for Friends

    We traveled that way for another three days. Lord Ather managed to teleport us about once every six hours, clearly paying a price with each successive spell. I forced him to take a longer break after the fourth jump for his own sake though he was clearly fretting over the delay. We didn't see a single Bladesmen the entire time; Ather did well at choosing the sites he set us down in.

    The constant wariness and continual teleportation took its toll on us humans as well. It didn't help that our travel eastward shortened each day by an hour or two, sending our internal clocks haywire. I regularly swept the area around us with my magical senses while Uncle Ather was recovering from each jump. Twice I sensed an enemy Lord's probe trying to pinpoint the disturbance Ather's spells were causing. Fortunately I was able to slip aside and avoid detection, but it kept me on edge - we could be found at any time and the only warning we would have was the crack of our foes appearing around us.

    We made our last jump shortly before dawn. Ather was clearly torn between excitement and fear, but the sense of disappointment I felt as he swept us up in his spell told me what he'd sensed from a distance before we arrived. I blinked a few times, trying to clear my vision, and found myself in a clearing covered in broken boulders. The moss on their surface showed that they'd been in place for many years.

I raised my eyes and saw Lord Ather staring sorrowfully at the cavern mouth across from us. Half of it was collapsed, its destruction the source of the stones at our feet. Blackened scorch marks and soot over the entryway showed that a great inferno must have raged inside, and deep scars in the cliffs nearby were clear evidence of Bladesmen magic.

"I failed them," my namesake said quietly as he fell to his knees, uncaring of the way his shin blades scraped against the fallen stones. He pointed upwards where a few exposed bones, clearly Bladesmen, could be seen. "I probably knew those sentries," he whispered. A moment later he leaned forward and vomited across the tumbled scree, the teleportation nausea suddenly proving too much for him.

I nodded to the soldiers and they cautiously took up positions around the clearing, keeping a close eye on the forest around us. The carnage here had been caused long ago, so I didn't expect to be attacked, but even so I wanted someone watching our back. I took a moment to let Ather recover somewhat then squatted down next to him. "From what I understand, they made their own choice," I said in what I hoped was a reassuring tone.

A tear formed at the corner of Ather's eye, something I'd never witnessed. He'd always been calm and collected even when Ikami had nearly killed him by accident - his broken forearm blade was a constant reminder of that event. "Cordell, my people deserved better than this. They were a free people, and to see that they fell here..." He ran his hands over the moss on the nearest boulder and continued, "It could not have been long after we left. I can only imagine how enraged the other Lords were. They would not have spared anyone."

I hesitated, not sure what to do next. "Do... do you want to go inside?"

He shook his head vehemently. "No, I do not think I could handle seeing what became of our settlement. Just ... give me some few moments, please."

I nodded respectfully and took a few steps back,

making eye contact with each of the other three and signaling for them to maintain their positions. For everyone's sake I closed my eyes and focused a quick spell to carefully cover the evidence of Ather's sickness. Just as I started to withdraw I felt a twinge from the direction of the cavern as though some spell was drawing my energy inwards. I cautiously sent my mind that way, making sure not to trip any unseen wards or traps that might have been left behind.

As I came near the half-collapsed entrance I found some dangling threads of magic moving slowly as though affected by an invisible breath of wind. They were definitely Bladesmen in origin and looked to be some kind of alarm or trap. On closer investigation I realized that they must be at least a year or two old, their power faded and weak - but still much more recently placed than the disaster that had taken place here. Their structure was crude, as though placed by a first-year apprentice who had little idea what they were doing.

"Ather?" I said quietly, fighting to hold my attention near the wards while forcing my body to respond to my will. "There's some spells near the entryway. Something is strange about them."

A moment later I felt his consciousness join mine, both of us staying some distance back and carefully examining the magical strings I'd found. *This doesn't look like the work of any Lord I knew of while I was here,* he sent to me with a sense of determination. *I think we should trip these spells and be ready to strike whoever comes. This might be a chance to hit our enemies where they don't expect.*

I'm not sure, I replied. *You, me, and three soldiers against a Lord and whoever he shows up with?*

The difference is that we'll be ready - and we can fall on them the instant they appear.

At the camp they didn't seem very affected by teleportation sickness. Uncle Ather, I'm not sure this is a good idea.

The sadness in his mind caught at me as he opened his emotions further. *Cordell, how would you feel if your family had been slain by our enemies? I need to do something, not just sit and wait and hope they don't kill us before your sister opens a way home. We can do this. I'll have a teleportation spell ready so if they show up with more than one Lord I'll get us out of here immediately, no questions asked.*

Sudden action wasn't like Ather but his despair was undeniable. I hesitated for a moment longer, then sent back a feeling of assent and pulled my mind back to my body. As soon as I opened my eyes I called to the soldiers. "Pull out your bows and Fuel-tipped arrows if you've got them. Ather's going to try to set a trap for an enemy Lord; we may have a chance to ambush them here and at least get something out of this trip."

They looked at one another with some surprise, then nodded and started picking their way across the broken ground back towards Ather and I. The older of the two men said gruffly, "You keep the magic off us as best you can and we'll give whoever shows up a lesson he won't forget."

I felt Ather tripping the wards a moment later. A shiver of cold air went through the clearing just as the sun started to break through the trees to our east. The three soldiers quickly strung their bows and nocked arrows, ready to draw and fire with the same smooth movements I'd seen a thousand times on the practice grounds. I gathered power inwards and set up some basic shields around the four of us, knowing Ather could handle himself. True to his word, I felt my namesake surround us with a teleportation spell ready to trigger at an instant's notice - though at the same time he pulled up his own reserves of energy for a quick strike outwards.

We waited, ready, for more than five minutes. Just as the soldiers started to relax their arms slightly Ather shouted a wordless warning and turned towards the top of the bluff above the cavern entrance where the sentry's bones lay stark against the grey stone. A bright flash and sharp crack announced the arrival of another Lord and I drew my breath, waiting to see if Ather would teleport us away or stay and fight.

Just back from the edge of the bluff I could make out at least six or seven Bladesmen heads, though in the dappled shadows of sunrise it was hard to make out any details. Without warning a piercing green lance of light carved down through the trees nearby, wobbling until it struck my shields. I tensed, hoping Ather would help reinforce my defenses, but my protections held on their own and I was able to throw the attack off to the side. I heard the groan of a tree behind us as it crashed to the ground.

In response, my companions aimed upwards and released three Fuel-tipped arrows nearly simultaneously. Their aim was true and I slipped my mind forwards to smooth the arrows' flight as Dad had taught me many years before. Just before they reached the top of the bluff my focus was suddenly swept up in a power I recognized as Ather's. Without warning he tossed the arrows aside so that they flew into the cliff face itself and exploded, sending shards of rock and dirt flying everywhere - except into the ranks of our enemies, who looked just as confused as I was.

"Wait!" he shouted, then repeated himself in the Bladesmen tongue. "*Wait, don't attack! I know you!"

Our opponent didn't hold back, though, and unleashed another blast at us. Ather's mind grabbed hold of the light and twisted it downwards, grounding it in the earth right before our small group. *I said to HALT! he sent in a frighteningly strong message aimed directly at the other Lords' mind.

I waited, tensed up for another attack, but it didn't come. After a few seconds where the only noise was that of branches falling behind us, the other Bladesmen hesitatingly approached the stark edge of the bluff.

"*Kaibo! Do you not recognize me?" Ather called out to the figures above.

Suddenly one of them gave a great whoop. "*Lord Ather? Is it really you?"

Ather gave a wide grin and shouted back. "*Damn right it is! Get down here and let me see you clearly!"

The other Bladesmen started working their way down the steep slope, moving a few yards to the side until they were able to slide down from one tree to the next. Most of them seemed the age of my parents or even older though two were a few years younger than I. The Lord in their group was no more than a teenager, watching us suspiciously with his shields raised high against any sudden attack. He had wild black hair and was close to my height, with gangly limbs proving that he had yet to grow into his full stature.

A Bladesmen with scarred forearm blades and tattered grey hair ran up to Ather as soon as he could. The two slapped palms together and clapped their forearm blades so that they echoed across the clearing. The newcomer, who I assumed was the Kaibo Ather had addressed, looked Ather up and down before saying, "*I can't believe it. It really is you."

The others jogged up behind with the young Lord arriving last. Kaibo bowed formally to him and his voice changed as he continued. "*Lord Ather, may I introduce Lord Sumi. Lord Sumi, you've heard stories of Lord Ather since you were a boy - I am proud to introduce him in the flesh."

With a hard look in his eyes, the boy bowed back slightly. Then, before anyone else could utter a word, he spoke in a high-pitched angry voice. "*So the Lord who abandoned his people has returned. What do you have to say for yourself?"

I cursed to myself as Ather's joyous expression fell. Not all of them, it seemed, were happy to have us back.

Chapter 19 – Long Term Plans

Kaibo stiffened at the youngster's words and clenched his teeth as though wanting to growl, but held his tongue after a moment's effort. Ather similarly took a second to regain his composure, then answered stiffly, "*It seems we have both been through many events in the last score of years. Lord Sumi, I would be happy to converse at greater length, but this might not be the best location to do so."

Sumi's eyes flared with anger, but he merely nodded and stepped backwards. "*Kaibo, you will vouch for this Bladesman?"

This time the older Bladesmen did not hold back. "*Lord Ather was the one who started the rebellion you're now part of. If not for him you'd be dead or with the others. Have some respect... Lord Sumi."

Ather held up his hand to silence the others and the teenage Lord visibly gritted his teeth when they instantly obeyed. "*I understand that your concerns must run deep. I would be willing to lower my shields while we teleport if that would make you feel safer."

Sumi slashed one arm through the air, barely avoiding striking his companions with his forearm blade. "*I can handle you with or without your shields up. What of these others? Human, I presume? Will you tell your pet human Lord to lower his defenses too?"

I cleared my throat and answered in the Bladesmen tongue. "*My apologies, Lord Sumi, but I am merely a common mage, not a Lord."

Ather's expression, stoic when enduring the young Lord's barbs, had darkened as soon as they became aimed at me. His voice grew stern as he spoke. "*Lord Sumi, this human standing next to me is overly modest. He is a Councilor, one of the rulers of their people, and I strongly advise that you behave diplomatically towards him. May I introduce Councilor Cordell... Cordell Ather of the City."

Kaibo and the other Bladesmen immediately bowed courteously, while Sumi frowned but ultimately nodded politely. "*Do all of your companions understand our tongue, or only the Councilor?" inquired one of the other Bladesmen, a woman who looked slightly younger than Kaibo.

"*We all do. Pleasure to meet you," the oldest human soldier said gruffly. All three had relaxed their draw, though I noticed that not a single one had released their weapons completely. I gave them a subtle hand signal and they started to unstring their bows.

"*That will make things more convenient," Kaibo said with a smile, clearly trying to repair the mood. "*I think Lord Ather is correct and we should retire to the encampment. Lord Sumi, we can trust Lord Ather completely, as well as his companions."

The teenager's eyes flickered back and forth between us, and after a moment's hesitation nodded and closed his eyes. I gestured the other humans to step close to make it easier on the Lords, not knowing how far we had to travel. Once we were huddled up I closed my eyes and switched to using only my magical senses. I could feel Ather's attention following Sumi's some great distance to the north, journeying on a longer trip than I was willing to risk. After a few seconds I could feel both of them focusing some power around us and I prepared myself for the sickening feeling of teleportation.

It felt different somehow when it happened this time. The ground stayed steadier though the spell itself seemed to happen over a longer duration. It was unpleasant, certainly, but by the time I opened my eyes and heard the last echoes of a familiar crack I felt less distressed than I ever had when using that particular mode of transportation.

Lord Ather looked much better as well. He was only slightly unsteady on his feet and had no signs of the usual nausea that Bladesmen suffered during the spell. I glanced around and made sure my companions had all arrived safely, then raised my eyes and examined our surroundings.

We had arrived in a small valley with steep, treacherous-looking sides covered in low brush and stunted trees. The air felt thin and chill, causing me to expend a tiny bit of power in warming myself magically. Each breath left traces of steam as though we'd teleported into the dead of winter. High mountain peaks stretched above us, a line of snow only a thousand or so feet above us.

Some distance up the valley I could see a collection of rude huts with traces of smoke rising from them. Plots of land covered in sickly vegetables surrounded the small village, where a few Bladesmen could be seen here and there working the earth. The nearest had looked up at the sound of our arrival and were slowly heading our way.

Next to me Ather bowed deeply to the teenage Lord. "*That is an extraordinary modification to teleportation. I feel much better than I ever did before, and I thank you for showing it to me."

The boy looked stunned at the compliment and looked down at his feet as he answered. "*It's nothing - I stole it from watching another Lord do it at a distance." When we started walking as a group towards the village, however, something had softened in his demeanor and he walked a little closer to Ather than I thought he would have before.

The Bladesmen we approached were dressed in dirty clothes and looked half-starved but were clearly excited to see us. We humans attracted strange glances but Ather was the object of main attention. Enough of them recognized him that whispers spread quickly throughout the village, and by the time we reached the largest hut an ancient Bladesman with sagging flesh was waiting in the road to meet us, leaning on a simple staff. His face broke open in a wide grin, an expression that looked foreign to his corpulent face.

Ather strode up to the elder without hesitation and gently clasped hands with him, clapping forearm blades together with a soft ringing noise. "*Igwer," he breathed, "*I cannot say how glad I am to see you."

I'd heard that name before - he had been one of Ather's advisors many years before who had chosen to stay behind and lead the rebels who remained here. He had to be at least seventy or eighty years old and life here had not been kind to him. Still, it brought a smile to my face to see the two old friends reunited with such obvious joy.

The old man's face crinkled with a wide grin. His voice, when he spoke, was frail and trembling but clearly happy. "*Lord Ather, I would bow if I could - but as you can see my knees are not what they used to be. It... it is very good to see you back."

My namesake smiled. "*You need never bow to me, Igwer. Let us sit somewhere and talk of what has happened to each of us over the last... twenty-three years?"

"*Has it been so long?" Igwer asked wonderingly as he tottered back into his hovel, waving for us to follow. Not many of us fit inside, but after a quick check around the three soldiers whispered to me that they'd be right outside. Ather, Sumi, Kaibo, Igwer, the Bladeswoman who had spoken back in the clearing, and myself squeezed around a small table. Stools were quickly passed in from outside so everyone could sit while we talked.

Igwer - with a pointed glance from Kaibo - first had Ather talk about what had happened after the Lord had left with the majority of the rebels over twenty years before. I'd heard the tale before, of course, but it somehow made it more real when I realized that at that very moment I was sitting on the human world where the story had started. Igwer and his group had heard nothing of the escape and Ather's success.

The Bladesman Lord talked about the world we'd traveled to - the world I'd grown up on - and the trials we'd gone through there.

Sumi's expression grew openly curious during the retelling, especially when Ather talked about how the retired Lords and their chokehold on that world had been overthrown. The teenager looked very young while he listened, more a boy than a man.

While Kaibo's expression was one of great relief as he heard about how Bladesmen and humans now lived together in peace, Igwer's face was unreadable. I mentally reviewed the little I remembered about him from Dad's stories; the older Bladesman had been against Ather joining with us humans from the beginning. From the current state of his people I wondered if he now regretted that decision.

It was nearly three hours before Ather was done, having touched only on the major points of the human-Bladesmen adventures. A small meal was brought, with none of the meat or cheese I'd grown to associate with Bladesmen preferences. I tried not to turn up my nose at the wilted vegetables and poorly dried berries, reminding myself that I was a Councilor and that this was likely the best food they had stored.

After lunch it was time for Igwer to speak. He cleared his throat, hawking up a foul-smelling ball of spittle into a nearby clay pot, before beginning his tale. "*So after you left, Lord Ather, there were about five hundred of us who remained as you know. We weren't sure whether we would ever see you again and had to prepare ourselves for reprisals. I sent several groups of scouts out to find a new place for us in case the cavern was attacked - you'll recall that we talked about that a few times. The rest of us set as many snares as we could around the outside and hunkered down to wait out whatever was going to happen.

"*When it came it was bad. Our pickets saw the teleportation flashes about two months after you'd left, a good ten miles away. There were at least fifty within the space of a couple of hours, so we knew thousands of soldiers were coming our way, all of them under the Pact. Those of us who had undergone the Pact before got out while we could, along with the youngest and those unable to fight. The spells you wove to suppress the Pact within us wouldn't hold against another Lord who wanted to reactivate it, you know."

His voice was already growing hoarse so with a quick glance Kaibo continued, his tone much stronger. "*I was one of those who stayed to fight. Our traps slowed them down, and of course they sent the commoners first - whatever you did to them when you left made those Lords right furious yet very cautious."

"*How did they find you?" Ather asked, leaning forward onto the table. His lone forearm blade was rubbing a scratch into the already worn wood; under normal circumstances he would have immediately noticed and apologized.

Igwer shrugged while Kaibo continued the story. "*We don't know for sure, but I suspect they caught one of our scouting parties and got them to tell. It was always a risk. Anyhow, them and their troops came charging right up to the cave. We tried to hold them off at the mouth but had to fall back. Some of us made it out through side passages before the Lords themselves made it up. I don't know for sure how the last fights went, but as we straggled out through the woods I looked back and all I saw was black smoke. Nearly two hundred of us died that day." The Bladesman shook his head as he remembered it.

After a respectful pause he continued. "*We all met up at a prearranged spot and figured out what to do next. Everyone was a mess. For two years we stayed in small groups, only reconvening every once in a while. Sometimes a group would never make the next meet and we'd all split up in a hurry, worried that the Lords were going to crash in and start blasting away. It happened twice like that, you see, and more free folk died."

Igwer nodded sorrowfully then took up the tale.

"*Those were tough times. Finally we found this valley and started trickling in. Only a hundred or so of us remained, although a few had managed to rescue children along the way before they could be taken by the Pact. One group found Lord Sumi here. He was just a babe, newly born, when they saved him from the other Lords - he would have been killed or forced into the Pact otherwise.

"*We sent out spies where we could and learned that the humans had escaped, though we never found out if you had made it with them or not. They talked of tens of thousands of Bladesmen killed in the battle. I tell you, though, that whatever you did left them scared. The Lords started recruiting newly born Lords instead of killing them. Based on what we know there's at least eleven Lords now, five of them young."

The teenage Lord nodded as all eyes turned to him. His high-pitched voice broke as he talked. "*I... I haven't had the training that they have. But I'm more powerful than any of them, I'm sure of it. I learned by watching their spells from a distance. I think they always thought I was just one of them - they often work as a group anyways."

"*From what our reports say, they had just about given up on you returning and had started to talk about killing newly born Lords again," Kaibo said grimly. "*The Pact is still strong, as strong as ever. Lord Sumi does not know how to dampen its effects in the way you managed to do, Lord Ather, but he's working on the best way to do it. Although with you back now..."

It was clear that everyone, Sumi included, expected Ather to step back into his old role. My namesake looked down at his hands for a moment, suddenly realizing that he'd scraped up the table. "*My friends... You have done well in surviving so long. The information you have will prove invaluable for us all. In our world we have learned how to completely dissolve the Pact, albeit slowly - it only works on one person at a time. Without capturing or subduing one of the Lords who built the Pact from the ground up, I fear we will not be able to break the spell across everyone in this world."

He took a deep breath and continued, looking directly at Igwer. "*I know you were not willing to trust the humans and our plan a score years ago, Igwer, but I ask you to reconsider that choice now. We can teleport back to our encampment with all of your people, where we have seven other allied Lords and many human mages as well. We need only to hold until Councilor Cordell's sister is able to open a portal back to our home world, and your people would be more than welcome there. Please, my old friend and advisor, I beg of you - have trust and come with us."

I glanced back and forth between the two of them. Clearly there was something major at play here; Ather needed this vote of confidence from Igwer. Perhaps it was the only way he'd feel forgiven for leaving his people behind, no matter that it was their choice to do so originally.

After what felt like an eternity, Igwer slowly nodded, his jowls shaking with age and emotion as he did so. "*This time I will come with you, Lord Ather. This time nobody will stay behind."

Chapter 20 – Abuses

It took only a few hours for the Bladesmen to assemble. The collection of items they chose to bring was heartbreaking - a ragged bundle of cloth that one boy held as a doll, the pathetic broken handle of an axe, and a battered pot which clearly served as a valued family heirloom. Everyone brought what food they could, but there was little to be had - these people lived day to day with no reserves for hard times.

Ather gently coaxed the younger Lord into a conversation about how best to handle the teleportation. It was clear that Sumi had never spoken to another Lord about magic before and he looked alternately terrified and falsely confident. I knew that my namesake would need to draw on Sumi's power to bring this many people through, but I feared that the teenager would refuse to open himself to Ather, making each jump difficult and treacherous.

Yet it took far less time than I'd thought it would for Uncle Ather to persuade Sumi to work with him. Once again I was impressed by his ability to teach and persuade; for someone who had no real teachers of his own while growing up he had a real talent for sharing the gifts of magic that they'd both been born with. The two of them stood in front of the mob, the older Lord only slightly taller than the younger. They looked little alike; Ather's skin contrasted darkly against Sumi's lighter tone while the teenager's wild black mop was a world apart from Ather's short, well-groomed hair. The only thing they had in common was a slight build, though there was no guarantee Sumi would stay so slim as he grew over the next few years.

I stood at the front of the press, ready to scout outwards using my magical senses as soon as we reappeared somewhere new. I felt Ather and Sumi communicating via mind to mind contact, readying their power to move the Bladesmen across hundreds of miles. The elder Lord had quickly grasped the alterations to teleportation that the Lords here had worked out in the last score of years, assuring that we wouldn't arrive with hundreds of Bladesmen drained and sickly.

When I sensed the two building their power I closed my eyes and called out to the group to do the same. Everyone fell silent a moment before the spell gathered us up, giving the familiar feeling of the earth shifting under our feet. I stumbled as I heard the sharp crack that announced our arrival, blinking away the flashing afterglow of the magic. I spun my mind out around us quickly, making sure that we were alone within at least a ten mile radius.

The first teleport had gone so successfully that the two Lords agreed to do another jump in an hour. The Bladesmen sat and rested in the small stony glen we found ourselves in while Ather and Sumi gathered their strength. I found myself next to Kaibo, who surveyed his kin with his arms crossed and a look of satisfaction on his face.

"*Oy, human, what do you think of our group?" he asked me without turning.

"*I think you've done well to survive for so long," I answered honestly. "*That said, I believe your people will do well with the safety and sanctuary our camp offers."

He thought for a moment, then continued in a lower tone. "*Lord Sumi is a good boy," he said, "*but he is just that - a boy. His whole life has been spent hearing Ather this, Ather that, and I don't think we ever really thought the two would meet. I'm worried about him - he's a Lord, but he still has a lot to learn, see?"

I nodded, wondering where the older man was going.

"*I'm too old to know how to talk to him," he said cautiously. "*I've tried raising him, but I know I'm a mentor, not a friend. Will the other Lords accept him? Will he be able to find those who he can relate to?"

"*I think so," I said with a slight smile. "*They are good people. I've known some of them for years, and they have proven solid allies and skilled in their works. I think being around his peers can only be good for him - if he's willing to learn from them."

"*That there might be the hard part," he muttered. "*Boy's got attitude. It comes from being the only Lord around." Kaibo sighed, raking a hand through his short hair. "*I suppose he'll learn, one way or the other."

Soon we continued on with another leap across the countryside. The sun moved a handspan with each spell, making for darkness after only three castings. We set up camp, the more experienced scouts among the Bladesmen supervising the rest of the civilians. Ather looked tired but happy, clearly feeling better than he ever had after teleporting. The four of us humans kept watch alongside the Bladesmen scouts amicably enough, though after the morning meal there was little food to be had for anyone.

After a quick conference we agreed to teleport another two jumps, then take a few hours to try and do some hunting. Ather warned that he could feel another Lord probing the area, having sensed our arrival the previous evening, but that he was doing what he could to shield our presence against anything but a directed search in this very spot. I had a private conversation with him and agreed to take over these duties between each jump so he could focus on gathering enough power to keep us moving quickly.

We traveled that way for two days, the only signs of pursuit being of a magical nature. I was able to slip the searches aside, barely, though I wouldn't be able to breathe easily until we were back at the main camp near other allies who could help out in case of an attack. I was petrified that at any moment we'd be found and an attack group would teleport into the middle of the mob of civilians we were escorting. Only about twenty of the Bladesmen had proven to have any training in martial arts, and despite the fearsome natural weaponry that every Bladesmen sported I knew they wouldn't last long against trained opponents.

During our travels we found just enough food to get by. Scouts would track down a few animals during the midday break - our human archers were a subject of much discussion as they helped the hunting parties - and we'd teleport the carcasses along with us until night fell. Between what was gathered in the dark and the butchered meat each evening we survived, though we never quite felt full. Still, I could tell that the Bladesmen were pleased to be out of their tiny valley and able to roam the area to hunt.

In about half the time we'd taken to travel outwards we made it back to our temporary home, even with so many people in tow. We teleported into the middle of the military camp at noon after Ather sent a signal to let the Lords on duty know we were coming. I'd never be able to forget the emotions of the Bladesmen who had been hiding on their own for twenty years when they saw thousands of friendly faces nearby, filled with joy to see them and concern about their well-being. Many of the older folk broke down sobbing while they met friends lost decades ago with hand clasps, while the younger Bladesmen simply stood in shock. They'd never seen so many people gathered at once.

Mom came rushing up only a few minutes after we'd arrived, looking much better than last time I'd seen her. She gathered me up in a tight hug for a moment, then stood back at arm's length and looked me up and down. "How was it?" she asked simply.

I smiled. "Look at these people, Mom. Over a hundred and fifty of Ather's rebels made it this long out in the wilds. We brought them back - and a young Lord who's not part of the rulers here."

Her eyebrows shot up. "Oh? I was wondering who that

was - he didn't act like someone you captured and brought back as a prisoner." She hesitated a moment, then continued, "I'm glad to see you safe, Cordell."

My response was to reach forward and give her another embrace. "How have things been here?"

She frowned. "Well, we've gotten organized, and we were able to gather a few days worth of supplies from what was abandoned before the City left, but we still have some major food problems. Even with rationing we don't have nearly enough to last. But that's a subject for discussion tonight after everyone's settled. You two returning with this batch will certainly raise spirits."

I paused for a few seconds, then asked gently, "Any sign from the other side that they're trying to reestablish the portal?"

"It's too early, Cordell, you know that," she said with a sigh.

I shrugged. "A man can hope, that's all. Here, let me introduce you to Lord Sumi."

The afternoon flew by quickly as the newcomers were settled. A dazed-looking Sumi was introduced to the other Lords as well as General Teyo and some of the other leaders in the camp. It was obvious that he felt out of place, but as a Lord he was immediately accepted into the highest councils despite his inexperience - a gesture that went a long way in helping convince him to throw his full effort in with us. Igwer and Kaibo joined us in the command tent as the sun was falling, half the people standing due to a lack of space.

The General started off as the last few Lords were still straggling into the meeting, again speaking in the Bladesmen tongue for everyone's convenience. "*Let me start by officially welcoming Lord Sumi, Igwer, and the others to the camp." The reunion earlier between Igwer and Teyo had gone unwitnessed within a private tent, but both men had tears in their eyes as they'd emerged, Igwer leaning on the arm of the still-strong Teyo despite the latter man's use of a cane.

Everyone bowed respectfully to Sumi and Igwer, the

teenager blushing and fidgeting in response while Igwer merely smiled like an elderly grandfather who has witnessed his descendents reach great success. Teyo continued, "*Their group has infiltrators throughout the hostile Lords' encampments, giving us information we may be able to use. We're still speaking and setting up new lines of communication. Our immediate concerns are twofold: First, to gather supplies for our continued survival until the portal can be reopened from the other side; and second, to keep the enemy Lords off balance for that same period so that they cannot unite and hit us as one."

Mom stepped forward and leaned against the map table before anyone else could reply. "*Lord Ather has informed me that with Lord Sumi's assistance we can change our spells of teleportation in such a way that Bladesmen are not nearly so affected. With this in mind, I would suggest using the strongest tool of our foes against them - the Pact itself. If our esteemed Lords can now move to and fro without needing hours of recovery, why not jump into their major cities and start ordering Bladesmen to attack and destroy their own homes? The Pact would force them to obey you, would it not?"

Ather and Wesnoq both frowned while Sumi looked openly shocked. Wesnoq, the eldest of the three though he looked like a man only slightly older than I, shook his head vehemently and responded, "*That would be an abuse of power we could not approve of, Archmagess. Those are innocent people - we cannot put them into the same state we currently find ourselves in, facing starvation and lack of shelter."

Mom glared at him. "*With all due respect, Lord Wesnoq, that's a pile of crap and you know it. This is a war here - pretending otherwise is foolish. It's a military maneuver, nothing more. Had I wanted to offend your sensibilities I would have suggested that you Lords start teleporting around and ordering commoners under the Pact to commit suicide."

A gasp rose from around us. I shifted nervously - Mom wasn't making any friends among the Bladesmen with the way she was talking. Truth be told, she was sending chills down *my* spine. Nobody had ever accused her of being weak or having any lack of ruthlessness.

"*Archmagess - Viala - we've known each other long enough that I know better than to take offense at your words," Ather said next. "*You're right; we are at war - but this is not a war we can win against the commoners. Their Lords are the ones we must strike. Without them, the millions of Bladesmen across this continent would have no anger towards us. We all understand that some of them will die in this conflict; this is regrettable but a fact we have to face. But to sow death among innocents merely to keep our enemies distracted is not a thing we can countenance."

"*Then at least use the Pact to get information from them. You can remove its effects from one Bladesmen at a time, right? Go out and capture highly placed commoners, bring them back here, force them to talk using the Pact, and then free them from its compulsion." Mom's voice was tightly controlled and I could tell she was trying to keep her frustration reined in. My mother had never been one with deep reserves of patience. She continued, "*Have them destroy only military supplies; that's a good start and wouldn't affect their survival."

The others around the tent looked at each other. Teyo cleared his throat and spoke. "*My people need little in the way of purely military supplies, Archmagess. You know this. We have no stockpiles of weapons and armor to strike at. The best we could hope for might be bedding and marching rations. That said, I will support the Archmagess in one respect - capture and interrogation is an acceptable protocol of war. Utilizing the Pact is far kinder than the harsher methods we might otherwise resort to. Lords, Councilor - what are your thoughts?"

Lord Fian, leaning on a staff and pure magical force to balance out his one remaining leg, raised his voice. "*I can support this as a course of action. We should not destroy the livelihood of innocents, but learning where food stores are and sending missions to capture at least some of them is surely a reasonable course of action." He nodded to Mom with respect.

The discussion continued and eventually it was agreed - missions would be sent out the next day to try and locate and capture ranking Bladesmen commoners and stored rations. Sumi still looked uncomfortable at the thought of using any part of the Pact but in the end simply nodded when asked for his assent. Teyo appointed three Lords to lead individual groups; I agreed to go along when Teyo asked for volunteers. The morrow would be an interesting one.

Chapter 21 – A Sense of Scale

  That evening I sought Dalt out among the long lines of white tents. We sat some distance outside the guard pickets and shared a glass of wine I'd bargained from a quartermaster who knew me well. Hand in hand, we watched the foreign stars wheel overhead without speaking for over an hour, the only noise that of the camp behind us drifting into the empty sky.

  Our time together was precious and for that reason rarely shared with others. I knew that many of the older humans of the City didn't understand relationships like ours, especially when Dalt was outwardly plain with little to recommend her. I'd learned the secret to her beauty not long after meeting her in desperate circumstances, though; her smiles, though rare, lit up the entire world around her in a way I could never explain. We were beholden to different nations and never questioned when the other had to leave; we were content to appreciate the time we were able to snatch from the world around us.

  As much as I wanted to stay with her I bid good night with a lingering kiss and left after midnight. My heart wanted us to go back to my tent together, but my duty as a mage and a Councilor demanded that I get a good night's sleep to prepare for a dangerous day.

  I awoke the next morning to the realization that it had already been more than a week since the portal had closed. Our initial despair had given way to determination and I even dared to hope that we might last long enough for Kami to open a way home. Although our new allies were few in number, their arrival and the subsequent reunions had lifted the spirits of the entire army.

My pack was still ready from the previous trip and only needed a quick airing and a few more supplies before I was ready to go out again. Mom had privately expressed her concerns with me leaving on another mission into enemy territory so soon, but at least out there I could feel like I was making a difference. Business here in camp was important, of course, but I felt penned up and useless every moment that I spent without actively making progress towards our survival. I recognized that I was one of the fortunate few with the option to go out but that didn't stop me from taking advantage of my privileges.

I headed out towards Wesnoq's tent not long after sunrise, accepting a steaming cup of tea and a plate of hard biscuits from a friendly Bladesman cook while making my way through the camp. The food steamed in the early morning air as I ate and drank, well aware that every crumb was valuable until we were able to secure more rations. I was licking the last traces from my palms when I arrived.

Much to my surprise Mom was waiting calmly with her own gear, chatting with Wesnoq about some of her childhood memories from this very place. As soon as I arrived she gave me a knowing smile and nodded.

"Mom?" I asked with a frown. "What are you doing here?"

"I convinced Lord Orove to trade out with me," she said. "He'll go with Mornali and keep the ex-rebel in check. I'll be going with you and Lord Wesnoq."

I spun a quick thread of thought out to meet her, not waiting for the customary polite pause before sending her a mental message. *What are you really doing here? You're not supposed to be coming with us, you're supposed to be working on protecting the camp against teleportation.*

There's nothing I can do on that front right now until Lord Bilak gets his plans written out, she sent back calmly. *An Archmagess will be of as much use as a Lord on this mission.*

Don't you trust me? I fired off immediately.

Her mental signal instantly changed, sensations of brittle anger coming through with her next words. *Cordell, I'm your mother as much as your Archmagess. We're all in danger every instant that we're here without Ikami. Do you have any idea how worried I was while you were running across the continent? If you had been with anyone but Ather I would have ordered you not to go.*

I bristled in response. *Don't go there. That's not a fight you want to have with me, Mom.*

It doesn't matter now, she sent back with a tinge of sadness. *Cordell, don't you understand? Your father and sister are an unimaginable distance away. You - and Ather, from a certain perspective - are the only family I can hold on to here. We may never get back. And if we don't, I'm not going to let you go off alone to die without me being there to fight to the end with you.*

It took some effort to not send another impulsive rejoinder, but I tried to calm myself down and see things from her perspective. I wasn't a parent, though deep inside I harbored a hope that someday Dalt and I might raise a family together. There was something about my leaving alone that Mom dreaded which I knew I didn't fully understand and I forced myself to cut her some slack. She was right that her presence would be at least as valuable as the Lord who had been slated to join our little group, and I had far more experience working side by side with her than with either Orove or Wesnoq.

I withdrew my line of communication leaving behind a feeling of resignation at her presence. Together we turned back to Wesnoq, who had been waiting patiently throughout the conversation he must have sensed. I bowed politely and spoke in the Bladesmen tongue. "*Lord Wesnoq, I am ready when you are. Do you know where we are to meet the group coming with us?"

He nodded. "*Towards the portal area. All three groups

will assemble there once ready." He led us through the camp, soldiers stirring all around us for the day's work.

A few minutes later we joined a milling squad near where the Portal had arched into the sky a week before. I recognized none of the group; three were human while the rest Bladesmen. Their sergeant, a tall raven-haired Bladeswoman with several battle scars obvious across her arms, bowed formally to us as we approached. "*Good morning and strong arms, Lords. My name is Sergeant Mona. I look forward to working with you today."

We bowed in return and Wesnoq replied. "*I understand that the General will have briefed you on our mission?" The soldiers nodded and Wesnoq continued. "*Excellent. I will be handling our teleportations back and forth; Lord Ather and Lord Sumi have shown me the necessary alterations to avoid the sickness we're all used to. Councilor Cordell and Archmagess Viala will worry about magical defense once we arrive as well as help me seek out a high-value target to capture. While we're there we'll bring back any food supplies we can find - but a ranking military target is the primary objective."

Mona looked us over as though appraising our value. "*I know that we are looking to avoid as much bloodshed as possible, but we'll be there to hold enemies off if we need to. We won't hesitate to kill if necessary - subduing them is up to the three of you."

The Bladesmen Lord frowned in reply. "*Hopefully that won't be necessary. If I give them a clear order, the Pact should force any attackers to stand down." Mom nodded in agreement and I remembered her story from long ago when Ather and another Lord had commanded a group of Bladesmen under the Pact to attack one another, resulting in every Bladesmen there rotating back and forth to try and comply with the latest order. I hoped things went as well as she expected; I was glad to have the extra arms with us just in case something went wrong.

I glanced around and saw that the other two groups

going out were having their own discussions nearby. Lords Orove and Mornali were arguing urgently about something I couldn't make out, and I had a flicker of worry over our two parolee Lords. The abrupt closing of the portal home had given them more leverage than they deserved.

Wesnoq spoke from next to me. "*If we're all ready we'll start heading out. Lord Sumi's people have identified some locations where we're likely to find military camps and we have three on our list to visit."

I sensed his mind flying off to the north and closed my eyes, readying myself for teleportation. A long minute ticked by in which I tried to listen to the conversations of those around me, doing my best to not fidget. With no further warning I was suddenly swept up in Wesnoq's spell, my body spinning through the magical aether for what felt like an eternity. We emerged back in the physical world with a familiar crack echoing around the terrain nearby.

It took us three jumps to reach the first area on Wesnoq's list. With Sumi's adjustments Wesnoq was still in fine shape, all the Bladesmen clearly impressed at how well they felt. We found ourselves in a high mountain glen, a chill wind occasionally gusting through the trees nearby. Although it was only early afternoon we decided to wait until nightfall for our raid. Mom settled down and sent her mind around the wilderness nearby while Wesnoq and I tried to scout out the target location from afar.

I let my mind follow the Bladesman's as he spun a magical thread northward. The mountains and hills fell away beneath us after a few miles and I could sense Bladesmen civilization far below, towns and villages spreading across a wide plain. A quick spell let me see the land as though from physical eyes as we sped along. The buildings were a strange mix of architecture; most of the towns had their central styles much like those in the City while everything erected in the last century was clearly of Bladesmen construction.

It hit me suddenly that this had once all been human territory conquered more than a century before. Even though we'd crossed most of the continent to meet Sumi and the rebels I'd never really seen the area we were traveling over; this time I was struck by the sheer scale of our world. I knew intellectually that the land here was only slightly larger than the main continent of the Bladesmen world, but it was an emotional impact to realize how many uncounted millions of humans had once lived here. Even with our successes in the Bladesmen world my race now numbered less than two hundred thousand. We could never reconquer this world alone; even if we slew the Lords who opposed us, this planet would never again truly be a human one. At best, the future of both worlds would be determined only in some small way by humanity.

It was a depressing thought.

As I followed my Bladesmen ally north, however, I decided that it wasn't such a bad thing. Couples like Dalt and I might help unify the two races over time; Kami's very existence proved that it was possible. Perhaps in a few millennia there would be no more Bladesmen and human distinction.

I was interrupted in my musings when Wesnoq's presence slowed to a stop. Below us was a large camp teeming with activity, set up perhaps a mile from a sprawling city. There were at least ten thousand Bladesmen already present with hundreds more arriving from across the plains. It took me a moment to find what looked like a command tent - no guards were posted, which puzzled me until I realized that the Pact would probably make them redundant.

When I kept the Pact in mind my entire view of the camp shifted. I could suddenly see the regimented order in the legions below; the soldiers weren't talking and joking the way I was used to. They never hesitated in their movements to wave hello to an old companion, and even the mess tent had a surreal look in the way the line snaked in and out without anyone stopping for conversation. This was the Pact truly at work and it made me shudder, bringing to mind a hive of ants more than a healthy gathering of people.

I could sense Wesnoq's distaste from next to me, and a moment later he signaled that it was time to return. I didn't wait to start spinning my mind back towards our bodies, wanting to witness the unnatural movements of these Bladesmen no longer than necessary. A few minutes later we were back to our little group and I opened my eyes.

Sergeant Mona saw me moving and walked over, squatting down nearby to be at eye level with where we sat. "*Did you find it?" she asked politely.

I shuddered while Wesnoq answered in an uncomfortable tone. "*Yes. It... it was obvious that they are well controlled by the Pact. I don't foresee any issues to teleporting directly into their command tent later tonight, but we should definitely expect a coordinated response right away."

Mom turned towards us from where she sat a few yards away. "*How many?"

"*At least ten thousand," I replied. "*More were streaming in all the time."

The Lord next to me shook his head. "*It seems clear that our opponents are already gathering an army for a direct strike at our camp. We are a thousand miles from the location of the portal; if they are assembling here they must have other camps much closer. How many do you think they will send at us?"

After a long sigh Mom replied. "*After last time? They'll send every last Bladesman on this continent if that's what it takes to break us. Millions of Bladesmen - and the Lords here would sacrifice them all to bring us down."

Chapter 22 – Stealth

We made our first move about two hours after sunset. Wesnoq gathered us close and told us to ready ourselves for the spell. He knew no way to prevent the distinctive crack and flash that came about as a side effect of teleportation, meaning that we'd be immediately detected as soon as we jumped in. We left our packs in the small glen, bringing only what we would need for the raid. The humans drew their swords while the Bladesmen lowered themselves into a fighting crouch facing outwards around us mages. I drew power into myself, feeling Mom doing the same to my side. The spell of teleportation was triggered upon us a moment later.

The moment I felt the world stop shifting I threw a thin shield around us even though I couldn't see anything through the bright afterimages that arced across my vision. I heard a surprised shout and the clash of bone against bone from my left; I twisted to face it and blinked furiously to try and get a clear view of what was happening.

We'd landed in the center of the command tent Wesnoq and I had spotted during our scrying earlier. Braziers in each corner provided dim light and heat, though one had already been knocked over spilling hot coals across the packed earthen floor. Scattered wooden wreckage attested to the presence of a table that had once stood where we had arrived - Wesnoq must have acted quickly to destroy it just as we materialized. I'd heard chilling tales of misplaced teleportations and was glad our ally was experienced enough to know what to look out for.

In front of me I saw two of our soldiers crossing forearm blades with two unfamiliar Bladesmen in officer's uniforms. I'd never seen Bladesmen battling one another up close and the sight was mesmerizing. Arms and shins struck at lightning speed back and forth, the combatants fighting literally face to face at times. Their natural weapons were short ranged but viciously quick. I had some practice with a sword, but without the advantage of its reach I wouldn't count on my chances facing a Bladesman hand to hand.

Wesnoq, still slightly rattled by the teleportation spell, saw what was happening and barked a quick order in the Bladesman language commanding everyone to back down. The Pact would ensure that the enemy officers recognized him as a Lord, and our soldiers took a step back to give them a moment to understand.

Instead, we all watched in stunned surprise as a near-identical mask of rage crossed each of our foes' faces and they dove forward with bestial screams, catching our men off guard and lunging towards Wesnoq.

I reacted barely fast enough to throw another physical shield in front of Wesnoq before they struck. They seemed to ignore the hideous wounds our men inflicted upon them as they dove through, pushing through the soldiers protecting the Bladesman Lord. Their natural weapons glanced off my spell with an audible screech that raised the hair on my neck. Wesnoq tumbled backwards from the impact, grounded but not injured thanks to my wards.

Mom slapped a thin shell of force around both of them at once, immobilizing them instantly. "What the hell happened?" she yelled, forgetting to speak in the Bladesmen tongue.

"Pact worked not," Sergeant Mona shouted back as she stepped forward to block the entrance to the tent. She switched to her native tongue and continued, "*Trouble's coming - get over here quick!"

Wesnoq climbed back to his feet while the other soldiers scrambled to the front of the tent with Mona. A moment later I heard fighting from the entryway as battle was joined; the canvas walls sagged inwards from the pressure of many bodies trying to fight their way inside.

The allied Lord shook his head and spoke quickly. "*Give me a few moments to set up a spell out of here. I don't know why they attacked me when I spoke - something's wrong. Viala, Cord, keep us safe!" He staggered and a blank look crossed his face as his mind leapt forth, trying to navigate a way back to our safe mountain retreat.

Mom and I looked at each other and nodded. I reached out with my mind and put up a temporary buffer of wind at the entrance to the tent; the resulting dirt and grit forced our soldiers a few steps backwards towards me. I expected their foes to similarly retreat outwards but hadn't accounted for the determination that drove them through the Pact. Three Bladesmen followed our people in, heedless of the grit that left blood streaming from their cheeks and faces. I had no idea how they could still see after walking through the flying gravel.

Meanwhile Mom was working to erect a more permanent barrier. I felt her spell wrapping the tent in an impenetrable wall of magical energy, cutting off the Bladesmen outside from reaching us. Every impact took a bit of her energy and focus to hold off, but she had plenty in reserve to keep us protected here for a good long time.

I drew on my reserves to throw a burst of wind at the three foes that had made it inside before Mom put up her wards but it barely slowed them down. Our people were still trying to pull back, conscious of their orders to not kill unless necessary, but the humans stepped forward with their longswords ready if I failed to stop the attackers.

"Close your eyes!" I yelled, hoping the enemies wouldn't speak my language and that enough of my allies would understand to protect themselves. I shut my own eyes and used magic to create a brilliant flash right in front of the oncoming

Bladesmen, the light burning through my eyelids as though it were bright noon. After I let it go I opened my eyes, blinking, to see the enemy Bladesmen staggering and clutching their faces. The insane anger was still there, but they could no longer make out where their targets were.

"*Can you rope them?" I asked Mona, trying to stay out of the Bladesmen's way. She nodded and a few minutes later the three were subdued, straining uselessly against the ropes that bound them to the tent poles. The two officers were still frozen in place by Mom's original spell nearby and I pulled them close so Wesnoq would make sure to bring them along with the rest of us. Once again I tried to take the gap in power between Mom and I in stride; I would never be able to split my focus three ways between difficult spells as she was right now - four, if you counted the personal wards that I could feel her maintaining.

We huddled close around Wesnoq's body, everyone wincing a bit at the continual battering on Mom's spell. Through the tent flaps we could make out the silhouettes of enraged Bladesmen; any of them that caught sight of a human seemed angered beyond reason. Some of them were slamming their bodies over and over against the invisible wall of force, hard enough to send their own blood flying backwards over their companions. Not a single one seemed to care.

I had only an instant's warning to squeeze my eyes shut again as Wesnoq's consciousness surrounded us. A moment later we reappeared up in the mountains near our packs, the cold air a shock on my skin. I staggered for a moment before putting up some magical lights nearby so we could all see clearly. Mom's eyes looked glazed; her link to the spells back in the camp had been broken by the teleportation and I knew she'd have a ferocious headache soon.

Everyone had made it back, although Mona and a few other soldiers would have new scars from the night's activities. Wesnoq, after a moment to regain his balance, went among them to heal injuries as best he could.

I waved a couple of the uninjured soldiers over to help

me bind the captured officers securely. Mom was still maintaining her spells on them, but the instant I sent her a mental communication that she could release the magic she did so with a sense of great thanks. A few moments later we had them bound securely to trees nearby, gags across their mouths to muffle the ceaseless screams that they didn't seem to tire of.

After ten minutes or so to collect ourselves and set up camp for the night, Wesnoq and Mom came over by me to look at our prisoners. Mom held a cool cloth to her head, obviously in pain, but didn't complain at all. The Bladesman Lord started performing some minimal healing on our captives, salving the wounds they'd suffered diving at him back in the tent. "*What happened back there?" I asked Wesnoq quietly.

He shrugged. "*I do not know, Councilor, but I intend to find out. I'm going to examine the spells on them. It was certainly a different response than I expected."

"*Same here," Mom added with a wince. "*I've seen Bladesmen under the Pact before; they always responded instantly. Something has changed. I'll back you up, Lord Wesnoq; I have more experience with the Pact than you do and perhaps I'll see something you don't."

He raised his eyebrow at her obvious pain but after a moment's hesitation only nodded. "*Councilor, can you keep a watch out around us? If any Lords get wind of our presence we won't get much warning before they hit us."

I nodded. "*No problem," I answered. I took a few steps away to where I could see them clearly and sat down against the tree where my pack rested. I pulled out a few strips of dried meat and munched on them slowly, watching Mom and Wesnoq focus together on one of the two officers. I closed my eyes and sent my mental senses outwards, passing where I could feel their powers prodding lightly against the mix of spells active on the Bladesman prisoner.

I spun my mind slowly around the mountains nearby, searching for any Bladesmen magic which might be seeking us out. I didn't dare go back out to the camp we'd visited; it was near the edge of my range at the best of times and I was just as likely to draw a Lords' attention back to my body as I was to sense anything useful.

Some forgotten memory at the back of my mind kept pulling at my focus, something about the Pact. I tried to remember what it was but couldn't pin it down. I had a vague feeling that Kami had said something before we left but the thought kept escaping me.

A muted shout drew me back to my body a few minutes later before I could remember what she had said. I fled back to the physical world and jerked upright, adrenaline coursing through my muscles. When I opened my eyes I saw Wesnoq falling backwards while Mom yelled something incomprehensible at the prisoner they'd been looking at. A moment later the officer stopped fighting and slumped forward against his bonds, clearly dead.

"Mom?" I shouted, pushing myself upwards. "Are you all right?"

She nodded, holding her hands to her chest and sitting down hard. "Yes, I'll be fine," she gasped. "Check on Wesnoq."

I turned to the fallen Lord and scrambled to his side. His chest rose and fell though he looked far more pale than I'd ever seen him. "*Lord Wesnoq? Can you hear me?" I said, then lightly slapped him across the cheeks.

At my touch he blinked a few times, then shook his head as though to clear it. "*Yes... Yes, Councilor, I can hear you."

Once I'd helped the two of them to more comfortable positions I squatted down nearby. "*What happened?" I asked.

Wesnoq shuddered. "*Your mother saved me, I believe," he answered in a shaky voice. "*Archmagess, perhaps you can explain it better."

Mom nodded and took a deep breath. "*The Pact... it got changed at some point in the last twenty years. We should have known they'd do something to stop us from using it against them like we did before," she said bitterly. "*It's keyed to only a few specific Lords now, not all of them. If another Lord gives an order the Bladesman will treat them like a human

- something to kill at all costs."

She took a pause to swallow some water from a flask, then continued. "*Even more than that - they left traps for us. I'm lucky they still haven't figured out how to trigger spells on human magic or it would have caught me too. A Lord who probes into the Pact and isn't involved in it... well, it could easily have killed Wesnoq. The backlash did the prisoner in, as you can see."

I shuddered. Every time I heard about the Pact it got worse. After my firsthand experience a few minutes ago I was coming to understand why Ather was so vehement about our need to return here and free his people from the clutches of that evil spell. I'd never seen magic that felt so cruel and foul as what had been done to the Bladesmen here - I had little doubt that the sight of the soldiers scraping and clawing to try and get into that tent would haunt my dreams.

Suddenly I remembered the thought that had been flitting around the edges of my consciousness. I spoke in my own language, turning towards my mother. "Wait - didn't Kami mention the possibility that the Pact might have been changed before we left?"

Mom looked at Wesnoq and blanched. "I had forgotten about that. It was over dinner when Dalt came over after Randell was killed, wasn't it? She was wondering if they might have - oh, damn. Why didn't we remember that?"

I shook my head. "It slipped my mind too. It didn't seem like a big worry - Kami was supposed to be here with us to deal with anything new that came up."

Mom looked at the second prisoner and sighed, continuing in the Bladesman tongue. "*I think if I take the lead on this one, now that we know what's up... I might be able to suppress the Pact somewhat, at least enough to get him back to where he can talk."

"*Tomorrow," I said and shook my head. "*Both of you are wiped out. Put him to sleep so he doesn't hurt himself overnight and get some rest."

For once my mother didn't argue with me and just

nodded. A short time later I pulled myself into my bedroll, shivering slightly against the cold night outside. I extinguished the lights over the camp, nodding to the two soldiers left on sentry duty, and tried to find a path to sleep which threaded through the horrors I'd witnessed that evening.

Chapter 23 – Information

  I woke with the predawn light, having achieved only a few hours of sleep. Every time my mind started drifting I saw the horrified eyes of Bladesmen, compelled against their will to attack me with every ounce of strength they possessed. The last time one of the faces was Dalt's and I sat up abruptly, shivering from more than the chill mountain air.

  The rest of our soldiers were already awake, talking in quiet tones while they readied the camp for the day. Our prisoner was still strapped to his tree insensate, forced into sleep by Mom's spell. I slowly pulled my gear together, trying to wake up, before accepting a small platter of gruel from Sergeant Mona. By the time I finished eating Mom and Wesnoq were starting to stir nearby.

  Within an hour the three of us and Mona gathered together to discuss a plan for the day. Wesnoq would back Mom in her attempt to dampen the Pact's influence on our prisoner so that we could interrogate him at length, this time prepared for the traps laid within his mind. Mona and I would keep watch in the physical and magical realms respectively in case any enemy Lords were searching for us after the raid last night. If we didn't have any answers by noon we would teleport back towards home, bringing our captive with us; none of us felt safe staying here any longer than that.

  I wished Mom and the friendly Lord luck, damning the

worry in my voice. After they'd started their work I sat down nearby and closed my eyes, letting my mind drift free of my body. I started by surveying the area from some distance above, invoking a spell that let me see into the physical world from my magical perch. Other than a few deer and a single bear a mile away I couldn't sense anything larger than a bird for miles in any direction. For a moment I watched the bear with wonder. It was a creature I'd known only from tales I'd heard growing up; I'd never really thought I'd have the chance to see one.

I switched my focus to purely magical sight and scanned the wider region around us. It was only moments before I sensed the attention of a Lord sweeping across the countryside. As of yet he was staying to the lowlands but at any time he might switch to surveying the wilder areas closer to our camp. I watched carefully from some distance off, trying to keep my own probes from being detected even though I risked losing sight of my opponent's spells.

After perhaps half an hour I could determine that his search was radiating outwards from the camp we'd raided the previous night. He had probably been doing so for hours. Taking careful note of where he was looking I turned and fled back into my body to warn the others that we might need to move sooner than planned.

I opened my eyes to see Mom and Wesnoq talking animatedly to our prisoner. His glassy-eyed expression showed that he wasn't fully conscious but at least they seemed to be getting answers. I took a moment to listen in, not wanting them to lose track or disrupt whatever magic they were maintaining to keep the Pact suppressed.

The enemy officer was speaking softly in a monotone voice, answering some previous question. "*Near... city in west... Aybel, military camp... orders received ten and half days ago..."

Mom and Ather looked at each other and frowned. "*Over ten days? You're sure?" Wesnoq asked quietly.

"*Very sure... told timing of importance... stockpile of food and bedrolls there... ready to march in a few more days..."

The prisoner's expression was slack, no emotion seeping through.

I suddenly realized why Wesnoq was so focused on the timing of what he'd heard. It had been just under ten days since the Portal had been attacked. This meant that the enemy Lords had started assembling their army not long after our first forces had come through, even before their initial attack.

Mom looked around the camp for a moment and I caught her eye. She nodded and slowly backed away from the conversation as Wesnoq started to inquire into troop numbers and which specific Lords had given orders. After Mom had gotten closer I spoke in the human language, just in case the prisoner could hear what I was saying. "Mom - there's an enemy Lord looking for us. He's scanning the area below the mountains, but I'd guess he'll start looking higher within the next two hours. We should get ready to go before that happens."

She nodded. "We got the Pact rewired - slightly - so that he's listening to Wesnoq's questions, but as you can see we can't pull it away completely. He's got a lot of information. Wesnoq is going to try and have the prisoner guide his mind precisely to where this other camp is that he's talking about - we might be able to make a raid later on and bring back some food or at least disrupt their plans somewhat."

"I'll keep my watch and try to give warning if they start coming closer," I replied. "How long do you two need?"

Mom thought for a moment. "Half an hour should do it, but we can move sooner if we need to. Let Mona know before you go back out." She gave me a quick hug and turned back to the captive.

I walked over to the scarred Bladesman sergeant and filled her in. The soldiers started putting their packs on so they'd be ready to go at any moment and Mona promised that they'd be prepared when we were. At that I nodded, leaned back, and sent my mind upwards again.

At first I couldn't find the enemy Lord's mental probe. I started to worry and scanned a bit farther outwards; this was a case where I didn't want to be surprised. Suddenly I sensed a magical presence some distance ahead of me and I slowed my own search, hoping I hadn't gotten too close. After a moment's cautious investigation I realized that I was witnessing three Lords mentally communicating across the miles. A more experienced mage might have been able to get closer and try to eavesdrop on their conversation but I knew that any attempt to do so was more likely to alert them to my presence than give me any information.

An instant later, much to my shock, one of the Lords' consciousnesses broke off from the conversation and slammed right into my mind before I could move out of the way. Our thoughts connected for a moment, tumbling together in mutual surprise, before I could pull my mental presence away and flee back towards my body. I dimly sensed the other Lord following me back and leapt back into my physical self, needing a moment to catch my breath before I could shout a warning.

"They found me," I yelled, then realized I'd spoken in my own tongue and repeated the statement in the Bladesmen language. I grabbed my pack and slung it over my shoulders, staggering as I tried to stand up too quickly. The other soldiers drew weapons and looked outwards, ready for a threat.

Mom looked worriedly at Wesnoq, whose mind was clearly far from his body. "He's still trying to find that camp-" she began before being interrupted by a familiar crack from the forest nearby. My stomach was gripped by fear as I fell back against a tree, frantically trying to clear my vision from the bright flash that seared across my face.

I felt Mom's shields snapping into place just as a deadly lance of light speared towards us. Between the bright spots flaring across my view I saw one Bladesman soldier struck, his body sliced in half in an instant before Mom's wards could surround the group. Her spell protected the next target, a human desperately backpedaling to get closer to us, but I could tell that Mom was having to throw out far too much energy trying to keep the whole group safe.

"Back me up, Cordell!" she ordered, and a lifetime of

training immediately kicked in. I fell to my knees as I sent every bit of power I could pull into her, letting her reinforce the defenses around our little group and halt the enemy Lord from striking any more of us.

We need Wesnoq, I sent to Mom on a spear of thought.

I can't bring him back right now, she replied grimly. I could tell how much focus she was having to maintain from the scant attention she could send my way. *Following the mind of someone who doesn't use magic while maintaining the complicated spells to suppress the Pact... He's already stretched thin.* She broke off for a moment to shift the direction of her shields as the enemy Lord tried to throw a burst of fire at us, but managed to twist it to splash into the forest nearby where the ground immediately caught flame.

If we don't get out of here soon we're all going to get cooked, I sent firmly.

I'll hold him back for a moment if you can try to pull his attention and give me some breathing room, Mom replied. I sent back a sense of agreement and withdrew my mind and my magical power, feeling her pull ever more furiously on her reserves as a result when the lance of light returned. The enemy Lord was seeking to find a crack in her defenses; I was worried that she had too many people to protect. I'd seen her fight back against a Lord if she only had herself or one or two others to shield, but we were too many for her to split her focus like that.

I took a deep breath and sent my mind forward, first trying to assess exactly what faced us. There were at least fifteen other Bladesmen with the enemy Lord, fanning out to flank us before charging. At least the flames our foe had started would hold them off from one side, I thought to myself grimly. Our soldiers would have to deal with the enemy commoners if they got too close.

I focused my attention upwards to the nearest trees around the Lord and slammed a jab of power forward. It was quite a distance for me to work at, but after a few seconds of repeated blows I heard a loud crack echo through the forest and saw the top half of a tall pine start to topple forward.

Physically grunting from the strain, I caught its weight with my mind and redirected it towards the enemy Lord.

I felt wrung out by the time I released the tree but had the satisfaction of watching the Lord remain unaware until just before it struck. He looked upwards in horror right before impact, breaking off his attack on our group, and threw a ward directly upwards.

Before I could see further results of my work my attention was pulled to the other side of the clearing, where I suddenly sensed the release of another Bladesman teleportation spell. A second enemy Lord appeared, this one with at least fifty commoners. I fled back into my body and called out to Mom, "Watch your left! There's another one!"

The first Lord was still dealing with the tree I'd dropped on him, fortunately, but the second one didn't hesitate before striking us with his own attack. A jet of flames shot forward, deflected at the last moment by Mom's shields, but not before catching our prisoner's leg. A cry of pain rang across the clearing and I felt the jolt of a broken spell ripple back and forth, though who it belonged to I couldn't tell.

I was torn for a moment, drawn between wanting to try and save the officer and needing to help our own soldiers. Despite my desire to save everyone I knew that I'd be stretched too thin if I tried to extend protection to our prisoner. Instead I darted a thin line of force forward with my mind, knocking some of the charging Bladesmen down before they could make it to our forces. I could sense Mom weaving another protective spell nearby. The enemy Lord tossed a blast into the ground in front of us, causing a hail of head-sized stones to slam into the magical defenses keeping us alive. They rattled off to the sides in time to reveal the second wave of commoners running in towards our lines. Flames surrounded us on all sides as the first Lord rejoined the battle, sending another superheated conflagration directly towards us.

Just as I was ready to give into despair I felt the familiar sensation of a Lord's teleportation building around us. "*Get in close!" I screamed, this time remembering to shout in a language everyone could understand. The remaining soldiers squeezed in as much as they could, the air heating uncomfortably as Mom tried to keep the white-hot flames all around from reaching our skin.

A moment before the heat became intolerable Wesnoq's spell triggered. I closed my eyes just before the resulting flash flickered across our little group. The feeling of cool air rippling across my face afterwards was like heaven. "*That was a little closer escape than I'd prefer next time, Lord Wesnoq," I said with a smile as I opened my eyes.

It took me only a moment to realize we were surrounded by rows of Bladesmen tents. Hundreds of enemy faces were turning to look at us after the crack of teleportation, each one transforming to a mask of rage as they recognized humans among them.

Chapter 24 – Clever Acquisitions

The friendly Lord crumpled to the ground in front of me, his eyes rolling back up in his head senselessly. Mom wasn't in much better shape but had the presence of mind to snap some physical protection around us before the enemy Bladesmen charged in. I glanced around, trying to find a place we could hole up for a moment, and spotted a large wooden warehouse only a few yards behind us.

"*Mona, grab Wesnoq and follow me!" I said quickly. I tried pulling more power into myself despite my building headache as I turned and led the group towards the nearest doorway. Howling Bladesmen started slamming into Mom's defenses, bouncing off like broken dolls in a way that struck me as more macabre than anything else.

As soon as Mom saw the direction we were going she focused a little more and threw a blast of wind ahead of us. The closing Bladesmen in that direction were thrown off their feet, giving us a clear path to advance through. In a rare bit of good luck for the day her spell also blew the door of the building inwards so I didn't have to slow as I entered the darker interior. It took my eyes a moment to adjust to the light, goosebumps prickling my arms from the chill air inside. Only a few high windows provided any illumination from the outdoors, dust motes visible in the thin beams of sunlight.

Once everyone had made it inside one of the soldiers

slammed the door shut behind us and leaned against it, panting and holding her side from an earlier injury. Mona dragged the senseless Wesnoq to a nearby box and leaned him against it while sending two other soldiers to take a quick jog around the building and make sure there were no hidden threats waiting for us.

    Mom put her hand up against the inside of the door and, after a moment's concentration, nodded to the soldier holding it shut. "*It's fine," she said in a tired voice. "*They won't get through anytime soon." As if to belie her statement, the door shuddered from sudden impacts as the Bladesmen outside caught up and attempted to bash their way in.

    I took a better look around the building as I tried to catch my breath. It was at least twenty yards tall and most of its volume was stacked high with crates and barrels. Packed earth provided a simple floor with a corridor left open all the way around the inside. The soldiers who Mona had sent off a few moments before came back after a few seconds, signaling that there were no other entrances to the building.

    I walked over to a crate near Wesnoq and pulled at the lid, curious to see what was inside. It took only a small burst of magic to pop its seal and open it up, revealing carefully packed rations of dried meat wrapped in some sort of wide tropical leaf. Mona, similarly giving in to curiosity, held up a wax-lined wheel of cheese from the crate she'd pried open.

    "*I think these are rations for the army outside," she said with a wide smile, the first time I'd seen her look excited about anything. "*Councilor, if we could take these back with us or destroy them..."

    "*We need to wake Lord Wesnoq up before we can plan on getting out of here at all," I replied. One of the soldiers was already gently propping a water skin up to the Lord's mouth, trying to revive him that way.

    "*What happened to him?" a young Bladesman soldier asked with concern.

    "*He had to trigger a teleportation without preparation," Mom responded from behind us. "*I imagine this was where the prisoner was guiding him and thus the only place Lord Wesnoq could send us in an emergency. Triggering a spell that potent too quickly is difficult at the best of times, and we were both still recovering from last night when we got hit this morning."

Her voice wavered near the end of her statement and I turned to look her over closely. Her face was pale, enough so to worry me. She saw my look and waved me away, saying, "*Oh, Cordell, I'm fine. Holding this door takes very little. Just leave me alone for now and try to help our ally here get back into shape to get us out of here."

I frowned and shook my head, muttering under my breath about her stubborn nature. After one more searching look I shrugged and turned away, wondering how we were going to get out of this one. A thought struck me and I called back over my shoulder, "*Mom - any chance you could reach a friendly Lord back in the camp to get us home?"

She laughed mirthlessly. "*We're far too distant. You know that. Not possible. Your sister could have, but then *she* would have just gotten us out of here on her own." I recognized the bitterness in her tone and sighed; it had been a long time since she'd sounded so jealous of Kami's power. Our situation was proving more stressful to her than she'd let on.

Wesnoq stirred and I knelt on the hard-packed dirt next to him. "*Lord Wesnoq?" I asked softly in the Bladesman tongue. After a moment he opened his eyes and blinked a few times, his pupils dilated hugely.

"*We aren't... where are we?" he asked, his voice struggling.

"*You teleported us," I replied in an even tone. "*Remember? You sent your mind out to try and find the enemy military camp."

He pulled himself a little straighter and nodded groggily. "*Yes, I recall... then there was a signal, something from my body at the camp..."

"*We were jumped by two Lords and some enemy soldiers," Mona said gruffly.

"*I just remember heat, intense heat, and teleporting whoever was nearby. Where are we again?" he asked, his voice clearing a little with every sentence.

"*You put us down in that camp," I responded.

His eyes grew wide. "*What? But there were thousands of Bladesmen there, I saw them." He shook his head for a moment and squeezed his eyes shut, then shuddered. "*Oh dear. I can sense them around this building."

Mona laughed. "*That seems an understatement. 'Oh dear' indeed." She paused, then continued, "*Can you get us out of here?"

He nodded. "*Yes, but I need some time to try and gather myself. The Archmagess seems to have things under control for now," he added with a nod towards Mom.

"*I can lend you some of my power," she replied, then added after a pause, "*I don't know how much I can give right now." I knew how that admission must have grated on her; she hated to show any weakness. The spell I'd sensed breaking back in the camp must have been hers.

Wesnoq smiled. "*Anything would be helpful, thank you. I have had the pleasure of assisting your daughter with spells, and if you are anything like her your help will be most welcome."

I stiffened, knowing what Mom's reaction might be in her current state. There was a long pause before she replied, thankfully in an even tone. "*Let us begin. The supplies here are rations, by the way - if we're able to bring any of them it would be exactly what the camp needs."

Just then the building shuddered with some impact on the far side. "*I'll take care of it," I said quickly and started jogging around the crates to see what was happening. Behind me I could sense them starting to focus their power, Mom sparing only a little to keep the door shut on the horde outside.

The sound of running feet behind me reassured me that I wasn't alone. I glanced over my shoulder and saw Mona and the young Bladesman following along. We turned the first corner and saw daylight streaming in through the wall perhaps twenty feet ahead of us. Natural weapons chopped and pulled at the opening, prying planks off of the wooden frame to make a gap large enough to enter.

"Crap," I muttered to myself and threw a blast of power at the first body I saw come through. It tossed them back out and gave us enough time to get up to the opening. The Bladesmen outside were eerily silent as though the Pact had stolen all ability to speak. I could see dozens straining to reach the wall where it had been torn open. We were lucky there were so many here; they were trying to squeeze inside in such numbers as to obstruct each other and give us a few precious moments to prepare.

Mona and her companion took up station in front of the gap, slashing and stabbing at any foes that managed to stick an arm or leg through. I gritted my teeth and threw a simple barrier over most of the gap, preventing them from pressing through the opening. "*That should hold them here," I said. "*I'll have to stay to maintain it. You two take a look further up and see if they're getting through anywhere else."

They nodded and trotted off towards the next corner. It took most of my attention to keep the wall up, each impact of the frenzied Bladesmen taking a little more of my energy. Everything I'd prepared was exhausted within two minutes and I started drawing deeper on my reserves, knowing I didn't have much more to give. I was about to shout for some help when I heard the sounds of fighting from the direction Mona had gone. Clearly this wasn't the only place the Bladesmen had broken through. After another minute I heard the scrape of bone against wood back towards the others and I knew no help would be coming.

We can't hold this place much longer, I sent out in a mental message. I couldn't spare the time to link up with Mom or Wesnoq directly, instead throwing it out in all directions. There couldn't be any enemy Lords nearby anyways or the building would have come down around us right after we'd holed up.

It was only a few seconds before I felt Mom's mind connecting with mine. *Buy us a few more minutes,* she sent. I could sense a deep exhaustion behind the words, but even so she sent me a trickle of power that I greedily drew on to reinforce my spell. As though at a great distance I could feel another presence drawing upon her abilities. I knew she couldn't afford what she was giving me, so I released my link with her and sent her back with a sense of gratitude.

    The energy she'd given me was enough to reinforce my spell for at least a little while. I put enough power into it to let it stand on its own for a few moments and glanced to my sides, trying to figure out what was happening elsewhere around the building. I heard the cries of battle and bone against steel, a sure signal that human soldiers were fighting somewhere nearby. A moment later I saw Mona turn the corner towards me, retreating one step at a time against three Bladesmen soldiers trying to throw themselves upon her. There was no sign of the young Bladesman who had accompanied her a moment before.

    I drew my sword and rushed to help her, pausing for an instant to reinforce the barrier with a few more measures of precious power so we wouldn't have enemies at our back. I caught up with her in seconds, shuddering when I saw dozens of cuts dripping blood all across her arms and legs.

    "*Get back!" I commanded her, throwing a burst of force forwards as soon as she was out of the way. The enemy momentum was stopped as though they'd struck a wall, two of them falling down completely while the other managed to stay on her feet. A wave of enemy Bladesmen turned the corner behind them, charging forward to catch up with their comrades as soon as they saw me.

    I lifted my weapon, knowing I had to keep my last scraps of energy to reinforce the spell keeping our backs safe. My head was pounding from the draw on my resources and I thanked the years of training that brought me automatically to a guard position. The length of my sword was a huge asset and I'd trained exclusively against Bladesmen - humans had no cause to fight each other when there were so many out to destroy us. Mona stepped back up to me, a grim expression on her face.

They came at us in a rush. I slashed at the first face to approach, cutting deep across her cheek and nose. Blood sprayed into the dusty air and she dropped to the floor without a sound. My blade flashed back down in time to deflect a stabbing arm blade, continuing its arc to stop the follow-through of the same enemy's shin blade. Mona lunged forward, impaling my foe with her own bone weapons, then dodged back to avoid a counter from the next Bladesman in line.

"*Keep retreating towards the others," I ordered, falling back one step at a time. I stop-thrust an oncoming enemy, but instead of stopping he simply clawed forward at my face with his arm blades. I couldn't withdraw my sword and had to let go, shoving the hilt hard to keep him from cutting me.

"*Councilor! Your weapon!" Mona shouted, then dove forward to retrieve my armament. She was rewarded with a long slice across her back, but she managed to pull my sword free from the enemy and stab them with her shin blades. Two other Bladesmen cut at her and she parried their blows expertly, somehow delivering shallow cuts in return. I'd seldom seen such skill and was glad she was on my side. She scooped up my sword and tossed it backwards; I managed to catch it just in time to avoid impalement. The grip was slick with blood but I tried not to think about it.

We took another step back together, fighting off the enemy soldiers who climbed over the bodies of their own people without an instant's hesitation. I kept getting in cuts that should have disabled or at least slowed them, but the Pact drove our foes to a desperation we couldn't match. A missed parry resulted in a deep stab to my left forearm and I hissed in pain, trying to keep my focus on parrying the incoming blows. Mona had taken more injuries as well, unable to outrange our opponents with her own equally-sized natural weapons. I had no idea how she was still standing, but the sergeant fought on with only a few grunts to indicate the pain she must be feeling.

Get everyone back here, Mom sent suddenly. I drew upon my last reserves and tossed a physical barrier into the corridor before us, then grabbed Mona's arm and turned to flee headlong towards the others. We passed the breach in the building's wall just as my prior spell faded and I heard more feet rush into the passage behind us.

I started to sense a familiar spell building ahead of us and tried to coax more speed out of my feet. I know we only had a few dozen yards to go but it felt like too far. "Wait!" I shouted desperately, knowing the spell would go off without us if we didn't make it in time.

A few steps more and the spell expanded past us, wider by far than the previous teleportation. I shut my eyes just as it triggered, the dirt floor spinning under my feet. A familiar crack echoed around us along with a bright flash and suddenly I was standing on empty air. I let out an involuntary scream as I started to fall, opening my eyes just as I hit grassy ground perhaps two feet below me. The impact was jarring and I sprawled forwards, catching myself on my hands as my sword went spinning away.

"Watch out!" came a shout from ahead of me in the human tongue and I instinctively spun to the right just in time. I felt the impact on the ground where I had lain a moment before and scrambled to my feet, blinking furiously to clear my vision.

We'd arrived in a wide grassy field with many of the crates and barrels from the warehouse in a pile next to me. Mona lay nearby, struggling to rise with two enemy Bladesmen standing over her. Another, the one who had tried to hit me a moment before, was pulling himself upright to attack me. My sword was nowhere to be seen.

The only weapon I had left was my magic and that was nearly exhausted. I dredged deep, trying to find another scrap of power, but only a feeble trickle responded to my call. I had to pick a single place to put it and I chose to throw it to Mona. My power was just enough to stop the blades coming down at her head, deflecting them to the sides.

My decision cost me. I tried to dodge out of the way of the Bladesman nearby but couldn't avoid his strikes in time. I felt the impact of his arm blade on my right bicep just as he kneed upwards with a wild kick. His shin blade caught my chest and I gasped, falling backwards, as a pain worse than I'd ever felt clutched at my heart.

The last thing I remembered was striking the ground with my vision going grey at the edges. The sounds of battle faded as though I was running away, and a few moments later only the sound of my heartbeat reached my ears.

After a few more slow thuds even that stopped.

Chapter 25 – Return

    I can't properly remember what happened next. My memory contained flashes of vision, with Mom and Wesnoq kneeling over me with faces of shock and concern. Hideous pain wracked my chest over and over until I wanted to give up and die. The unnatural sensation of magically forced healing lingered through all of it, leaving aches and pains around wounds I didn't want to think about.

    When I finally came to and felt like myself again the sky was dull and grey with a chill wind blowing across my face. I was swaddled in bedrolls like a newborn child, barely able to move. Tall cliffs of stone towered over me disappearing into mist a hundred feet or more above.

    "Hello?" I asked weakly, my throat dry and sore.

    "Cordell?" Mom's voice replied from somewhere nearby. A moment later she stepped up to where I could see her face. It was shockingly pale and her hair seemed more grey than I remembered, though it very well might have only been my perception. "Was that you?"

    I smiled and nodded, coughing a moment later. "Water, please?" I rasped. Soon the bedrolls were being pulled back while a flask was pressed to my lips. I drank greedily, the ice-cold liquid feeling like the first drink I'd had in weeks.

    Once I could move I slowly sat up and leaned against the rocks behind me. There were only five of us in view - myself, Mona, a human soldier, Lord Wesnoq, and Mom. After a few more swallows from the flask I asked, "Are we all that made it out?"

Wesnoq and Mom looked at each other. The Bladesman Lord answered in his own language. "*We have two lookouts in the rocks nearby... but yes, many had to be left behind."

"*What happened, exactly?" I inquired. "*The last thing I remember was the grassy field right after you got us out of the warehouse."

"*Lord Wesnoq teleported us and as many of the supplies as he could to a field a few miles from the warehouse," Mom replied quietly. "*By the time we could gather strength for the spell together, enemies had broken through and were mixed in with our people. A good dozen of them came through with us."

"*I was knocked down to almost nothing by the rapid teleportations," Wesnoq continued. "*Even with Lord Sumi's modifications, jumping that fast is very draining on us Bladesmen. I couldn't help in the fighting. Our people fought bravely but as you yourself saw the Bladesmen under the Pact's influence fight without fear or notice of their own wounds."

Sergeant Mona had walked over during our talk and chimed in, bowing her head respectfully as she spoke. "*Your mother says that it was your spell that saved me there. You have my thanks. We fought well together - without your sword I wouldn't have made it out of the warehouse."

"*What she's not saying," Mom followed up, "*is that she held two of them off despite her wounds when they tried to attack me from the back. If you hadn't saved her, Wesnoq and I would both be dead right now."

"*We still lost several before the enemy Bladesmen were all taken down," Wesnoq said after nodding in agreement. "*I was barely able to summon enough power to stabilize your wounds and we had to wait almost two hours before I could teleport us out of there. Eventually I was able to get us a few more hops away. We reached this spot up in the mountains, where we've been resting before the next jump."

"*I don't know that it was worth losing good soldiers," Mom added, "*but we brought a lot of supplies with us. Wesnoq has been transporting them separately - they're in a valley a ways down the mountain right now. It's enough to extend the entire army's rations by at least a week. That's a pretty big deal."

We were quiet for a few moments, all of us considering the results of our mission. I wasn't used to thinking in military terms; I felt like a cold bastard to even consider the calculation of lives for food and whether it was a good trade. That was a job for generals, not me. I shook myself out of my thoughts and asked, "*How far are we from getting back to the camp?"

Lord Wesnoq answered immediately. "*At least five or six more days. Two have passed since the battle. It's taking much longer to get back - I'm having to expend a good deal of power to transport the supplies each time, and to be honest I'm still not completely recovered from the battles."

"*Mom, how close would you need to be to call for some help?"

"*I can try reaching out after another few jumps," Mom said after a thoughtful pause. "*There's a lot of supplies, though - they'll need to send several Lords to bring them back quickly. I'm worried that we're not safe - that's why we're so far from the crates; if they find those at least they won't find us right away. If the other groups haven't returned, they may not be able to risk sending any more Lords out to help us teleport back."

"*What about the *Harmony* or the *Origin*?" I asked, struck by the thought. "*They could carry most of the supplies and meet us hundreds of miles from the camp in a few hours."

The Bladesman Lord mulled the idea over for a few moments. "*I could handle teleporting the supplies up to the deck much easier than jumping them all the way back."

Mom nodded. "*No offense, Lord Wesnoq, but you're not in very good shape right now. Honestly, neither am I. We both need a few days of rest. Get us a little closer and I'll try to get a ship sent out." She turned to me and continued,

"*Cordell, I'm weak enough that I'll need your help to send a message all the way back to the camp."

I nodded, pleased that she'd asked. The energy I could contribute was only a fraction of her own, but it meant much to me that she was willing to admit that she needed my help. Asking for assistance was a rare thing for her.

We gave Lord Wesnoq another two hours to rest while I slowly walked around to stretch my limbs. I felt physically weak but my mind was ready to leap forth. Unlike the others, I hadn't had the strain of watching constantly for enemies over the last two days. The magical healing from Wesnoq had saved my life and gotten me most of the way back to health; I was sore but everything remaining from my wounds would heal over time.

The shadows were stretching far to the east when we started to make our way back down to the supply cache. I waved off offers of help as we carefully climbed down a small game trail through the rocks. When we turned the last corner and saw the pile of crates and barrels stolen from our foes I was impressed - Lord Wesnoq had managed to bring a huge quantity with him, though clearly at some cost. I almost laughed at his expression when he saw the food, as though he'd come to hate bringing it along with each spell.

By the time he triggered the teleportation I was no longer laughing. It clearly strained his abilities to transport so much so quickly, and after the familiar flash I opened my eyes to see him fall forward clutching at his head and wincing in pain.

"*It's too much for him," Mona said softly to me as another soldier rushed to his side with some water. "*I think he gets worse each time. I always thought Lords were omnipotent back in the old days before you humans made them listen to us commoners, you know. It is an education to see both what they can and cannot do."

"*Where were you from?" I asked.

She shrugged. "*A nation that is no more. Does it matter? Our Lords ruled over us with cruelty, and your Lady

Ikami ended that. We came to fight the rebels and continued through to this foreign world. Yet despite the strange air and the blue sky here I wouldn't change what has happened, not for anything." She smiled, making her scars crinkle oddly. "*Do you know, commoners like me now run things in my land? I do not think you humans understand the depth of loyalty you have inspired in people like me."

With that she walked away to look for a place to lay our bedrolls for the night, leaving me tongue-tied. It was a strange monologue from the taciturn Sergeant. I realized that I knew nothing about her despite the days we'd spent around each other. I'd have to think carefully on her words when I had more time.

"Cordell?" Mom asked from my side, taking my elbow and pulling me away from where Wesnoq sat, shaking and pale. "We're still a lot farther than I'd like, but I think we need to try reaching out to the camp. Lord Wesnoq... I'm afraid he's pushing himself too hard." She shook her head. "*It reminds me of Archmage Wendel when - well, let's just say we need to either give him a few days to recover or leave the supplies behind if we're going to rely on him to get us home."

I nodded. "I'm game to try it if you are. Do you have any idea where we are?"

She took a deep breath. "We're still at least fifteen hundred miles from the plateau."

"That's way too far, Mom!" I blurted out. "No way will we be able to get a message through."

"What are our other options, then?" she demanded. "Leave the supplies behind? You and I both know the camp needs them. Wait for Wesnoq to recover? I've felt the Lords who are looking for us probing day after day. They're going to find us sooner or later and we can't take another pounding like we did when we were trying to interrogate that prisoner. We've got to try, Cordell."

I looked at her face and saw the desperation in her eyes. It wasn't like her and shocked me into realizing that we were in a much more precarious situation than I'd been thinking.

Slowly, I nodded assent. "Okay. Let's try this, then."

We found a comfortable place to sit down and let our bodies relax. "I'll take the lead, but don't hesitate to push me or send me whatever you can if I start slowing down," Mom instructed. "It will take either ship quite a while to reach us, so we should look for a place a few hundred miles closer to meet them. If we give Wesnoq a day or so we can link up with them there, I hope, and if not then we can redirect them here."

"Who are you going to try to reach?" I asked.

She shrugged. "Anyone I can, honestly. If we're lucky someone will be watching a few miles north of the camp. If not... well, let's hope fate is kind to us this evening."

Side by side we closed our eyes and sent our minds journeying out of our bodies. I linked up with her quickly; it was just like it had been back when she and Dad had taught Kami and I lessons as children. I hadn't been an apprentice for years, though, and she didn't wait for me as she spun a thread of pure thought far to the south. As we leapt forward I tried to keep track of the miles and the landmarks we crossed, switching my view to and from the physical world.

Mom, do you see that river bend ahead? I sent after a few minutes. *We're probably two, three hundred miles from the others by now. This would be a good meeting place.*

Mom sent a feeling of assent. *An airship should be able to identify it - the river goes fairly straight east and west except for that one curl. Good eyes. Now we can really get going.*

With that she leapt forward faster than I'd sensed anyone send their mind - other than Kami, of course. I could only hang on to the sense of her presence, no longer able to keep track of our location independently. This was a journey only an Archmage - or a Lord, I supposed - could make, beyond my skills and power.

It was hard to keep track of time and before long I couldn't tell if we'd been journeying for minutes or hours. The thread of power connecting us back to our bodies had become too thin for me to follow and I had to trust that Mom could get us back when it was time. Periodically she sent a sensation of need and I'd feed her some of my magical power; I knew that it wasn't much compared to her own but it was enough to strengthen her a little bit each time. Still, I started to worry that it wasn't going to be enough - I was rapidly running dry and I had no idea if we were even close.

I started to worry when she started to ask for more than I could give. Finally, when only the faintest trace of power remained leading us back to our bodies, I had to refuse her request - I had nothing more to give. My mind was exhausted and it took everything I had just to remain focused on where I was. Losing track of that would be deadly, I knew; that was one of the first lessons a mage learned when leaving their earthly vessel behind.

Then suddenly we stopped. I felt dizzy, fighting to maintain my concentration and just hold position without wandering. To my delight I felt the presence of a Lord nearby - against all odds we had found someone!

And then, in a deadly tone that dashed my hopes, I felt the other presence call out to us in the Bladesman language. *You are a long way from home, humans. Tell me, why should I not simply snap your minds off from your bodies? I can sense your fatigue and weakness.*

I felt Mom's despair before she answered. *I know you... from a long time ago. You are the Lord who captured Kenton, from whose citadel we took the plans that let us escape this world.*

Lord Hannon, yes, that is me. It is a pleasure to meet you, humans. And so very, very lucky for me...

Chapter 26 – Twists and Turns

Mom tried to shake free and dart back towards our bodies, but the Lord easily seized us with his mind and held us firmly in place. We were both overextended, too weak to fight back. I felt terror of a depth I'd never experienced; my mind felt exposed and naked before the enemy Lord.

Now, what are you doing reaching back from so far away? mused Hannon. *You communicate very well in a civilized language for humans. We've all been extremely curious why you came back.*

We have nothing to say to you, Mom sent coldly, trying to project more power than she had. *Those who imposed the Pact are our enemies. From what Kenton said of you, you have little interest in our kind anyways.*

The Bladesman sent a condescending feeling towards us. *I remember him, the simple human mage you call Kenton. He was unwilling to tell me much, but he must have learned from me. The items you stole were very valuable, you know, but in a strange way they also showed respect. But killing my fellow Lord in my own castle... that was very bad for me, you know.* He tightened his mental grip while communicating, then relaxed when he suddenly realized what he was doing. *I'm sorry, I have no wish to mistreat my... guests.*

It was one of your own who did that, Mom shot back. *The Bladesmen you hold in thrall... they've had no choice in what you've done to them. I'm just glad one of them was able to strike back.*

You have no idea what the Pact means to us, he sent sternly. *Nor do you understand what has happened since you humans left. Many things have changed in the last score of years.* He hesitated, then continued in a calmer tone. *This Kenton whom you seem to know so well... did he tell you the terms of the Pact as I communicated them? Did he tell you why the Pact was originally made?*

He told us that the Pact was supposed to end when my kind were no longer a threat, Mom replied. *I see that you failed to disband it after we left. Had you done so we would have parlayed with you and your fellows and there would have been no need of a battle. Instead you have left your kin enslaved, held captive-*

I HAVE NOT! the Lord thundered back, his blast of power almost knocking us senseless. *We were not all of one mind on this,* he continued after a moment. *That, in fact, is why I was roaming outside of your military camp. I was hoping to intercept a human presence, as I cannot be sure of the Lords you seem to have brought back from... wherever you went.*

I sent a private thought to Mom with the trickle of power I had remaining. *What's happening here?*

I have no idea, she replied, feeling as exhausted as I. *We have to play along for now - if he doesn't let us go I don't know what we'll do.*

She turned her attention back to Lord Hannon, who continued as soon as he felt our minds focusing on him again. *Before I continue I require your answers to several questions. It is in all of our best interests if you answer them honestly - you humans, unlike us Lords of the Pact, have been known to lie.*

Mom started to bristle but I sent her a calming sensation and she waited patiently for the Bladesman's first question.

May I assume that by bringing other Lords back you reached my homeworld, the land from which I was torn as a child?

Yes, Mom answered simply.

And may I further assume that you have come to some sort of accord or alliance with the Lords there, or are you under their sway? Or - and for a moment he paused, continuing in an incredulous tone *- *are they under yours?*

Mom hesitated before answering, then replied, *We are allies with the Lords that accompanied us back. They are here of their free* will.

You are holding something back, Hannon snapped. *What is it?*

There were wars, Mom admitted. *We came out on top. That does not mean the Lords with us are captives, however; all of them agree with our perspective that Bladesmen commoners should have equal say in their fate to the Lords.*

Almost all of them, I corrected her. *Two of them were defeated, it's true, but they have come with us to make amends and join our cause.*

Lord Hannon pondered this for a moment. *My last question - what are your aims here?*

They are as I claimed a moment ago, Mom responded quickly. *Simply to end the Pact and allow the commoners free will again. That is why the Lords wanted to join us. Many more would have come as well, all volunteers, had you not closed our portal.*

In that case, the Bladesman replied slowly, *I would make you an offer. As a token of my goodwill I will release your minds from my hold here no matter what you agree to - I would not have you say 'yea' simply out of a feeling of duress.*

Make your offer, Mom sent back with a sense of guarded anticipation.

There are things of which you know nothing, changes and ripples among the Lords who maintain the Pact. We are not all of one mind; we never were, though we fight with common cause when provoked. He hesitated, then continued, *The Pact has gone on too long. Some of us wanted to hold with the original purpose and disband it once you humans departed, but we - I - was overruled. Now... now I would speak with your group as a potential ally.*

I could feel Mom's shock and quickly jumped into the conversation. *I am a diplomat for the human camp and can speak for them in this. If you are willing to meet under a flag of truce we will treat with you with open hands. All of us - humans and Bladesmen alike - would rather have peace than war.*

Hannon sent a feeling of sarcastic humor. *Oh, do not doubt that you will have war, human. I am alone in this matter now. Take this message of truce back to your camp and I will look to meet you again, mind to mind, in a week's time near this same place. Until then, I offer you a token of good faith. First, I will give you both more power - you are clearly overextended.* He offered up a wellspring of his own energy; Mom and I both started siphoning it off immediately. I could feel my strength returning quickly and realized just how close we had come to disaster.

*Last, before I leave you - you have a traitor in your midst. One of the Lords who came with you has been working with our group for some time before we struck your camp. He gave us the knowledge we needed to close the portal so quickly. I do not know who it is - they did not communicate with me - but be warned. Ferret out this betrayer before we next meet or I will not dare join you. With that, and one last burst of power, his mind was gone.

Renewed, Mom and I waited until we were sure that his presence had left us. *That was incredible, if it's true,* I sent to her. *What do you think?*

She paused, considering for a moment, before responding. *According to what I remember your father saying, Lord Hannon wanted to destroy the City so the Pact could be ended. He thought it was a foul thing, but necessary at the time. He was also the first one who told us that Lords bound by the Pact could not lie. I... I think I believe him, though I'm not sure yet. I need to think.*

I sent back a feeling of agreement. *For now... is this enough strength to reach the camp, do you think?*

She didn't send anything back, merely swept me up with her mind again and sent us hurtling across the miles. After an interminable time, our mental threads stretching far behind us, she suddenly slowed and we met a more familiar mental presence. Much to my relief, it was Mastermage Sciani on a skiff some fifty miles north of the camp. After a quick conversation telling him of our need, Mom and I departed and fled back north towards our bodies.

By the time we opened our eyes it was late, the stars twinkling overhead in the cool evening air. I sat up and stretched, my muscles aching. Mom and I looked at each other with unanswered questions between us, but nothing to discuss right now. We both needed to sleep on our thoughts before either of us could come up with any answers.

After a long night with little rest I awoke to the sound of Lord Wesnoq talking with Mom in low tones. I approached them politely as soon as I'd relieved myself and had a cup of water, waiting for them to acknowledge me before joining their conversation.

"*Good morning, Councilor," the Bladesman said when he looked up. I nodded and sat down as he continued. "*The Archmagess has appraised me of your plan. I think it sounds reasonable. I may need both of you to lend me your strength to jump to that river bend, as one night was not nearly enough to rebuild my reserves."

"*Of course," I replied quickly. "*Are you sure you're feeling up to even that?"

He shrugged. "*It will end with getting us all home much faster, will it not? Nearly a day?" When Mom nodded, he continued, "*The food is needed back at camp - and the sooner we return, the better for all of us."

I looked at Mom and sent her a quick mental message. *Did you tell him about our meeting with Hannon?*

No, she replied in the same manner without returning my glance. *We can't trust any of the Lords right now - we need to talk to the other humans and General Teyo back at camp before anything else.*

I frowned and looked down at my hands to disguise the movement. *Lord Wesnoq has been with us for a long time. Kami is sure of him. The traitor has to be one of the two rebels we brought through.*

Not necessarily, she fired back. *Later. Wesnoq is starting to wonder what we're talking about.*

When I withdrew my mind, the Bladesman was waiting patiently. He had, of course, sensed our contact but was too polite to inquire what it was about. "*I just wanted to see how Mom was feeling," I stammered to fill the empty air, but my words fell lamely even on my own ears.

He raised his eyebrows skeptically, then shrugged and turned back to Mom. "*As I was saying, the loan of your strength will again be needed. Give me an hour or so to prepare, then the two of you can join me and we can get underway."

"*Would you rather try it in two smaller jumps?" Mom inquired.

"*No, I think it's best to do it all at once. I cannot say how long I would need to rest to jump again afterwards." He sighed and continued, "*I'm sorry, my friends. I have nothing more to give."

I tried to reassure him. "*You've already done more than any other Lord could be expected to."

After a few more minutes of conversation Mom and I stepped away to inform the others. We made our way back to the huge pile of supplies where Wesnoq started to gather his strength. The sun slowly climbed over the ridgeline to the east, warming the air suddenly as it fell upon us. Working quickly, we tried to reorganize the pile to be as compact as possible so the transport spell would be a bit easier on Wesnoq.

When we judged it had been long enough we sat next to the Lord and started to pull up every scrap of energy we could afford. Mona and her charges pulled in around us, watching warily for any signs of danger. I closed my eyes and sensed Wesnoq's presence ready to spin forward, launching us to our destination in the blink of an eye. The spark of his mind seemed dimmer than usual, reflecting the deep exhaustion of his power from teleporting too much too fast.

Let us go, he sent to Mom and I a few minutes later. I called out to warn the others and shut my eyelids, linking up with Wesnoq and Mom and opening my reserves for his use. It was a simple exercise, one that mages learned in their first few years of education.

A burst of magic flared around me and I looked around, shaking my head to clear the ringing in my ears from the loud crack of teleportation. We found ourselves on the grassy field we'd surveyed from above the evening before, the stack of supplies piled high around us. Wesnoq gave a deep sigh and slumped forward, but remained conscious enough to wave us off and merely ask for his bedroll.

I helped Mona and the others set up a nearby perimeter

while we waited for our ride to arrive. When I walked around the rear of the supply cache I stopped for a moment. The back row of crates was sliced cleanly in half where Wesnoq's power had failed, their contents spilling out across the grass.

    I shuddered, trying not to visualize what would have happened if one of us had been standing there instead.

Chapter 27 – Difficult Questions

We patrolled the small field for the next few hours as the sun strode across the sky. Wesnoq slept the whole time, insensate to the world around him. Mom and I spent turns spinning our minds outwards to ensure no enemy Lords were probing nearby; neither of us wanted to be ambushed again.

I was searching some distance to the south when I sensed another magical presence approaching from high in the sky. My hopes were confirmed when I carefully surveyed the new arrival and recognized Mage Biala, a confident middle-aged woman who had fought in the war with Rainshye over twenty years before. I switched my view to the physical world and felt a surge of relief as the massive silhouette of the *Origin* leapt into view. Biala and I traded a quick moment of contact and I zipped back into my body, calling out the good news to everyone.

We lined up and watched the skies, eagerly awaiting the zeppelin's arrival. Mona was the first to spot the dark speck in the sky many miles away. Within a few minutes we could clearly make out the sails, billowing under a fine wind holding firm from the south. At ground level we could barely feel it but the airship was making good time using both its engines and its masts.

As soon as they made it within about a mile a smaller skiff detached from below, descending rapidly to our position as we waved to it. The *Origin* circled above, its ballista manned and ready should any enemies appear. I recognized the navigator on the skiff - Eresani, one of the few Bladesman who had trained as pilots. He was about my age and we'd both grown up in service to the City, casual acquaintances through the years.

"You're a damn fine sight to see!" I called out in the human language.

He laughed and set the skiff to hover with its keel just above ground level. Two crew tossed ropes down that we quickly secured with iron stakes and ladders were thrown over the sides. I was the first person aboard and clasped hands with Eresani, grinning wider than I could remember.

"Sorry it took so long," he said with an answering smile. "We hit some bad oncoming gusts coming out of the camp last night, but a few hours ago we hit this lovely wind and made up a lot of lost time." He looked over our small number and immediately sobered. "Where's the rest?"

I shook my head and he looked down respectfully. "I'm sorry to hear that," he said softly. "I knew one of the men who went with you. That's... well, let's get you folk back home."

"Thanks," I replied. "We have a lot of supplies to get up to the *Origin*. Are you the only skiff?"

He nodded. "One of the other teams hasn't returned either, so the General was worried about sending any more support than we needed to. He thinks we might get hit again while we're light on firepower and wants us back as soon as possible. We were hoping Lord Wesnoq could jump the supplies up to the airship's deck."

"I'm not sure that's going to happen," Mom said, joining us after a slower climb up the side of the skiff. "He's in bad shape. We can ask, but it would probably go better to get the *Origin* down here at ground level and get things up to the deck by hand. Cordell and I can help move things at that point."

"In that case, can you pass word to Biala? Saves us a trip back and forth," he pointed out.

Mom nodded and got a distant look in her eyes; a

moment later the airship above us started to descend.

    The *Origin* was massive, one of our newest ships of the line. It stretched four hundred and fifty feet long, the biggest single construction that the City had ever produced - larger than the Council building itself. The craft boasted thicker armor than our other airships and had two separate balloon chambers inside so that if one were ruptured it wouldn't immediately crash to the ground.

    It was large enough that half of the airship stuck out over the river when it settled to a rest nearby, hovering perhaps ten feet off the ground. The rope catwalks on the bottom, usually used only to tether and access any skiffs it might have tied alongside, rested gently on the grassy plain.

    The captain, a man I knew only distantly, came down to help supervise the effort. I shook his hand and ensured that his crew got Lord Wesnoq up into the craft first, placing him in the captain's stateroom to continue resting. With my magic helping buffer the trip he didn't wake up once, even as two volunteers helped me guide him carefully through the narrow corridors and stairs of the ship.

    Once I was sure he was settled into place I made my way back out onto the deck. It was bustling with activity. The soldiers and crew moving back and forth made the ship feel like a beehive; I could sense the deep purpose in everyone's stride. Crew were climbing to and fro with crates and barrels in their burly arms. I saw that the captain had sensibly organized the two sides of the craft into opposite directions of travel - one up and one down. Mom was floating dozens of containers at once up through the air to lower them gently onto the deck. I looked over and waved, and together we coordinated to get even more loaded onboard as quickly as possible.

    It took perhaps an hour before everything was secured. The airship had dozens of tiedown ports built into the wooden planking and hundreds of yards of rope were brought out from lockers below deck to make sure nothing would shift during our flight. We started ascending even before the process was finished, the engines rumbling to life in a smooth purr as we slowly spun around to face back south. Within minutes we had accelerated to fly through the air as fast as a bird, the sleek prow of the zeppelin slicing through the air like a knife.

The skiff tied up below - it was more efficient to keep it tethered close and have the *Origin's* larger engines pull it along. It felt good to be safe again, away from the days of unending stress and danger. I stood by the starboard railing as the sun went down. The rushing air felt good against my face, reminding me that I was on my way back to friendly territory.

Biala came up to stand beside me, the two of us watching the sunset wordlessly until its crescent slipped below the horizon. She let out a sigh and shook her head. "Damn, I missed that," she said sadly.

"What do you mean?" I replied curiously.

She gestured towards the western horizon. "The sun here is so much brighter and more vivid than on the Bladesman world. It's been almost exactly half my life and I'd forgotten how amazing the sunsets looked back here."

I laughed. "It just makes me feel like I have to shade my eyes more than I'm used to."

The older woman looked searchingly at me for a moment. "You grew up on the Bladesman world, I know. This place must feel foreign to you. For me, though, it's the most astonishing feeling of coming home after a long exile away. I don't know if you can understand."

"I try," I said hesitantly, "but I think you're right. The air here smells strange, the color of the sky is weird, and even walking around feels a little different. And magic... it works differently, even though it's subtle."

Biala nodded. "Your mother and I, we both missed this place. You and the Lords are here to help free the Bladesmen from the Pact. I respect that - it's a worthy cause. You need to remember, though, that for many of us there's much more at stake than that. Even after so many years away, this is still home to me - and I can see it in Viala's eyes, too, sometimes." She paused a moment, then seemed to change her mind about what she was about to say and simply followed with, "Good evening. Try to get some rest. We still have many hours to go."

I wasn't sure what to make of the conversation and mulled it over in my mind as the stars began to come out above me. The foreign constellations reminded me of just how far I was from home. I shivered suddenly, feeling the icy wind cutting through my clothes. I wound my way across the deck to the forward stairs and went below to the cabin I'd been assigned, glad to follow Biala's advice even if I wasn't quite sure about the rest of the conversation.

I awoke to a banging on the door and Mona's familiar voice yelling for me to get up. "*It's nearly dawn, and they say we're about to arrive," she called through the door when I groggily asked what was happening.

"*All right. I'll be up soon."

The banging stopped so I supposed that she must have moved on. I pulled my clothes on and rubbed my forehead, brushing my bangs back out of the way. They were getting long - I'd have to ask Dalt to cut my hair again. There was something sensual about the way she used her forearm blades to gently part my hair... I shook my head and reminded myself that I was supposed to be getting out on deck.

A few minutes later I emerged into the predawn twilight. Sailors were moving back and forth with great purpose, raising the sails from where they'd been helping drive us along all night. I rubbed at my eyes and stepped up to the foredeck where I saw Mom and the captain talking.

"Oh, good, you're awake," Mom said with a smile as I approached. "We're almost there - did someone tell you?"

"Mona got me," I replied curtly. "She wasn't very polite about it."

"Have you ever seen her be polite?" the captain asked, raising his eyebrows. "I've met her a few times in the last couple of weeks. Brusque woman, that."

"I made contact with Lord Abel," Mom continued. "Lord Wesnoq is still asleep. Abel and Ather will help us unload once we get to the main camp."

I nodded and turned to the captain. "You and your

crew made good time. I wanted to thank you again for coming to meet us."

He waved the compliment off with a smile. "Happy to give you folks a lift. Besides, I'll be eating out of these rations too - I had a good reason to come out and snag you."

It wasn't long before we could make out the sides of the plateau in front of us. I saw the *Harmony*, still little more than a black dot, patrolling and keeping watch for attackers. After only a few more minutes we could make out the rows of tents that made up the camp, with thin spirals of smoke reaching out where morning campfires had been started.

Between the two Lords, Mom, and a collection of human mages we made short work of getting the crates safely back on the ground. Ather and Abel teleported most of them right off the deck, while the rest of us carefully levitated the rest down to the ground. After that, the remnants of our small expedition made our way through the *Origin* to the bottom catwalks and climbed down to the skiff. As soon as we were released the massive airship lifted back up to rejoin the *Harmony* in keeping a watch on the countryside nearby.

It felt good as I jumped off the skiff's side onto solid ground a moment later. I smiled and clasped Ather's forearm as he strode up to meet me. From behind him I saw Dalt running up with a wide grin. "Damn but it's good to be back," I breathed, suddenly overcome with the emotions I'd been holding in for the last few days. She and I embraced carefully; I'd learned early on in our relationship how to avoid getting skewered by her shin blades. It resulted in a hug that was a strange mix of Bladesmen and human customs, but it worked for us and it felt so good to have her warmth in my arms again.

After a few moments she pulled away, still shy about any public show of our affections. Out of the corner of my eye I saw Mom watching us, something unreadable on her face, while Ather was grinning openly at our display.

I held tightly to her hand as we made our way to the command tent where Ather said Teyo was waiting for us. Most of the soldiers waved in a friendly manner when they recognized us, though a few looked away embarrassed or stared darkly as Dalt and I walked hand in hand through the camp. I didn't care anymore, I realized; we'd hidden our feelings for each other for too long. I looked at her and smiled, drinking in the sight of her beautiful Bladesmen face.

She stopped when we reached the tent. "That your place, not me," she said haltingly in the human tongue. "I need to get back."

I nodded and let go, trailing my fingers over the back of her hand as I released. She paused for a moment before turning away and whispered, "*I missed you, Cordell," in her own language. Then in the flash of an eye she had disappeared down one of the long rows of tents.

I ducked into the pavilion, where the side flaps had been pinned up to light the interior brightly. Mom was already talking to the grizzled general, giving him a report of our mission - everything except our conversation with Lord Hannon, anyways. I chimed in where it was needed while Ather and Abel listened in. Teyo asked some penetrating questions about our choices but at the end he simply nodded and concluded with, "*It sounds like you had a difficult time but did the best you could. The supplies you brought back will be extremely helpful."

"*Has there been word from the other groups?" Mom asked.

"*Lord Jabnoss returned yesterday," Ather replied. "*They had some light contact but came back after the Bladesmen he tried to order turned on him, much the same way as those you encountered. There's still no word of Orove and Mornali."

I frowned. The thought of being down two Lords was not a pleasant one.

Mom hesitated, then asked gently, "I'm sorry, Lord Abel, but I need to ask you to leave for a moment if you don't mind. I need to talk to the General and Lord Ather privately."

The dark-skinned Bladesman Lord frowned, then after a moment's thought simply shrugged and left the tent without another word. Teyo and Ather both waited, clearly puzzled as to why Abel had been sent away.

Mom closed her eyes for a moment and I felt her wards encircling the tent, creating a barrier impermeable to sound. "Something else happened while we were out," I said quietly in the human tongue - both Ather and Teyo were quite fluent in it and it was another way to help foil any traitorous Bladesmen who might find a way to listen in.

When Mom opened her eyes I continued. "We met Lord Hannon when trying to reach back here. He'd been searching around, trying to find a human mage he could link up with."

Ather visibly stiffened at the mention of Hannon's name, but I kept going. "He claimed that one of the Lords with us had contacted the ones here and given them information about the portal that let them close it. Hannon - Lord Hannon, rather - says that he's sick of the Pact and the other Lords that keep perpetuating it no matter what, to the point where he's willing to work with us if we can uncover the traitor among us."

Teyo frowned. "This could be a trick, a way for them to convince us to fight among ourselves."

Mom shook her head. "I don't think so. He had the two of us in his grasp and could easily have killed us. Of all the Lords here, Lord Hannon is one who knows to respect what humans are capable of - I don't think he would have released us unless what he claims is true. There's also the fact that the Lords who made the Pact say they can't lie, and so far as we know that's never been proven otherwise."

Ather tapped the fingers of one hand along his other forearm blade. "I understand why you sent Abel out, but why not me?"

Mom reached out and gently laid her hand on top of his. "Ather, I've known you for more than half of my life. If you've turned traitor against us then we should just give up now and let them win. No, I refuse to even consider you under suspicion."

He smiled and bowed his head. "Thank you, Viala. That means much to me."

"The Lords Bilak and Mornali are the obvious suspects," the General said thoughtfully. "Lord Randell's cohorts are not the most willing of allies."

"I agree," Mom said, "but until we know for sure one way or another we can't speak of this to any of the other Lords. If the traitor hears that we're looking for him..."

Ather nodded, but said cautiously, "That said, once the other Lords find out they will be quite offended."

"That can't be helped," Mom said with a shrug. "They'll just have to suck it up and live with it."

"We're supposed to parlay with Lord Hannon in a week, but only if we've rooted out the traitor," I said.

"Then we've got a job ahead of us," General Teyo said decisively. "Let's figure out how we're going to do this."

Chapter 28 – Tension

    Our little cabal spent the next two days trying to figure out who had turned against us. Mom, Ather and I each took shifts sending our minds to follow the various other Lords in the camp with us. It was perilously difficult; we had to spend hours with our minds away from our bodies, trying to stay close enough to sense if our target tried contacting the enemy Lords without letting ourselves be spotted. I went to bed each evening with my head ringing from a furious headache. Dalt would spend an hour rubbing my neck and shoulders to help me relax; the promise of stealing time with her each evening was the only way I could convince myself to go out in the morning.

    I was assigned to watch Lord Abel, the weakest of the Lords and one we were fairly sure was on our side. I didn't take any offense at the task; Mom and Ather would both be better at tracking the stronger Lords than I. Still, there were a couple of times that his mind darted to and fro suddenly where I was sure he'd sensed my presence. He didn't do anything suspicious; far from it, in the time I watched him I became sure that he was a diligent servant to his people. He truly cared about them in the way we wished every Lord would.

    Lord Wesnoq woke up after nearly forty hours of sleep. He would need a few more days to get back to full strength, but he'd saved us many times over and Mom and I both expressed our deepest appreciation to him. We didn't tell him about what had happened with Lord Hannon, but Ather agreed with us that he was the least likely Lord to work with our enemies.

On the third morning Lord Mornali returned alone. He was physically unharmed but clearly exhausted when he teleported into the middle of camp shortly after dawn. I met him and the other Lords, along with Mom and Teyo, in the command tent not long after he'd come back. All of the Bladesmen sat on stools while I stood near the entrance, the cool air from outside blowing on the back of my neck.

"*Lord Orove is dead," he said in the Bladesmen tongue as soon as everyone was there. "*We were ambushed by three of the enemy Lords. He and the other soldiers were struck down within seconds; I managed to teleport away just in time."

General Teyo bowed his head. "*He was a good man - it was only due to his efforts and research that I am now free of the Pact. How did they find you?"

Mornali shrugged. "*I don't know. We made our way to a military camp after five days of searching. They are assembling hundreds of thousands of commoners to come down on us. Orove and I abducted an officer and ordered her to tell us where we could find their supplies. She immediately started to talk but soon afterwards the enemy Lords teleported in and hit us hard. From there I had to jump across the countryside alone - it was not a pleasant journey."

Lord Wesnoq frowned. "*Wait - you successfully used the Pact to order the commoner to speak?"

The onetime rebel nodded. "*Of course. That was our plan, yes? She started to tell me everything we needed to know, or rather would have if we hadn't been struck."

Mom and I looked at each other and had the same thought. "*It's all right, Lord Wesnoq," I said quickly. "*I think we need to let the rest of the camp know about Lord Orove and give him a general moment of silence to show our respects."

"*But-"

"*Please, let us come back to this conversation later,"

Mom said, laying a hand on Wesnoq's arm. "Lord Mornali clearly needs some rest."

Mornali nodded stiffly. "*Yes, I think that would be best. Shall we all meet at dusk?" At Teyo's assent he bowed and left the tent. The other Lords followed him, talking worriedly about Orove's demise and how it would affect our magical defenses. Mom held Wesnoq back and Ather stayed as well when he saw us waiting.

"*What was that?" Wesnoq asked once the others had left.

"*I'm sorry," I said, "*but we had to interrupt you. You were going to tell him how the commoners had reacted to your attempt to use the Pact, right?"

He nodded. "*Yes - I'm very curious how the Pact didn't cause them to attack him the way it worked for us."

"*It's because he's turned against us," Teyo growled. I'd never heard him sound so furious; the older man had always been a paragon of patience and wisdom in my experience. "*The Archmagess and the Councilor here encountered one of the Lords of this world and spoke at some length. They were warned that we had a traitor who gave away the secrets of Lady Ikami's portal, but we did not know who it was."

"*Until now," Mom said with venom on her tongue. "*That bastard Mornali sold us out and killed Orove. I'd wager anything on it."

Wesnoq laughed bitterly. "*Now I understand. The Lords Abel and Jabnoss came to me last night and said that they'd sensed someone watching them over the last couple of days. They were worried that the humans were going to turn against us. You were watching all of us, weren't you?"

"*Well... not you," I said lamely. "*You were the least likely to have turned against us."

He just shook his head. "*No, I understand. In your situation I would have done the same thing. Lord Jabnoss will be quite offended, though, I warn you now."

"*He'll live," Mom replied dryly. "*We need to catch Mornali red-handed and pin that bastard down. Ather, you and

I can trade off watching him. Lord Wesnoq, can you help too?" She turned to me and continued, "*I'm sorry, Cordell, but we can't risk him sensing our presence..."

I smiled. "*It's all right, I don't mind. It will give me more time to rest up and see to the camp."

Mom gave me a knowing look and nodded. "*It's settled then. We'll start immediately."

Wesnoq stood up. "*Let me take the first watch. I haven't done anything useful in days and I need to start pulling my weight again."

"*Call on the other Lords as soon as you sense him making contact," General Teyo stated firmly.

I left the three of them talking about how they would catch the traitor and trotted through the camp looking for Dalt. She wasn't with her countrymen from Ganshe; they said that she'd gone to check in with the camp quartermaster for supplies. I started walking in that direction when I was suddenly rocked with the sense of strong magic from back towards the portal.

I staggered into a nearby tent pole and held it tight, closing my eyes and spinning my mind outside of my body. Using my magical sight I could sense dissipating energy from somewhere nearby. Several other presences were questing around as well, and I spotted Mom back towards the center of camp. I linked my mind up with hers and was almost thrown out by the intense anger emanating from her.

What happened? I asked.

The bastard got away, she replied curtly. *He made a move before we expected it. Wesnoq was watching him carefully. Mornali went out and made contact with some enemy Lord to the north. Wesnoq tried to catch him but was not back up to full strength yet and the scum wriggled free. He teleported out after trying to blast Wesnoq to bits.*

Is he all right?

She sent a sense of safety. *Yes. Ather threw some protection around him just in time to deflect the attack.*

I replied with a feeling of relief. We couldn't afford to lose any more Lords at this point. *What now?*

The four of us will inform the other Lords and the human mages what's happened. You don't need to be here - it's going to be an ugly conversation and I think it will be better for you if you can stay out of it.

Thanks, I sent back. *I appreciate it. Let me know if you need my help, though. As a Councilor.*

She withdrew, leaving behind a sensation of wry appreciation. I didn't envy her talking to the other Lords, and while a part of my mind said I should be there I knew she was right. I'd do better dealing with them if they didn't associate me with that conversation in the future.

I managed to catch up with Dalt and walked her back to the Ganshe contingent. We went slowly, happy to share a few extra minutes of conversation. We agreed to meet for dinner that evening; I figured we deserved a few hours away from the camp together. Dalt had plenty to do with her group and we parted for the time being.

After that I didn't have anything in particular to do so I headed back towards the clearing where the portal had once stood. I sat facing it and spent a few hours fruitlessly examining the area magically, hoping to catch a spark from home or some other signal that Kami was working to rebuild it from her side. Our only hope was still to hold out until she could find some way to reopen our path home.

Unsurprisingly, there was nothing new to see. Nobody knew what was happening back on the Bladesmen world. The closing of the portal might have sent devastating feedback through to the other side, crippling my sister. I'd never heard of such a massive spell being broken, and having had a few of my own magics sundered I could only shudder at the thought of how Kami must have felt when the portal went down.

It had only been a few hours since Mornali's departure when I sensed the familiar feeling of a teleporting Lord right in front of me. I opened my eyes after the flash and crack of teleportation to see a short Lord I didn't recognize, blood streaming from a slash on his cheek and livid red burns crossing his shoulders.

A moment later the allied Lords responded to his

presence. Beams of light lanced down the length of the camp pathways and converged on the newcomer, crackling and smoking where they met his protective spells. He cried out something unintelligible, throwing up new wards, just as Ather and Jabnoss teleported into the clearing nearby. They raised their arms and blasted forward with their own attacks, determined to get revenge for Orove.

Chapter 29 — Parlay

"Stop!" I heard Mom shout from somewhere nearby, her voice magically augmented to echo from one end of the camp to the other. "Hold off, damn you all!"

The attacks flickered out one by one. The foreign Lord had fallen to his knees, clutching at his head with both hands. I could sense the wisps of his wards surrounding him; a few more seconds of attacks would have wiped them away and destroyed him.

A moment later Mom rushed into the clearing on a gust of wind, her magic propelling her forward at great speed. She came to a halt near Ather and waved to get the newcomer's attention. "*You're Lord Hannon, aren't you?"

Ather frowned, then gaped as he recognized who he'd attacked. "*Oh, damn," he breathed. My heart felt like it jumped in my chest; I hadn't realized that I'd been holding my breath ever since the first flash of teleportation. I steeled myself and stepped forward, reinforcing my magical defenses just in case I was attacked. I could feel Mom throwing some additional power into my wards as well and I sent a quick feeling of thanks to her for it.

"*Lord Hannon?" I said as I approached him. "*I am Councilor Cordell Ather of the City. We spoke several days ago. Are you all right?"

He looked up, blinking, then slowly climbed back to his feet. I could feel him drawing together more power to rebuild his shields but held up my hand to the others to tell them not to resume their assault. "*Lord Hannon, if you have come here in peace we will hold off," I said cautiously. "*But you must speak if we are to parlay."

He let out a short, gruff laugh before responding. "*There is little left for me to treat with, human. Come closer and I will show you what has happened. This way you will know I am not deceiving you."

I could feel Mom, Ather, and the others stepping up behind me and felt reassured by their presence. Other than General Teyo, I realized, there really was nobody else to make diplomatic efforts with the native Lords here - we'd never really expected them to do anything other than fight. I nodded, struggling to control the trembling in my limbs, and stepped forward into his reach. His hands went to my temples and I closed my eyes, forcing myself to trust that the others wouldn't let him hurt me.

After a moment my mind was flooded with images, accompanied by a blinding agony. I cried out and staggered, but waved my arms to signal that everyone else should hold back. I had to fight to get my mind to recognize what Lord Hannon was doing and not lash out; I knew that this was the same way he had once shown Dad a direct view of history many years before. Slowly I brought the pain under control and made an effort to focus on resolving the images the Bladesman was trying to show me.

I was in the great hall of a castle the likes of which I'd only heard about in stories. Its stones gleamed with the ceaseless toil of a dozen Bladesmen servants wiping them down all around me. Gathered on a dais before me were ten Lords, two of whom I recognized: Mornali and Hannon.

This happened only a few minutes ago, I heard from the air behind my presence within the spell. I could feel a deep anger in his tone.

The Lord Hannon in the vision spoke, his voice seeming strange to me. I realized that the Bladesman must be projecting an image from his own mind in such a way that he was replaying the scene with the way he heard his own voice. I'd never really realized how different we must sound to those around us compared to what we hear in our own skulls. I shook off the odd thought and strained to make sense of what was happening.

"*You would bring this new Lord into the Pact? Lord Dantiel, you are the only one who has spoken with him before he arrived a few minutes ago. How can we trust him among us?" shouted the diminutive Lord who was showing me the scene.

A taller Lord, haughty-looking with rich robes, responded in a brusque tone. "*Don't play coy now, Lord Hannon. I informed everyone that one of the invaders had contacted me. We were all aware - I was just the one who actually knew his identity and contacted him directly. What did you think was going to happen when he left their camp?"

Lord Dantiel, Hannon's disembodied voice spoke from next to me. *This next one is Lord Kaji.*

A darker-skinned Lord chimed in. "*Really, Lord Hannon, this long-lost cousin of ours has already shown his worth several times over. Without him we never would have closed down that cursed portal - and he says he has more information on their attempts to reopen it. How can we *not* add him to the Pact, as we have done with the younger Lords in the last few years?"

Hannon growled his reply. "*You fools, we should have dissolved the Pact before this became an issue. I tell you - had we destroyed these magics when the humans fled a score of years ago they never would have attacked us when they returned. Don't you understand? *They are our only way home!* You younger Lords may not feel it, but those of us who were stolen from our own world over a century ago want to get back!"

The other Lords looked at each other uncomfortably, then Mornali gave a little nod and spoke up. "*That world has been corrupted by the humans too much. I was with the last band of Lords who tried to resist their influence and we lost, much like the humans have here. With the Pact you have a paradise here - there is nothing for us in our own world."

"*Don't you see, Lord Hannon?" asked one of the younger Lords, who could have been no more than fifteen years old. "*This is our home now. Let the humans have that one. We can crush their force here once the commoners are all assembled and be done with them forever - if they lose this force Lord Mornali says they are unlikely to send more."

Hannon looked around, his face flushed with rage. "*What has become of you? Are you all so drunk on the slavery of our kin that you forget why we made the Pact in the first place? Do none of you wish to return to our homeland and find those who we remember from our childhoods?"

None of the older Lords would look him in the eye save Lord Dantiel, who just shook his head sadly. "*I'm sorry, Lord Hannon, but none of us agree with you. With the assistance of Lord Mornali and the slaying of one of our enemies' Lords, our forces are even more overwhelming than they were before. Do you stand with us or against us? There is no longer any middle ground - we need suffer your deviant views no longer."

Hannon stared back with despair. "*Then I give up on all of you. I will find a way back home with or without you. I will no longer put up with your cruelty - even if it means working with the humans and everything they've done to us."

"*That, I fear, we cannot allow," Lord Dantiel said in a deceptively mild tone a moment before he threw up his arm and slashed a beam of deadly light at the shorter Lord. Hannon was ready, though, and his defenses held as he fired back with a gout of flame. Within seconds the room had erupted into chaos, the other Lords scrambling to get out of the way or throwing in with more attacks on Hannon. Mornali was one of those who fought, throwing himself at Hannon's unprotected side and slashing with his forearm blades. One cut deeply into Hannon's shoulder before a flash of light and sound announced a teleportation and my view went dark.

A moment later the Bladesman's hands came away from my head. "*And now you know," he said quietly, still breathing heavily - with fury or exhaustion I couldn't tell.

I nodded and carefully stood up, still feeling like a knife was rattling around inside my brain. His methods were painful but direct, and I was convinced. "*Give us a moment," I said before bowing and turning back towards the others. A moment later I connected my mind to theirs, feeling Mom and all six Lords save Sumi waiting for me to make contact.

I quickly related what he'd shown me, letting it sink in for a moment before sending anything else. Mom replied first, sending her words in the Bladesman language for everyone's benefit. *He is obviously wounded and has the bearing of a prideful man defeated. Kenton met this Lord long ago and never saw any deception in him, even though he was our enemy at the time. I believe him.

*I do too, I sent.

Lord Ather sent a sense of agreement. *His story has the ring of truth indeed. We know Mornali is working against us and he had no way to know it as well unless he was really there. From what I know Lord Hannon has always wanted to find a way to end the Pact, though he felt it was necessary at the time. Humans in the past treated him and the other Lords here very badly.

*I know I am not the most trusted among you, Lord Bilak sent, *but - for obvious reasons - I have to believe that one who once fought against you can be accepted into your ranks if he truly repents and wishes to join your side. Beyond that... if you remember, Lady Ikami stated that if she could work with a Lord who was part of the Pact she may be able to break the entire spell. This could be that Lord.

Wesnoq gave a feeling of assent. *We cannot forget that without Lord Orove, and with Mornali having joined our foes, we are at a sore disadvantage in power. We will need this Lord Hannon if it comes to an all-out fight. Does anyone disagree? After a few moments of silence and a few more signals of agreement - some of them reticent, but still there - Wesnoq sent his thoughts again. *I will speak to Lord Sumi and General Teyo. Councilor, will you officially accept Lord Hannon into the fold?

I nodded and stepped back, breaking my link to their minds. Mom gave a last trickle of power that helped calm the ringing in my head as I parted from them. I turned around and approached our visitor once more. He was waiting patiently, his hands crossed in front of his body and his wards raised high although he showed no signs of aggression.

"*Welcome to our united forces, Lord Hannon," I said with a deep bow.

He blinked as though he hadn't been expecting that response, then gave a stiff nod in return. "*I will not claim to be comfortable among you humans," he growled, "*but I will endeavor to work with you as best I can."

"*Let me tell you exactly why we're here and what we're waiting for," I suggested, motioning for him to walk alongside me back towards the command tent. The others broke up and went their separate ways, although I could feel at least three Lords unobtrusively watching us with their minds from a distance. Hannon must have noticed but he didn't say anything about it - he seemed to realize that he wasn't in much of a position to complain about surveillance at the moment.

After several hours of conversation, in which he met General Teyo and was officially introduced to all the other Lords as well as Mom, I gave him over to Sergeant Mona to get settled and went to find Dalt with relief. She was with her troops and after a moment's conversation we walked towards a quiet spot outside the guard perimeter. I told her about my day along the way, speaking in the human tongue to help her practice. We sat down and played with the grass in the gathering twilight as I wound up my story.

"Can we trust him?" she asked when I was finished.

I shrugged. "I don't know, honestly. He's clearly uncomfortable around humans - he couldn't hide it very well although at least he made an effort. But at the same time he *feels* truthful; I don't know how else to describe it."

"How well you know Orove?" she asked, switching topics.

"Not very well. Not as well as I would have liked, anyways. He was integral to figuring out how to break the Pact back home."

She nodded, picking at the short grass near our feet.

"Cord... do you think we make to out of here? We seem to losing more than we be gaining. I am worried."

I turned to face her and took her hands, pulling her back up to her feet. "We have to trust in Kami. I've never seen her fail at something she really, truly wants. Our part is just to last long enough. I can't really do anything *but* believe that we're going to make it - the alternative would be to give up."

Dalt looked away for a moment, then turned back with a smile. "She is going to be angry, very angry, when she comes back. Right?"

I laughed. "Extraordinarily so. And our enemies aren't going to like that experience one bit, are they?" I had a sudden mental vision of my sister flying through a new Portal with the energy of a hundred Lords at her fingertips, wagging her finger at the Lords of the Pact and chastising them sternly in a voice that would echo across the entire continent.

We held each other for hours before returning to camp. I couldn't bear the thought of losing Dalt now that we were just starting to form a life together. I tossed and turned for hours before falling asleep, unable to keep from worrying about what was going to become of us.

Chapter 30 – Fortification

    The next two weeks dragged by slowly. Lord Hannon was an invaluable source of information; with his help we were able to launch several small raids and capture supplies to keep ourselves well fed. Twice we disrupted an enemy military camp to the point that it disbanded, but we all knew we were just playing for time - for every Bladesmen commoner we forced to start regathering supplies, a thousand others prepared to march on the plateau.

    After one of our groups was ambushed and half the scouting force slain General Teyo put a moratorium on venturing too far afield. The enemy Lords were starting to draw a net around the Plateau, a half dozen of them constantly watching for miles around such that it became harder and harder to teleport past their vigil. When Lord Jabnoss reported that the farthest camps had started to march towards us, a hundred thousand strong, General Teyo looked grim and had no response.

    We worked on fortifying the Plateau as best we could. It was clear that the enemy would approach from the north, and we decided to join battle in the same place where the City's forces had bought time to escape almost exactly twenty three years before. Mom muttered that it felt like we'd come full circle in a tone that didn't sound promising. Without a Shield Wall up, we couldn't stop them from pounding the Plateau from all directions. We had significantly more firepower this time - but so did they.

At least with Bilak's help we were able to construct a network of spells that would prevent teleportation on and off the plateau by our enemies. We discussed at some length whether to include Lord Hannon's magical signature in the spell, such that he would be able to freely teleport along with the rest of our forces, but eventually we agreed to allow it. As General Teyo wryly noted, we would need every scrap of advantage we could get no matter what its source might be.

The top of the plateau was surveyed by engineers and the Lords started impregnating it with defensive spells. We didn't have any Fuel to spare - it was all in use on the airships and our ranged weapons - but two weeks of weaving magic resulted in some very potent wards that might make the difference when battle was joined.

We had one more discussion about hitting the enemy hard before they arrived, but the various Lords were unwilling to harm enemy commoners who were only obeying the Pact unless absolutely forced to do so. Hannon seemed pleased by this although Sumi and Bilak had to swallow their objections along with Mom. General Teyo was clearly of two minds on the matter but eventually threw in with the other Lords. No fighting would happen until our opponents made it to the plateau itself. It was still possible that we could hold out until Kami made it through and broke the Pact, which would make any deaths a waste.

Lord Ather and Mastermage Sciani worked with the other Lords and human mages on some of the same battle plans we'd used in the battles with Rainshye when the humans had first come to the Bladesmen world. The Lords here had only fought airships once, and then only the earliest model. Lord Hannon helped explain the best ways we could use their capabilities to surprise our opponents when they arrived.

The biggest problem, we all knew, would be the sheer quantity of commoners under the Pact. All over the continent millions of Bladesmen were on the move, with only a bare minimum left in their homes to keep a semblance of normal life running. Within weeks they would arrive in a giant tide at the plateau, a faceless mob driven to insane acts of suicide by the magics that compelled them to fight. Even if our soldiers were able to fight them face to face without worrying about the enemy Lords, our arms would grow tired long before they ran out of bodies to throw at us.

While surveying the perimeter of the camp one afternoon with our newest recruit I asked Hannon whether he was tempted to rejoin his old allies. He thought about it for a moment, then shook his head. "*I've spent more than a century just wanting to survive and return home," he replied quietly. "*For most of that time I've felt like I'm betraying my principles. I'm not going to pretend I like mingling with you humans, but I feel... cleaner... on this side of the battle. For the first time in many years I'm doing what I should, and I believe I'd rather die fighting alongside your kind than go back to using the Pact again."

It wasn't exactly a strong endorsement of our alliance, but I had to admit it was a better response than I'd expected to hear.

Those of us in the camp who could wield magic met almost daily to talk tactics. The enemy Lords, stolen from their homeworld as youths, had plenty of experience with brute force attacks and smashing the ancient human armies with combined spells. Compared to some of the Lords we'd brought with us, though, they were rank amateurs. Lord Wesnoq was older than any one of our enemies, with some of the other Lords - Jabnoss and Fian among them - more than three hundred years old. They had centuries of experience battling their own kind, and they shared wily techniques and subtle spells with all of us. It was the first time, I think, that humans had ever heard of many of their methods, and it was a truly eye-opening experience.

A good example was when Lord Sumi asked why we didn't simply teleport large boulders directly out of the earth and drop them from a mile above our enemy's heads. Abel answered him. "*Besides the fact that they could easily redirect the falling boulder towards our forces, young Lord, you must remember that it takes some time to gather strength and proper aim for a teleport. While doing so you leave yourself open for an attack - but a strong Lord will do worse; they will redirect the power of your spell without you ever knowing it."

"*Doesn't your battle doctrine involve teleporting groups of soldiers in and out of the fight? How is that different?" pressed the young Lord.

"*For one, we always drop them some distance from the enemy Lords, not right on top of them, for just that reason. It's always easier to sense a spell directed right at you. Even so, it's risky, very risky, every time we do so. Councilor Cordell here was witness to one occasion when a teleportation was intercepted and redirected. The Lords attempting it were quite gruesomely spread over hundreds of yards when we managed to turn their spell against them."

I shuddered at the reminder. It had been a terrible battle to witness and I'd always hoped I'd never see its like again. Now, however, it felt like an apocalyptic war was headed right towards me and there was nothing more I could do to turn it aside.

The confidence granted by our superior skill was mitigated somewhat by the knowledge that Lord Mornali was quite possibly educating his new peers with his own two hundred-odd years of experience. This meant that none of us were quite sure what we'd face - it might be no more than a batch of strong but ill-trained Lords, or it might be an overwhelming barrage of well-wrought magics.

With everything going on around us Dalt and I barely saw each other. It felt like a clock was ticking, every sunrise making our time together shorter - but there was nothing we could do other than steal a few moments here and there when we could. Her people did what they could to help facilitate my visits but I had great difficulty putting aside the demands on my time as both a Councilor and a mage.

At one point in a late night council, General Teyo raised a difficult question to Lord Hannon. We had talked as a group for more than three hours, going over possible airship attack routes around the likely battlefield.

"*Lord Hannon, I must ask something I know you will not want to hear. Among us you are the only Lord still empowered by the Pact to command the commoners who are coming to attack us. If it comes to it, and there is nothing else we can do... will you order them?"

The diminutive Lord looked grave as he replied. "*I do not honestly know, General. I loathe the Pact; it is the symbol of everything I hate in the Lords I used to work with. But to use it to avoid bloodshed... this is a very difficult question indeed. My voice would lock them in position as the other Lords countermanded me. Even if I did so, I warn you - any use of this time to slaughter them in their vulnerable state would cause me to fight you with as much zeal as I now strike back against the Lords I grew up with."

The General nodded. "*I understand that. We have no desire for blood from those under control of the Pact."

"*These humans can be bloodthirsty, General," Hannon replied quickly as though Mom and I weren't there. "*They will lie and cheat to get what they want. Will they obey your orders in this, or will they merely slaughter my people while they are helpless?"

Mom stiffened next to me but I laid a cautionary hand on her arm. She pulled back, though not without a dark look at Hannon.

"*I trust them with my life and the lives of my fellows," Teyo replied calmly. "*The humans who betrayed you died generations ago, Lord Hannon. At some point you must give up this ancient feud and treat with modern humans without your preconceived notions."

Hannon frowned and stood up abruptly. He glared at us, then swept from the tent without another word. Teyo and Ather sighed together, then went back into the prior conversation.

Sumi and I practiced together on the deck of an airship every few days to get him more used to working with human mages. Once I'd broken past his teenage sullenness I found him to be wonderfully quick of mind and even likable, though he had an endlessly dour mood that was at times off-putting. Kaibo was often with him, helping ensure that the Bladesman Lord was willing to learn the lessons we were trying to impart. Given another decade Sumi would be a valuable ally for the City somewhere, I decided, but I wasn't sure any of us were likely to live that long.

After we'd been on this world for just over a month our evening conference started with dire news. The enemy vanguard was drawing near and was now only a day's march from the edge of the plateau.

More than two hundred thousand Bladesmen commoners, and ten Lords, would arrive to destroy us on the morrow. Even if we somehow managed to drive them off, the Lords would only return a few days later with millions more commoners at their backs.

Chapter 31 – Dawn

    We tried a few last attempts to parlay with the enemy Lords but they rebuffed any mental communications. After they tried to ensnare and trap Lord Ather during one of these the General ordered no further attempts at dialogue be made.

    As the thirty-third day since our arrival dawned I made my way over to the *Origin* as per my preplanned assignment. Once on board I found Dalt, leading her contingent of Ganshe scouts, and gave her a tight embrace not caring who saw it. Lord Fian was with us as well, leaning on a cane though at times he was clearly using magic more than physical strength to make up for his missing limb.

    Mom and Ather were on the ground leading defensive efforts along with Jabnoss and Fian. Lord Hannon was with Lord Sian on the *Harmony*, while the remaining Lords were scattered among our forces where they held the top of the bluffs at the edge of the plateau. The other human mages were embarked on the skiffs that flitted around the larger ships of the line like gulls circling an albatross.

    From two thousand feet up in the air our enemies could be seen as a dark wave on the horizon making their way in a dozen columns through the forest. They inched closer, the unmistakable magical signature of their Lords huddled together in the center of their army. I judged they'd be in position around noon and passed this information on to the other mages.

Our entire army was calm but not hopeful. General Teyo tried to be optimistic but had never lied to his soldiers about the odds we faced. The portal behind us showed no signs of life, meaning that we'd have to hold out as long as possible and cross our fingers.

It could be weeks before Kami opened our way home, and I feared we didn't have any more than a few hours.

A bolt of light seared up out of the forest below towards one of our skiffs circling far out over the enemy lines, missing cleanly at the extreme distance. Its vile green glow signaled that battle was about to be joined. The sailors around me looked grim but determined, as though glad that the waiting was finally over.

We'd talked at great length about the prior battle that had occurred here many years before, with Lord Hannon able to fill in much from the perspective of the attackers. At that time there had been far fewer Bladesmen commoners and we'd had a lot more Fuel to work with. We'd focused more on the enemy soldiers at the time, trying to delay and defend the top of the bluffs without much that could really hit the enemy Lords.

For this fight we wanted to change those tactics and strike directly at the enemy leaders as much as possible. With their army forced to come up the broken earthen ramp leading to the bluffs, our soldiers could hold off the enemy commoners for days if magic wasn't involved. We would still fall in time, of course, but we'd last a lot longer that way. With that in mind, we were leaving the enemy Bladesmen soldiers to our own forces on the ground and had planned for a series of strikes on their Lords. If we could force them off the battlefield we'd gain a little more breathing room, at least until we were overwhelmed by the Bladesmen tide which now stretched across most of the continent converging on the plateau.

The outer skiffs dove and bobbed across the sky, their design far more agile and nimble than the ships we'd first brought to bear prior to our flight to the Bladesman world. Enemy lances of light speared up from the forests below and tried to connect with our ships but couldn't land more than a glancing strike. Their paint was barely blistered by these attacks, and while they didn't inflict any damage they were an excellent distraction as the Bladesman vanguard approached the plateau.

The forest was thicker near the ramp, the trees short and scrubby after only twenty years of growth. Their forebears had become the hull of the *Lord of the City*, our first zeppelin that had brought Mom and Dad back with the tools to save our race. The oncoming enemy lines slowed down, having to fight their way through the young trees for the last few yards.

Our forces stepped up once our foes emerged from the treeline. The two armies paused for a moment as though taking each others' measure.

Their only approach to the top of the bluffs was the broken, boulder-strewn remains of the earthen ramp the enemy Lords had raised in the assault many years before. It had been rent nearly in two by the City's fuel supplies, but time and weathering had evened that out somewhat. Erosion from the top of the bluffs, where battle scars had stripped away almost all of the vegetation, had created a shallow bowl around the ramp. It would still be a difficult approach where attackers would have to scramble up the walls one at a time, but we faced the very real possibility of Bladesmen under the Pact throwing themselves against us to create a ramp of bodies up the side of the bluff. It was a hideous concept, but one that Lord Hannon had assured us was very real - it had been contemplated in the last war and would surely be an option for them this time.

I could feel the allied Lords on the ground forming overlapping shields across our lines, ready to repel any attacks from below. Meanwhile, I started to gather power into myself while Lord Fian did the same next to me. It was an action I knew to be repeated all up and down our lines, our way of readying ourselves for battle while soldiers strung their bows and Bladesmen did a last round of sharpening on their natural weapons.

The Bladesmen below started to clamber their way up the rubble, a few dozen climbing faster than the others. Our lines were disciplined, not a single arrow loosed too early. Even after weeks of preparation and herculean fletching efforts our archers had less than one arrow for every three Bladesmen approaching us, and by now we all knew that Bladesmen under the Pact would ignore anything but the most grievous of wounds.

I kept a wary magical eye on the cluster of Lords and their approach. They stayed some distance back, still trying to pin down the skiffs thousands of feet above them in the air. So far as I could tell they had put no magical defenses in place over the front of their lines. I frowned - the point was coming soon where we'd have no choice but to start slaughtering Bladesmen who had done nothing wrong other than be compelled by the Pact, and their leaders didn't even care enough to try and stop us.

Within minutes the first commoners had made their way to the top of the bluff. General Teyo gave his sorrowful order, magically amplified by Mom, to slay any that reached our lines. With pikes and longswords, the first cluster was thrown off the edge and tumbled to their deaths on the boulders below or was trampled underfoot by the hundreds coming behind.

The slaughter was needless and wasteful - but something we could no longer avoid.

Come closer, I mentally urged the enemy Lords. They approached slowly, maddeningly so, making sure that at least ten thousand of their soldiers stayed between the plateau and their position. Our plans required them to reach a certain point, right about where the older trees started to change over to the younger ones.

Finally, after hundreds of Bladesmen had reached the top of the ramp and been thrown back down, their leaders made it to the designated target zone. I signaled our helmsman while Lord Fian sent a quick mental message to the other ships. Within seconds we had turned towards the battle and were racing over our enemies, engines thumping below us at full power. From every direction the circling skiffs started to converge with us while the *Harmony* paralleled our track a hundred yards to the east. Lord Fian put his strength into shielding our massive hull with Lord Sumi doing the same on the *Harmony*.

For this first attack, we'd decided to unload the full power of our airships at the enemy Lords. They were ready to handle a magical attack and outnumbered us in sheer power - so we'd capitalize on the resources they didn't have.

Our opponents saw us coming, of course. There was no way we could have hidden the entire force of airships on a clear day like this one. They concentrated their wards upwards, ready to deflect whatever we could throw at them. And, truthfully, it might have been enough to stop our assault - but they hadn't counted on our ace in the hole.

From their camouflaged positions up in the mature trees dropped two dozen Bladesmen in a tight circle around the Lords. They'd hidden there all night, barely daring to breathe. As Bladesmen, they hadn't set off any magical alarms when our foes had swept the area for spells or human spies. None of the army passing below had thought to look directly up, instead focused on our forces awaiting their approach from the bluff.

They were all volunteers, knowing they were on a suicide mission from the moment it was proposed.

I could sense them under the trees using my magical sight, their presences dim next to the blazing potency of the Lords clustered together. Together, they charged inwards with wild yells decrying the Pact and the evils these Lords had perpetuated.

Other than Mornali, the Lords' natural reaction was to try and order the attacking commoners to halt. The traitorous Lord, on the other hand, didn't hesitate and started throwing lances of light into the Bladesmen who had suddenly appeared all around them, killing half a dozen in seconds. During those same seconds, the other Lords were struck speechless, unable to comprehend Bladesmen who didn't obey their orders instantly. Just before they made contact the Lords shifted their defenses to focus on the immediate threat of being slashed to ribbons, their attention pulled away from our airships.

As soon as we felt their overhead cover weaken, each mage ordered their ship to open fire. With rippling twangs and snaps a dozen Fuel-tipped ballista shots, each one as tall as a man, shot into the enemy leaders below. More than two hundred archers contributed fire from the zeppelin decks, the skiffs banking to give their passengers a better line of fire.

The aerial onslaught took only two heartbeats to land. The result was a furious roar and a shock wave that sent the skiffs flying to the side, their navigators fighting to regain balance. Even the massive bulk of the *Origin* shuddered from the impact. The explosion lit the entire valley with a stark white light, causing a momentary shadow brighter than that from the early sunlight.

I caught the railing to keep my balance and leaned over the side, trying to see what had happened below. The *Origin's* captain was smart enough to order us back over our own lines right away in case our attack hadn't had the result we hoped for. A rising cloud of black smoke obscured my vision and I switched to my magical sight.

A huge crater had replaced the forest for fifty yards in all directions from the blast. I could sense a few Lords but over the next few seconds they all winked out in tiny blips of teleportation. Our fusillade had driven them off the field early, thought we had no way of telling if there had been any long-term damage.

A cheer went up from the deck as the smoke started to clear and the crew could see the damage we'd inflicted. I raised my hands and called for a moment of silence to remember the brave volunteers who had made the attack successful, feeling a pit in my stomach as I looked at the carnage below. Bladesmen bodies lay scattered in all directions from the explosion, and I couldn't help imagining one of them as Dalt's.

Just as I had this thought she stepped up next to me and leaned on the railing as well, a grave expression on her face. "*How much damage did we really do?" she asked quietly, slipping into her native tongue.

"*I don't know," I replied in the same tone. "*Many of

them lived - I could sense them teleporting out to regroup. At least we've got some more time."

She shook her head and pointed to the ramp below just as we crossed over our own lines. "*They're not stopping, see? Even with the Lords gone."

During the few minutes of our attack more Bladesmen had made it to the ramp and it was now covered in a living carpet of bodies. Our soldiers were throwing their enemies back easily but I could sense the terrible despair and sadness of our forces. Winning against such a foe was proving more demoralizing than losing would have been.

Chapter 32 – Dusk

Lord Fian kept watch over the battlefield as the rest of us convened for a quick mental conference once all airships were back over safer territory. Lords and mages gathered together in a confused welter of emotions, from exultation by Lord Sumi to resignation from Lord Hannon and dismay from Mastermage Sciani. By mutual assent we waited for Ather to begin.

*Our strike looks to have been quite successful, he began in the Bladesmen language. **The volunteers who gave their lives spent them well. Of the ten enemy Lords I sensed under their shields, two were seriously wounded and may have been slain. All of the rest were either injured or stunned by our assault and fled the field.*

*It was an effective use of your air power, Hannon added.

Mom jumped in with a sense of wariness. **The Bladesmen commoners here are still compelled by the last command they were given under the Pact. Lord Hannon, can you order them to leave or at least stand down?*

*That will likely only buy us a few hours until they start to return, he warned.

*Nevertheless, we need every moment we can pull together right now, Lord Abel advised. **Please - it is far kinder than having our soldiers continue to slaughter them as they reach the top of the bluffs.*

I felt our newest ally leave the conversation briefly and vaguely heard a magically enhanced voice call out across the countryside. A moment later his presence rejoined us. **It is done*

- I have told them to scatter and go back to their previous lives.

*They'll be back soon, when your order is overridden, Ather gave with the mental sense of a sigh. **Still, it is appreciated. We must do what we can.*

*What will we do when they come back? asked Sumi. Even in this ethereal conversation he sounded young.

*We will fight, the Mastermage replied simply. **I would guess, based on our experience back in the Bladesman world, that we have at least six to eight hours of respite before the Lords who fled are ready to direct another army. Perhaps a full day, if they gather another force of commoners. Lord Jabnoss, you've looked farther out to the north - how long do we have?*

*Within forty-eight hours the next major group of commoners will arrive, he replied. **More than a quarter million Bladesmen. They have only limited supplies with them, but the Pact will compel them no matter how hungry they may be when they arrive.*

*Then I suggest we land and take a break while we can, Lord Ather sent back decisively. **Lord Jabnoss, please relieve Lord Fian within the hour and keep a watch northward. When the enemy Lords come back, we'll fall back to our secondary plan of attack. Thank you, everyone.*

Mom and I lingered after the others had split up, waiting until their mental presences had gone back to their bodies before communicating in our own language.

Mom? How were your defensive spells down there?

They barely touched us, she sent back. *You and the others on the ships did a great job beating them back. It won't work again, of course, but as a first strike it was damn effective.* After a moment's hesitation, she continued, *I just wanted to see how you and Dalt were doing. You know that her group may need to be teleported in as a strike force if it comes to that point.*

I know, I replied soberly. *We've talked about it. She has her job and I have mine. None of us are very safe at this point, and we just have to hope for the best. It's not easy.*

She left with a sense of hope and I returned to my own body. The ship was already angling down. Dalt was waiting next to me patiently, long since having recognized when my sense of self wasn't present. We held hands without speaking for some time.

The next few hours passed slowly. The enemy commoners fled into the woods and soon disappeared from view, leaving behind hundreds of dead just from the few minutes we'd fought. The friendly Lords and airship crews rotated out, keeping watch from their respective vantage points for any signs of trouble. Dalt and I both elected to stay on board the *Origin* for the time being.

Just after noon Lord Jabnoss flashed a mental alarm across the plateau. I jumped upright from my seat on the foredeck and called out to the crew to be ready, feeling the engines throttle up almost instantly. We started to rise in altitude and shift slightly past the edge of the plateau. Soldiers manning the ballistae twisted them into a ready position though our enemies were as yet unseen.

I closed my eyes and sent my mind outwards, trying to track in on what had triggered the alert. Sure enough I could sense the power of several Lords somewhere to the north though I couldn't make out what they were trying to do. It didn't feel like a direct attack, though I couldn't say exactly why I felt that way. I looked back towards the camp for a moment just to make sure I knew where the other mages were, and just at that moment the enemy spell triggered.

With a crack and a bright flash nearly a hundred Bladesmen commoners teleported in. The spell had gone awry though - as promised, Lord Bilak's defenses kicked in and stopped their spell from landing where intended. Instead, the enemy Bladesmen materialized a thousand feet above the bluffs, right where the woven teleportation wards ended. They looked around, obviously shocked, and immediately started to fall.

I watched, horrified, unable to do anything to stop the inevitable. Even if we'd been close enough we couldn't have caught them - they would have fought us the moment we rescued them. Instead, our entire army watched them plummet to the rocks far below.

It was the first time I'd heard real terror in the voice of

a Bladesman compelled by the Pact.

I shuddered and fled back to my body, keeping my eyes closed as soon as I was there. Their screams echoed in my mind, along with the hideous sound their bodies had made upon impact with the ground below. They must have hoped to throw their soldiers deep into our camp to sow chaos and destruction. Surely they couldn't have expected only a hundred Bladesmen to do significant damage.

Suddenly I realized with a sickening feeling that there must be more coming. I opened my eyes and jumped to the railing just as another crack echoed across the forests. Another group of Bladesmen appeared in the sky and started falling. A few seconds later a third group appeared as well, destined for the same fate.

"What the hell are they doing? Don't they realize it's not working?" I shouted.

"I think they must not," Dalt replied from behind me in my language. "They keep think these group attack our camp."

"They're just dying," I said in a hollow tone as another group teleported in. "For no reason at all. They're killing their own people... for no point."

"Tell them!" Dalt commanded. She was right - and no matter what I couldn't just sit by and watch this happen. I closed my eyes, feeling Dalt hold me up as I leapt outwards. I flitted to where I could sense Mom and Ather watching the futile teleportations and linked up with their minds, feeling a horror similar to my own.

We have to tell them to stop, I sent. *They don't realize what they're doing.*

Ather sent a sense of agreement, but Mom held back. *Can we?* she asked warily. *Last time we tried to parlay they attempted to catch our presence away from our bodies. Yes, what they're doing is terrible - but would they really believe us if we tell them it's not working? This is war, Cordell. They're spending power doing this instead of -*

Stop right there, Mom, I cut her off. *This isn't right. We can't countenance this just because it gives us some fleeting 'tactical advantage'. That's a pile of crap and you know it. Hundreds of people are dying right now - we can't let this continue!*

If we back up Lord Hannon, he should be safe communicating with them, Ather added. *They know that he cannot lie. Your son is right, Viala - we cannot use this as a method of warfare. Just because these aren't humans doesn't make it right.*

That's not why I'm saying it, Mom sent back angrily. *I've defended Bladesmen along with humans for more than half my life now. Don't accuse me of racism, Ather. You know better than that.*

Are you saying you'd feel the same way if those were humans dying out there? I asked with accusation in my tone.

If our enemies were as overwhelming as the Bladesmen here? Damn right I would. A frosty sensation accompanied Mom's words as she continued. *You both know me well enough to recognize that I'm willing to do whatever it takes to win. If that means enemy troops - whoever they are - need to die, then I'm not going to cry. Thousands of Bladesmen are going to die so that the rest can be freed - and that's if we manage to live through this. There's no way around it.*

Once again I saw Mom as though a wide gulf separated us. I understood what she was saying, and I could even accept its rationality on some basis. I simply couldn't agree with her end justification. *I'm sorry, Mom, but all that doesn't make it right to just look away while they continue to slaughter their own people. Yes, we'll fight back - but this isn't a fight. This is a waste. Ather, I'll help you and Hannon however I can.*

He hesitated, then replied, *I'll ask him. I'm sorry, Viala - we are old friends but I have to side with Cordell on this. I won't ask you to help with something you think to be wrong, but neither can I sit back and watch this.*

Mom abruptly left our presence, leaving behind a feeling of anger and despair. I waited for Ather to bring Hannon into the conversation, giving a mental flinch every time I felt another flash of teleportation behind me. By now a thousand Bladesmen had to have been sent to their deaths.

Seconds later I felt Ather's presence rejoin me along with Hannon and Abel. **I've explained things,* he said immediately in the Bladesmen tongue. **We'll go right away. Everyone, lend your strength to Lord Hannon and be ready for them to try and catch us. Flee if* *it becomes necessary.*

We flitted northward, led by Hannon's consciousness. He took us directly down the path of the repeated teleportation spells, flying across close to a hundred miles in minutes. Soon we were over the enemy force Jabnoss had warned us about, a sea of Bladesman spreading across a wide valley. The enemy Lords were casting from the center of the group, small groups of three Lords each gathering their power to trigger the spells. They ceased as we approached, sensing our presences clearly - we hadn't tried to disguise our passage.

Lord Hannon tried to make contact with one of the enemy Lords, but his attempts were rebuffed. I sensed a group of four Lords circling around to try and cut off our retreat. Frustrated, I threw out a blanket message to all the Lords nearby. *Damn you all, we come with a message that will help you! Will you not pause long enough to listen?*

This got them to hesitate for a moment. It was a major breach of normal etiquette for communicating mind to mind, but I didn't really care right now. We could sense them conferring among themselves, then a familiar presence approached warily, clearly watching for a trap.

Lord Mornali, Hannon sent coldly.

Hannon, I presume? We met only briefly. I'm surprised you let a human speak for you. From what I've heard that doesn't seem like your way.

Your pathetic attempts to insult me will do you no good. I have made my choice and will live with it. Heed our message: your assaults are futile. They are failing to arrive where you think due to the teleportation shielding spell that I understand you helped devise.

Mornali paused, clearly stunned. *Oh, sh-*

We left immediately before they could regroup and decide to try and trap us after all. Lord Hannon led our little group back down the thread connecting us to our bodies. *I have the feeling Lord Mornali is going to be in trouble with his new allies for forgetting about our wards,* Ather sent as we flew along. *We talked about them weeks ago - he had to have known our plans. We're lucky he forgot.*

Before we split up Lord Hannon gave a sense of satisfaction and even thanks, though it was colored by a bitterness I recognized as being due to my race. I tried not to take offense; it wasn't so different from how many of the Bladesmen Lords had treated humans before getting to know us better. This particular Lord might never come to enjoy our presence, but for now he was tolerating us - and that was good enough for me.

Chapter 33 – Night

Once I'd returned to the airship and had a chance to assess the battlefield I was both awed and horrified by the carnage down below. More than two thousand Bladesmen commoners must have died during the course of the day. Their bodies lay broken and lifeless scattered across the rubble at the base of the bluff, thrown away by their masters to no effect.

Or rather, as I found out shortly, very little effect. One of our soldiers had perished as well, pulled over the edge by one of the Bladesmen climbing up earlier. The cold logic in my mind told me that this was the only ratio that would let us win this war; my heart recoiled at the thought of so much slaughter continuing on. I talked to Dalt on deck for a few minutes, trying to work out my feelings about what had happened or at least explain them to a sympathetic ear. Other soldiers and sailors moved around us quietly, leaving us to our own devices. My beloved's presence was the only comfort I could find in the day's events.

We were fairly sure that the enemy wouldn't try anything else for some time. I took a ride on a skiff back down to the camp and rested for an hour or so, going over the day's events in my mind. After several hours I was summoned to the command tent along with the other Lords. Its sides had been pulled up so that the afternoon sunlight illuminated everyone around me without any need for torches or magical lights. The angle of the light had the unfortunate side effect of making everyone's face appear gaunt and wasted. It didn't help that Ather had a hurt expression for some reason, but I didn't have time to ask what was wrong.

General Teyo started off, speaking in the Bladesman tongue. "*I understand that in the next two days we'll be faced with a much larger force of commoners. Is this correct?" After Jabnoss nodded, he continued, "*I must commend everyone on the coordination of our airship strike. I doubt such a tactic will work as well again, but it has purchased us valuable time."

"*We have a few more tricks up our sleeves," Lord Fian said flatly.

"*Yes, but our enemies are still legion," Hannon growled. "*I doubt you truly understand the numbers facing us. Every five years, to reinforce the Pact, we assemble hundreds of thousands of commoners from throughout the continent. Until you have seen that sea of faces stretching across miles of grass you will not know what is coming. They will not break so easily next time, and if even one Lord remains on the field I cannot simply command the army to leave again."

Lord Abel spoke next. "*Even if we drive off this batch, there are dozens following. Millions of Bladesmen are converging on our position over the next two weeks."

"*Lady Ikami stated that it would take her longer than that to rebuild the portal," the General observed. "*What options do we have other than try to hold this location until she arrives?"

"*None," Ather replied quickly. "*None whatsoever. We cannot flee with the army fast enough to escape the net that is tightening around us. Nor can we expect any hope of clemency if we surrender. We have to fight as long as we can and give Ikami every moment possible."

Our newest ally looked quizzical. "*I have never met this supposed wonder from your world and have no reason to put faith in her. A spell was used to transport the humans away from this world twenty years ago. Why do you not simply repeat it?"

Mom laughed. "*We got extremely lucky that it worked

before and we only have one Archmage this time. You weren't here last time we talked about this, but trust me, it's more of a crapshoot than trying to just hold the damn plateau."

"*Is there nothing to be done to help this portal from our side?" asked Hannon. "*If we are relying on it..."

Mom and the other Lords traded looks. "*Once you meet Ikami you'll understand," Ather answered after a moment. "*All of us together, working for a month, could not hope to replicate what she can do in a minute."

"*Wait a moment," I said, grasping hold of an idea that had been bouncing around in my head ever since Hannon's initial comments. "*Kami had to spend a lot of effort building the initial path for her spell before triggering it. We can't do much about the portal itself, but maybe we could make that first part easier. Could we build a beacon large enough to attract her focus from across the worlds?"

Nobody answered for a good thirty seconds, rolling the concept around in their minds. The General merely shrugged and sat back on his stool, waiting for the mages to answer. His senior officers had similar expressions to his, unsure whether there was any hope to be found in this new direction.

Finally, Mastermage Sciani spoke up. "*I believe the Councilor may have hit upon a way to help. It would have to be strong and focused. I doubt we could reach the Bladesman world, but it's possible we could make it much easier for the Lady to find this one. It would alert everyone with any sensitivity to magic for thousands of miles around, of course."

"I don't think our location is any mystery to the Lords here," a human mage muttered behind me.

"*What would this effort require?" Teyo asked.

"*Most of us to start, that's for sure," Lord Ather replied. "*But once we got it going... perhaps two Lords and some human mages at a time could keep it going?"

The General considered this for a moment before answering. "*That would be a noticeable hit to our combat effectiveness, but I believe Lord Ather is correct that we have few options if we hope to ultimately prevail. I judge it a worthwhile expenditure of our resources. Does anyone disagree?" After nobody spoke up, he continued, "*Then it is decided. We have a short breathing space now that we should use wisely. Lords and Mages, please begin the process as soon as you are able."

After a short while longer the meeting broke up. Teyo signaled to me to wait while the others shuffled out of the tent and I hung back, curious about why he'd want to speak to me privately. He waited until almost everyone else had left; only a few Bladesmen soldiers were within earshot to let the tent sides back down. When he spoke, it was in my own language.

"Councilor, I heard that you led an effort to contact our enemies earlier today."

I nodded. "I did indeed, General. I had planned to give you a written report on it later this evening." I didn't mention that I'd hoped by delivering it in writing I wouldn't have to face this very conversation.

"You know that I instructed no further contact be attempted with them a few days ago," he said in a somber tone. "This was a risky maneuver to take."

"I'm sorry, General, but in my judgment there was no time to reach you and sort things out before we went. We had sufficient power to escape if they tried laying a trap."

"Don't get me wrong, Councilor, I do not disagree with you. But I need you to understand my position. I trust you mages, the Lords, and my officers to make the correct decisions on the battlefield. What happened today was a terrible thing and reaching out was the best way to stop it. At the same time, I do not have the information I need to do my job unless I know what my people are doing - and right now you and everyone else in this camp is under my command."

I swallowed and nodded, hating the sudden sense of awkwardness that gripped my gut. My gaze went down to Teyo's feet, unable to look him in the eyes.

"I needed to know as soon as you got back, and I needed to hear it from you, not some soldier onboard the airship who overheard you talking about it with your damn girlfriend afterwards. Other than Ather, these other Lords don't really believe in my authority over them. If you, your mother, and Ather don't show any respect for the chain of command, why do you think they're going to?"

It felt like my stomach had dropped down to my ankles. "You're right, General, and I apologize. I should have come to you right away."

He sighed and I looked up. The General suddenly looked old and worn, showing all of his sixty-odd years. "Councilor, I've known your parents since before you were born. I've helped direct the defense of the City since we became part of it and fought in two wars on its side. Even in the direst of moments the situation has never been this bad. Our allies are far less certain than they appear, and I fear that if we do not hold firm to the structure of this camp some of them may break and flee. Even worse, more may take Mornali's path. I still do not trust Lord Bilak, and Lord Hannon's presence is dubious at best. They absolutely must see examples of proper military behavior or I'll lose the tenuous grasp I have over them."

I'd never seen the situation from that perspective before. From my position it had always seemed like the Lords just agreed with whatever the General laid down. Now that I thought about it, Ather and Mom had always been the ones to lead the consensus to what the General wanted. He was right - if the other Lords didn't work with the group plans in battle we'd soon be in even worse trouble.

"I'll not soon forget this lesson, General," I said. "I understand what you're saying and will not let it happen again."

"That's all I can ask, Councilor," he replied in a tired voice. "Thank you."

I nodded and left the tent, still feeling pained about what I'd done to him. Teyo had always been a constant figure in my life and it hurt to have worked against his position, even inadvertently. At least now I understood why Ather's face had looked so pinched when I came in; Teyo must have had the same conversation with him before the meeting.

The rest of my evening was spent back on board the *Origin*. Nearly every other magic wielder in camp was focusing together to create the beacon we hoped would help guide Ikami, but we'd needed a couple of us to keep watch just in case our enemies tried some new spell to reach out across the miles. I volunteered for the duty, not wanting to spend the next few hours with my mind entangled with those of the other Lords and mages.

Instead I stayed on patrol far to the north, flitting back and forth over the forests and hills to try and sense any Bladesman incursion. I could sense some of the last commoners who had been ordered away by Hannon earlier, but no Lords in either body or spirit. The world seemed peaceful for a few more hours at least.

The time passed by swiftly. I took breaks only long enough to relieve myself and have a few bites to eat, preferring the distraction of searching for enemies to the thoughts rattling around in my head. As the evening went by I felt an itch growing back at the camp, until at almost precisely midnight a brilliant sense of *presence* erupted back where the portal had once stood high. The beacon was lit and it was all I could do to focus on anything else, its magical signature seeming to wash out the real world.

After some time I was able to partially filter it out but doing so quickly gave me a headache. I managed to stay on patrol for another hour before having to give in to my fatigue and pain, withdrawing to an officer's room on board the airship and collapsing into a cot for the night. Another human mage took over my watch, clearly struggling to make way against the brightness of the spell behind us.

I awoke to bright light streaming in from the room's single small window, much refreshed. Within half an hour I'd made my way back down to the ground and had a short breakfast with Dalt. Afterwards I made my way through the camp and found Mom sitting over a hot cup of tea, holding her head in her hands.

"Are you all right?" I asked, concerned that she'd put

too much into building the beacon.

"What are you looking so cheery about?" she said tiredly.

I shrugged. "A full night of sleep did me a world of good. Did you get any?"

"You're damn lucky you're not an Archmage right now, son of mine," she grunted. "Unlike you I can't just flip off my magical senses. That spell is everywhere around us. I don't think any of the Lords were able to sleep either."

I blinked, then tried opening my mind and looking at the magic around me. The immediate sensation was one of drowning in light as though I'd been thrown into the center of the sun. I shut those senses down and staggered for a moment, catching myself against a nearby tent pole. "Wow," I gasped, "you weren't kidding."

She shook her head. "This is terrible. Your sister damn well better sense it. At least the enemy Lords will be just as blinded by it when they come close. That's something."

"Why don't you and some of the other Lords go out on one of the airships? It gets better a few miles out."

"That's a good idea. I'll grab Ather and we'll give it a shot." Mom looked up and spotted the *Harmony* circling not too far away. "If I hurry I can catch up before it heads too far out on patrol." With a wave she took her tea and started walking quickly towards Ather's tent, wincing with every step.

I made my way to the portal location and spotted Lords Jabnoss and Sumi laid out on cots near one another, two human mages nearby. All four looked drained and pale, their minds clearly out of their bodies. I reached out and shook one of the mage's shoulders, offering to trade out. He gladly agreed and staggered off to get some rest.

I took a deep breath, laid back, and plunged into the spell.

Chapter 34 — Brightness

The experience of being part of that beacon was something I could never forget. It felt like being swept up in a maelstrom of power, focused not on manipulating the physical world but simply existing. The spell didn't take much energy to fuel but the mental focus required to keep it up was grueling.

Most of its energy came from the Lords. We humans added a certain flavor to the magic, a unique signature that helped send the signal further into the void back towards the world I thought of as home. I couldn't tell if it was doing anything useful, but I swore I felt someone searching around the edges of the spell from a distance farther than I could imagine. I soon found that I wasn't the only one to report such a sensation.

None of us could manage it for more than a few hours at a time, so the next two days became a trial of endurance for everyone involved. I didn't know who had it worse - we human mages could at least turn off our magical senses and get some solid sleep, while Mom and the Lords had to put much less power into the spell but were constantly hounded by its potency no matter where they went. The only way they got some fitful rest was by embarking on an airship to the far end of the plateau fifty miles distant.

By the time dawn came on the third day of the beacon we were all exhausted. I was worried about how much longer we could keep it up, but it was our best chance to survive and the feelings of fleeting contact we'd all sensed gave us some hope that the spell was working.

On that same morning the second enemy army came within view of the bluffs. This time their lines stretched to the horizon, a gathering of impossible proportions. My mind simply couldn't grasp the idea that there were nearly a score of armies this same size approaching the plateau. It felt like everyone in the world must be assembled below as I looked down from the deck of the *Origin* far above.

The enemy Lords had once again grouped up some distance back. Nearly fifty thousand commoners separated us this time. They'd learned from their prior experience and had the advancing army completely destroy the forest as they advanced. The result was akin to watching a massive tidal wave overwhelm the countryside, miles of woodlands cleared in hours as the enemy approached. The logs were dragged to the rear, the incomprehensible labor of two hundred and fifty thousand soldiers used with no regard for the consequences.

It was early afternoon by the time their vanguard drew to a halt just outside of arrow range from the bluffs. I heard the soldiers around me muttering, stunned by the realization of just how many people a quarter million really was. It was a sight to shake our confidence to its core.

If every one of our soldiers fought without injury for a day we'd be lucky to bring a tenth of them down.

We searched the magical spectrum only sporadically, each venture outside of our bodies partially blinded by the presence of the massive magics behind us. Our only consolation was that our enemies must be experiencing the same obstacle.

Our foes bound their magics together into a potent ward surrounding them on all sides, a hemispherical construct that shimmered visibly in the warm air. They were taking no chances this time and spared little energy for offensive spells, not wasting power to try and strike at the skiffs zipping above them. The beacon worked against them in this matter as well; I could only imagine how bad their aim would be right now.

A single command rolled across the miles, empowered by magic to echo off the bluffs even though the enemy Lords were a good two miles away. The Bladesmen assembled down below began to charge forward, eerily silent as the Pact forced them to obey. Within minutes they began to clamber up the ruined earthen ramp and over the bodies of their comrades from the battle three days before.

Our soldiers easily held them back just as they had in the first battle. Bladesmen commoners reached the top of the bluff only to be thrown back onto the soldiers following them, often sending two or three at a time tumbling to their deaths down the hill. Lord Hannon tried his own command to have our enemies halt but he was easily drowned out by the magically augmented orders of his onetime allies. He couldn't get any of his words to take hold over theirs and soon gave up, conserving his strength for the inevitable magical battle to come.

For hours the leaders of our enemies held back, letting their army do the work for them. Thousands of Bladesmen were sent pitilessly to their deaths, futile waves not even making a scratch on our forces. Our own men and women started to rotate out as their arms grew tired and they needed a rest. The airships rode the winds back and forth, unable to do anything useful to help. The slaughter continued unabated; there was nothing we could do but keep throwing our enemies back one by one.

Felled bodies started to pile up. It looked like our worst fears were true; the Lords of the Pact were willing to throw their entire army away simply to raise a ramp of flesh and overwhelm us slowly.

When they made their first real move we were caught off guard. Lord Wesnoq had been watching for an attack but was clearly exhausted by his work on the beacon. Its magical presence overwhelmed his senses and he missed our enemy's subtle spells working underground. Without any warning the earth suddenly started to shudder and break, heaving upwards for a hundred yards back from the bluff.

Shouts of alarm came from our soldiers as they lost their balance, a dozen toppling from the top of the bluff to fall screaming among their enemies below. Hundreds of attacking Bladesmen tumbled to their deaths as well or were swallowed whole by the rising tide of dirt and stone.

It took several seconds for our Lords to respond. I shut my eyes, holding tight to the deck rail, and sent my mind leaping forward. The brilliance of the beacon was nearly overwhelming and I had to fight for a moment before I could sense anything at all. I could dimly feel the *Origin* wheeling under me to aim a barrage at the enemy Lords, trying to distract them from their spell. The presences of four friendly Lords dashed towards the destruction being caused on the ground below. I felt their minds collide with those of our enemies, fighting to break their magic before our foes succeeded in raising a wide causeway to give their forces easier access to the top of the bluffs.

I wouldn't contribute much there so instead I spun my senses forward to try and sense how many Lords were still holding up their wards. Frustratingly, they had enough power available that at least three were still keeping their defenses empowered enough to throw off the arrows already raining down from above. The *Harmony* fired three massive ballista shots into the cluster of Lords but they splintered uselessly into shards of wood a dozen yards overhead. I sensed the soldiers on board my own craft loading the more potent Fuel-tipped bolts and grimly hoped these would have a little more effect.

From my magical vantage point I watched the artillery pound home, loosing a shockwave that scythed into the bodies of common soldiers near the knot of Lords. It took nearly half a minute for the resulting debris to settle enough that I could determine how the Lords had fared. To my dismay their magically armored shell had held firm. A crater pocked the earth before it, a curving dirt wall unnaturally held in place where the blast had bounced off their wards.

Seeing this I was struck by an idea. Fighting to focus against the blinding draw of the beacon behind me, I forced my mouth open and dimly heard myself shouting to aim for the enemy Lords' feet. Our crew started to reload the ballistae as quickly as they could, years of training coming through in their discipline and teamwork. In less than a minute another load of Fuel-tipped bolts was ready to fire.

This time they slammed into the ground before the Lords' protective shell. No magical protection slowed them as they plowed into the earth and exploded, setting off a series of blasts that dug deeper into the ground with each impact. I felt the outpouring of energy towards the bluff stop as our enemies fell forward and rolled into the hole opened beneath their feet. It might not have been far enough to harm a Lord but it was startling enough to break their focus.

We were suddenly thrown off balance as the *Origin* heeled sharply to the left. One of the enemy Lords had decided they'd had enough of our meddling and was firing a bolt of deadly green light up towards us. I'd seen this type of attack many times in my life, but this was the first time I'd seen it curve - normally these beams flew straight and true, burning into whatever they touched. Today, though, it twisted and warped, pulled towards the all-consuming beacon we'd ignited with the power of our minds. The shot missed cleanly and blinked out a moment later. I imagined that the enemy Lord was as surprised as we were by this development.

I pulled my mind back into my body, ignoring a budding headache, and leaned forward to see what had happened at the front of the battle. The enemy spell had raised tons of earth most of the way up the cliffs, meaning that enemy Bladesmen had only a few feet to climb to face the blades of our forces. We still had an advantage but it had been cut drastically.

Our opponents started firing blasts of energy into the air, trying to figure out what was happening with their spells. Every one went off course and flew back towards the camp. I could only hope that the Lords and mages currently powering the beacon were safe from whatever stray spells were flying their way.

Before long some of our enemies had started to learn how to shield their attacks and protect them from the warping influence of the beacon. The *Origin*'s captain sent us back towards friendly lines just as we started to take hits, glancing blows by enemy fire scorching lines across the thick planking protecting our vulnerable engines. The skiffs proved more difficult to target but I could see the *Harmony* lose a sail a mile away, the rigging sliced cleanly in two by a well-aimed blast from below. Torn white canvas fluttered slowly downwards, landing amidst silent enemy commoners waiting for their chance to run into the slaughter at the bluffs.

Our army started to loose arrows at the oncoming foes as they made ground. Now that they had a shorter distance to climb it proved necessary to use our archers to keep our front lines from being pulled down. This was a bad sign - despite the tens of thousands of arrows we'd prepared, our bowmen couldn't keep up with the ongoing assault for long - and due to the Pact it took a clean kill to disable the oncoming Bladesmen. No amount of pain or injury would stop them from their assault.

I switched back to magical sight and felt the Lords tangling down below. Our side was attempting to collapse the earthen ramp while the opposing forces were working to keep it intact. Between those holding the beacon and the enemy Lords keeping their protection intact, little ended up being accomplished by either side with nobody having overwhelming force over the others. The ground shook and moved every few seconds but the advancing commoners merely picked themselves back up and continued to press forwards towards our lines.

Twice when we started to lose ground I felt friendly Lords pull our enemies' minds into the wards we'd prepared over the last two weeks. The resulting magical feedback knocked our foes temporarily off balance, buying time for us to regain firm control over the edge of the bluffs. It was a war of attrition we couldn't fight forever.

I shook my head, blinking a few times to let my eyes

transition back to the mundane world. Behind me I heard the ship's captain talking in urgent tones about how we only had a few more volleys of Fuel-tipped ballista bolts. I looked over my shoulder and saw a hundred grim-faced archers taking shots over the railing where they could, but I didn't see a flicker of hope among them.

Chapter 35 – Visitors

The stalemate continued for another hour. Sporadic forays of magic were made from each side without any major gains; it was clear that Mornali had conducted a crash course on skillful use of magic with his allies over the last few days. Their advantage in sheer numbers was at least temporarily countered by the defensive spells we'd placed on the hillside below us, although those wouldn't hold out forever. Meanwhile the massive Bladesman army continue to charge forward and die en masse while trying to climb the last few feet to our soldiers. The ramp was a scene of carnage, blood flowing freely over the earth where it had been turned to mud. Our forces still held the top of the bluff but fatigue was starting to take its toll. Every few minutes another friendly soldier was pulled down to be hacked limb from limb.

We held a quick mental conference to try and decide what to do. Our plans had involved small forces of friendly soldiers teleporting in around the enemy Lords to launch quick attacks but they kept so many thousands of commoners packed around them that there was simply nowhere to set our groups down. Continued harassment from the skiffs and airships did nothing more than waste arrows and bolts against their nearly impregnable defense. Eight enemy Lords were reinforcing their protective shields, reaching out only to fire the occasional beam against an airship that drifted too low or counter any friendly attempt to magically disrupt the army assaulting our lines. Our mages were spread too thin by the beacon and the need to keep watch over our own forces; if we tried to coordinate a magical attack with too many Lords at once we'd leave our battle line open to the mercy of our enemies. One solid magical strike would open the entire ridgeline to our enemies.

Mom and the other Lords kept trying more subtle attacks to get inside the enemy shield, but none of them worked. There were simply too many of them able to counter our assaults. Every minute that went by meant more Bladesmen commoners slain and a few more of our forces weakened.

We can't keep this up for long, I sent to Mom after the others had gone back to their bodies to try and come up with some new answer.

If we had half a ton of Fuel we could break their defenses open, she replied with a sense of deep exhaustion. *We're killing them a hundred to one and it's still not enough.*

They've decided to wait us out, I agreed. *Should we drop the beacon?*

What's the point? she answered bitterly. *They have nine Lords. We can throw every scrap of magic we have at them and we might fight them to a draw. The airships can thin down the commoners but without more Fuel we can't break their Lords. We can leap around the continent and disrupt their camps but there's too many of them.*

They'd give up the entire continent to stop us, I realized.

Mom sent a sense of assent and continued, *Do you have any idea how much this campaign will cost them? They've abandoned most of their farms and industry. The few left behind won't be able to feed this horde alone. They expect millions of Bladesmen to die here... and they don't care.*

I withdrew from the conversation with a mental shiver. How could we win against such a foe? Kami was our only hope now, and the beacon was our best chance to help her arrive sooner.

As though linked to my thoughts, a massive magical eruption triggered back in the camp. I felt it even without my magical senses active, the airship shuddering under the impact of a great gust of wind a moment later. "What the hell?" the navigator cried out behind me as he fought the wheel for a moment until the shockwave had passed.

The armies below had fallen into disarray, thousands on each side knocked down. Our pilot ordered us towards the beacon immediately. I tried switching to my magical sight but gave up in an instant, some unnatural fog clouding my ethereal view.

It took us only minutes to come in view of the camp. The entire crew held their breath and leaned forward, craning their necks to see what had happened. I felt a sharp stab of disappointment when I saw that the portal had not opened - I'd had a hope that Kami had somehow made it through early.

The disappointment changed to stunned amazement a moment later. As the *Origin* came in view of the camp's center we saw that tents had been leveled for a hundred yards radiating outwards from where the portal had originally stood. The shade over the mages taking part in the beacon had collapsed; we could not make out if those underneath had survived. There was a peculiar shimmering hanging in the air, very different from Kami's portals, that I couldn't quite focus on. It seemed to twist my eyes and play tricks on my vision as we drew closer.

Without warning the shimmer began to bend outwards as though something gigantic was pressing against it from the other side. A hazy figure of gigantic size swam into view as though seen through a layer of water, its featureless face glowing with a fell light. My view felt warped somehow as though I was able to see its mile-tall height despite the fact that the shimmering below was only the size of a man. The creature's head flickered to and fro as though analyzing everything it saw. Some artifact of its appearance made it feel hideous and alien, as though its very existence violated the laws of nature. I heard shouts from down below as another gust of wind slammed outwards, sending everyone on board grabbing for the railing as we spun in place. I could only imagine how bad the impact was down below.

"What is that thing?" shrieked a crewman nearby, his

eyes bulging as he stared in shock at the monstrosity trying to make its way through below us.

A burst of flame slammed into the shimmer below, causing the figure within to recoil in pain. Fian stalked towards it supported by his cane, having crawled out from underneath the collapsed tent from whence the beacon had been maintained. The creature responded a moment later, sending a searing line of energy through from the place beyond into the proud Bladesman Lord.

His shields lasted only a fraction of a second before he was obliterated. Lord Fian's ashes sprayed across the camp, fluttering through the air to land softly on the ground.

The grotesque figure suddenly flickered backwards as though pulled away and disappeared, leaving the shimmering to fade away within a few moments. We descended immediately, hoping to help any survivors of the pressure wave that had been triggered by the creature's appearance.

I threw my mind outwards to find Mom, the mysterious magical fog having vanished with the figure's departure. *What happened?* she sent urgently, her attention flashing back and forth between the camp and the continuing onslaught at the bluff.

I think the beacon attracted something other than Kami, I replied quickly. *Fian is dead.*

She absorbed this information for a moment before responding. *I'll tell the others. You do what you can there.*

After I opened my eyes I went searching on deck for Dalt. I found her and her group about to descend to the catwalk below to help out in the camp. We held each other wordlessly for a moment, then let go so we could do our jobs.

I ran to the command tent as soon as I reached the ground to find it surrounded by soldiers trying to lift heavy crates of supplies that had knocked it down. Pulling on my reserves of energy I threw my arms forward and used magical force to toss the obstructions aside. The soldiers looked up with surprise before nodding in thanks. A few moments later they pulled General Teyo and Mage Biala out of the debris.

Biala was dead, her spine crushed. Teyo was alive, but his arm hung at an unnatural angle and two of the small bone spikes around his face were broken off.

His eyes found mine, lucid though I could see the pain behind them. "*What happened, Cordell?" he asked calmly. "*Did they get behind us somehow?"

I shook my head. "*I don't know, General. Something showed up at the center of camp and... Lord Fian couldn't stop it, but I think he may have driven it away."

He bowed his head. "*We may have lost this battle, Councilor. If that happens again..."

Without warning I felt the earth begin to shake beneath my feet. The hairs on the back of my head stood up and I switched my view away from the physical world around me. My stomach clenched as I felt another massive accumulation of magical power growing back towards the center of camp.

I spun without another word and started running towards the portal clearing. The only thing I could think of was Dalt's presence near the ship. If something tried to come through again and triggered another blast of energy we'd all be dead.

As soon as I came into view of the airship I started to wave it off frantically. "Get away!" I shouted, using magic to amplify my voice. An officer looked down curiously, then recognized me and turned to signal the pilot. In moments its engines started to accelerate and the massive zeppelin began to rise off the ground, surprised soldiers looking up at it from below. Those who had understood me grabbed the arms of those who hadn't and started to flee from the portal area. In less than a minute I stood alone, feeling the magical power in front of me continue to build. The air itself started to crackle and hum, swirling around me fast enough to pick torn pieces of canvas off the ground.

"What are you doing?" I heard Dalt shout from behind me. She jogged up next to me before I could motion her back.

"I'll do what I can to stop this," I yelled back, raising my voice over the gathering wind. "Get out of here before that thing comes back!"

She shook her head. "If you stay I do too," she called out stubbornly, then continued more fluently in her native tongue. "*Damn it, Cord, if a Lord couldn't stop it you don't have a chance!"

I looked at her helplessly. I was the only one with any magical ability in the area; I had to do what I could to keep people protected. "*I'm sorry, Dalt. There's nowhere safe anymore. I love you." I shivered as the wind grew into a gale and continued in a low tone. "*I wish we had had more time."

She stepped up and leaned forward to kiss me hard, then spun and raised her arms into a fighting stance. Whatever was coming, we would face it together.

The air in front of me began to glow in a tall line at least three times as high as the earlier shimmering had been. Sparks and flares of energy spun around it where flecks of dirt and dust touched the building heat at its core. Growing pressure forced me back a step as I raised my arm to shield my face.

I forced myself to reach an inner calm. Time seemed to slow down as I drew every scrap of power I could from my reserves. I reached out for any magical energy I could leech from the world around me, mustering everything humanly possible. I knew it wouldn't be enough to stop whatever was creating the spell opening before me, but it was all I had.

The immense magic suddenly exploded with power, throwing both of us down onto the ground. I had to close my eyes at the intense light; it was like staring at the sun. Heat washed over me. I threw a shield around Dalt and I to protect us from whatever was coming and curled up around her, hoping I'd have just enough left over to strike back. The world was torn apart by a sound the likes of which I'd never heard, tossing the ground beneath us as though the plateau was no more than a clod of dirt.

I looked up and opened my eyes as soon as the light dimmed, knowing I'd have only one shot at whatever had come through. High above me I saw the air itself tear open and darkness pour through lit only briefly by the light of a thousand foreign stars.

A single figure soared into our world from the rift, arms held wide while the winds whipped her cloak wildly. A terrible light illuminated her eyes and pits of darkness surrounded her hands as though Hell itself had been summoned forth. She looked thin and scarred but I recognized her immediately.

Kami had arrived, and she was angry.

Book 3

~ Ikami ~

Chapter 36 – Damage

    A portal linking two worlds was a spell beyond anything a Bladesman Lord or a human Archmage had ever imagined. It was without question the most powerful spell I had ever cast, and was likely the single largest release of magical power either world had ever seen. That I survived the backlash of its sudden destruction was nothing short of a miracle.

    The magical feedback from its closing knocked me out immediately. One moment I was watching supplies go through, curious why Dad was shouting and running towards the portal, and the next I was falling forwards against the hard earth wondering why it was coming up to meet me so quickly.

    It was two days before I woke up; I can only imagine how bad a shape I would have been in if I'd stayed conscious. Every mage knows the pain of one of their spells being broken. One that powerful would have killed a normal Lord or Archmage straight out. Even after my short coma I had a terrible headache and felt drained and weak when I tried to tap my inner wellspring of power.

    I tried to throw off my covers and stand up but the attempt left me dizzy and winded. I had to sit back down before I'd gotten my balance. I reflected that the only other time in my life I'd felt this weak had been in this same place, after I'd destroyed the City of the Lords and nearly died in the process. My body was almost invulnerable to normal damage - but I was reminded yet again that "almost" was not "complete".

The irony of being in this same situation in the same place would have made me laugh at another time. Just then, however, it was incredibly frustrating.

Gregor was waiting next to me when I woke up. He explained what had happened, as far as they knew - something had collapsed the portal from the other side. He didn't tell me about Dad, though; I didn't find out about his injury until I was able to stand up and look around the infirmary an hour later. Dad's left hand was gone, a bandage in its place at the end of his wrist. For a moment I had a flashback to the accident where Dural had died years before. The nightmares from that day had mostly vanished but once again I was transfixed, watching Ather's arm blade shatter from the power I'd unleashed. I shook it off, refusing to let myself fall into despair again - I'd had enough of that to last a lifetime.

By the next morning I was up and about, refusing to stay put no matter what anyone said. Physicians had never had much to say to me and the same was true now - I recovered faster than they could explain or understand. When I finally stepped out into the chill morning air the camp was abuzz with activity. Soldiers bustled to and fro but I sensed a lack of purpose in their actions, as though they were moving just to have something to do. After a shiver I warmed the air around myself instinctively and went to find General Sanato.

"What are you doing to regain contact with them?" I asked without preamble the moment I found him. He was eating breakfast next to some of his officers at a rough wooden table and took a moment to finish chewing before he looked up and replied.

"Waiting for you," he replied in a level tone. "In case you've forgotten, you're the only one that can reach that far."

I flushed and glanced away for a moment, hugging my arms across my chest. "Of course," I stammered, "but the camp is busy... doing what?"

He leaned back and spread his arms, one hand still holding his fork. "Honestly? Nothing. Nothing at all. Ikami, it's a damn good thing you didn't go through to the other side. I hope you recognize that General Teyo was right and give him your sincere apologies if we ever meet him again. Or any of them, for that matter."

"Don't say that," I snarled. "My mother and brother are over there."

"Along with thousands of others," he replied angrily and stabbed his silverware in my direction. "Don't get uppity with me, young lady. I've known you since you were in diapers and you're not going to impress me with bluster. Shut up, sit down, and think about what you're saying for a moment."

I opened my mouth to snarl back, then shut it and sat down feeling foolish. A bowl was set in front of me and I started eating woodenly, cursing my addled wits. Of course I was the only one who could do anything about the portal, and I must have looked like an ass approaching Sanato the way I had.

"I'm sorry," I muttered after a few bites.

"Apology accepted," he answered quietly. "Look, Ikami, I have to give the soldiers here something to do. The Lords have been itching to start trouble ever since you were knocked out. They're a fractious bunch at the best of times and... well, we were worried about what might happen when you weren't around for a bit. I declared martial law in the camp to keep things tamped down. It sounds ridiculous - we're already a military encampment - but it's the only thing that kept the Lords in line. It worked for now, but I'm damn glad you're back on your feet to show them that you're still in control."

I frowned. "They should know better than to start anything," I said.

He shrugged. "Oh, don't get me wrong. There's plenty of Lords who were willing to step in and help keep the peace. But too many are ready to jump back to the old ways at the first sign that you might not be able to enforce the City's will here." The General shook his head helplessly and shrugged. "But that's that and here we are. The question everyone needs to know is... can you open another portal?"

I closed my eyes and leaned back for a moment. My mind flitted outwards, gauging the power over the hill. I was barely able to buffer my mind from the boiling power there, proving once more how frail I still was. Even so, I could tell that much of the reservoir of ancient spells and still-burning Fuel had been depleted. The power was building again already, but it had a long ways to go before I could draw enough to cross the distance between worlds again.

"Weeks," I answered when I opened my eyes. "Months, more likely." I shook my head to try and clear the remaining cobwebs. "Look, General, give me some time with a few of the Lords here. Maybe we can come up with something faster."

He nodded. "Just remember, Ikami, that we have no idea what's happening on the other side of that portal. If we're going to rescue them, sooner is better than later." With that he pushed back from the table and stood up, raising his hand in a salute before leaving.

I jumped into the task immediately. Lords Haren, Lim, and Mavue worked with me hour after hour to try and find a better way to relink the two worlds. They had me go over the spell I'd used piece by piece, quickly demonstrating a strong theoretical grasp of the magics involved. After the tenth time we'd walked through the entire casting end to end I stood up and started to pace. "This isn't helping!" I shouted, needing to vent my exasperation. It had been three hard days of study with no visible progress.

Lord Lim shook his head and answered in the Bladesman language. "*Lady Ikami, we're learning as much as you are here. These spells are beyond any of us individually, and most likely even all of us as a group. We've already devised some ideas that should - in theory, at least - help improve your methods. The problem is that we simply have no way to practice them ourselves."

"*I know," I answered in the same language while running a hand through my hair. I realized it was growing longer than usual; I needed to trim it back. "*I'm sorry, Lord Lim. I'm just tired of talking and I want to be able to do something."

He nodded. "*Perhaps, Lady Ikami, you should let us

put our heads together for a while. Your power seems to be fully returned, yes? Have you considered fueling the crater's energies yourself?"

I cocked my head to the side, considering. "*No, I hadn't. You know, that's not a bad idea - the energy feeds on itself in such a way that I could probably fuel it quite a bit faster than it grows naturally."

Haren smiled. "*We've talked among ourselves about the possibility a few times already. Please, try it for a while and let us know. That would help while we try and work out a few more ways to streamline the portal creation."

I said my farewells and headed to the edge of the camp. I trudged up across the dusty soil through the thin grasses, feeling their dry leaves trail against my feet. There was something satisfying about walking instead of flying that made me feel more grounded both mentally and physically. When I reached the crest a strong breeze struck me, sending my hair whipping fitfully around the small bone spikes framing my face. I looked down into the crater where smoke bubbled from fractures in the glassy ground, feeling the magical power pressing against me eager to take more.

Raising my hands together I summoned my own energy and sent it forth. The crater's force sucked it up eagerly and I gave it freely. I stood that way for hours, my nearly inexhaustible reserves feeding the maelstrom of magic below.

This became my daily routine over the next two weeks. I'd spend the morning working with the Lords to perfect the portal spell, sometimes opening small rifts back and forth to the City to demonstrate some new technique and let traffic through in both directions. In the afternoon and evening I'd commune with the crater's power, standing alone on the hills that used to border the parasitical community I'd destroyed two years before.

On one evening about twenty days after the portal had closed Dad came to stand next to me partway through my vigil. He stood silently, his right hand clasped over the stump of his left wrist behind him. I was rattled - I'd barely talked to him since his injury; he'd spent much of the time back in the City keeping the Council occupied.

After a few minutes I stopped sending my power into the crater and stretched, working the knots out of my shoulders. "Hi, Dad," I said awkwardly.

"How are you doing, Ikami?" he asked quietly.

I shrugged. "I feel helpless," I answered after a moment's hesitation. "Look at me - I'm supposed to be the most powerful person in the world, able to solve all problems with a snap of my fingers. And now I'm as useless as everyone else. Mom and Cord are stuck somewhere, maybe dead, and I can't get us back there to help them."

Suddenly I realized tears were rolling down my cheeks. I sniffed and tried to wipe them away but they were followed by more and a moment later I found myself in Dad's arms, bawling like a child. My body shook with sobs. I felt like this wasn't me, I couldn't be acting like this, but a part of me felt a huge relief from releasing some of the tension of the last few weeks. Dad was safe; he didn't care if I showed weakness.

Finally I stood up and wiped the last few drops off of my cheeks. "Sorry," I mumbled, looking away.

He laughed. "You're so much like your mother sometimes, you know," he said. "It's okay to show that you care, Ikami. We're all worried about them."

I turned back towards him, still sniffing every few breaths. I motioned to his arm and asked, "How is it?"

Dad shrugged and held his wrist out, looking at it as though for the first time. "It's... strange. I keep reaching for things without realizing my hand's not there anymore. The number of times I've knocked papers off of my desk... I'm getting used to it. It's fine. I think Viala will miss it more than I will." He wiggled his eyebrows lewdly to punctuate this last remark.

I couldn't help myself and laughed through the tears. "I don't want to hear about that, Dad!"

He chuckled. "It's good to see you smile again, my dear. You're too serious for your age sometimes."

We stood shoulder to shoulder for some time after that, our shadows stretching away from us until they reached across the entire crater to dissolve against the steam rising from its center. Finally, just as the world started getting dark, we walked back to the camp together.

I settled into my cot that night feeling more positive than I had for a long time. I was going to find a way to make things better, I vowed, no matter what it took.

Chapter 37 – Healing

I woke up the next morning refreshed and ready to go. Dad and I met Lord Haren for breakfast and I asked a question that had come into my mind overnight.

"*Lord Haren, you've worked on some remote scrying spells, right? Could you use a spell to look back in time and see exactly what happened on the other side of the portal when it closed?"

He frowned. "*We know many spells to look around the world, and some to look at things that have already come to pass, but I don't know of any way to tie accurately the vision to a particular place or time. Some other Lord may know a way. I am sorry."

Dad raised his eyebrows. "*Actually, I know a Lord who could do so. Unfortunately he happens to be an enemy of ours. Lord Hannon, in the human world, once had me participate in such a spell. He spent decades perfecting it. So it's possible, at least."

"*I fear we do not have decades right now," Haren observed dryly.

I stirred my morning gruel idly with a thread of mental energy, my mind flickering over possibilities. I had a great store of magical knowledge that I'd stolen from my biological father, but a quick review of it showed me nothing that would apply to the current problem.

"*We still haven't solved that other problem," Haren

said with a frown.

"*What's that?" Dad asked.

"*Well, we used the sword of yours to guide me to the human world before, right?" I said. "*We were talking yesterday that I'd have a lot easier time if we had another one. But I can't think of anything else that has the same properties - made by humans, with only human magic on it, and protected from this world's magical influence."

"*The Council building?" suggested Dad, then he immediately shook his head. "*No, never mind. It's had plenty of Bladesmen spells put on it over the last few years, mostly from Ather."

"*Are there any plants from your world that have grown successfully here?" the Bladesman asked.

"*I don't think so," I answered with a sigh. "*Certainly none that have been protected from this world's magical flavor."

"*We still have some of the wreckage of the *Lord of the City* preserved with magic... wait, damn. That's Ather's spell too."

The three of us sat in silence for a few minutes, eating slowly as we rolled ideas around in our heads. Suddenly Dad sat bolt upright and grinned. "*I've got it!" he shouted. Heads at nearby tables turned to look at us curiously.

"*What?" I prompted impatiently.

"*The Council table. Think of it - the damn thing is more than a hundred years old. It was built by human hands in the human world, and it's been protected by spells from every Archmage since the founding of the City. If anything would serve as a beacon back to our world, that's it."

I nodded. "*You're right. That's great, Dad!" I frowned for a moment. "*It'll be destroyed, if the last spell is any indication."

He shrugged. "*I'm Head Councilor. We can make a new one if I order it. Look, there's nothing else that will work, right? Do it."

"*It's a start. Last time I needed another Archmage to

cross the distance though."

"*Well, I'm no Archmage, but you can use me if it will work."

"*Dad - that's risky. You're strong for a regular mage, don't get me wrong, but I really need an Archmage for this."

He raised his eyebrows. "*We don't have one, Ikami. I'm the best you've got." His voice changed and took on the tone of Head Councilor for a moment as he spoke in his native tongue. "Make it work."

I nodded. "*I'll get the table here today," I answered. "Let me keep pumping power into the crater. I can feel it getting stronger very quickly now. Tell the General I'll be ready to try in a few more days and to have everything ready."

"*Everything?" Lord Haren asked quizzically. "*What does that mean?"

"*It means that any Lord that's not here to help will get his ass kicked," I stated. "*It means we're getting our people safe no matter what it takes."

I had to meet with the General in person the next day to convince him I was serious. I wanted every single Lord on the continent here to help me build the portal this time. This wasn't a moment for half-measures, not when the crater really needed another month to build energy before trying the spell again. I wasn't about to let any Lord get away from this responsibility; I sent a mental message reverberating across the continent which gave no room to back out.

Over the next few days Lords started arriving, many of them grumpy but none willing to challenge me. Dad took the opportunity to work on new diplomatic efforts which helped take the heat off my peremptory summons. Meanwhile I dragooned the closest allies of the City into helping me fuel the power down in the crater. They seemed frightened by my single-mindedness at times; I didn't give a damn what they thought so long as they assisted.

Finally, almost exactly five weeks since the portal had been closed, the last stragglers had arrived and I was ready. A voice in the back of my mind told me that there still wasn't enough power to ensure I could connect the portal with the right destination, but I told that voice to go to hell and hoped that my prior mental journey to the human world would make this one easier. It was the only chance we had; I couldn't wait any longer knowing that every day made it less likely we'd find our family and friends alive on the other side.

Shortly after dawn I had every Lord on the continent assemble on the hill crest looking down at the ruined City of the Lords. It was an impressive sight; more than a thousand Lords in all had replied to my summons. There were some I'd never met, and seeing the destruction I'd wrought two years before seemed to inspire appropriate awe and fear to make them stay in line. I couldn't afford to give any ground, not now when I needed everything they could supply.

Dad stood next to me with the Council table between us. I ran my fingers lightly over its scarred surface; the massive artifact had seen generations of Councilors come and go. It was sad to say goodbye to what had become a constant fixture of our history, but I would have thrown anything at this spell if it improved the likelihood of success.

The incantation went off much as it had before, at least the first part. My work with the other Lords had helped me devise a way to trigger the portal as soon as I found my way to the human world, far superior to the two-part method I'd used previously. I opened myself to all the power below me, feeling it flow into and through me in a godlike swelling of magic. When every Lord there submitted to my mind and offered up their own energy I was emboldened with a swift sense of victory - but I couldn't let myself get distracted from the business at hand. In moments I sent my mind flying outwards away from this world.

Dad gave me the first anchor point, his distinctively human magic leading me back towards his birthplace. It was as though an ethereal thread, so weak that only I could sense it, connected him with the planet of his origin. His power wasn't enough, though, and I was forced to pull upon the Council table earlier than I had the sword. The table levitated up into the air, then vaporized into a puff of dust as I used my mental power to rip apart its component atoms and lead me to the place they'd been put together.

Once more I led a group of Lords on a journey through darkness the likes of which we couldn't truly comprehend. We travelled across uncountable miles, the distance greater than our minds were capable of handling. Several of the weaker Lords dropped out quickly, exhausted in minutes as I had to draw upon their energy rapidly when the crater's powers proved too weak.

I knew we were in trouble before we'd made it halfway. Some of the other Lords were holding back a portion of their power, unwilling to offer up everything they had. I took mental note of this but couldn't spare the focus to rip their energy out forcibly. That was a last resort I hadn't yet reached. Dad held firm, keeping his mind focused directly on the human world without wavering for an instant.

Our pace faltered just as I started to sense something from far ahead. I pushed onwards, beginning to feel my own exhaustion building in the back of my mind. A powerful spell tickled my magical sight, as yet nothing more than the merest smudge of light - but it was enough for me to push forward with the right direction. More Lords dropped out of the spell as I wrung the last scraps of power from their reserves.

I sped onwards, following the dual threads of Dad's mind and the Council table towards the beacon illuminating the universe from ahead of me. I reached its edge just as Dad's energy failed and he vanished from the spell, leaving behind an exhausted apology. He'd given more than he should have and in the back of my mind I worried about what condition he'd be left in. Then there was no time to think as I grasped the mental beacon full of familiar power that lay before me.

This was a signal I knew. Lords and mages I'd spent years working beside were calling me towards them, giving me a lifeline without which I'd never had been able to make it. I rushed down the path they laid with the remaining energy at my back, flitting forwards at impossible speed. As the blur of stars streamed past me I paused for a moment, sure that I'd felt some other foreign presence nearby - but I couldn't take the time to look. I pressed onwards, knowing I was close.

And suddenly I was there, my mind at the source of the beacon just as it flickered out. The place felt familiar and I anchored a mental link to the soil of my parents' home world. My mind slipped back across the black void to my body and I released my grip on the Lords who had made it all the way with me. As soon as I opened my eyes I raised my arms and cried out to the universe, tearing the very fabric of reality to connect the two worlds once more with a portal a hundred feet high.

Hostile magic flickered beyond its shimmering surface and I felt a flash of fear. A battle was underway and I was on the wrong world to help. This time I wasn't going to stay back, no matter what anyone said. I felt reinvigorated by my success and called out to the other Lords to guard this side of the portal against any who would interfere with it.

I reinforced my reserves with the last scraps of energy in the crater and lifted myself into the air on the power of my mind. My magic whipped around me to form wards sufficient to hold off a score of Lords and I sped forward, ready to save - or avenge - my family. I raised my arms and let loose a primal scream of anger. It was time to visit the human world and set it to order.

Chapter 38 – Settling Accounts

The transition through the portal seemed to take forever. An inky void flashed across my vision as my body was teleported over uncountable miles. Once more I felt another presence watching me, as though there were something else observing the portal. A bright flash of light flew past and then I was on the other side.

My magical senses were on full alert as I scanned the surrounding area. A few miles away a furious battle was expending prodigious reserves of magic, with Lords I knew involved on both sides. I immediately recognized Mom's signature on one of the closer defensive spells and felt a dizzying sense of relief. Human mages sprinkled the area nearby and I felt a fading sense of Bladesman magic from immediately below me, as though the last wisps of the beacon were wilting away.

Next I took a look around the physical world with my own eyes. The sun was brilliantly yellow above me, illuminating a bright blue sky the likes of which I'd never seen. A military camp spread in all directions around me, many tents knocked flat from some recent impact. The nearby paths were nearly empty - the entire force seemed to be at the battle I'd sensed a moment ago. The *Origin* - it could be no other airship with its massive bulk - was less than half a mile away, moving at full speed as though fleeing from the portal I'd opened. Two figures were on the ground below me and my heart jumped as I recognized my brother and his chosen mate.

I swooped down to ground level in an instant and grabbed Cord up in my arms, spinning him around while both of us laughed and cried. "You're still alive!" I shouted, while at the same time he celebrated my arrival by whooping out loud. We took a few precious seconds to revel in each others' company before I pulled Dalt into the embrace as well. She seemed surprised but I didn't care.

Cord pulled away and took a breath before speaking. "Kami - you have to get over to the battle and stop them. We're getting pounded out there now that Lord Fian... well, I'll tell you about that in a bit."

I nodded and stepped back, preparing to take flight once more. Dalt called up to me and I paused for a moment. "*Wait - there's an enemy Lord on our side, and Mornali is working against us!" she yelled. I waved my thanks and turned to speed off towards the battle lines. I threw a quick shield around myself to render my presence nearly invisible, at least without close examination.

It took only seconds to reach the edge of the plateau. I recognized it all from Mom and Dad's stories over the years. Below me I saw our forces fighting hard to hold the ridgeline. They were opposed by a moving carpet of Bladesmen crawling over the slain bodies of their comrades, pushing forward up a wide earthen ramp. Rivers of blood streamed off its sides, carving small channels in the freshly turned dirt as they wound downwards under the inexorable pull of gravity.

When I raised my eyes I faltered for a moment. An endless horde of Bladesmen filled my view, stretching back from the plateau for miles. From my height I could see two additional armies arriving through the hills many miles distant. In my entire life I'd never imagined so many people could exist in one place. It made the City where I'd grown up seem like a child's dollhouse. The entire population of Rainshye, a mighty nation to the north of the City back home, might have equaled the Bladesmen within my view.

Some distance back from the front line I spotted the

enemy Lords clustered together. A visible shield arced over them to keep them safe from our airships; I could see tendrils of their magic sweeping outwards to deflect any spells our forces tried to fire off. Mornali's signature was easily detected near the front of the small knot and my anger returned in an instant.

"Traitor!" I called out in my native tongue, using magic to amplify the word so that it echoed off the mountains leagues to the north. The battle paused for a moment as all eyes turned to me where I flew a thousand feet over the battle lines. Those commoners under the Pact kept advancing, unable to disobey their last orders, but I threw a barrier of pure force across the front of the entire bluff for a mile in either direction that did the job quite nicely. I dropped the spells that had kept me invisible and pointed to the Lords below me.

They might not have understood my language but they recognized a threat when they saw one. Almost every enemy Lord below launched an instant assault on me, Mornali alone holding back with a look of utter terror. Nine beams of sizzling energy connected with my wards, crackling with power enough to rend an airship in two or blast another Lord from the sky.

I laughed and threw my arms outwards, my protective spells barely rippling under the attack. When Mornali's mind flickered outwards to try and find an escape route I casually reached down with a tendril of power and caught his mental thread firmly. Trying to teleport while I had him trapped would kill him as surely as any attack.

"*Time to answer for what you've done," I roared to the rebellious Lord. It took only a moment to shatter their protective spell into a thousand pieces. Half of the Lords fell to the ground writhing in pain; I ignored the others' continued attacks and physically wrenched Mornali into the air. He clawed backwards, trying desperately to stay with his new allies, but not a single one reached out to help. In a moment I held him in front of me with magic, grasped firmly a thousand feet above ground with nothing but air under his feet.

"*Lady - Lady Ikami - I swear -" he started, babbling,

but I only raised a finger and waggled it before his face.

"*Speak again without being spoken to and you will regret it." I said sternly. I sensed Mom and the other friendly Lords drawing a spell around our foes below; it took only a moment's mental examination to recognize that it would prevent them from teleporting away. I sent a quick message of thanks to Mom, promising to talk more in a moment, before returning my attention to the terrified Lord suspended next to me. When I spoke I made sure that my voice would be heard by everyone involved in the fighting below.

"*Now, Mornali, I have the feeling you had hoped you'd never see me again. We gave you another chance, a parole in which you could have redeemed yourself. Instead I find you on the wrong side of this battle. Do you have any explanation whatsoever?"

His eyes darted left and right, then up and down, while his mouth worked as though trying to find some phrase by which he could save himself. I gave him a good thirty seconds, then shook my head sorrowfully. "*I see. You do not. I know that right now you fear death. You're worried that I will drop you to the ground, or burn a hole through you, or some other similar punishment. Well, you don't have to worry on that account. Too many have died in this place."

I looked around and addressed everyone more generally, continuing on the same train of thought. "*Too much blood has been spilled here! Lords of this world, I order you to command the Bladesmen under the Pact to stand down immediately. Failure to comply will result in your immediate and irrevocable destruction."

One of the enemy Lords didn't get the message and instead lanced out towards me with a giant ball of flame. I glared down at him in response, slapping the spell aside with little effort. It required no more than a furrowed brow and a few moment's concentration before the enemy Lord simply crumpled to the ground. Trails of blood leaked from his ears. The massive brain trauma I had caused through his personal wards wouldn't kill him, but I doubted he would ever recover fully. At the moment I didn't particularly care.

"*Any others?" I called out angrily. A moment later a hoarse voice, shaking in fear, echoed across the countryside with an order to stand down. The massive swarms of commoners came to a halt immediately, some of them falling forward onto each other from their momentum. This evidence of the Pact's power was a chilling reminder of what we had come to stop.

I turned back to Mornali and continued, making sure to speak in the Bladesmen tongue so my message would not be lost. "*Lord Mornali, once of Randell's rebels, you have broken your parole and attacked those who gave you a second chance. I hereby find you guilty as a traitor. I would leave this to the Council but we have no time for that measure; if they find my judgment inaccurate I will willingly comply with whatever they order. In this case, I doubt that will be a problem."

Before pronouncing the punishment I'd decided on I looked him over carefully for a moment. This man was not solely responsible for those who had died below - a grim total I had no desire to determine right now - but I had little doubt that he held a significant amount of responsibility. I sent a mental tendril of communication down to the friendly lines below and found Mom and Ather watching intently. A moment later the three of us opened a joint line of communication.

Oh, Ikami, it's good to see you, Mom sent with genuine happiness.

I'm glad to be here, I replied warmly. *We'll talk more later - for now, I need to know what happened with Mornali.*

He gave them what they needed to close the portal so quickly, Ather sent in a somber tone. *The rebel was working with them from the instant he stepped through your portal.*

That's what I needed, I answered. *Thank you. I'll deal with these Lords and then get back to you. Oh, I saw Cord - he said you had another Lord with you?*

Lord Hannon has joined us, Mom confirmed. *He's part of the Pact - can you end it if he assists? He would be more than willing.*

This was a story I'd have to find out later. *Yes. Get him*

ready to help. With a parting sense of caring I pulled my focus back into my body, watching Mornali still struggling helplessly in the air only a few feet away. I continued speaking from where I'd left off only a moment before.

"*Mornali, I strip you of your title. No longer shall you be addressed as Lord. Your power is forfeit and the rest of your life will be spent as a commoner, subject to the vagaries of normal life." I closed my eyes and pushed my mind forward; this would take both a delicate touch and a surge of power beyond that of any normal Lord. A moment later it was done. Mornali let out a terrifying scream as he felt his magical senses crumble. The part of his mind that allowed him to harness power, that which Lords were born with and commoners were not, had been forever burnt from his brain.

I let him down to ground level where he immediately started raving and roaring. He fled through the press of bodies towards the hills. I had no idea if his loss of sanity would be temporary or permanent; either one was well deserved.

My sentence had shocked the Lords on both sides of the battle. I could feel them communicating furiously in small groups. Destroying the ability to use magical power was a secret I'd learned from my natural father when I'd stolen his knowledge but had never had the will to use. Faced with Mornali's actions, however, it seemed appropriate. I knew it was something that would forever separate me further from the Bladesmen Lords I had to deal with but right now I didn't give a damn what they thought.

"*And now for your Pact," I announced grimly. "*This abomination of a spell has gone on far too long. Lord Hannon, I require your assistance. Do you give it willingly?"

A short Lord whom I'd never met strode to the front of the bluff and called out his agreement. His face was flushed with righteous anger; Mom must have briefed him while I was dealing with the traitor. I wafted the foreign Lord through the air much more gently than I had Mornali and bowed politely once I'd brought him up to my altitude. He bowed in return and spoke quietly so that only the two of us could hear.

"*I have heard much about you, Lady Ikami," he said in a guarded tone. "*Are you truly ready to end the Pact so quickly?"

"*Yes," I replied immediately. "*It's what we came here to do. Now, I could rip your link to the Pact out of you by force, but I'd much rather do this cooperatively. Mom - excuse me, Archmagess Viala - says that you are willing to destroy the Pact? Even though you were one of those who created it in the first place?"

He nodded gravely. "*Yes. Its purpose is done and the other Lords have corrupted it into a spell of slavery and servitude. It should never have gone this far."

"*And you realize that once this is done I will never allow it to be remade, yes? You will need to serve yourself and work to find a place in the world we will build here."

The Lord laughed. "*I want to go back to the world you have come from," he answered bitterly. "*This was never my home and I have no desire to stay."

"*On the Bladesman world we are working hard to break down the caste system by which Lords enforced their wills over the commoners," I pressed. "*You will find no easy life over there, if that's what you imagine."

He shook his head. "*I will find a way to move on. I cannot countenance the Pact anymore, it is that simple. Let us make an end to it."

This Lord intrigued me. He stood firm with his principles in a way that reminded me of many of our staunchest allies from the Bladesman world. I nodded and spread my arms wide. "*Simply focus on the spells that you used to build the Pact. I can do the rest."

Before starting, I mentally thanked Lord Orove and Lord Jabnoss for the work they'd done on breaking the Pact over the last few years. General Teyo owed his mental freedom to them, and now I hoped to extend that across this entire world. I closed my eyes and focused on the spells woven deeply around Lord Hannon.

The sheer complexity of the Pact was daunting at first.

For most of my life I'd relied on pure magical power to avoid the need for subtlety, but between Mom and Uncle Ather I'd learned much in the last two years. It had been a long and painful path to accept that I still had a place as a student to their skills and experience. Without their foundational training I never would have been able to untangle the threads making up the Pact on this world.

A nearly invisible magical filament connected Hannon to each individual Bladesman under the pact. The sheer quantity was impossible to grasp; millions of tendrils spiraled out from his ethereal presence in all directions. Much stronger ties bound him to the other Lords on the ground below. I could only imagine how they'd designed the Pact so that it had survived transport back and forth to another world for those individuals cursed with its presence.

The technique devised by Orove and Jabnoss hadn't tried to untangle every part of the Pact. That would have proven impossible; I could have spent weeks working on removing individual Bladesmen from the spell without making an appreciable dent on the population here. Instead I went straight for the source. If the Lords here had their threads to the Pact broken, the entire foundation for the spell should crumble all across the planet. Lord Hannon willingly offered up his connection to the spell, an initial link that made this method possible.

I focused strongly and pulled all of the Lords' links to the Pact together. It took some careful focus to sort out all the different spells active on them but finally I had what I needed grasped in front of me trapped under the power of my mind. I knew my attentions must have caused considerable pain to those Lords who were resisting, but Hannon showed no complaint as I pulled at the spell that he had spent most of his life building. The Pact was built in such a way that any damage to the spell would be mended by drawing on the strength of the Lords who remained with it, rebuilding the connection of all involved. The only way to break it completely was to strike at each of its sources of energy at the same time.

I took a deep breath, focused my power, and severed all of the Lords' links to the Pact simultaneously.

Chapter 39 – Rebuilding

A bright green light flared around each Lord involved in the Pact. Screams rent the air from ten throats as a rushing wind built in seconds. Just as it felt like the entire battlefield must erupt into a huge cyclone the pressure broke with a crash akin to a thousand whirlpools collapsing at once. An omnidirectional gust of wind flew outwards, taking with it the power held in the Pact for more than a century.

Every Lord involved crumpled to the ground save Hannon. He alone had not resisted, though I could tell that the backlash would give him a nasty headache for days. A half dozen of the others had perished with the breaking of such a massive, long-lived enchantment. The others flopped on the ground unconsciously, tremors of power causing them to twitch uncontrollably every few moments.

The Bladesmen commoners below hesitated collectively, many wavering as though a support had been pulled from under their feet. It was as though the entire world was holding its breath below me as I hung motionless a thousand feet above the horde. After nearly half a minute a cough echoed from the bluffs, breaking the silence. A Bladesman somewhere in the army below apologized, clearly embarrassed.

It was as though a dam had burst. The commoners started talking to one another, voices joining in until the battlefield thundered with conversation. There was no coordinated cheer or loud celebration of freedom; instead the individual Bladesmen started off with the simplest of introductions. They gave one another their names, for the first time in their lives free to say or not to say whatever they liked around the Lords in their midst.

Those nearest the Lords looked at their onetime rulers, clearly unsure what to do. They backed off, leaving a dozen yards of clear ground around the dead or prostrate Lords. I could see them start to argue; some were pointing and yelling at the comatose Lords with clear hostility. I drifted lower, curious to see what form of justice they would enact. I would not have blamed them one bit if they had executed their slavers then and there.

One, a stern-looking young woman, looked up and noticed me coming closer. She called out to me and waved; I couldn't understand her over the innumerable voices nearby but it was clear that she wanted to talk. A moment later I settled to earth nearby, crossing my arms and nodding politely.

"*You... You did this? You freed us from *them?*" she asked in the Bladesman language.

I nodded and replied in kind. "*Yes, though not without help from many others. My name is Ikami. How do you feel?"

"*This is a new feeling," she said slowly, motioning to the hordes around her. "*We have many questions... but first we must decide what to do with *them.*" The woman made the word sound like an epithet as she pointed to the Lords nearby.

"*Kill them!" shouted an angry-faced man from nearby.

"*We would be no better than they are," an older Bladesman called back. "*Let those who freed us decide what is to be done!"

The woman who had originally called me down nodded in agreement. "*Please. Take them away and deal with them. We have no more use for them. When they awaken tell them that if they return we will cut them apart, no matter how many of us they take with them."

I was no diplomat but I could imagine Dad's response.

I bowed deeply and replied, "*Your prudence shows great wisdom and restraint and I will let the others know about this. Can you work to organize yourselves somewhat? We will want to help you get back to your lives but we cannot talk to all of you at once. Are there any leaders?"

She shrugged helplessly. "*Our leaders are slain or deposed, laying before you here. They allowed no others to help them."

"*That's not true," the older man replied sternly. "*The officers led when they were not around."

"*But do we want to allow them to lead us now?" she shot back. "*They worked with... with *them!*" Her tone left no question who she was referring to.

"*You need to decide," I answered both of them. "*We can advise and help but we are not here to replace one set of tyrants with another. Please, do what you can to keep everyone safe for now. We will talk to you soon."

With one more bow I took to the air again, hauling the unconscious enemy Lords behind me on a cushion of wind. I looked up and realized Lord Hannon was still high above, spinning slowly in place as he watched my progress. A moment later he was floating beside me as we proceeded back towards the cheering faces at the bluff.

"*You did well, Lady Ikami," he said quietly. "*I will never be able to express my thanks sufficiently for what you have done here today."

"*Help Cord figure out what the hell to do with these people," I laughed. "*You're the only one here who can tell us about how commoners live their lives on this world. There's the better part of a million folks down there who don't look like they have a lot of food with them and who are a long ways from home."

"*Your young face belies your wisdom," he answered gravely. "*Yes, I will help with this, even if it delays my return to my home."

A few moments later we settled a short distance behind the battle lines. I let my cargo down nearby and waved the friendly Lords to attend to our enemies. Cord disembarking from a skiff not far off and he and Mom caught up to me at almost the same time. The three of us embraced tightly, holding each other in silence for a good minute. It felt as though a huge weight had lifted off my shoulders, an iron mountain that had set in ever since the portal was closed a month before.

Eventually we stepped back, looking over each others' faces. Mom looked older; so did Cord, as though each had gone through some crucible during their time here.

"Kenton?" Mom asked quietly, as though she feared to hear the answer.

"He was almost through the portal when it closed," I answered quietly so that only they could hear. "He lost his left hand, but he's recovered fully and is doing fine."

Cord gasped. "Wait - I remember seeing that!" He turned to Mom and glared accusingly. "Did you know it was his the whole time?"

She nodded slowly, tears welling up in her eyes. "I'm sorry, Cordell, I just couldn't tell you. We had too much to deal with here. I was just so worried that he hadn't made it."

"Oh, Mom," he whispered in a stricken voice. "You didn't have to keep that to yourself this whole time."

Mom just shook her head and wiped at her eyes with the back of her hand. "How did you get the portal reopened so quickly?" she asked in an obvious bid to change the subject.

"I told every Lord on the continent to get their asses to the crater and help out," I said with a laugh. "And every day for a month I pumped that damn crater full of as much energy as I could spare. We worked out some improvements to the portal, too. Even so, we barely made it. If you guys hadn't built that signal I would have missed and we would have had to wait another month to try again."

"You didn't have the sword anymore. What -" Cord began, but I interrupted him.

"The Council table. They'll have to build a new one."

He rolled his eyes. "Some of the Councilors must have hated that."

"Do you really think Dad gave them a choice?" I asked incredulously. "You know how he gets when he's determined. They didn't even get to vote on it."

"Did you bring any Fuel?" Mom asked. "We should protect the damn thing better this time."

I shook my head. "No, but that's a good point. I have some Lords guarding the other side and I'll get some through to hold this one. We'll wrap it so tightly in wards that nothing could break it." I turned to Cord and asked, "What were our losses here?"

"Lord Orove was killed by Mornali, the bastard," he replied grimly. "We lost a few hundred soldiers, human and Bladesmen alike. Mage Biala and Fian... they died right before you came through. We should put up those wards right away."

I looked back and forth between the two of them. "What do you mean? Are there more Lords out there?"

Cord looked down uncomfortably. "The beacon we built... it drew something else. Something mean. Kami... it reminded me of you, the way it used power. It barely twitched a finger and Fian just exploded. I think the only reason it left is that it sensed you were coming."

Something twitched at the back of my mind. "Wait - Cord, did it look like a burst of light?"

He nodded. "More like a person made of light, yes. Did you see it?"

"I may have, on the way here through the portal," I replied with a frown. "You're right. We'll have to talk more later, but for now we should protect the portal. I don't want to have to rebuild it a second time."

A few minutes later the three of us had set down near the portal again. Two more ships of the line had already come through and soldiers were offloading boxes of supplies - General Sanato had wasted no time in reinforcing this side. I flicked through the nearest crates with my mind in a moment and felt my senses prickle at the feeling of Fuel. Cord popped back through the portal to talk to Dad and warn that side while Mom and I started to craft the strongest protections we could from this end.

It took us about half an hour and two crates full of Fuel before we were satisfied. Working with Mom felt satisfying in a deep, primal way; the Archmage part of me exulted in working with a kindred spirit. The portal now shimmered with an unearthly blue light around its edges, visible proof of the impenetrable wards we'd built.

"I need a few minutes before we start on the other side," Mom said before sitting down heavily on one of the empty boxes. She wiped her brow just as a soldier ran up with a flask of water. Mom nodded her thanks and drank, then offered me some as well.

"How are you doing? Really?" she asked while I drank deeply, the cool water refreshing.

"Tired," I admitted. "I pushed hard, really hard, to rebuild the portal this fast. If you hadn't held them off this long... if they'd gotten through and shut down your signal even an hour earlier I wouldn't have seen it. I don't know everything you've been through but you lasted a month against overwhelming odds."

She nodded and held her hand out for the water. "It was rough over here. There were a couple of times I didn't think we were going to make it. We definitely didn't think *you* were going to make it this quickly. The beacon was a shot in the dark, the only thing we could think of that might help you out."

"How's this Lord Hannon?" I asked, passing back the drink. "How long has he been with you?"

"Maybe a week? Two?" she answered, shaking her head slowly. "He seems solid enough. He's got some serious problems working with humans but I think he'll get over them in time."

I stood up and stretched. "Let's get this done with, Mom. Dad will want to see you, and I want to talk with Ather and the other Lords here. Ready?"

She nodded and we stepped up to the portal. It didn't quite reach the ground here, but it came close. We both took a look over the shielding spells we'd built, just out of habit; when we realized what the other was doing we both smiled. Sometimes we really acted like mother and daughter; a pleasant surprise whenever it happened.

Mom started to gather power to lift herself awkwardly into the air, but paused before triggering the spell. After a moment's hesitation she turned to me and asked, "Mind giving me a lift?"

I replied with what felt like the biggest grin I'd ever had. "Sure, Mom," I answered easily, and floated us both back through to the Bladesman world.

Chapter 40 – Research

Dad was nowhere in sight when we emerged from the portal and despite Mom's obvious anxiety to see him we set to work immediately. It took us a little longer this time, mostly due to both of us feeling exhausted, but when we were done I could tell that she felt as relieved as I. Neither of us wanted to go through another experience like that again, cut off from our family for weeks without knowing if they were alive or dead.

Not long after we'd finished Dad strolled up with Cord, the two of them talking animatedly about the horde of commoners on the other side of the portal. He held his arms behind his back until he could hold Mom, squeezing her tightly. They both had tears in their eyes when they separated.

"Show me," Mom ordered. He raised his left arm for her inspection, pulling back the long sleeve that covered his scarred wrist. Mom examined it carefully but could find no flaw in the magical healing the Lords here had performed.

"I'm sorry," she whispered a moment later. "I tried to hold them off as long as I could, but -"

"Shhhhh," Dad said to comfort her. "I shouldn't have charged at the damn thing. What's done is done, and there's no sense blaming anyone over it."

A loud sob drew our attention from the direction of the portal. We all turned to see Lord Hannon falling to his knees, a cry torn from his throat as he touched the soil of his homeworld for the first time in more than a hundred years. He let loose a wordless wail, a plaintive cry that simultaneously spoke of relief and agony.

Dad gave him a moment to run his hands through the dry earth then walked up and bowed politely. Hannon looked up, tears staining his face.

"*Lord Hannon? It is good to see you again, this time in better conditions," Dad said solemnly in the Bladesman tongue.

The Bladesman focused on Dad's face, taking a moment to recognize the man in front of him as the boy he'd talked to more than a score of years before. He slowly pulled himself to his feet before bowing deeper than I'd ever seen a Lord go. He replied in the human language, his words strangely accented. "Kenton. I remember you. You've learned to speak a civilized language, I see." He glanced at Mom to see her glaring at his words and smiled. "But look, I can speak a civilized tongue as well, remember?"

Dad laughed. "Then let us speak in the human language here on the Bladesman world. Let me be the first to welcome you home after a very long time away."

"Thank you," the short Lord said in a husky tone. "I never expected to meet a human here, but life takes strange turns." He cleared his throat and gestured back towards the portal. "I am needed back there to help the commoners return to their homes, but I had to come through just for a moment. Now, if something happens, at least I've felt the earth of my home once more before I die."

My father raised his eyebrow. "Well, as an ally of the City, we have no intention of letting you die anytime soon. We're sending help through as fast as we can organize it. Food, shelter, anything the people on that side need we will try to supply." He hesitated, then continued, "I look forward to having a similar experience soon. I've wanted to return to my world ever since we left as well. You might be surprised at how much our journeys have paralleled each other, Lord Hannon. Let us work together now to repair the damage our races have done to one another on both worlds."

Hannon started to speak in a respectful tone. "Your words are -" he began, but was suddenly interrupted by a loud roar from the portal. The area brightened visibly, our shadows thrown starkly away from the portal by a hideous light. A figure built of pure illumination stepped through and looked around curiously. Before any of us could react it glanced at a nearby skiff and twitched one finger. A tremendous burst of power leapt between the figure and the small airship. The zeppelin disintegrated into a burst of wood and blood, a dozen soldiers dying with the blast in an instant.

Screams rose from around me as I threw up a defensive wall too late to safe the skiff. Cord slapped at the creature with a gust of wind but it passed through it as though the creature wasn't there. Dad and Hannon both took a precious instant to raise their own defenses while the glowing figure turned to look at my brother.

"No!" I screamed as it blasted forward with a surge of energy. This time my spell came up in time to stop the attack, although Cord took enough of a hit to send him sprawling in the dirt. The creature's strike was stronger than any I'd ever felt from a single source, my defensive shield buckling under the strain. I blinked, not used to facing such power. Only once, when under assault by more than a hundred Lords, had I ever felt such an impact.

Hannon slashed his arm at the creature, releasing a deadly beam of green light. The destructive spell simply merged with the glowing figure with no visible effect. Dad tried something else, some sort of shadowy spell that I didn't recognize, but it seemed to do no more than Hannon's attack. It turned its featureless face at Dad, shifting patterns of light giving it an alien expression.

"Hell no," I muttered under my breath. I wasn't about to let it hit us again. I smacked at the creature with a full barrage of energy, striking it again and again with power sufficient to slay a dozen Lords. The power of my mind smashed and tore at its luminous body. It staggered under the assault, sparks flying off of its skin. The creature's head spun to face me, the smooth glow looking somehow furious. For the first time it was showing a real reaction.

When it struck back I was thrown to the ground. The power was intense, stripping layer after layer of my shields away. I cried out as several of my defensive spells were sundered in an instant, the backlash making my skull ring like a bell. After a few agonizing seconds I gritted my teeth and threw more power into my wards to hold the creature off for a little longer.

Suddenly a series of blasts rocked the creature off balance and it stopped its assault. It looked up at the line of Lords that had crested the hill nearby and shuddered. From my position on the ground I struck it with another attack built of pure magical force, sending it sprawling for a moment. I sensed surprise from it, as though it hadn't expected to find opposition here.

For a moment its mind connected with mine and I felt it sending something unintelligible. It wasn't just another language; instead it seemed as though it was trying to connect to my mind directly and not quite finding how to communicate. It gave a sensation of a great wrath from antiquity, as though it was here to destroy every Bladesman and human it could find.

An instant later it vanished with the crack of teleportation. For a moment I tried to follow its path with my mind but I quickly realized it had used enough power to travel thousands of miles in a single jump. Nobody other than I could have done such a thing, at least not until now.

I gasped, taking a painful breath, and pulled myself back to my feet. "What the hell was that thing?" I moaned, rubbing my bruised ribs.

"I think that was the same creature that killed Lord Fian," Cord replied in a similar tone.

"It took both you and a hundred Lords together to drive it off," Dad said, surveying the area carefully. "Whatever it was, I'm impressed."

I sent a quick mental message to the Lords who had come to our rescue thanking them and promising to share everything we knew on the unknown attacker shortly. I was glad that so many had stayed here; I hadn't expected that I'd need their help after opening the portal. Or, to be honest, that they would come to our defense.

"It's still on this world somewhere," I warned. "We need to be vigilant - I'm not sure where it's going to go next. Cord, what do you know about it?"

He shrugged helplessly. "Nothing. It popped through right before you built the portal and vaporized Lord Fian in an instant. We'd sensed something watching the beacon over the last couple of days, and I assume that was it."

I shuddered. "If it wasn't, and there's more things out there, I don't want to know about them."

Several other Lords we knew well trotted up together from where they'd helped drive the glowing figure away. Lords Lim, Haren, Jabnoss, and Mavue had all helped me on and off over the last month in determining how to reopen the portal. "*Thank you, all of you, for the assistance," Dad said as soon as they were within earshot. He bowed deeply to show his appreciation.

They bowed back in a similar fashion. Lord Haren spoke first. He was a short Lord with dark brown skin and black eyes that gave him a permanently dramatic appearance, one of the few Lords I'd ever met from the eastern continent. "*I too am glad we were nearby. To witness such a thing, well, I never imagined meeting such a visitor."

Lord Lim bobbed his head, looking thinner than ever. "*Quite an historic occurrence indeed. I have a suspicion that this creature may have something to do with the shared history of our race and yours, Councilor Kenton. Its magic felt like none I have ever felt - except for that of the Lady Ikami." He nodded politely in my direction.

"*And you think this indicates a link to me?" I asked, unsure where he was going.

Haren leapt in before Lim could reply. "*As you know, both of us have studied the human race thoroughly over the last few years. I agree with the honorable Lord from Tanekyth.

The attacker's spells had a certain unmistakable flavor. Lady Ikami, like it or not, that creature is like you - and to defend against it we must learn more about our shared history." He took a deep breath and bowed to Lord Hannon in way of introduction. "*I apologize for the abrupt nature of this request, Lord Hannon, as we have not been properly introduced. I understand that you worked on magics to view selected portions of history on the human world. With your help, and the power of the Lady Ikami backing us, I believe our answers can be found in the past. I propose that we journey back in time to witness the initial emergence of Bladesmen upon this world."

Chapter 41 – A Vanished Past

With no other ideas on where we might learn more about the mysterious attacker, Haren's plan was agreed to immediately. Dad and Cord went to talk with the other Lords to give word on this new threat, spreading the little knowledge we had. Supplies continued to pour through the portal where General Sanato was finally able to coordinate with General Teyo on what had suddenly become a relief mission. Lord Wesnoq worked with them to communicate with the vast hordes of Bladesman commoners who had been torn from their homes and forced to march on the plateau, now left adrift with the sudden destruction of the Pact.

Only a few hours later four of us - Lords Hannon, Haren, Lim, and myself - were seated together in a small tent, warmed against the evening chill by a glowing brazier of charcoal. Mom had initially tried to join us until Hannon had informed her that including her human magic in the spell would do nothing but give her tremendous pain. He had barely been able to show Dad a vision of the past long ago; Mom's magical presence was simply too powerful - and too human - for him to feel confident in including. She had argued for some time until Dad had come along and hauled her away, telling her she was needed on his end of things. He gave me a wink as they left; I slipped him a quick mental message of thanks to go along with my plea for help a few minutes before.

Our little cadre closed our eyes and sat back in unison.

We'd talked only briefly about what we were going to try here. Lord Haren would lead the spell based on his research of how to look many millennia into the past. Hannon supplied the knowledge of how to target a specific place in time, solving the problems Haren had run into before. Lord Lim had the greatest knowledge of Bladesman history on this world and would help direct Haren's magic based on what had long since become myth and legend. I was there simply to supply raw power. All four of us, if the spell worked as expected, would be able to view what Lord Haren saw with magical eyes.

Our minds met in the center of the tent. Haren began weaving his spell immediately, the three of us watching passively. I offered up a link to my power, far more than Haren had ever had available at once. He was overwhelmed for a moment until I slowed the flow of energy down to a trickle. After that he was able to twist it into the complicated magic he was building in front of us. Before long he invited Lord Lim to help, guiding the spell far into the past.

Fragmented images started to flicker before our mental vision. One moment we saw two Bladesmen armies smashing into one another and the next we witnessed only primal forests stretching as far as the eye could see. Events flashed by faster than we could make sense of and Haren called for the final participant to enter the spell.

Hannon, the youngest Lord of the three, started to exert pressure upon Haren's magic. The visions slowed down, lasting longer and longer until after a few minutes we were left with a single image. We were hanging suspended in the air over a barren desert, only a few scrubby bushes in sight far in the distance where huge birds circled on hot updrafts.

Too far back, Lim instructed. *Move us forward a few centuries so I can figure out when we are.*

Under Hannon's guidance our view flashed again, the world seeming to speed around us at an incredible velocity. The desert strobed between day and night until it blurred into a single grey twilight. Suddenly Lim called for a halt and things came crashing back into focus. The instant change in apparent speed made my vision swim for a moment.

Now we're getting closer, Lim sent with a sense of satisfaction. Below us we could see small bands of Bladesmen roving across the desert. *They're coming from the north. Go that way.*

We flew forward for some time, Lim ordering minor course corrections as we progressed. Before long we crossed over the edge of the desert into a rolling grassland, where we came into view of a small Bladesman town. *This is it,* he crowed. *Evecath. The first Bladesman city. Its location has been lost for thousands of years.*

Haren's excitement was palpable. *Then we simply need to go back farther, right?*

A moment later the world started to flicker and speed by once more. The town below us shrank to a tiny village, then suddenly disappeared. Hannon moved us forward again without prompting, this time slower. Before long I sensed a surge of Bladesman magic building from below with my magical sight. *Wait,* I sent. *There's something there.*

Our journey slowed back down to normal speed. It was midday in what looked like summer. The grasses stretched for miles in every direction, the thin edge of a forest on the horizon to the north opposite the dusty air of the desert far to the south. *I don't feel anything,* Haren sent. *We need to go farther.*

No, I replied before Hannon started us moving again. *I feel a Bladesman spell somewhere nearby.*

We're in a vision - how could you feel such a thing? Lim asked, startled by my claim. I sent back a feeling of uncertainty and indicated patience. This was new territory for all of us; I was used to manifesting abilities that others didn't understand. The four of us watched the empty grassland, our mental presences side by side in this vision of the past.

Without warning a bright spark appeared in midair perhaps a dozen yards above ground level. It slowly traveled down to the waving grasses below, leaving a glowing trace in the air behind it. When it touched the ground it left a smoky burn and the grasses withered for ten feet in every direction from the sudden heat.

I felt another surge of power and the glowing line started to wrench outwards, opening a gaping hole in reality. I recognized the spell well - it was a variation on the portals I'd built many times before. This one was clearly coming from somewhere not on this world; the power pouring through was immense.

Soon we could see through the shimmering portal to the far side. Our view was hazy but what we saw was unmistakable. A battle of apocalyptic proportions was underway, the very earth wracked with open fissures and chasms. Some were spouting lava into the air while others let forth great gouts of superheated steam. Thousands of people were locked in deadly melee, while perhaps two dozen indistinct figures floated above the fray releasing brutal blasts upon each other. The sky was dark red, clouds backlit in all directions by flames. It looked as though their entire world was burning.

A figure made of pure darkness fell through the portal, followed by a horde of Bladesmen fleeing for their lives. Most were commoners but some were clearly Lords based on the visible wards around their bodies. The first arrival threw blast after blast of pure energy through the portal above the heads of the Bladesmen coming through, trying to hold back another shadowy being on the other side. I had no idea how he got his spells to pass through the portal; that was a trick I'd never figured out.

I gasped as I suddenly recognized some of the figures fighting on the far side. The shimmering surface of the portal gained a momentary clarity, allowing me to clearly identify several as humans. There were at least a half-dozen Archmages leading many mages in coordinated magical strikes against the last of the Bladesmen as they tried to flee through the portal. The shadowy figure that led the humans sent one massive burst of power through from the far side, striking the creature made of darkness that had first opened the portal and now lay panting in the grasses here.

The smoky figure that had led the Bladesmen through was quite simply broken by the attack. It let out one strangled cry, then its portal wrenched closed with a hideous scream. The last few Bladesmen were cut in two by the abrupt vanishing of their method of transport. The Lords who had made it to this side tried to revive their patron but had no luck. We watched for a few minutes more until the Lords started to organize their comrades and plant the first seeds of what would eventually become the settlement of Evecath, then swept away from the scene and returned to our own time. A few moments later we opened our eyes as our minds returned to our bodies.

Nobody said anything for some time, churning over the sights that we'd witnessed. Lord Hannon was the first to speak, his tone containing a great bitterness. "*So," he said in the Bladesman tongue, "*humans have been after us since our very arrival in this world."

I frowned and answered in kind for the benefit of the other Lords. "*We know nothing of the context of what we saw. For all we know the Bladesmen attacked first and simply lost the battle, fleeing to end up here on this world."

"*We would not have -" began Hannon before I interrupted him

"*None of us know what happened, that's all I'm saying!" I said, exasperated. "*Look, Lord Hannon, I understand that you have had your quarrels with humans. We have to look at this with open minds and lay aside our prejudices. Yes, it appears that Bladesmen came here to flee some cataclysmic war. Yes, humans were involved. Beyond that we can draw little from what we witnessed."

"*Actually, I think we can draw a number of conclusions," Lord Haren said in his soft voice. "*Both Bladesmen and humans were led by figures of darkness who possessed great power, yes? Did they not remind you of a certain visitor we had recently?"

I thought for a moment. "*You're right," I replied, chastised by the realization that I'd missed the obvious. "*Other than the substance they appeared to be created from, they had much in common with the figure of light that attacked us earlier."

Lord Lim nodded. "*Indeed. In addition, I think we can all agree that the world we viewed through the portal in the vision was not the human world, yes? We were witnessing events perhaps ten thousand years in the past - but even over that time I do not expect that world to have recovered from what we saw."

Hannon blinked, then spoke slowly as though he was contributing only against his better judgment. "*Which means the humans were likely eventually driven to their own world just as we were forced here."

"*Which also means," Haren continued in an excited tone, "*that we may learn more by going to the human world and repeating this exercise."

I frowned. "*You're likely correct, but I fear that our history - that of the humans, I mean - was lost when we were forced back to the City. We have no equivalent of Lord Lim for human legends to guide us in our visions."

Our newest ally fidgeted uncomfortably, revealing some inner discomfort that I was surprised to see him show. After a pregnant pause he spoke. "*That is not quite true, Lady Ikami. Over the last century *I* have become an expert on what human culture was like before we destroyed it. I believe that I may hold the knowledge you need to learn where the human race came from. In fact, I am sure of it."

Hannon and I looked at each other, measuring one another's will with our stares. Finally I nodded, showing respect that he was willing to volunteer his help on what in some ways was a purely human matter. I was about to speak when all four of us rocked backwards, caught off guard by an immense release of magical energy from somewhere far away.

The creature of light was striking again, and this time there was no one nearby to stop it.

Chapter 42 – Power

We ran out to meet the other Lords and nearly crashed into Mom right outside the tent. Arguments immediately broke out as the Lords assembled in the center of camp. Most of them wanted to teleport to their home nations as quickly as possible to make sure everything was safe. Others pointed out that doing so one at a time was certain suicide against a creature of such immense power. Before long everyone was looking at me, waiting to see how I would combat this threat.

I took a deep breath. It shouldn't be surprising, after all; I'd placed myself in the position of ultimate enforcer for the entire Bladesmen world. Mom glanced at me and opened her mouth, but I just shook my head. I knew what I had to do. "*I know you are all worried," I called out, amplifying my voice so it could reach the entire camp. "*Those urging caution are right to do so. I have already engaged this creature once. I mean no offense, but it is a match for any of you individually. Only by staying in a group can you hope to drive it off."

After a moment's hesitation, glancing over the faces looking at me expectantly, I continued. "*I will locate this creature and do what I can to kill it or force it to flee. At a minimum, I will find out where it is right now and call for assistance. We must work together in this. While I'm gone, work with Lord Hannon - he is from the human world and during his long exile there has developed new ways to teleport that may ease your journeys." I had no idea if the alterations the

Lords there had developed would have any effect on this world, where magic worked slightly differently, but it would keep them occupied for a while so they wouldn't stray.

Mom's mental presence tapped urgently for my attention. I linked up with her mind and she started addressing me in an authoritative tone. *Ikami, you can't head off on your own. Whatever this thing is it has you outmatched.*

It caught me off guard last time, I replied stubbornly. *Besides, nobody else can jump around fast enough or far enough to catch this thing. We can't just let it start killing people while we're hunkered down here. That was a losing battle against Randell and it's a losing tactic this time.*

Then bring me with you, she sent in the same tone. *Teleportation won't slow me down like it would a Lord. I can help.*

I considered it for a moment, then sent a sensation of disagreement. *I'm sorry, Mom, but even your shields won't stand a chance against that type of power. I can't afford to try and keep us both protected. I have to do this alone.*

Dammit, Ikami, I just spent a month dealing with your brother pulling the same kinds of stunts! Don't make me watch my other child run off where I can't help!

Mom, I sent gently, *at some point you have to let us go. We love you. Let that be enough to hold you until I return.*

She withdrew, leaving behind a feeling of hurt. It pained me but I couldn't have given any other answer. We were both cut from the same cloth; I knew with absolute certainty that she would have made the same choice if our positions were reversed. She just needed time to see that.

With that I sent my mind spinning outwards from my body. The massive release of energy was continuing from somewhere far to the west. We weren't far from the ocean, so it had to be coming from one of the other continents. I frowned, recalling back to Mastermage Dural's lessons on trigonometry many years before. A few moments later I teleported several hundred miles to the south, leaving nothing behind me but a flash of light and a tremendous crack echoing through the camp.

Now I could sense the energy from a different angle. It

wasn't appreciably weaker, but I wasn't sure how much I'd be able to sense distance that way. The ongoing release of magic was now slightly northwest. I sent my mind snaking southwards clear to Lord Abel's nation of Seratore and jumped to a small coastal village I knew well, where Cord had sallied forth with Abel several years before to come and find me at the City of the Lords.

The houses built of bamboo and reeds were peaceful, the inhabitants busy on the fishing boats which were the main source of industry here. I'd made sure to bring myself in on the far side of the River Gan, almost half a mile wide here, so as not to disturb anyone unnecessarily. From this point the release of power felt slightly further off, even more to the north and west.

The location puzzled me. When I thought about the directions in which I'd sensed the creature's magic and tried to calculate a location which would intersect all three lines I came up blank. The western continent didn't stretch that far north. There was nothing there but empty ocean stretching for thousands of miles.

Then it struck me. There *was* something in that direction, something quite significant. If I was right, the immense release of power was coming from the island where I'd dropped Randell's remaining unrepentant rebels a couple of months earlier.

It made sense. If our attacker was bent on killing Lords, then on that island he'd find the biggest group outside of those of us at the crater. I took a deep breath and closed my eyes, pulling up as much power as I could. My mind flickered into the soft ground nearby, reaching lower and lower until I sensed a thread of Fuel in the bedrock deep beneath the river. In instants its energy was mine, converted into magical power through my human heritage. Suddenly I was brimming over with vigor. I pulled my mind out of the earth and sent it flying northwest towards my foe.

For three thousand miles I raced across the waters far below. I didn't bother looking at the physical world, instead focusing on any traces of magical power around me. After what felt like an interminable journey the island came up over the horizon and my fears were confirmed - I spotted a blazing beacon of light ahead of me, incredible amounts of magical force pouring into the ground beneath it. It could be nothing other than our alien aggressor.

In a moment's release of energy I teleported my body to catch up with my mind and I was soaring a thousand feet over the ocean waves beneath me. A pillar of black smoke a mile high rose into the air over the island's sole peak, with a glowing spark floating above visible even from this distance.

I sensed no signs of life from the island surface.

The creature seemed focused on total destruction of the land below it. The small island was perhaps five miles across and already the entire surface seemed ablaze. An area which had once been a wide meadow was scoured down to the bedrock, while once-verdant forests were nothing more than blackened trunks giving up the last of their life to the flames which consumed them even now. Nothing could have survived the hellish inferno.

At this point I had no desire to follow what I'd always been taught was the honorable method of battle. I didn't challenge the creature or declare war on it - it had already done that in spades. Instead I shielded my own power as much as possible and crept up behind it, staying away from what I hoped was its face. Risking detection, I readied as much power as I could bring to bear at once. I raised my arm and released a destructive torrent of energy from a hundred yards away, the air giving way before my assault with a shriek and a flare as the very elements of the world were rent asunder under the fury of my attack.

The figure of light was caught completely unaware. Sparks flew from the impact and it was sent spinning, great gouts of flame and energy spewing from its back. My spell was immense, strong enough to break the shields of a dozen Lords at full power.

I didn't give it any chance to recover, following up with

a far more powerful version of the standard attack of a Lord. Instead of a single beam of focused light I summoned forth a twisted skein of energy, no wider than a book. I sharpened it even further down to the thickness of a blade and slammed it home into the creature. Had it been recognizably human or Bladesman I would have struck it right at the base of the skull - an instantly fatal blow.

The figure of light let out a howl of pure anguish as more sparks flew. I nearly sliced the damn thing in half before it managed to get up enough shielding spells to stop my attack. I tore at it with a barrage of energy but nothing further managed to get through its wards.

It twisted to face me properly and reached out as though to gather in sunlight. For a moment darkness washed across my vision, every scrap of solar power drawn into the creature's grasp. The deep rents in its body started to slowly knit together, though the creature was obviously in agony from the effort. Even without facial features I could tell it had been deeply wounded. I slammed more power into its defenses, trying to bring them down and finish the creature off.

My foe refused to go down without fighting. It focused for a moment and sent a bolt of red-hot energy flying at me in return. The spell collided with my wards with an impact like a bolt of lightning, sending me off balance for a moment before I could recover my bearings. My ears rang from the thunderclap and I shook my head to clear it for a moment.

I wrenched a huge stone free from the shore of the island far below, wanting to try a purely physical attack to see if it had any more effect. I used the power of my mind to accelerate it straight up, crashing into the creature's defenses where the boulder broke apart into a hundred shards. My enemy was rattled by the attack but I didn't manage to break any of its spells. In return I was smacked by another gout of flame and had to focus on rebuilding the strength of my own wards for a moment.

We paused and glared at each other, panting, as we hovered a hundred yards apart. Or at least I glared. I could only assume it was giving me the equivalent; its lack of eyes made it difficult to tell. The deep wound in the creature's side oozed liquid light that sputtered out in midair a hundred feet below.

In some ways it was an extraordinary lesson to face something as powerful as I was. By now I was certain that we were almost evenly matched in terms of pure power. I wasn't sure what to do; this was something I'd never had to deal with before.

I sensed the figure of light reaching out with its mind for some new attack. I threw my focus forward, trying to understand its intent, but managed only to get my mental presence directly into its path. Our consciousnesses collided for a moment and the world went sideways.

Whatever this thing was, it didn't think at all like I did. I sensed a similar confusion to my own; at least it wasn't doing any better at making out my thoughts than I was its. Fragments of understanding flew across my mind, most too brief for me to grasp. I grabbed hold of a momentarily clear thought; a familiar-looking figure of darkness was the object of its attention. I yanked out another fragment of meaning from the thrashing thoughts; the dark creature it was looking for had somehow bred, or built, or created the Bladesmen.

Suddenly I realized that the creature thought *I* was that figure, just disguised. It thought that I was the Bladesmen progenitor!

Just as I understood this the creature managed to pull its mind free. An instant later it had vanished with a muted pop, air rushing in to fill the void where it had been a moment before.

I gasped, realizing suddenly just how winded I was from the brief battle. A quick glance showed that there was nothing worth saving on the island below me. I wasn't going to shed any tears over the rebel Lords, but the island had been teeming with wildlife only a short time before. The peaceful creatures living here hadn't deserved this.

From what I'd gathered during my brief foray into the creature's thoughts, the fate of this island was what it had planned for our entire world. If I didn't stop it, I had no question that it would be able to accomplish its goal.

Chapter 43 – History

    I made it back to the portal in a single draining teleport, arriving exhausted from the battle and the journey. It didn't take long to convey what I'd learned to the others; while they were glad the creature had been driven off they were aghast at the fate of the marooned Lords. Many Lords went off to confer while Mom, Cord, Lim, and Haren stayed nearby.

    "*We need to see what we can learn from the human world as soon as possible," Haren fretted. "*Lady Ikami, when do you think you will be able to help another scrying spell?"

    Mom frowned. "*Give her a little rest first -" she began, but I interrupted her before she got too far.

    "*Lord Haren is right, Mom. We need to keep moving on this. I have no idea how long that creature will take before it attacks again, and every moment I'm in the human world we risk that it starts another rampage here. Get Lord Hannon and some Fuel, please, and I'll be ready in a few minutes."

    My brother looked me over with clear concern as the Lords bowed and left. "Are you sure about this, Kami?" he asked in our own language.

    I shrugged. "I don't think we have a lot of choice. That thing wants to kill every Bladesman and human in both worlds. The only lead we have on learning where it came from - and hopefully how to stop it - is to see how humans arrived in their world. If you have a better idea, believe me, I'm all ears."

    He sighed and shook his head. "I wish I did."

We looked at each other helplessly, then Mom gave up and turned away muttering something about her stubborn daughter. Cord gave me a slight smile and headed off just as the three Lords I was waiting for approached from another pathway through the camp. A few moments later we were back in the human world with its strange smells and colors.

Wesnoq happened to be standing nearby talking with Generals Sanato and Teyo. The stately Bladesman Councilor looked more battered than ever after the events of the last month but he was the type who wouldn't lie down while there was work to be done until the day he died. I led my little group over to them, waiting politely until they asked us to join their conversation. Both of the military men gave a sidelong look at Hannon but seemed to accept him based on the help he'd given earlier. I knew that Teyo, long held under the compulsion of the Pact, had to be experiencing internal ambivalence at Hannon's presence. My respect for him only grew as he dealt with Hannon simply and professionally.

"*Good afternoon," Teyo said with a bow to all of us. "*We heard about the attack in the Bladesman world. Are you worried about more strikes here?" he asked politely, instead of asking me point-blank why I wasn't back there protecting the City and our allies.

I shook my head. "*I'm fairly sure that I hit our enemy hard enough that he'll need time to recover. No, we have some reason to believe that we might gain more information by casting some spells here."

"*Then by all means, let us not impede your progress," he replied with a smile. "*Lord Wesnoq was just finishing up here - do you need his help?"

"*It wouldn't hurt," I answered. He was clearly curious about what we planned, and Wesnoq had been one of few Lords who had always treated me respectfully as a peer. Most of the others, especially since my destruction of the City of the Lords, didn't dare get familiar with me.

We moved a short distance away so we wouldn't obstruct the constant traffic moving through the portal then sat down together on a small patch of untrammeled grass. Despite my deep weariness I indicated my readiness to Lord Haren. Wesnoq didn't ask any questions and simply closed his eyes, joining our mental presences a moment later.

As before, Lord Haren led the spell while we others waited to join until we were needed. Before long all five of us were spinning through the centuries, a visual history of the human world flashing by in a blurred confusion. Once we'd gone back approximately ten thousand years Lord Hannon was able to slow the spell and anchor us to a particular moment. The spell was pulling on my reserves, but with the Fuel the others had brought it wasn't too much for the moment. Wesnoq was happy to help support the spell with his own energy as well, although his contribution was by nature far less than what Haren was relying on me to supply.

I think we're a little too far, Hannon sent with a hint of uncertainty. *And we need to go east quite some distance - my research indicates that human culture originated on the other coast.*

Our vision began to fly eastwards, traveling over wide forests and open plains. There was no sign of civilization anywhere. Soon we were in sight of the eastern ocean, its open waters crashing against a rocky beach.

Lady Ikami, can you sense any magic in the vision, as you did in the Bladesman world? Lim queried. I could feel Wesnoq's intense curiosity at this question but he politely held back for now, content to witness what was to come.

Not yet, I replied. *Let's try going forward again, but slowly.*

Time began to flicker by. The ocean waves became impossible to distinguish as night and day blurred into one another. We'd gone forward perhaps fifty years before I felt something prickling at the edge of my consciousness. *Wait,* I signaled.

The Lords in control of the spell slowed our progress down once more. I started giving slight corrections - move us northwards, go forward a little farther, now a little west - until the sense of impending magic was as clear as I could get it. Finally I signaled that we should let the spell proceed at its own speed for a moment. Our perspective was about a hundred feet above the shoreline of a wide lake. Reeds waved slightly in a fitful breeze while tall birds stalked the grasses nearby.

It was only a few minutes later that a light appeared in the air before us. This time the portal appeared much faster, ripping the air open like a wound between worlds. The same battle we'd witnessed previously could be seen in the background. There seemed to be many fewer figures in sight; the conflict was clearly being won by the glowing figures flying to and fro in the distance who were firing indiscriminately at anything on the ground.

A shadowy figure crawled out of the portal, the bottom half of its body completely gone. Shreds of darkness twirled into nothingness behind it as though its remaining form was held together by a tenuous grasp of magic which might fail at any moment. Hundreds of humans leapt through behind it, spilling out from the portal in all directions. They were clearly glad to have escaped the burning hellscape behind them. Many openly wept at the verdant world they'd come to, while others screamed epithets back at their enemies in the other world and wailed over those they must have left behind. Their language was almost understandable, although many of the words had changed over the years from what we knew today.

The portal started to waver and shake. Bolts of lightning arced between its rim and the lake surface nearby, causing the few birds who had stuck around thus far to take wing with loud complaints. A last few humans made it through before the spell collapsed with a falling cloud of sparks.

The dying figure called weakly to its followers and a small cadre stepped up, clearly the leaders of this beaten group. Three were Archmages based on the ability I sensed within them, while the others seemed to have no magical sensitivity at all. The shadowy creature spoke quietly at some length, answering a few questions from the humans. Its dissipation seemed to be accelerating and within minutes it waved the others away. A last few wisps of shadow flew into the air, and then it was gone.

*Go back, Lim ordered. *Let me listen to that again.

The vision froze, then spun backwards and we watched the whole macabre thing again. I could feel Lim's mind focusing closely on the words which were spoken, and he seemed to have some sense of understanding. This time, while the portal was open, I studied it carefully and got a sense of direction from the magical threads trailing off into the distance.

After we'd gone through the scene a third time Lim sent, *I can get bits and pieces of what the creature is saying before it dies. This language was passed down in ancient texts, or at least a little of it. It's telling the humans something about a 'revolution' and to defend themselves. There are clear cautions against enemy Bladesmen following through. He hesitated, then continued, *I'm fairly certain that this creature claims to have created the humans.

*Which would agree with the idea that that other one created the Bladesmen, Haren replied excitedly.

Wesnoq gave a more cautious feeling with his statement. *It does not inspire confidence to think of our races as having been 'created' by something else.

*This is a question many human nations had fought over in the past, based on the histories I put together, Hannon answered. *Did our people not worry about the question of origin on our world?

*There was rarely time for philosophical discussion among the warring nations, Wesnoq replied. *Perhaps in the City of the Lords they had time for such follies.

*No matter what, I interjected firmly, *this tells us quite a bit. We saw the humans and Bladesmen fighting each other, led by their respective figures. We saw the creatures of light driving humans through the portal here. Now we have one of these glowing figures in the Bladesman world. What can we do about it?

The others paused for a moment, thinking over my question. Finally Hannon contributed an answer. *There were others of these glowing things through the portal. Many of them. Do we think the one we are fighting today is the only one left?

*Ten millennia have passed, Lord Lim replied. *We can only hope so.

*Going through the vision several times let me study the portal *closely,* I sent. **If I had enough power... I might be able to open a portal to that world. If it still exists. Perhaps we can get more information there.*

The others gave a mental shudder at the idea. **Wouldn't that just invite more enemies to our world?* Wesnoq asked.

*If one found us, more will someday, I replied stubbornly. **Who knows what we'll find on that world? Both Bladesmen and humans may have come from there. It may be that we can find answers there as to why we're so similar. It may be that we find that the other glowing figures are long gone and we only have this one to deal with.*

*And if we don't? asked Hannon.

*Then we make sure we only send a small group, I snapped back. **No more wholesale invasions with fleets of ships and tens of thousands of soldiers. Look, we have to find out more about this. We can't afford not to.*

*Even if you could get the others to agree, Wesnoq continued, **where would you get the power you need?*

*Simple, I sent. I knew a vicious undertone was leaking in, but right now I didn't care. **We capture that other creature and use its power. Everything we need is right there, we just need to hold it in place. The Lords are already assembled. Together, we can stop this thing and take what we need from it.*

Chapter 44 – Wrath

I knew the others weren't fully persuaded but none could come up with a better option. I contacted the Lords working here in the human world and asked them to join us back on the Bladesman side of the portal. By the next morning I found myself back in the world I'd been born on, addressing the entire known population of Bladesmen Lords. Those from the other three continents had straggled in during the short time since the Portal went back up.

On Dad's advice we'd chosen a bare grassy area not far from camp. I stood a short ways up the hill which masked the crater of the City of the Lords from our view with the others below me in a natural amphitheatre. The assembled power of almost twelve hundred Lords was awe-inspiring; the City of the Lords itself hadn't boasted this many. The mysterious glowing figure would have a hard time dealing with this force even without my presence, and together I was certain that we could put an end to its threat. Many of the Lords seemed impressed by the meeting; nobody could remember any gathering so large without fighting breaking out from age-old rivalries.

Every airship that could be assembled floated nearby, Fuel-tipped bolts loaded in each ballista. Five ships of the line formed a V shape in the air while dozens of skiffs darted around them, their decks covered with soldiers holding explosive arrows. Mom and the other human mages - including Dad and Cord - stood in a small group off to the side. Power sufficient to destroy continents had assembled here. Surely it had to be enough to deal with one enemy. I knew that *I* wouldn't want to face this group alone.

By now everyone had heard my report of the rebels' fate and understood that our only chance was to stand together. My hope was that the creature would respond to an open challenge. Lim had supplied me a few broken words our foe might understand, but I knew that my mental tone would be felt no matter what language I used.

"*Prepare your defenses," I called out, amplifying my voice to reach everyone. The rumble of conversation stopped as every Lord raised their shielding spells high. Half of the assembly coordinated to raise a massively potent ward around the entire group while the other half prepared a spell to snare and capture the creature if it appeared.

Seeing that everyone was ready I slowed my breathing and pulled in as much power as I could hold. I wanted to be prepared as soon as our enemy appeared. When I was fully focused I sent a pulse of mental energy out to draw attention, then fired off a signal strong enough to reverberate around the entire globe.

Ka'lech na Thala-tal, I started. Lim felt reasonably sure that this was a common opening to conversation though he didn't actually know what it meant. The words thrummed through the ether in every direction, only the Lords' defenses keeping everyone present from being overwhelmed by their power. I followed in the human language, letting my frustration and anger from the last month come through. *You want to fight us? We challenge you to face our assembled might.* I continued with a statement in the Bladesman tongue. *We will hunt you to the edges of any world you flee to. If you are here to destroy us, we're all in one place now. Come and get us.* Finally, I sent another statement from Lim that he'd assured me was an insult of some form. *Danivel na tor-Kanit. Chinabi el Van-noth!*

I let my mind sink back into my body, blinking a few times and taking a few breaths to recover. I hadn't held back on the sending, wanting the creature to feel every fragment of my rage. I was relying on its arrogance and could only hope my anger would draw it in. Everyone waited, our eyes and minds searching in all directions for any indication of power. The crater was almost quiet at the moment with much of its energy being pulled off to keep the portal to the human world open.

One minute passed, then another. Lords started to look at each other uncertainly. After five minutes some of them started to mutter to each other. *This isn't working,* I sent to Mom.

Do you have - she began before being interrupted by a blindingly bright light in the sky above us. A crash like thunder announced a massive teleportation. Everyone else blinked furiously, trying to regain their vision. I simply abandoned my body and used my magical senses to see what had arrived.

The glowing figure was there, fully healed from our battle the previous day. It held a giant slab of stone as large as a hill balanced easily on one hand. Our foe looked tiny against the quarter mile long chunk of granite, many times larger than our biggest airships. The massive block blotted out the sun; the figure's innate glow lit the ground beneath starkly.

Its face turned to me, then it raised its arm and simply dropped the entire thing on the assembled Lords before darting out of the way.

LIFT! I cried out mentally. I whipped out the magical power I'd assembled and caught at the falling stone. Untold tons of rock slammed into my spell and I felt my body stagger. I slowed its descent but couldn't quite hold it in place - my mental force hadn't been braced quickly enough. Suddenly I was joined by dozens of Lords and I felt the impossible weight stabilize.

By the time we had it steady the creature was already attacking. It sent hideously strong blasts of power into the assembled Lords over and over. Their combined defenses held it off for the moment but every attack sent shivers through the entire assembly. Sparks and bolts of lightning flew in all directions from the assault. I caught a momentary sense of surprise and frustration from the glowing figure, as though it hadn't expected this level of coordination.

The other Lords and I heaved together and the stone slid backwards over my head to slam down into the crater behind us. It felt like an earthquake; the earth shuddered under the impact and many people lost their footing. As soon as the rock was out of the way the assembled airships had a clear line of sight and began to fire.

Their biggest difficulty was the figure's size. Flying a hundred feet in the air, the creature had no difficulty dodging the first few bolts. They exploded harmlessly on the ground a mile distant, sending puffs of dirt into the air far from their target. After a moment the human mages started steadying the flight of the massive ballista bolts as they'd been trained, guiding them home into the glowing figure.

Three bolts struck at almost the same time. The explosions were brutal, sending shards of light and flame spinning in all directions. Our enemy was caught off guard; I had the feeling it hadn't expected any physical attack to scratch it. The creature let loose an audible howl as it wobbled from the attack, one of its legs nearly detached at the knee. Light seemed to drip out from the injury like blood, fading to nothingness before it struck the ground.

I sent a signal to the Lords to release their readied spells just as the creature decided it had had enough of the airships. It raised one arm and slashed at the *Lord II* a quarter mile distant. I sensed a flicker of invisible magic but nothing seemed to happen for a moment. A second later, my heart caught as the zeppelin exploded into a cloud of wood and cloth. The entire airship was vaporized in an instant. I tried not to think of how many people had been onboard.

I had probably known many of them.

Enraged, I fired a potent bolt of magical force into the figure to get its attention. My attack skidded off the side of its defenses and it turned towards me, releasing its own blast in return. My wards held firm against the assault, a burst of bright blue sparks flying high into the air.

The distraction was enough for the Bladesmen below to

send out their own spell. Five hundred Lords threw threads of magical energy around the creature. At first it didn't even notice, individual strands of magic burning into ash as they touched its defenses. After a few seconds there were dozens, then hundreds. It started to lash outwards, breaking ten strands at a time and leaving the Lords staggering in pain as their spells were sundered, but the others piled on faster than it could tear free. The figure tried to strike here and there at the Lords to draw the attack away but their defenses - reinforced with additional shielding from Mom and the other human mages - barely wavered.

    I threw my own power upwards, twining an immensely potent thread around the figure in both the magical realm and the physical world. A mental burst of power yanked it tight while the other Lords kept piling spell after spell onto it. The glowing creature's struggles were getting weaker as we wrapped it firmly in layer after layer.

    As it stopped attacking, trying only to burn away the magical bonds we'd wrapped around it, I sent my mind up to meet it. The creature refused to let my presence in but despite its mental walls I sensed astonishment and disgust. I had no means to force my way into its mind despite how much I would have loved to learn what this creature knew and where it had come from. At that moment I had no care what the cost would be; I just wanted to cause it pain after watching it so casually kill so many.

    Frustrated, I grasped hold of its spirit and started wrenching at its power. The creature fought with me in a mental duel the likes of which I'd never experienced. Had it been free there would have been no way I could have pulled at it like this but its efforts were hampered by the hundreds of magical threads holding it in place. I felt its mind darting outwards for a moment, trying to teleport away, but I sent a stunning blast of mental force into the creature and forced it back into its body.

    A moment later I started to tap into its energy. Its reservoirs were immense, noticeably deeper than my own. The flavor of its magic was somehow both Bladesman and human at the same time, with many unfamiliar sensations mixed together.

As soon as I'd fought my way in and opened a path to the energy it held within itself, that power started pouring outwards. It was a raging torrent, a waterfall that I could only catch with a single bucket. The Lords behind me grabbed onto drops here and there where they could but much of it was lost into the world around us. I gritted my teeth and held close, trying to direct as much as I could into the portal. It would store it up like a battery for as long as I needed it to.

Be careful, Kami, Cord sent, exhausted, as he watched what I was doing. *There's too much there, even for you.*

I couldn't spare the concentration to reply to him and only sent a sense of understanding. As I grew more accustomed to the creature's power I was able to siphon more of it off, much like I'd used the power in the crater to build the portal in the first place. I put all of my focus into keeping the flow open. In minutes I had funneled more energy into the portal than I could have gathered in a year.

I realized my attention had wandered too far just as the creature gave a sense of triumph and vanished. The Lords' spells broke asunder as its presence disappeared. It hadn't teleported out in the way we were used to, but used some other method of transport to go much further - without question it had left this world far behind.

My mind slipped back to my body and I looked around myself, dazed by the experience. Many Lords were moaning in pain and several lay lifeless on the ground - our enemy had slain them during the struggle with one of its attacks that I hadn't even noticed.

I received a sudden call from Lord Wesnoq, circumventing the usual protocol for allowing someone to politely accept or reject a mental communication. *Be alert,* he warned me with a sharp tinge of fear. *Some of the Lords are-*

My ally was suddenly cut off and I couldn't tell why. I raised my wards as high as I could, trusting his words implicitly.

My wits were returning slowly, too slowly, and alarms were ringing in my skull that I was missing something.

A moment later bursts of light flickered among the Lords below. Deadly green beams sliced among a dozen Lords and half of them fell to the ground as their defensive spells broke. Wisps of smoke rose from burned bodies as voices called out in shock, a moment too late to do anything.

We dealt with it, Mom sent a moment later with a sense of satisfaction just as Lord Wesnoq spoke in a forbidding tone.

"*Do you fools not know what you are doing?" he cried out. "*For those who are not aware - and there are few enough of those - some of our fellows here had decided to attack the Lady Ikami while she was recovering from the battle. They tried to take advantage of the situation. Do you not see that she defended us - all of us! - against an outside force?"

He took a deep breath, his face red with anger. "*We Lords are strong, and we are stronger together than apart. None would dispute this. But the old days are done. They will never return, and good riddance." Wesnoq turned to me and continued. "*Lady Ikami, please know that while several Lords wanted to combine our force to destroy you, more than half of the assembled Lords defended you while you were focused on our enemy."

I suddenly realized what had just happened. The Lords here had felt their strength and those who still regretted the new way of life had tried to convince the others to attack me. Had they done so while I was distracted they likely would have killed me before I could have stopped them. This gathering of power was too strong for even me.

Wesnoq wouldn't lie, though. If hundreds of Lords were willing to stick with me and fight on my side, we were doing better than I had thought in bringing them around to the ways of the City. I released my breath and bowed, sending a wave of thanks to all those who had held firm. "*The creature is gone from this world, now," I called out to the group below. "*But there may be others out there and this one may return when it has regathered its power. We have to work together against our common foes. I could not have stopped that thing alone - and neither could you Lords. Only while unified can we defend both worlds."

Nice speech, sis, Cord sent. I could almost see him grinning at me.

Shut up, I replied with a sense of exasperation. *You're distracting me.*

"*Tomorrow I plan to journey to what may be the home of both of our races - and our enemy. With luck we will find a key to defeating them forever. Until I return, I ask that you guard the portals and keep them safe from interference. Many have died here today and we cannot forget their sacrifice. Together, we can prevail!"

The speech felt pithy to me, even ridiculous, but cheering erupted from around me. I'd found a way to unite the proud, fractious Lords on a common cause. If only it hadn't taken an enemy to do so, I thought to myself, but in this case I would take what I could.

Chapter 45 – Destinations

I slept deeply that night, better than I had expected. The next morning arrived with a sense of purpose keener than any I'd ever felt. The time had arrived when I might have a way to learn how my two parent races were connected. It had taken years of effort and the deaths of many I cared deeply for but the day had finally come.

For this journey I gathered those I trusted most. We met near the portal to the human world shortly after dawn and I looked around at these, my closest friends. Uncle Ather was there, of course, along with Mom and Cord. Dad would have come if I had asked, but I knew that despite how much he hated to see us leave again he had too much to do here. The people of both worlds needed him as Head Councilor more than I needed him as a mage.

Lords Lim and Haren were there as well. Haren was shivering absently, having forgotten to put a warming spell around himself. A moment later Lim looked over and built one for him with a slight smile. I might have asked Hannon to join us for his unique viewpoint but he was already back in the human world working hard to atone for the sins of the Pact after so many years. Lord Wesnoq was coming with us; I'd always felt close to him after our training sessions back in his home nation of Illonye when I'd journeyed to the City of the Lords. It felt like a long time ago now, and I'd made good use of the wisdom he'd collected for more than a century.

We were taking a skiff through to the other world and old Gregor would serve as pilot for us. He was well past sixty by now, his hair thin and gray, but I wouldn't have had anyone else guide my way. His mind was still sharp and his arm strong from years of steering the airships that had been born from his innovative imagination.

Last but far from least my brother's woman was coming with us. I still knew Dalt less than I would like but I expected that soon I'd be calling her sister-in-law. She was good for Cord and had a cunning eye from her days fighting against a cruel Lord. Anyone who could outwit one of them for years at a time without any magic was all right by my book.

"You know," Cord remarked as we waited on board the skiff for everyone else to climb up the sides, "we've got everyone here. Think about it - a Bladesman commoner, several Lords, and humans of all varieties - Archmages, a regular mage, and, well, Gregor." He grinned. "It's quite a collection."

"I hadn't thought about that," I mused. "Perhaps it'll bring us luck."

A few minutes later everyone was on deck looking at me expectantly. I cleared my throat and started speaking in the Bladesman tongue for the benefit of Haren and Lim - most everyone else understood the human language well enough to get by. "*Good morning. Thanks - all of you - for coming with me. I'm not at all sure what's going to happen here but... well, I can't think of a finer group to journey into the unknown with."

Gregor leaned forward and slapped my back with a wide grin. "No problem, girlie," he replied in his own tongue. Lim and Haren looked a little shocked that he would treat me so familiarly but I just smiled back to the grizzled old engineer. I knew him almost as well as I knew Ather.

"*I'm going to open a portal to... well, somewhere. Ten thousand years ago that entire world was burning. Now? I have no idea. If some of the glowing figures show up, get the hell out of there as fast as you can and I'll collapse the portal behind us. Otherwise we'll look for clues as to why these things are trying to kill us. Okay?"

Nobody had any questions, which meant it was time for me to bring about the spell I was uniquely capable of constructing. I took a deep breath and reached my mind out towards the portal to the human world. Right now it was bursting with energy, enough to keep it open for scores of years even if the ruins of the City of the Lords suddenly stopped generating power. I tapped into the fresh reserves and sent my mind spinning outwards, following the threads I'd sensed while viewing the past from both the human world and this one.

It was different from the previous times I'd tried to cross the gulf between worlds. This time it felt as though there was already a path laid to my destination, an ancient gateway that was just waiting for a little bit of power - and a certain type of talent - to reawaken it. Before I knew it I had reached my destination, the great void already behind me with its impossible distances and inky blackness. I couldn't make much out from here, save that it didn't feel like it was still burning.

I twisted the power I'd captured into a new portal not far from the old one, anchoring it to the strange place I'd found. I had no doubt that this location was close to where the battles we'd seen in the past had ended. Watching the shadowy figures build their portals had given me some new ideas and I constructed this one in a way which should make it more resistant to attempts to shut it down by anyone other than me. I hoped that's what I was doing, anyways, but it certainly felt stable enough when I was done.

By the time I'd returned to my body and opened my eyes Gregor already had the skiff accelerating towards the rift a short distance away. Air was audibly hissing through it though I couldn't tell in what direction. The military forces here had been warned to stay well away from this one and four trustworthy Lords would watch it and make sure nothing tried to get through from either side without their recognition. I held firmly to the wooden railing as the airship sped up, the wind rushing past my ears as the rift grew in size.

A moment later we passed into it.

The feeling of disorientation was smoother this time as though the portal were welcoming us in. Perhaps I simply imagined it but the journey seemed quicker too. We emerged in an instant, the skiff nosing forward into a foreign world.

The first thing we all noticed was the air. It seemed suddenly dry and terribly thin. Everyone started coughing at once, gasping as though there wasn't enough atmosphere to take a good breath. I struggled for a moment, then spun my mind back through the portal and encapsulated a huge bubble of air. Crossing through a portal with my focus like that was perilous, but I had no choice. In seconds I'd brought the breathable atmosphere from home back through and surrounded the airship, keeping it in place with a thin wall of force.

"Thanks," Cord gasped, his face returning to its normal color. Now that we could breathe properly I had a chance to look around and examine the place I'd brought us so far to see.

I was greeted with an endless vista of gray and black. Barren stone lay in every direction. Gray hills of bare shale lay ahead of us, while black gravel coated the ground directly below. Dark dunes lay off to the side, composed of sand so fine as to more properly be termed dust. The sky was a dull reddish color and a thin haze kept us from seeing the source of the light. If this world had a sun it couldn't penetrate the dust clouds above us.

Nobody spoke for some time. The only sound was a whistling wind blowing fitfully past our ears and the slow thump of the engine running beneath us at low speed.

Finally Dalt broke the silence. "*What happened here?" she whispered.

"Hell," Mom answered quietly, not thinking to speak in the Bladesman language. "This entire world... it's been burned to ash. There's nothing left."

"*This is what comes of unrestrained power and war," Wesnoq said in a low tone. "*This... this is what our world would have come to in time if the City of the Lords had not been removed."

"Anywhere in particular you want to go?" Gregor asked, not bothering to hush his voice. It sounded stark and grating in this place. Lim and Haren frowned at him but didn't say anything. I looked around helplessly - no direction seemed better than any other.

"Give me a moment, dear," Mom said, laying her hand on mine where it gripped the railing. She closed her eyes and I felt her mind spinning forward, darting off into the distance. A moment later the Lords did the same, each searching in a different direction. I kept my mind in my body, trusting them to do their job while I made sure the skiff was kept safe.

A few minutes passed. Gregor and Dalt were clearly cold so I lent them a bit of magical warmth. It didn't seem to stop them from shivering no matter how much power I put into it. We stayed in a hover not far from the portal, ready to turn around and dart back through if needed - but nothing showed up. After some time Mom opened her eyes and spoke. "I think I found something. Head towards the hills ahead of us." As the airship started to move forward the others returned to their bodies and shook their heads one by one, indicating that they hadn't found anything of interest in their searches.

We pushed on, Mom calling out directions to Gregor. He didn't dare push the engines to full speed; he said that they were sucking in a lot of dust as it was and it was keeping their temperatures higher than he would like. It felt like we were creeping over this desolate place at a slow crawl though I knew we were still moving three times faster than anyone could run.

The countryside moved smoothly below us for perhaps an hour while we traveled. It was hard to tell the passage of time here; the light seemed to come from all directions equally in the ever-present haze. Eventually we drew near to the slate hills and Mom slowed us down. She looked closely at the ground below until finally she called out excitedly and pointed to a particular section of crumbled stone.

"I don't see anything there," I said, puzzled.

"No, I see it too!" Cord replied. "Look - some of the stones are regular. That can't be natural!"

Sure enough now that he'd pointed it out I could see what Mom had brought us to. Some of the stone looked like it had been shaped, though it had been weathered to such an extent that it was hard to tell it apart from the surrounding shale. "Take us down, please," I asked Gregor.

Within five minutes we were all standing on the ground where Gregor had found a solid place to set the skiff. I expanded the bubble of atmosphere and carried it with us as we disembarked. We walked up to the regularly shaped stones a few hundred yards away. Ather stepped forward a few more paces then stopped, a curious expression on his face. "Listen," he called to us before stomping his foot.

The slate sounded hollow. There was a void beneath us.

"*Lady Ikami? Can you clear a passage through?" Haren asked, clearly excited. I nodded and asked everyone to step back. After a moment's focus I could clearly sense what Ather had found - a square emptiness, clearly unnatural. I pulled on my innate power, twisted some around the slate, and triggered a teleportation spell to move it a hundred yards behind us.

It didn't budge.

I frowned and tried again, pushing harder this time. For a moment I could feel it resist me, then with a protesting squeal the slab of stone moved - but not nearly so far as I'd intended. It reappeared only a few feet behind us, popping into view with a flash of light and a loud *whomp* sound. A gust of air and dust pushed into us as it fell onto the gravel.

"*Be careful with your spells, everyone," I said loudly. "*Something's not right with magic here."

"*It's been used up, I think," Wesnoq replied. "*I was sensing it earlier. This entire world - it feels as though every scrap of power was wrested out of it. These wisps that we feel now... I think they're what has come back in the last ten thousand years."

"*Can you imagine what it was like at the worst?" Mom asked, visibly shuddering. "*There must have been no power at all available. Only the strongest could have done anything."

At least I know why Dalt and Gregor kept shivering

when I tried to warm them, I thought to myself. The damn spell didn't work.

Haren had, with some effort, built a dim light to float alongside him. He was looking down into the dusty hole I'd uncovered, waving to us to join him. We obliged, lining up at the edge and looking into a room that must have been covered for millennia. It was walled with exposed stone although lines of white powder along the walls indicated that at some distant point in the past there must have been some other surface present. Anything that had once been inside had long since settled into dust, small piles of gray and black the only indications of anything at all.

"*Why don't we try scrying into the past here?" Lim asked, raising an eyebrow. "*Think of what we could learn!"

Ather shook his head. "*How much energy it would it take to go back even a hundred years? It would be too dangerous, I think, and we all need to be on our guard. I would recommend that we try other means first."

"*Something's shining," Haren pointed out. Indeed, a tiny metallic glimmer gave proof that despite the best efforts of time some remnant of civilization had survived. I reached out with a tendril of energy and carefully pulled on whatever it was. A few moments later we were all clustered around the shiny chrome plate I'd brought up. It was covered in spidery writing, each character no more than a tenth of an inch tall. Haren and Lim pored over it, arguing over certain words and meanings.

"*Do you understand it at all?" I asked.

"*Yes!" they replied in unison, one voice high and one low.

"*Well, somewhat," Haren amended. "*This is the same language as I've found in our most ancient records. I confess that our command of it is... imperfect... but we will do what we can."

"*I will try to translate as we go through," Lord Lim continued. "*Let me begin. I will extrapolate where I need to, if I do not comprehend some meaning."

He cleared his throat and began to recite off the tablet.

"*I find myself locked away in this pit, unable to escape with the others who are fleeing nearby. I do not know if anyone will ever read this, but the world above burns and I can do nothing else than write down what I know. Nothing remains intact except stone and metal, so that is what I use for this last pathetic message.

"*We rebels are losing. The others ordered that we stay here, on this world, and wait for another race to grow in power so that they may become our peers. But we have found no other races in all our searching and so we gave up. There are no traces of intelligent life in all the universe save for us, and we could not bear to be alone.

"*So half of us rebelled against the edict. From our own people we created new creatures, at first to join us as equals but soon we found that they could not equal our abilities. They were made servants, pawns, and before long the newer races were being bred for battle. Those who hewed to the old ways attacked the new races, trying to wipe them out and censuring those who had created them. We refused to stop and thus began our war.

"*We might have won if we had fought alongside one another. But rifts appeared in our own ranks. Soon we were creating races to fight not only the others but ourselves. Dozens have been created that I know of, likely with scores more I have no contact with or which have already been destroyed." Lim paused for a moment, scanning, then nodded. "*Many strange names are listed here. Both Bladesmen and humans are described, let me skip ahead to those... Yes, here.

"*Another race has natural weaponry built from the bone of their arms and legs. They are to have a ruling caste, which can command magic, to lead the others in battle. Their creator has a long-standing feud with another, who built a separate race named humans. These creatures spread their magical abilities around more evenly but are just as skilled at war. The two races..." Lord Lim paused for a moment, his already gaunt face turning stark white. He continued in a shaking voice. "*The two races were created specifically to destroy one another alongside their patrons and finally gain an upper hand between the two rivals."

"So it's true," I whispered to no one in particular, suddenly recognizing just who and what I was. "We were created from the same source... and destined to battle one another to the end. Our races were never meant to join together in harmony. And that... that means I am an accident."

"Kami - don't say that," Cord replied quickly. "You've done more to bring peace to both worlds in two years than anything that had been accomplished in all of history beforehand. I'd say that's a pretty good track record."

I glanced at Mom to see her gazing at me with tears in her eyes. For a long moment we shared a look. At that moment I could see that she hurt for me, that despite all of the pain I'd caused her during my long childhood she was my mother and that was all that mattered. The memory of her own trauma - the agony of my birth - was completely and finally gone, diluted by time and her love of me to a distant memory.

Chapter 46 – Answers

It was a shock; I'd only seen her cry a handful of times in my life. We didn't need a mental link for me to know that she was thinking of my origin and my biological father, a Bladesman she'd never actually met. It reminded me that although I might be something unique, there were many who loved me and didn't give a damn where I came from. Right here, I was surrounded by my friends and family. It changed me in an instant, the realization that nobody there was fearful of me and they all cared for me as a person, not just an object of power.

I reached out my arm and took my mother's hand, smiling at her to show that once and for all I wasn't afraid of who I was. She and Dad were the only parents I needed to know. In that moment all of the slights and jealousy that had come between us over the years were healed and forgiven. Here on this barren world of ash and dust we had finally found common ground.

Ather and Cord were the only ones who really understood what had just passed between Mom and I. Both gave a solemn nod to acknowledge it while the others looked on with puzzlement. I just smiled and waved to Lord Lim to continue with his recital of the tablet. He cleared his throat and moved on after one last glance to make sure I was all right.

"*There are many other descriptions of what they term 'lesser races' but I do not recognize any of them. After those...

yes, here we are.

"*The battles have continued for years. Many of us have been slain and only a few are left. Our enemies have transformed themselves into beings of pure energy so as to continue their battle against us, but I fear they do not recognize the consequences of this. Many of our side have changed their own forms as well. There are almost none left of our original selves. We have truly destroyed our own race with this war, no matter who comes out on top.

"*Now the entire world is on fire. Some of us have tried to escape to fallow worlds we know of. I could not make it in time to join any of them. Outside I sense the entire planet consumed by battle. Every bit of magic is being torn out of the land to fuel these wars and soon there will not be enough for me to survive. I will perish before long, leaving behind only this record that none will ever read.

"*The world is ended, the world is ended. Death will take us all and there will be none to continue our works. The universe will be emptied and it is all our doing."

Lord Lim had reached the bottom of the plaque. He shrugged - there was nothing left. The Bladesman flipped it over idly only to spy more writing on the back, albeit much more ragged and clearly in a different hand.

"*I cannot make out many of these words," he said after a moment's study. "*It looks like the tablet was encountered some time later and added to by one of the victors - presumably those who had fought against the creation of the new races. It states... something about enduring wrath against their foes who escaped?"

Haren leaned inwards and nodded. "*I believe you are correct. This phrase here - I think it says that they will track down every race which was created and bring them... to extinction? To destruction?"

Gregor frowned and spoke in badly accented Bladesman. "*It's the same damn ending either way. I don't think the exact word matters so much. The glowing bastards - they want to kill us all because they think we're leftovers from this ancient war of theirs." He spat onto the dry earth, indicating what he thought of that.

Lord Lim looked closely at the last few words. "*Here - it ends by stating that these races which were created for battle will die in violence 'like what they were made for'." He glanced up. "*That's it. That's all there is."

We looked at each other gravely. At least now we knew what we were dealing with.

"*To carry a grudge for ten thousand years... they are singleminded indeed," Dalt said with a sigh. "*Is there no way to convince them that we want nothing but peace?"

I laughed bitterly. "*The one I made contact with... well, I don't think it was very interested in listening to us. They believe we need to be eliminated from the universe and will stop at nothing to do so. Hell, they didn't want us to be around in the first place - they probably just think of it as cleaning up the trash."

"*I'm not sure there is much more for us on this world, Lady Ikami," Wesnoq said after a moment's hesitation. "*Should we return to our own? At least we can defend ourselves somewhat there."

I nodded, kicking at the gravel idly. He was right. There was nothing here that would help when the glowing figures came back - and now we knew that they were certain to do so.

We walked back towards the skiff slowly. I let the others go on ahead, looking over my shoulder at the empty room one more time. Something kept itching at the back of my mind that I couldn't quite understand.

"*They're coming!" Dalt shouted suddenly, pointing far into the distance. A glint of light betrayed the presence of one of our enemies and my stomach dropped as though I'd been punched. With a shock I realized that the itch I'd been feeling was the sensation of strong magic headed this way. Everyone realized at the same time that we were too far from the skiff to climb on board in time. I called out for everyone to pull back and cluster up around me.

"*There's another," Ather said quietly, pointing in a

different direction. It was recognizable as a glowing figure speeding towards us at great velocity. I turned in a circle and spotted an even dozen.

We were trapped.

"*I'll sue for parlay," I said quietly. Everyone knew it was a lost cause and those of us with magic started pulling what bits they could into themselves. Mom cursed that she hadn't brought a bucketload of Fuel with her, but she sapped what she could from the skiff's engines leaving it with a dangerously low supply. She would be the only one with anything near her usual reserves of strength.

I raised myself up into the air to meet the oncoming foes on an equal footing. When one had come close enough I sent my mind out and tried to present myself for open communication.

I was brushed aside. The only response was a mental slap that sent me spinning.

By the time I'd returned to my body an incoming blast had already splintered my shields. It was a less powerful attack than I'd faced on the Bladesman world but my defenses were similarly weaker due to the lack of available power here. Two more glowing figures arrived a moment later and joined in the assault. I sent out a blanket plea for peace to no response.

Their onslaught smashed my defenses to shreds. Sparks flew in all directions and I cried out involuntarily as my wards shattered. I'd barely been a match for one before; three were too much for me. I dove for the ground as a last desperate measure to avoid a final blow that might very well have killed me.

A few other figures had drawn close enough to attack and sent spells flying into the others. Mom raised a glowing blue shield that caught the attack and barely deflected it. Almost all of her extra energy from the Fuel was used up stopping that one barrage and I knew she couldn't hold out against another.

Two more spells came in and we were sent flying. I saw Haren thrown behind me, screaming, his leg on fire. I fell face first into the gravel and only my inherently tough skin kept my face from being grated apart. An immense pressure held me down so that I couldn't rise; the best I could manage was to twist my neck to see what had become of my comrades.

What I witnessed filled me with despair. Lim was crawling across the broken shale, his back bleeding profusely from a hideous open wound. Wesnoq was prone and unmoving; whether unconscious or dead I couldn't tell from my position. Ather, Mom, and Cord were hunkered down under a shield that the three of them were trying valiantly to keep up. Dalt was standing helplessly next to Cord, her fists clenched. Gregor was nowhere to be seen.

One more bolt of blazing red power slammed in and both Mom and Ather fell to the ground. Cord went down to his knees, unable to keep the shield up on his own. I tried to scrape up enough power to escape the spell holding me pinned but there simply wasn't enough around for me to do anything. I called out wordlessly to my family to no avail. A moment later my brother fell backwards, senseless, as his final defenses were wrenched apart by our attackers. We had been defeated in seconds, barely even putting up a fight.

The dozen glowing figures hovered above us, their light shining brighter than the sky. They looked down, pitiless, and started pulling in power for one final attack to obliterate us all. One descended slowly and held its arm out towards Cord, ready to blast him into dust. I screamed, trying to reach out towards him, but there was absolutely nothing I could do. It was like my worst nightmare had come true.

Dalt stepped between Cord and the figure, raising her arm blades in defiance and growling out a challenge. The sheer ridiculousness of the act seemed to confound the creature. She had no magical power, no defenses against the pending attack whatsoever. I sensed it reaching out with its mind carefully, trying to detect some trick, but there was nothing to be found. Dalt was simply unwilling to let her lover die. She screamed out a wordless insult and crouched down as though to jump up and strike, never mind that her enemy was a dozen yards above ground.

The creature seemed completely mystified by what it faced. It must have suddenly realized what was below. Here was a Bladesman - a powerless commoner, no less - defending a human mage. If what we'd just learned was true this would be a situation they'd never expect to encounter.

Another figure floated down next to the first and I felt the two conversing. A moment later I recognized a fading scar of darkness around the new one's waist with a fresher line across one leg. It was the foe we had fought earlier, the one which had barely escaped the combined efforts of all of the Lords on their homeworld. It cocked its head, then suddenly reached out with its mind and sent a clear question to Dalt. It must have picked up the Bladesman language from my mind just as I'd stolen some part of its intent.

You stand to defend your mortal enemy. Why?

Dalt didn't seem to know how to respond. She'd never felt mind to mind contact, I realized. I had no idea how to make contact with someone who had no magical talents; the creature was using some mechanism that was beyond my experience. She blinked a few times, then answered verbally. "*I love him. The only way you will kill him is if you go through me first. Now either get down here where I can fight you or get it over with - but I'm not stepping aside."

The figures conversed among themselves again, and then once more the interpreter sent a message. *I have now seen your races working together twice. Yet the progenitor of your race is here beside you and some of the non-bladed ones still live. Has she captured them? Are both these races now slaved to her?*

I am not the one you seek, I shot back. *I am born of the union of both races. Those who created us are long since turned to dust - we are not responsible for their sins.*

My response sent obvious consternation among the creatures. Before long I felt their minds examining me closely, studying and probing me with magic in ways that felt deeply uncomfortable. There was nothing I could do but endure it until it ended.

It matters not, the figure finally replied. *We are here to cleanse the universe of the lesser races. Your two are the last to be removed.*

Wait! I sent. *Can you not see the evidence that our races are no longer warlike against one another? We have come to peace despite our origins. Our entire races have changed. Can you not do the same as we? And am I not proof that we might rise to join you as peers?*

This last statement clearly shocked them. Lightning-fast communication raced among the creatures for some time. I could barely breathe from the pressure on my back but fought to remain conscious, aware that the fate of both my parent races was being decided right here.

I had a sudden hunch based on Lim's earlier translation. I closed my eyes and used every scrap of power I had remaining to scan as far and wide as I could. No matter where I looked, I couldn't see any sign of more of the glowing figures. I decided to gamble and sent one more message to them.

You are all that's left, aren't you? When you became what you are now you lost the ability to reproduce. If you destroy our races, you will forever be the only ones to inhabit this world or any other. I hesitated, then continued, *I can join you, and in time others of the two races will do so as well. Do not give up on your only chance for companionship. You do not need to be alone anymore!*

The glowing figures paused and conferenced together one final time. My entire body tingled, not knowing if my next moments would be my last. Finally they spoke once more.

Never again did we expect to meet one like us. Your existence gives us hope - hope we have not felt in a very long time. These races will be watched for as long as it takes. Know that we have not lifted your sentence - but for now, it will be suspended.

Should your races once again come to battle we will know our hopes were for naught and you will be destroyed.

Should more like you come to pass, peacefully, then we will know equals for the first time in ten thousand years and more.

With that final statement, all twelve vanished in bursts of light and muffled pops.

Chapter 47 – Fate

I gasped as the hideous weight on my back was lifted. I'd come close to blacking out, fighting with everything I had just to stay conscious. Groaning, I climbed up to my hands and knees and slowly levered myself upright.

"*Is everyone there?" I called out, my voice sounding thin and hollow. I looked around - Dalt was crouched over Cord, clearly worried, while Mom and Ather were picking themselves up out of the gravel. Wesnoq was still motionless. Haren was about twenty yards away, moaning, and I couldn't see Lim or Gregor.

I staggered over to Lord Haren. He was clutching at his leg and for a moment my chest seized up. Shockingly white bone was visible through the charred flesh of his calf. The blast that had sent him flying had at least cauterized his wounds, the rational part of my mind mused, while the rest of my thoughts shuddered at the horrific injury.

"*Can't see right," Haren said, clearly dazed. "*Leg still there?"

"*It looks bad," I said slowly. I reached forward with the few scraps of power I could muster and infused his head with some extra energy. It wasn't much, and I'd never been a good healer, but it was just enough to help clear the fog from his eyes. He gasped with pain as clarity returned to his face, but nodded to show that he was in control of himself.

"*I'll... I'll do something about it," he said, gritting his teeth. "*Find Lim?"

I nodded and stepped away. It was suddenly clear from the concern in his eyes that the two of them were a couple. I didn't know how I'd never recognized it, but it suddenly made sense why both of them spent so little time in their home nations, preferring to research together at the City or in Illonye. I could only hope that Lim had made it through - I'd hate to have to break Haren's heart. I looked around, trying to find the missing Lord, but could see no sign of him.

Instead I made my way over to Wesnoq. I couldn't see any obvious injuries but he was barely breathing. Something was seriously wrong inside of him. "*Uncle Ather!" I called out, waving him over to me. He'd just gotten back to his feet and came running as quickly as he could. "*Wesnoq - he needs help," I said. Ather nodded and closed his eyes, falling to his knees as he looked into his fellow Lord's body.

Shaking my head side to side to try and clear the residual confusion from my thoughts I staggered to and fro looking aimlessly for Lim or Gregor. After a few moments I got angry at myself. What was I doing looking with only my physical senses? I closed my eyes and sent my mind outwards, detecting Lim a moment later. He'd been thrown beyond the airship. A minute later I was standing over his unconscious body, looking at the terrible wounds on his lower back.

A moment's investigation showed me that while the tall Lord had survived the impact his spinal cord had been completely severed right at the waist. I shuddered when I detected the broken shards that were all that remained of his pelvis. Carefully floating him on a cushion of air I returned to the others where they had gathered around Haren. Wesnoq was awake and standing, clutching his side.

"*Lim!" Haren cried out, trying to stand up. Mom caught him as his leg collapsed, sitting him back down and telling him softly to stay put. "*Lim, can you hear me?"

I passed the hideously wounded Lord over to Ather, shaking my head when he met my eyes. Cord was leaning against Dalt, her arm around his shoulders. I gathered them both up in a hug, then turned to Dalt and whispered, "*You saved us, you know."

She had time to look surprised before I pulled away. I left the others to deal with the injured and sent my mind out looking for Gregor again. I was starting to feel fear that I couldn't detect the spark of his life anywhere nearby. Gathering what power I could, I floated into the air to get a better look.

Before long I found the man who had saved the City with his invention of the airships many years before. Gregor's body lay peacefully at the bottom of the chamber where it had been thrown, looking for all the world as though he'd laid down for a nap. I settled down next to him and laid my head on his chest, but my fears were confirmed when I could detect no heartbeat. The greatest engineer of our times was dead.

It took us almost an hour before we managed to get everyone on board the skiff. Ather hadn't dared move Lim and Haren before he and Wesnoq could perform as much healing as possible here. I lent them my power; it regenerated in this barren world faster than either of theirs. Lim would never walk again, while Haren's leg was unlikely to ever fully heal. The others would be all right, although Ather confided to me that it had been a near thing with Lord Wesnoq - an artery in his brain was torn in the attack and only quick magical healing had saved his life.

Gregor's body was carefully laid out near the prow of the skiff and wrapped up in a spare sail. Cord shed the most tears although Mom and Ather both wiped a few away. The others hadn't known him well though they accorded him full honors. My brother took charge of the skiff and got us moving back towards the portal home.

It was a long, painful trek. After Gregor's worries on the way out, Cord didn't dare run the engine at more than half speed. Even then it choked a few times, almost dying out before it managed to recover. I didn't know what we would have done if it had completely failed - Gregor was the only one who could have fixed it. Eventually, the rift back home came into view and we limped our way through it to the other side.

I knew I'd feel differently someday, but in that moment of transition I hoped this would be the last view I ever had of the pitiless black void between worlds.

Returning to the Bladesman homeworld - my homeworld - was like coming back to spring after a long dark winter. A profusion of color struck our eyes, the violet sky standing starkly against the pale brown grasses of the steppes. The twilight air felt impossibly fresh and the sudden influx of magical power was invigorating in a way impossible to describe to anyone without sensitivity. The tightness across my chest, in place since I'd been crushed against the sandy ground, finally gave way to relief.

Cord advised that we gather the Generals and the Council first to tell them of what had come to pass. We left Lim, Haren, and Gregor's body in the care of the camp medics while the others assembled. Mom and Ather gave a quick briefing of what had happened; I stood silently nearby, bereft of words by the events of the day. After only half an hour we determined to address the Council and the Lords together on the morrow and adjourned, everyone going to their own tents to be with their own thoughts for the night. I was jealous of Cord and Dalt's companionship, curling up around myself until I could fall asleep late in the evening.

By the next morning I'd brought everyone back home to the City where we gathered in the plaza before the Council building, still under repairs from Randell's attack. It felt like a lifetime ago. My spirits had recovered overnight after much soul-searching. We had crossed a threshold, though the price had been hideously high. Both Bladesmen and humans now knew their place in the universe and had a direction to travel towards. Never again would petty wars be fought over such questions as whether one race was better than the other.

I stood there in the center of the City where I'd grown up, this place built by humans that was now the political center of the Bladesman world. Both parts of my dual heritage were in evidence in the faces before me. Dad had his good arm around Mom's shoulders, hugging her tight, while Uncle Ather and

Cord were deep in discussion next to Dalt. Lord Wesnoq talked to Nina, another engineer who had worked on the original airship design, and the tears on her face were clear evidence of the subject of their conversation. Lords and Councilors stood everywhere around me talking peacefully; not a single voice was raised in anger or rang with tones of battle and conflict.

The scene was far from the fractious meeting that I'd led after the City of the Lords was destroyed two years ago. On that occasion the assembled Lords of the continent had split on whether to keep fighting each other and the City or bow to my orders and put down their arms for the greater good of all. In that short time the ways of the retired Lords had been thrown aside. Bladesmen commoners had a say in their own fates all across the four continents of this world. The same was now true of the commoners on what had once been the human world.

I glanced over to where Lord Hannon was talking animatedly with a group of Lords who served as ambassadors from their home nations here in the City. A human Councilor was nodding vigorously, and while the newcomer wasn't exactly rubbing shoulders with the Councilor he wasn't shying away from conversation with one of his longtime racial enemies either. By now I was sure that he'd fit in well here within just a few years. The sins of his past would never be forgotten, but he had already proven that he sought redemption for them.

Just then the dull reddish sun cleared the top of the Council building, sending rays of light to illuminate the plaza directly. The violet sky above us was clear with just a few traces of high clouds scattered here and there. Two airships were visible in the distance on trade routes to distant nations, the faint echo of their mighty engines reaching our ears.

It was time to begin my address.

I lifted myself into the air on the power of my mind and waited a moment for conversation to settle. Every eye in the plaza turned to me. By now I'd grown accustomed to speaking to large gatherings and I bowed politely, floating backwards in the air until I could see everyone at once. When I spoke I did so in the language of this world, augmenting my voice so that it was clear from one side of the assembly to the other.

"*Good morning, Bladesmen and humans of this world. The sun rises today on a momentous occasion. Today, I can announce, three worlds are at peace."

A wave of hushed voices spread through the crowd below. Few of them had even heard of a third world before that statement.

During our predawn journey back to the City I'd talked with Dad, Cord, and Ather about what to say. Dad had coached me on much of the wording, giving me assistance I sorely appreciated. We'd agreed that revealing the true origins of our races would be too big of a shock. That knowledge could disseminate over time across the continents; there was no need to make an issue of it now. Our decision colored the words which followed.

"*We all know of the glowing creature which struck us without warning a short time ago. Yesterday, a small group volunteered to join me on one last attempt to find these creatures and negotiate peace with them. They are remnants of a long-lost race of which few are left. When they witnessed a Bladesman commoner willing to stand firm and defend her human consort from certain death they realized that our two races are no longer at war.

"*Through the brave efforts of my companions, our foes were convinced of our peaceful ways and agreed to join us in a mutual concord. So long as Bladesmen and humans refrain from battle amongst themselves this foreign race will hold off from interference on either of our two populated worlds. Their own world was long ago rendered barren and lifeless from unending war on an apocalyptic scale - and we can never let such a thing come to pass here."

I took a deep breath and paused for a moment. The faces below were both concerned and understanding. "*From here we can see a clear way forward for both of our races. The Bladesmen on the human world need help and many humans of the City wish to return to the world they were born in. The

Council would welcome any who wish to give assistance to our brothers and sisters there. The portal I have built between the two worlds is permanent, and over time we expect both sides to benefit from commerce and trade back and forth."

Until now everything I'd said had been talked about with my family. What I was determined to say next was a private decision, one that I knew would disappoint many. Cord would understand but I wasn't sure Mom and Dad could. I looked at them down there and knew that I'd never fit in here like they did. My fate lay elsewhere.

"*My presence helped bring about an end to the tyranny of the retired Lords, and it has been my threat - or promise - of force which has kept the more fractious nations at heel. But those purposes are necessary no longer. Randell and his group of rebels are either destroyed or paroled. The Lords who enacted the Pact and refused to release their kin from slavery have been stripped of their power. Our mysterious attackers are now willing to give us a chance to prove ourselves. My purpose here is done.

"*Someday, more people like me will be born. I will be back to help guide them and train them in how to live with so much power. But until that day I am leaving this world. My place is out there, among the other worlds, where there may be scattered remnants of other races hunted by the glowing figures. If I can help bring them contact and peace I will.

"*The fate of this world is yours to manage now."

The crowd below stood in stunned silence, unsure how to react. Mom was the quickest; in a split second I felt her mind in contact with mine urgently requesting communication. Cord, Dad, and Ather were right behind her. I opened myself up to them, but only in one direction so they could hear what I had to send to them.

I love you all. You are my family and I could have hoped for none better. I met Cord's eyes and continued, *I have to do this. I won't be gone forever - I'll come back someday - but this is not my world. Goodbye... and thank you.*

My brother looked back with clear sympathy in his eyes.

It was the last thing I saw before turning up to the sky where my destiny truly lay. In the space between two thoughts I was gone from the City, a hundred miles straight up with a bubble of air held around me.

I wasn't surprised when a glowing figure appeared next to me a moment later. *Have you come to join us?* it sent.

Yes, I replied. *Not forever - but both of us have much to learn.*

We left the Bladesman world behind without another look.

Epilogue

~ Cordell ~

Epilogue

"Cordell - where'd she go? Did you know she was leaving?"

Mom was panicked, a haunted look in her eyes. I shook my head slowly. "No, but it makes sense. Mom - you know she was alone here. She would never find an equal on this world, or on the human one. It was never fair to expect her to spend her life without peers. She would never have been truly happy." Saying it made me realize how long I'd known that someday she'd leave us for something more.

"She has us," Mom cried out. "Isn't that enough?" Dad made a soothing sound and laid his good hand on her arm.

"Viala - I know why this hurts," he said quietly. "I think coming to terms with you was what let her realize she had to let us all go. The two of you fought on some level for years, but now you're at peace. Be glad that you found that with her."

Five of us had formed a tight knot in the middle of the crowd. Ather had thrown a shield around us so that we were isolated from the rest as they tried to understand what had just happened; I thanked him with a quick nod of my head. My parents held each other tightly while a sob escaped Mom's throat. I heard her whispering something about how she'd finally found her daughter only for this to happen.

I put my arm around Dalt's shoulders and pulled her close. She knew what it would mean to lose my sister, but I reminded myself that like Kami had said it wouldn't be forever

- we'd see her again someday.

I looked at Dalt and raised an eyebrow. She nodded - it was time to tell Mom, Dad, and Uncle Ather what we'd known for a few days now. I cleared my throat to get their attention first. "Besides, Kami will have to come back at some point. In a few months she's going to be an aunt."

I looked around at my family, their faces suddenly transformed by excitement and happiness. I sent a thin thread of thought into the air above me, not knowing whether Kami would receive it or not, wishing her luck. Her family would be here waiting whenever she came back. Until then - well, we all had things to do.

About the Author

Bryan Lee Gregory lives in the Pacific Northwest with his son and wife. He has been creating new ideas for stories from a young age and writing since 2009. Bryan has worked professionally in the software development industry since graduating from The Evergreen State College in Olympia, Washington in 1999.

Bryan has written the three novels of the *Bladesmen Lords* series: *Lord of the City*, *City of the Lords*, and *Worlds of the Lords*. Learn more about these books and other projects by Bryan at his website:

http://www.bryanleegregory.com

Made in the USA
Charleston, SC
14 January 2015